A SKY LIKE BLOOD

KINGDOM OF BETRAYAL
BOOK ONE

EVERLY FROST

Frost, Everly
A Sky Like Blood

Cover design by Claire Holt with Luminescence Covers
www.luminescencecovers.com

For information on reproducing sections of this book or sales of this book, go to
www.EverlyFrost.com
everlyfrost@gmail.com

DISCOVER THE EVER REALMS

Seven series. One world.

Suggested Reading Order:

Bright Wicked
Storm Princess
Assassin's Magic
Soul Bitten Shifter
Supernatural Legacy
Dark Magic Shifters
Kingdom of Betrayal

In the space between heartbeats,
anything is possible.

PART ONE
THE BEAST FROM THE ASHES

TEN YEARS AGO

CHAPTER I
TEN YEARS AGO

At any moment, the beast that my people created will break down the throne room door. Then the shadow of death will come for us.

I huddle behind the Silver Throne, the malice in its metallic surface surging through my body while I try to shield my brother and my sister from the screams outside the throne room.

I don't have enough hands to cover their small ears. Not enough arms to comfort them. I want to tell them I'll keep them safe, that I'll die before I let anyone hurt them, but my mouth is too dry to speak. The pain in my body is too sharp.

The malice in the throne is too strong.

I would choose to hide somewhere else—anywhere else—but it's the only structure in the room that we can shelter behind.

On the other side of the throne, the floor is a wash of black marble that stretches two hundred paces to the door. The room is cold, shiny, and empty.

That was the way our leader liked it.

A distant *thud* makes me jump, my arms closing more tightly around my siblings.

It won't be long now.

My little sister, Tamra, is frozen in my arms. She's nine years old—seven years younger than I am—and she's small for her age.

Her face is upturned to mine, her pale-green eyes wide with fear and her silver-blonde hair matted with blood. Her scalp is bleeding from our mother's sharp fingernails. There are scratches across her shoulders and down her arms, also from our mother's grasping hands.

Her twin, and our brother, Gallium, huddles against my side. His head is bowed and pressed to my shoulder, allowing me to cover his outer ear with my left hand. He's shaking, and his breaths are short and fast. He's not too old to show his fear. Not too proud to seek safety in my arms.

He, too, wears bruises on his arms and legs. Along with a cut across his cheekbone. My parents caused those, too.

Their faces, wild with panic, flash through my memory. They grabbed Tamra and Gallium, intending to use their bodies as living shields, as if the idea of killing helpless children could deter a beast.

But I stopped my parents.

I fought them like I never fought them before, using every part of my body to fight back, to wrench my siblings away from them and turn *myself* into the shield, taking every punch and kick they rained down on my back and head when I refused to let my brother and sister go.

I would not let them use my siblings to steal a few extra moments of life.

Backing away from me, my mother had screamed at me. "You've killed us, you worthless bitch."

It was an irrational scream, full of fear and panic, as if I was somehow responsible for the death they had brought on themselves.

As if they could somehow escape their own doom.

I refused to hold my tongue, snarling back at my parents like the beast they feared. *"You killed yourselves."*

Their faces were cold and blank. Nothing I said ever mattered.

I was their failure. Their shame. If they thought they could drain the life from me to give them strength, they would have, but I was less than worthless. I would contaminate their power and make them weak.

Now, Gallium's small voice, muffled against my side, stops my fear in its tracks. "I'll fight beside you, Asha."

I close my eyes and let my tears fall, hating that they drip onto his hair and down his forehead, mingling with his blood.

I may have saved him from our parents, but I merely delayed the inevitable.

Finally, the screaming outside the throne room stops.

I thought I would welcome the silence, but it's horrifying. It means my people are dead.

All of them, including my parents and our leader—the Blacksmith named Malak.

It was Malak who created the beast that has now risen up and killed them all.

I fight the tightness in my throat and whisper as softly as an exhalation. "Shh. Quiet now."

Tamra closes her eyes as I lower my head to hers and press my cheek to her forehead. I relax my hand against Gallium's ear, cupping his face, trying to calm him with a gentler touch.

He shudders his next breath and then we're as still as we can be.

It won't matter.

The beast will hear our heartbeats and know where we are—

A *crash* at the far end of the room makes me flinch. It's the sound of wood splintering, followed by clattering across the floor.

A low growl sounds in the distance. A seething breath drawn in and out.

Then, the beat of steady footfalls drums in my hearing, each one slow and deliberate. Coming closer.

The beast's shadow falls across us, a thickening darkness.

I brace for the cut of his claws and the tear of his teeth. I wait for the painful death, suddenly shaking so hard that Tamra starts to cry. Quiet sobs.

I don't dare look up. I don't want to see the bloody claws that are coming for me. I want only to fill my mind with the presence of my brother and sister and every memory I have of them.

The beast's snarl is low and soft and sends a shiver down my spine.

"Fear," he says, as if he can taste it in the air. He pauses before he continues and now there's a hint of surprise in his voice. "But not hatred."

My heart is beating out of control.

I wasn't expecting him to speak—wasn't even sure if he'd be capable of logical thought.

It seems impossible that he hasn't killed us already.

Maybe we have a chance. Maybe—

No.

He'll kill us. He has every reason to turn this room red with our blood. Every right to want vengeance for what was done to him. It's only a matter of time. Maybe less than a few heartbeats.

I force sound through my lips, barely forming audible words, but I'm determined to speak the truth. "I can't hate you."

"Then you pity me," he snaps.

"No!"

My denial rings out like a shout, my voice no longer quavering as I look up into the face of my enemy for the first time.

He towers over me. His bare chest is splattered with blood, his pants are torn, and his breathing is harsh. The bloodied strands of his hair fall across his eyes, the gore so thick that I can't tell what color his hair is.

He was once human. That was before he was transformed by magic that used to be pure and good but had become twisted and dark.

Transformation magic. Blacksmith's magic.

But my eyes are widening because he's much younger than I was expecting.

He can't be more than a year older than me. Maybe seventeen at the most.

This is the beast my parents were so afraid of?

His lips curve upward, rising a little higher on the left. His sharp teeth glint. He turns slightly into the light and the disparate color of his left eye glints at me.

It's as if he's challenging me to lie to him.

"I have no pity for you," I say, refusing to look away from his beastly features.

His forehead creases, his gaze raking across me to the children I'm protecting, then back to me. His eyes bore into me for a long moment, and I can't imagine what he's trying to pull from me. My fear, my imperfections, my determination to protect my siblings. My... *strangeness*...

He shakes himself, and his features harden. "Give me your hand."

"No."

His lips rise again. It's a dangerous smile. He enunciates each word as he repeats his order. "Give me. Your fucking. Hand."

7

"Only if you let them live—"

He moves so fast that I barely follow his movement. His arm snakes out, his hand closes around my right wrist, and he wrenches me upward.

I try to hold on to my siblings, but Tamra and Gallium tumble from my arms and land on the hard floor. They try to reach for me, but I'm already too far away.

The beast has dragged me several paces from the malicious throne before I can even attempt to get my feet under myself.

His strength and speed shake me to my core.

I'm screaming, but not for my own life. "These children have no power. Let them live!"

The beast grinds to a halt, suddenly staring down at my hand.

My right hand.

Even through the strands of his hair, I read his confusion.

My right hand is where my power should be. But I'm not like other Blacksmiths.

My right hand is powerless.

Instead, my power lives in my left hand—a power that is barely functional. When I was first given a Blacksmith's hammer in a ceremony that should have allowed me to access my power in full force, it had barely sparked.

My parents declared me 'defective' and that was the end of it.

I wasn't permitted to touch a Blacksmith's hammer or tools again. Not that I didn't try.

All Blacksmiths need their hammer to access their power—and all Blacksmiths are possessive of their tools—but no matter how many times I managed to access a hammer, nothing ever happened.

The puzzlement on the beast's face now tells me he can't make sense of the absence of power in the hand he's holding, and I'm not about to enlighten him about my left hand, even though it's next to useless.

I can't predict what he intends to do next, but he's paused, and I can't waste this opportunity to speak. "These children can't hurt anyone. *Please*. Let them live."

I don't dare look away from him, even though my brother's and sister's sobs break my heart and I'm desperate to comfort them.

"No power?" The beast stares at them. It's as if he's trying to read the presence or absence of power in their young bodies across the distance, and maybe he can.

After all, Malak gave this beast all the senses of a predator.

"You are the children of Kalith and Ayla Silverspun," the beast says, his eyes narrowed. "Your parents were two of the most powerful Blacksmiths to stand at Malak's side. How is it possible that your brother and sister are powerless?"

I risk a glance back to Tamra and Gallium, who are huddling beside the Silver Throne, clutching each other, their young faces white with fear.

"My parents gave them as a gift to Malak," I say, fighting the hope rising within my chest, knowing that the beast could still strike my loved ones down within seconds. "Malak drained their power for his own purposes."

The beast straightens a little at this. Then he glowers at my right hand. "What of your power?"

My response is bleak. "Malak didn't want mine."

I should have been happy about it. But when my parents offered up the twins as a sacrifice, I wanted to take their place. I wanted to help them, but I also wanted to be rid of my faulty power.

Even if I could have convinced my parents to give *me* to Malak instead, I knew why Malak wanted my brother and sister weakened.

They had already demonstrated more power than my

parents ever had. Malak saw them as a threat. He wanted them neutralized, but killing them would have caused dissent among his followers. He found a way to take their power without alienating other Blacksmiths, and my parents went along with it.

The beast turns my hand over, the harshness of his breathing increasing. "I sense your hatred now."

I grit my teeth and let my anger flow. "Malak was a monster. So were my parents."

"As am I!" the beast roars. "Do not forget it!"

He wrenches me all the way upward, but this time, I'm prepared.

My left hand was pressed to my thigh, but now it shoots forward, my palm flat as I aim for the location of his heart.

I hope only that whatever magic was used to transform the beast's body will somehow trigger my own. All I need is to summon enough strength to drive this beast to his knees and escape him.

In the back of my mind, I know it's futile.

No Blacksmith had ever summoned their power without their hammer and their tools. And this beast killed all of them.

The speed with which he pulls me toward him creates enough force that my outstretched arm nearly breaks between us—it should have broken—except that his reflexes kick in and he stops moving the second that my palm presses to his heart.

Skin on skin.

But I have nothing. No miraculous surge of power that could save me.

Instead, I sense the heavy beat of his heart beneath my palm. The slickness of sweat and blood. A reminder of the lives he took on his way to this room.

The crease in his forehead deepens, but his grip on my right wrist gentles.

"You're left-handed," he says.

I expect him to insult me, call me 'weak' or 'worthless,' but he doesn't.

The thick silence outside the throne room is suddenly broken by cheers of jubilation, a rising cry that grows in strength until it's a roar that drowns out the quiet sobs behind me.

The humans are cheering. They must be free now.

This beast has liberated them from decades of tyranny.

The fight drains out of me. I have nothing left.

I was born a Blacksmith. So were my brother and sister. We are hated for the crimes of our people, and soon the humans will swarm into this room. If the beast doesn't end us, the humans will scream for our blood.

He's all that's standing between us and them now.

"Please," I whisper, never releasing him from my gaze. "Have mercy for these children."

The anger in the beast's voice tears through me. "You beg for mercy, but where was the mercy for my family?" His grip on me tightens. "When I fought to save my father's life and my brother's life, where was mercy then?"

I'm breathing too fast. I can't control the pounding within my chest.

"Then take *my* life," I whisper. "Take my life in front of your people so that they can be done with their vengeance. Let your justice end with me. Not with these children."

His eyes widen at my request, and his breathing stills.

Once again, his gaze seems to pull at my thoughts, and with a deep sense of powerlessness, I remind myself that he can hear my pounding heart, smell my fear, and sense the weakness of the sputtering power that won't save me.

His lips finally part. He's about to declare our fate, and I wait for his agreement.

I pray for it.

CHAPTER 2

The beast's voice is quiet and sounds more human than it did before. "I accept your bargain. Come with me peacefully, be true to your word, and I will make sure your brother and sister live long lives."

My shoulders slump with relief, a strange feeling, given that I'm now facing death.

The beast's fingers slowly uncurl from around my right wrist. He releases me, but he doesn't step back. My left palm remains on his chest for a moment longer while I take an inexplicable sort of comfort in the mercy his heart has lent me.

Then I grasp the temporary freedom he's offering me and hurry back to my brother and sister.

I kneel and scoop them into my arms. "You're safe now."

Tamra raises her eyes to mine. "Asha?"

I try not to choke as tears threaten to spill from my eyes. "Yes, my darling?"

"Please don't die."

I pull back a little, smoothing the bloodied strands of her silver hair. "Always remember that you are strong."

I draw Gallium closer as I hug them both. "Always

remember that if you love someone with all your heart, you've already won any battle that might come your way."

The sound of cheering is drawing nearer. The throne room is located on the southern side of the castle, and it sounds as if the humans have reached the courtyard at the center of the castle grounds.

My voice becomes more urgent. "Listen carefully: Do everything this man tells you. No matter what. Can you promise me that?"

Tamra's big, green eyes rise to the beast, who towers over us, even though he remains several paces away.

She is the first to nod. Gallium is much slower.

I take their hands as I rise to my feet and turn to face the beast. "We're ready."

He has prowled closer to me now, but despite his proximity, I can't read his expression at all. The fall of his hair doesn't help.

"Follow me," he says.

It surprises me that he doesn't grab me, and that he's trusting me to do as he says, but I suppose he's already proved that he's faster and stronger than me.

I could never outrun him or beat him in a fight.

I keep Tamra and Gallium close to my sides as we pad across the cold floor in our bare feet. They're wearing little more than their nightclothes. My own white dress is thin. I'd managed to pull on the children's jackets before our parents came for them, but that was all.

Ahead of us, the beast navigates between the broken shards of wood, and I pick both of my siblings up, an awkward task, so that they don't get splinters in their feet. I decide that a little discomfort as I carry them is better than risking damage to their feet. They may not be able to outrun the beast, but if something goes wrong, I want them to have a chance against the humans.

In the next moment, the beast swings back to me, plucking Gallium from my arms and lifting him over the wreckage.

My protective instincts kick in. I'm ready to demand that the beast give my brother back, but my shout dies in my throat when he puts Gallium safely back on his feet on the other side of the door.

The beast meets my eyes across the distance. "I made a promise to keep them alive," he snaps, as if my concern were insulting to him. "I intend to keep it."

"But I'm not dead yet," I whisper.

His big hand lands on my brother's shoulder. "Even so."

My brother stares up at the beast with wide, green eyes.

The beast growls down at him. "You will walk with me."

I don't know anything about the beast, only that he was Malak's prisoner and the last in a long line of humans to be subjected to Malak's magic, but the beast mentioned a brother. I can only imagine that it was a younger brother, given the way he hoisted Gallium up so expertly, as if he had carried a child many times before.

Now the hand he closes around Gallium's small shoulder makes me shudder.

I've bought my siblings' lives with my own, but I won't be here to protect them afterward.

Picking my way carefully to the door with Tamra in my arms, I place her down on the other side of the wreckage.

The beast is already leading Gallium away down the corridor toward the far open doors, from which the roar of human voices is coming.

My focus shoots to the other end of the corridor. It looks like a dead end, but there's another way out: a door hidden behind the golden tapestry that hangs against the wall. It leads into a small room with a trapdoor in the floor. A set of stairs beneath the trapdoor leads down into a narrow tunnel. The tunnel then connects to the sewage system, which flows to the swamp beyond the eastern edge of the city.

Outside the city is a wasteland.

It wasn't always so. Before Malak rose to power thirty years ago, this human city was surrounded by lush forests and fertile farmland that stretched for miles and miles, all the way to the ring of mountains that circles this land in the far distance.

Or so I heard.

For as long as I've been alive, there has been nothing but wilderness out there. The land was scarred by my people's magic, the life drained from the trees and soil over the decades. The natural habitat of the forest animals has been decimated.

The eastern swamp is particularly dangerous. It has come to be known as "the Sunken Bog" because the trees have slowly descended into the muck. Within the bog, there's a poisoned lake that the humans call the *Toxic Thirst*. Ingesting water from that lake leads to rapid dehydration and ultimately, death.

Making it to the trapdoor is only the first hurdle. After that, we would have to survive the harsh environment beyond the city.

Even if we made it through the mountains and reached a village or a city in the north, we would only find enemies there. According to the books in the library that I read when I was younger, there was a time when Blacksmiths traveled far and wide, forging peaceful alliances with other kingdoms.

But when Malak rose to power, he destroyed all alliances and ordered every Blacksmith to return home. Any Blacksmith who defied him was hunted down and killed. He concentrated the power of Blacksmiths here, in this city, and demanded complete loyalty. Now, I have no doubt that any human who lives in the north would fear us. Hate us. Hunt us.

Those are not the only threats we'd face.

In the last month, there were growing whispers among the Blacksmiths about a new danger rising in the wasteland outside the city because of how much magic had built up in the land out there.

I don't know what the new danger is, but it was the first time I'd seen my ever-confident parents look worried.

Well, that is, until the beast killed Malak.

Up ahead, the beast pauses, watching me as I hesitate.

Oh, but he was clever when he picked Gallium up under the guise of helping him. Because now he's holding Gallium's hand, and if I try to escape, I can only save Tamra.

If she and I live, our brother will pay the price.

I see the way Gallium is leaning away from the beast, ready to pull his hand free, but he's barely tall enough to reach the beast's waist. He won't stand a chance.

I give Gallium a firm shake of my head.

I'm not sure if he'll obey me, but with a dark glare up at the beast, he stops tugging.

I keep walking toward the beast, along the dark corridor, and across the walkway outside it, past the tall, black pillars and out into the moonlight.

The humans are surging into the courtyard through the portcullis on the other side. They're all carrying makeshift weapons and their bodies are bloodied in some way or another.

The Blacksmiths will not have died easily.

As soon as the beast appears, someone in the approaching crowd shouts. "It's the Vandawolf!"

A cheer goes up among the humans and they begin chanting, "Vandawolf! Vandawolf!"

I suppose that's his name. Whether it's the one he was born with, I might never know.

Even though I can't hide, I try to stay in his shadow, but it doesn't take the humans long to notice Gallium walking beside him, and then me and Tamra walking behind.

Our silver-blonde hair must be like multiple beacons in the dark, catching the moonlight.

When they see us, their shouts of jubilation turn to jeering.

The Vandawolf heads for the large, black table in the center of the courtyard.

This courtyard was Malak's open-air forge and the table was his anvil. It's made from a titanium alloy and is easily wide enough for two humans to lie side-by-side with their arms extended.

On the right-hand side of the table is a large, titanium bowl, also waist-height, filled with crimson-colored coal—the blood-red coal that Blacksmiths use for their forge-fire. It's mined in the eastern mountains and hauled down to the city.

All metal must be fired and beaten with a Blacksmith's hammer before it can be transformed at that Blacksmith's will.

Until last night, this bowl had burned with a wine-red flame. Now it's cold and dark.

On the left of the table, sitting close together, are two large, metal cages, both big enough for a human to stand up in.

The closer to the anvil we walk, the stronger the malice in its metal grows. Just like Malak's silver throne, Malak used this anvil as a conduit to his power and for the transference of magic between living things.

The anvil, forge, and cages take up enough space that the humans don't seem to know how to organize themselves around them. Nobody seems to want to come past them. As they continue to surge into the courtyard, they spread out until they fill the other side of the yard.

When the Vandawolf turns toward the table, no longer between me and the crowd, a pebble sails at me out of the throng. It misses me by inches, the clatter as it falls to the ground drowned by the din.

Tamra gives a soft cry and I pull her closer, trying to predict where the next assault might come from, hoping to make myself a shield between her and the throng.

Another pebble flies toward me, this one coming right at my face.

CHAPTER 3

I barely have time to flinch before the Vandawolf's hand shoots out.

He snatches the pebble from the air.

There's a sudden silence as he stops walking, his fist upraised, his fingers closing around the stone.

The grinding of rock fills the quiet.

Then he opens his fist, allowing the dust to float away in the breeze.

"Quiet your rage," the Vandawolf snarls into the silence. "And trust that justice will be done."

He takes another step toward the anvil, but Gallium tugs sharply on his hand and digs in his heels.

That anvil is where Malak took Gallium's power.

When the Vandawolf bends to him, his eyes narrowed, Gallium shakes his head rapidly side to side. "Not there."

The Vandawolf glances back to me, his focus dropping to Tamra, who has turned her face against my side, away from the anvil, while I hold her close.

My skin is crawling this close to the table and my instinct is to move away from it, but I'm stuck where I am in case the Vandawolf thinks I'm trying to escape.

He turns back to Gallium. "Why do you refuse to approach this table?"

Gallium shudders. "It's evil."

The Vandawolf leans back a little, as if in thought, before he bends to Gallium again, his voice quieter now. "I need this anvil tonight. But tomorrow, I promise I'll destroy it. You have no need to fear it any longer."

Gallium stops tugging as sharply against the Vandawolf's hold, but the terror remains in his expression when he looks at the table.

"Go back to your sisters," the Vandawolf says to him, straightening and giving Gallium a nudge toward me. "Asha knows what will happen if she tries to run."

Gallium darts to my side, and I pull him close, keeping my distance from the menacing table. I wish I could stem Tamra's tears and take away Gallium's fear, but nothing can change the past.

I flinch when the Vandawolf leaps up onto the anvil, as if the malice seething within its surface has no effect on him. Maybe it doesn't. Or maybe he's capable of ignoring it.

He raises himself up to his full height, standing tall before his people even while the strands of his hair continue to conceal the left side of his face. The beastly side.

"This is where Malak did his work," he says, gesturing to the mangled shackles attached to the table's surface. "This is where the wolf died. And this is where I was changed."

He's talking about an actual wolf. A real-life animal whose soul, strength, and nature was merged with his.

There was a time when Blacksmiths worked alongside humans, helping them expand their city and its infrastructure. In the time of peace, Blacksmiths used their transformation power to alter the shape of specially hammered metal into weapons and pieces of machinery—all for the good of humankind.

But then Malak discovered he could alter the nature of organic material. He could change the fundamental characteristics of living beings, not just metal.

He and his followers, including my parents, used their power to overthrow the ruling human king and annihilate the human army, triggering a reign of terror that lasted thirty years.

They pushed their magic to its extremes, starting with the environment on the northern side of the city, scorching the land with the intensity of their power. Then they turned the eastern side into swampland. They were sensible enough not to destroy the farmland to the south, but soon enough, they began experimenting on humans and animals, trying to combine the two.

They wanted to become gods.

Many humans died, but not the Vandawolf.

"Malak killed my family," the Vandawolf says as he looks around at the humans. "I feel your pain because it's my own."

The humans murmur quietly, many nodding their heads.

A man in the front row shouts, "All Blacksmiths must die!"

I recognize this man despite the mud and gore masking his features. His name is Braddock. He's tall, although not as big as the Vandawolf, and bulky through his chest, arms, and legs. Malak kept him as a laborer for hauling coal and chopping wood. Like all humans, he wasn't treated well. The blood may hide his scars, but he has plenty of them.

Braddock holds an axe tightly within his right hand, the weapon's head resting on the black, pebbled courtyard.

At his shout, the murmurs within the crowd grow louder.

Standing next to Braddock, a woman with tightly-braided brown hair takes up the cry. "Kill the Blacksmiths! Kill them *now!*"

As soon as she shouts, the crowd surges forward, spilling around the forge and the cages on each side.

My heart leaps into my throat and my hands tighten around my siblings.

I'm preparing to run despite the Vandawolf's threats, willing myself to believe that we'll make it to the trapdoor, when the Vandawolf roars so loudly that I freeze to the spot and the hairs on my arms stand on end.

"You will not harm them!"

His roar is like a physical shove against the wash of human bodies, bringing the crowd to a standstill before they can make it around the obstacles on either side of the table. Many of them flinch. Some of them drop to a crouch. Even Braddock hunches low to the ground.

The Vandawolf's lips draw back from his teeth, revealing the sharpness on the left side. His rage is like a hot brand, each word he speaks searing my senses.

"On this day, I have slaughtered Blacksmiths both young and old," he shouts at the humans. "I have covered my hands in blood, and they will never come clean."

He thumps his chest. "*I* have done this. *Me.* And now I am done with it."

He keeps the crowd within his sights as he points at Gallium and Tamra. "Anyone who hurts these children will answer to me."

A man hunching in the front row near Braddock speaks grimly into the hush. "Why do they deserve your protection?" he asks, revealing a chipped front tooth as he grimaces. "They're Blacksmiths."

"They were victims of Malak's cruelty. Just as you were," the Vandawolf says. "He placed them on this very table, took their magic, and left them powerless."

The Vandawolf's gaze passes over the crowd before his focus lands on me, a short, sharp glance.

His voice softens, but now it's raw and hurt. "They are children. Caught up in a war that was not of their making. Just like my brother was."

At the mention of his brother, every member of the crowd quiets and all murmurings stop. Even Braddock slouches, his head bowed.

"We have a chance to show mercy that wasn't shown to us," the Vandawolf continues. "I understand how difficult this is. But I ask you: Who will take these two children into their home and raise them?"

The silence is so sharp now that it burns my ears.

Another woman—this one with a scar across her forehead—who's standing in the second row calls out. "How can we invite them into our home when they could kill us in our sleep?"

"I know what I'd do with them," Braddock says, pointing his axe in our direction.

"That's right," says the woman with braided hair. "They might not have power of their own, but they're still Black-smiths. And besides, Malak used his power on them. How do we know they don't carry his evil spirit within them now?"

The Vandawolf has let them speak, but now he asks, "What would you do with someone who has suffered Malak's power?"

I consider him carefully. It's a loaded question, given that Malak used his power on the Vandawolf too, but the humans seem too overcome with emotion to realize it.

"We should kill them!" the woman with the braids replies.

This time, the Vandawolf doesn't roar. "Then you should kill me, too."

There's a shocked silence as the humans seem to realize what they were saying.

The man with the chipped front tooth splutters loudly. "It's different with you. You were human."

His use of the past tense doesn't seem lost on the Vandawolf.

The Vandawolf's lips rise, but it's not a smile. His growl

vibrates through the air. "I was human, and now I'm not. These children were Blacksmiths, and now they're not."

He moves closer to the crowd, stopping only a step from the edge of the table, and now his position means I can't see his face, but his threat sends a shiver racing down my spine.

"Do not imagine for one moment that these children are more dangerous than I am."

The humans stare up at him. He fought for their freedom tonight. Killed every other Blacksmith, just like he said. No doubt the humans were part of the fight. But perhaps only now are they realizing the full extent of the changes in him.

I wonder if they will continue to trust him, or if they will come to hate him for what he has become.

All I'm sure of is that I won't live long enough to know the answer.

Another male voice speaks, this one from within the crowd. "We will raise the children."

The crowd parts, and the man steps through with a woman close at his side. They both look exhausted. Their clothing is ragged, and their features are marred with blood. I'm sure I've never met the woman, but I know this man.

His name is Kedric, and he was enslaved to my parents. He was serving food to the gathering of high-level Blacksmiths on the day I picked up a hammer for the first time. He saw what happened behind closed doors afterward. My parents didn't hide any cruelty from their servants.

Unlike many of these humans, who have never set foot inside the castle grounds or even laid eyes on me, Kedric knows my name, and he knows my brother and sister, too.

A spark of hope lights inside me, but it fades quickly. My parents didn't treat him well. I'm not sure how I can trust that he won't take his revenge on my family once I'm gone.

When he and the woman stop in front of the table, Kedric turns in my direction, and it's as if he's explaining himself to me when he says, "This is my wife, Maybelle. Our ability to have children was taken from us."

He squeezes the woman's hand. Like most of the humans, her hair is brown and so are her eyes. She's a little shorter than her husband and her frame is thin. I imagine she was kept as a servant in one of the other Blacksmith households, since it was common practice for humans to be separated from those they loved.

She also looks me in the eye across the distance. "We will raise these children as if they are our own. Without harm or hatred."

There is no guile or malice in her speech, and I believe her.

My eyes suddenly burn with tears. I bite sharply on my bottom lip, swallowing the sob of relief choking my throat.

This is a greater mercy than I was expecting. All I can do is give Maybelle a nod before I crouch to my brother and sister, struggling to speak. "Go with Kedric. Stay close to him and his wife. They will be your family now. Trust them and nobody else."

Gallium is shaking his head vehemently, his body stiff in my arms. "No, Asha, I won't go. I want to fight."

My heart is breaking again, but I rally. "Good," I say, gripping him hard with one hand while continuing to hold Tamra close to my other side. "Fight to *live*. Fight for Tamra. Fight for your new family. Show them that you are honorable and that your heart is good. But don't look back. This next battle is mine, and only mine."

My brother's expression darkens. "No—"

I gasp as the Vandawolf plucks Gallium right out of my arms, holding him tightly despite his kicking. He passes Gallium to Kedric, who has quickly moved up to the side of the forge.

I spin to Tamra, whose eyes are wide. She's shaking her head, her lips trembling.

I press my forehead to hers, hoping only to calm her. "Keep your brother safe. Protect each other. Always—"

She's gone in the next second, whisked up into the Vandawolf's arms.

I cover my mouth with my hand, suppressing my cry, barely able to hear the Vandawolf over Tamra's cries.

He speaks quickly to Kedric and Maybelle as he passes Tamra to them. "If anyone causes you problems, come directly to me. Now, take the children out of here. Quickly."

"No!" Gallium shouts, struggling in Kedric's arms.

Tamra screams as she tries to free herself from Maybelle. "Asha!"

Kedric and Maybelle hurry away, veering as wide as they can around the other humans, managing to hold on to the children even as my brother and sister try to get back to me.

My siblings' sobs fade as they disappear into the distance.

Then they're gone, and my arms are left empty and aching.

I try to gather myself, to cage my emotions, but my shoulders are hunched, my hands are shaking, and there's nothing I can do now but wait for my end.

CHAPTER 4

T he Vandawolf has barely turned back to me when Braddock calls out. "What of the woman?" He points his axe in my direction again and I feel the rake of his eyes down my body. "Who gets to take her?"

I wrap my arms around my chest, reminding myself: *This will be over soon.*

"Nobody should take her!" the woman with the braids snaps. She has been vocal about ending me from the start. "Those children may have been innocent of their parents' crimes, but this one is old enough to be complicit."

She would be correct if she were speaking about any other Blacksmith. We start learning our craft at the early age of five. At sixteen, most Blacksmiths start working independently.

Not me.

The Vandawolf is only two steps away from me now.

The glint in his eyes demands my attention. "Asha Silverspun has offered me her life," he says, paying more attention to me than to the crowd.

I'm unsettled by the dangerous curl of his lips. The impossibly calm rise and fall of his broad chest.

Breaths of air that I'm counting down now.

I expect him to grab me, drag me up to the anvil, take the axe that Braddock is offering, and end me.

"Asha Silverspun's power is mine from this day forward," the Vandawolf says.

I wait for him to make a move toward me, confused when he simply tips his head to the side as he continues to contemplate me with a satisfied smile on his lips.

"Until the day she dies," he finishes.

His declaration is quiet but certain, and it makes my forehead crease.

I blink at him, waiting for him to tell me that the day I die is today.

That the time is now.

The humans also seem to be struggling to understand his intentions.

The woman with the braids calls out again, this time incredulously. "Surely, you don't mean to let her live."

The Vandawolf doesn't hesitate. "Asha Silverspun will stay with me."

Instant rumbles of dissent grow within the crowd and gain strength despite the Vandawolf's clear intention to maintain control of this situation.

He seems unmoved by the increasing uproar. In fact, he seems more interested in my reaction than the humans'.

The blur of sound washes over me as I try to focus on him through my confusion. Now I'm the one trying to pull the thoughts from *his* head, trying to process the meaning behind his intentions.

I told him to take my life.

I asked him to be done with his vengeance, and he agreed.

But I never imagined he would do anything other than end me. It didn't occur to me that he might interpret the offer of my life to mean that I would become *his*.

And for what reason?

Unless... he's simply playing a game with me.

Giving me hope that he wants to keep me alive before he tears me apart. Because that's what my people did to the humans. The Blacksmiths brought humans hope, gave them prosperity and the tools they needed to build their city. They'd *helped* the humans, before Malak ripped it all away and delivered violence and death.

Is the Vandawolf showing me mercy? Or is this torture?

The corners of my mouth turn down and the crease in my forehead grows, my thoughts becoming defiant in the face of his confidence.

I replay his speech inside my mind.

Asha Silverspun's power is mine until the day she dies.

I'm not sure if he can hear me over the din of his people now, but my anger forces its way past my lips. "I don't have any power to give you—"

It takes him a heartbeat to respond to my rage.

He crashes into me so fast that the breath is knocked out of me.

"No power?" he snarls. His arms close around me and within seconds, he has lifted me onto the anvil, where he forces me to stand within the circle of his arms.

It's the last place I want to be.

Anywhere but in contact with this cruel metal that seethes with hatred and brutality.

"No!" A scream tears through me as the pure malice in the table floods through my bare feet and up into my chest, squeezing my lungs, choking my throat, and cutting like knives at my insides.

The pain reaches my mind and turns to fire. A flame that threatens to consume me.

"I can't be here," I cry. "Not here!"

The Vandawolf's arms are like steel around me despite my cries.

I'm peripherally aware that the humans have flinched. They're a sea of wide eyes. Their voices are immediately silenced and their faces are ashen.

It doesn't matter to me what they think or feel now. The dark malice within the anvil is slicing through me over and over like claws tearing at my soul.

I thrash, needing only to get away. "Let me go!"

The Vandawolf's face is like stone. His snarl is just as cold. He continues to hold me to the spot, and I can't escape.

I can't run from him.

I gasp for breath, and just as quickly, fear turns to anger.

It's a cold rage in the face of too much pain. He warned me he was as monstrous as Malak and now I feel the truth of it. "You *are* a monster."

"Do you think I don't feel it?" he roars back at me. "Do you think I don't feel everything? I hear the screams in this metal. Smell the blood. Do you think it hurts you more than it hurts me?"

I don't.

I know his pain is greater than mine, but I'm mindless now.

Snarling at him, I fight back the only way I can, dragging my fingernails down his chest as far as I can while he's crushing me against him.

I'm sure I've drawn blood.

He responds with a growl, but instead of letting me go, he drops to his knees, taking me down with him. As soon as my weight lifts, I see my chance to wrap my legs around his waist and break contact with the anvil.

I cling to him, a shudder of relief passing through me, but it doesn't last long.

One of his hands wraps around the back of my head and a

heartbeat later, he tips me back onto the table, his full weight pressing me down.

This time, I can't even shout. The contact with the anvil is too much for my body to handle. I can barely hear him through the roaring inside my mind.

"Take the hammer!"

I have no idea what he's talking about.

I'm thrashing hard against him. My vision is blurred with pain and tears.

But then...

Then I see the tools nestled deep in the surface of the anvil on my left.

Malak's tools.

His titanium hammer, titanium tongs, and three bands of black metal about an inch wide and five inches long that sit in an orderly row beside the tongs.

The metal strips are known as medallions. They can be instantly turned into weapons or used as a conduit between a Blacksmith and some other material. Most Blacksmiths wore theirs as armbands while carrying their hammers on their belts. The tongs were usually left in the forge, used only for working with the fire.

All of the Malak's tools rest in neatly carved grooves in the top of the table. They're easy enough to scoop out, but also securely stored, and their dark color causes them to blend into the table's surface. Camouflaged from a distance.

"Pick up the fucking hammer!" the Vandawolf shouts at me.

I shake my head violently. Touching the hammer will be ten times worse than touching this table.

"What do you want from me?" I cry, shoving at his chest. "I already offered you my life."

His response is low and deep. "And I accepted it."

Hot tears pour down my cheeks, but my lips draw back

31

from my teeth with pain and rage. I'm as caged as the wolf whose soul was merged with his. "Do you want me to prove how weak I am?"

"You are neither weak nor vulnerable," he says, his eyes narrowing. "But you will remember that I have spared your family in exchange for your life."

He leans in closer as if to punctuate his meaning. "If you want your brother and sister to continue breathing, you will obey me."

CHAPTER 5

I drag a deep breath into my chest. If the Vandawolf wanted me to fear for my family, then he's succeeded.

Twisting, I try to create enough space between myself and his chest so that I can reach for the hammer with my right hand.

"With your left," he snaps.

I glare back at him before I switch hands, now sliding my left arm free.

It's an easier task, and it only takes a moment for my arm to extend far enough that I can reach the tool.

I glare defiantly up at the Vandawolf, my teeth gritted against the pain, my breaths hissing between my teeth, as my fingers close around the hammer's handle.

It's cold to touch, an icy temperature that sends a new shudder through me.

"Are you satisfied?" I ask through clenched teeth. "I'm weak! Incapable of—"

I gasp as light explodes around me.

My vision ignites as if a new flame has been lit within my mind and everything else around me fades.

All else is instantly inconsequential.

Nothing matters except this power.

It surges from my hand through my arm and into my chest, making my arm glow silver against the table. The strands of my hair glisten like fine silver metal where they spread across the surface. And the pain at my back recedes, becoming insignificant compared to the wild desires now shaping my thoughts.

The Vandawolf dominates my vision, the raw energy within him calling to me like a wolf's howl. The predator that was merged with him burns in my vision.

Oh, what a beautiful beast he is.

I slide my right hand over his heart, counting the strong beats.

I want... no, *need*... to connect with the beast within him and shape it. Change it. Recreate it.

Take control of the light and the dark.

Manipulate the metal beneath my back.

Dominate the body pressing down on mine.

Shape this man to match my needs.

Make him mine.

Perfectly mine...

The Vandawolf releases one of my shoulders and grabs my left wrist and it's only then that I realize I've raised the hammer to his chest.

His biceps and chest muscles strain as he pushes back against me, keeping the hammer at bay—but only just.

In the same beat, it dawns on me that the power surging through me has made me strong enough to shove him off me.

If I want.

My lips part. A soft smile.

Maybe I don't want.

I'd rather take my hammer to him and finish Malak's work...

With a roar of effort, the Vandawolf wrenches the tool from

my hand. To take it from me, he has to pull backward, lifting me from the table and plastering me up against his chest.

For the briefest moment, my legs wrap fully around his waist. My center presses up against him, my face is only an inch from his, and I inhale the alluring scent of sweat and blood and wolf.

In the next moment, he disarms me.

The second the hammer leaves my hand, the warmth of power abandons me. Cold reality returns.

A reality in which I struggle to comprehend what that dark, twisted power had done to my mind.

With a gasp, I jolt backward, unfurling my legs and scrambling away from the Vandawolf—and the hammer—now that he isn't restraining me.

I end up crouched several paces away from him, my nightdress tangled around my legs, my heart beating hard, and my focus flicking from the hammer in his hand to his face.

The pain I felt from the table is gone.

I'm still aware of it, the malice and hatred, but it doesn't hurt me anymore and...

That doesn't feel like a good thing.

Something has shifted within me, and now a cold fear is building.

My power came to life, and it was beautiful and terrible, both at once, and I didn't want it to end.

Opposite me, the Vandawolf grips the hammer so hard that his knuckles are white.

"You're not powerless," he says. "You simply weren't given the right tools."

I want to ask him how he knew that Malak's hammer would trigger my power. And *when* did he realize it? Was it the moment that I pressed my left hand to his heart?

Before I can speak again, he rises to his feet and turns to face his people.

The humans have remained silent and wide-eyed. Even Braddock has put down his axe. But now they shake themselves.

"Our battles aren't over," the Vandawolf shouts, taking control before anyone can speak. "Danger is coming from the wasteland. The Blacksmiths scorched the earth, the trees, and the very sky above us with their magic, and now it festers in the ash they left behind."

It's the same threat that my parents whispered about. A new danger. One that frightened them.

A danger of their own making.

The Vandawolf's next words drive a chill into my heart. "The Blacksmiths were afraid of what is coming, but we will not be."

He half-turns to me, his eyes glinting. "Because Asha Silverspun will fight these battles for us. From this moment on, she is mine to command. Her life. Her body. Her mind. Her *power*. They are mine. She will defend this city and make amends for her people's crimes."

I clasp my shaking hands in my lap.

Even though I don't know how it's possible, it's clear that the Vandawolf triggered my power for his own purposes. I promise myself that I will always remember that any act of mercy he shows me is never as it seems.

As he finishes speaking, there isn't a single objection from the crowd. The concept of making me pay seems to appeal to the humans, even to Braddock and the woman with the braids, who both wear cold smiles, as if I deserve what's coming.

"Now, go home," the Vandawolf says more softly. "Tend to your wounds and look after your families. Tomorrow, we begin rebuilding our homes."

The humans are slow to disperse, murmuring and casting glances back at me and the Vandawolf. But if any of them have any lingering thoughts about his decision to keep me alive, they don't say so.

Finally, the courtyard is empty, and I'm lost to a future I can't control.

Above me, a cloud moves slowly across the moon, casting me into shadow. I remain on my knees, my arms curled close to my chest, staring down at my empty hands. They burned bright silver, full of power, and now the skin across my palms appears gray and dull.

I don't expect the Vandawolf to answer me, but I ask anyway. "How is this possible?"

I can't understand why Malak's hammer—the tool of a monster and a murderer—triggered my power when other tools never did. The Vandawolf must know why, or he wouldn't have forced me to pick it up.

He places the hammer back into its groove on the anvil, so close to me that it's almost as if he's goading me to grab it.

But that will only cost my brother and sister their lives.

I will never disobey this man while he holds my family's safety in his hands.

He crouches to me and, for the first time, he draws aside the curtain of his hair, fully revealing his wolf's features.

I don't flinch.

I make a vow to myself that I will never look away from this man. I will face him. Always.

The Vandawolf exhales slowly as the cloud cover casts him into shadow with me.

He speaks in a low rumble and in his voice I hear violence and determination. His will to survive. "Before I killed Malak, he gave up all of his secrets to me. Even the secrets he kept from his own people."

I wait for the Vandawolf to continue, my hands slowly closing into fists, as if I could fold up the power I experienced and put it away from me forever.

Whatever power I have, it will only be wielded at the Vandawolf's command.

I am his until the day I die.

The Vandawolf lowers his voice to a bare murmur, and his words leave me cold when he says, "Malak was left-handed, too."

PART TWO
THE CAGE IN THE SKY
PRESENT DAY

CHAPTER 6
PRESENT DAY

The scent of rain makes my blood run cold.

A single crimson drop splashes onto my left shoulder, sinking through the gauzy, white robe that clings to my body. The cold droplet trickles down my chest, a path like ice, but I make no move to wipe it away.

Sudden moves are a bad idea in the Vandawolf's presence.

He stands with his back to me, one big hand gripping the balustrade at the side of the stone tower where he keeps me.

A sheen of sweat glistens across his naked back from his broad shoulders to the top of his pants, his muscles tensing when he tips his head to study the boiling clouds gathering above us. Moisture clings to the ends of his unruly hair at the nape of his neck, the movement of his head sending droplets across his shoulder blades.

He's changed a lot over the past ten years. His chest is now impossibly broad, his shoulders wide, and his muscles honed. He has scars he didn't have the night I first met him.

But much has also stayed the same. His temperament, for one. His wolfish nature, for another.

I can only guess what he was doing before he stormed into my room just now. Training new soldiers, perhaps.

When the rain threatens to fall, he drops everything. He comes straight to me, even though I've remained his enemy.

Not to ask for my help. No, never that.

He comes to send me out to fight to the death.

The wind picks up, swirling across the balcony and bringing with it the scent of the blood-rain. From this vantage point, we have a full view of the northern side of the vast human city that sprawls around the Vandawolf's castle—a city that contains both darkness and light, safety and danger. It took years to rebuild what the Blacksmiths had torn down and now the city thrives.

But beyond it, the wasteland has remained as dangerous as it was the night the Vandawolf claimed me.

From the balcony, we can see out past the unbroken wall that circles and protects the city, all the way to the scorched field that stretches for miles into the distance.

It's a field burned by magic. Littered with blackened, skeletal tree stumps that crumble at the cut of a sword.

The ash is so thick out there that it looks like snow churning in the wind.

It hides the bones I've added to it over the years.

"The attack will come from the north," the Vandawolf says, without turning. His voice is a low growl, a hint of the savage beast that lives within him. "The attack will start over there, near the edge of the Sunken Bog. I sense it."

I have no reason to question his judgement. He has proven time and time again that he has the same sharp eyesight and sense of smell as a wolf, along with a wolf's speed and agility— strengths that he will use against me if he thinks for a second that I might betray him.

What's more, he will be able to sense the intensifying

magic in the air as well as I can. A resurgence of the transformation magic with which the Blacksmiths scarred the earth.

Another crimson raindrop falls from the churning sky. This one lands on top of the stone balustrade next to the Vandawolf's hand. He doesn't flinch or acknowledge the blood-red stain spreading across the worn gray stone, but I have no doubt that he's aware of everything around him.

Nothing escapes his notice. Not the raindrop. Not the stifling charge of magic in the air. Certainly not the sudden hitch in my breathing as my heart pounds harder within my chest.

The rain always has this effect on me, the magic in the air tingling down my spine, making me aware of the power I can't access without the tools that the Vandawolf keeps from me.

So I wait. I force myself to remain quiet. Ready for his command.

I only shout when he tells me to shout. I strike when he tells me to strike. Every move I make is subject to his needs.

Even when he sends me outside the city walls to fight for my life and for the safety of the humans who live in the city, I act according to his most fundamental ultimatum: kill or my family will be killed.

The icy wind hits my body and chills me to my bones. It plucks at my robe and loosens the sash. The garment is in danger of coming apart at the front, but it wouldn't make any difference. I'm wearing only sheer underwear underneath it and the material conceals none of my curves.

The Vandawolf requires me to wear these clothes when I'm alone with him because it means I can't hide any weapon on my body.

I'm freezing, wishing for a blanket, but still I wait for him to give me the command I know is coming.

He finally breaks his silence, but not to give me the order I was expecting. "Fear doesn't suit you, Asha."

He hasn't turned, so I'm not sure what he's thinking, but he rarely comments on my mental state. It irks me that he thinks I'm afraid when the emotion I'm feeling right now is far more complex.

A mix of anticipation and dread. Need and hope. Terror and determination.

I *should* feel nothing but fear, but it's only when he sends me beyond the city walls that I glimpse any kind of freedom, even if it comes with the threat of death.

Unsettled by his declaration, I tip up my chin. "Give me my hammer, and I'll show you that I'm not afraid."

It wasn't meant to sound like a threat—not to him, anyway —but I immediately recognize that he could take it as one.

He turns, a dangerous snarl lifting the corners of his lips and revealing the permanently sharp, canine tooth at the left side of his mouth. A wolf's tooth. His left eye is amber and almond-shaped. The eye of a wolf.

The first time I saw him, his wolf's features were masked in blood. I'd caught only a flash of teeth and recognized the different colors and shapes of his eyes, the unnatural and wolfish texture of his hair.

Later, the details of his transformation were clearer.

He is partially and permanently changed on the left side of his face while the rest of him—what I've seen, anyway—is human. Often, he will conceal his animal features from his human brethren by allowing his unruly hair to fall across the left side of his face. Every strand of his hair is an ashen shade of black. The darkest gray. In some lights, it's as if he wears a crown of darkness on his head. In other lights, his hair glints with hints of silver. Touched by magic.

He never hides his wolfish features from me, especially when we're alone.

"Give you tools, and you become enslaved to the magic that binds you," he snarls.

I can't deny it. Connecting with my magic changes my impulses. It's alluring and seductive, calling me to push the boundaries of what it can do. What *I* can do.

I don't hold my tongue in time.

"I'm enslaved to *you*," I bite back. "Since you determine when I wield my power and whom I wield it against."

Oh... fuck.

I can only blame the magic in the air, the irrepressible charge that shivers across my nearly naked form and reminds me of the power that is so close, yet so inaccessible to me right now.

My regret at speaking out is instant.

So is his response.

He darts forward, demonstrating how agile and strong he is when he lifts me off my feet and pushes me up against the wall at the back of the balcony.

Without access to my magic, my reflexes are human, and I've barely got my hands up before he pins me against the rough stone, every sharp edge of rock pressing into my skin.

For some reason, he chooses to wrap his big hand around the back of my head before I hit the surface. I guess it's because he can't afford to risk knocking me unconscious right now.

I'm acutely aware of soft tearing sounds as the flimsy material at my back scrapes against the stone. Intensely aware of the heat of his body pressed against mine, the sheen of sweat across his chest soaking into the front of my robe, and the muscles in his thighs pressed to my legs.

The crush of his body is so forceful that my chest is compressed, and I hold my breath, but never once do I look away. I made a promise to myself ten years ago, and I've kept it.

His amber wolf's eye is bright with bloodlust. The wolf that became part of his nature must have been wild, untamable... *savage*. But then, it was not well treated.

Still, there's a line he's never crossed with me. He may

make me stand nearly naked in his presence when we're alone, but he's never forced his touch on me in any manner other than as a warrior.

His right hand closes more tightly around my left shoulder —a threat I immediately recognize since I wield my magic with my left hand.

"One day," he says softly, more softly than I was expecting, "I will find a way to free you from your magic."

For a moment, I sense a hint of regret in his voice. After all, I was born this way. I didn't choose to be a vessel to the twisted magic that tore our world apart. I didn't take part in my predecessors' crimes or have any influence over their decisions.

The Vandawolf's expression hardens. "If I can't find another way, I will rip your magic from you like I cleaved it from the others of your kind."

He means it literally and I fight my shudder.

All he has to do is cut my left hand from my body and my magic will be at an end. Such a simple but gruesome way to stop a Blacksmith from accessing their power ever again. He must have discovered this on the night he killed my people. I'll never know if he found out by accident or if Malak somehow let it slip.

To this day, I don't know who the Vandawolf was before Malak imprisoned him. I've pieced together small pieces of information. He was raised by his father. Apparently, his mother died—or disappeared. The stories vary. He had a brother, a few years younger than him. His brother was Malak's last failure before he succeeded with the Vandawolf.

It's ironic to me that Malak's obsession led him to create a human who could defeat him. An experiment so successful that the Vandawolf was stronger and faster than Malak could have ever been.

The Vandawolf liberated the humans, and I went from one cage to another.

It wasn't long after that first night that the Vandawolf devised multiple uses for me, and not all involved fighting battles in the wasteland.

There was a time when I believed that light could defeat darkness, but I soon came to understand that darkness merely replaces itself.

"One day you'll end me," I say with utter certainty as his hands tighten around me. "Until then, I'm yours to command."

Sliding his hand down my arm to wrap firmly around my left wrist, he eases back and pulls me away from the wall. His other hand is tangled in my silvery-blonde hair and is slower to leave me.

"Kneel," he orders me, still gripping my left hand, but his hold softens, no longer painful. Not like the first time he grabbed me when he was covered in the blood of my people, his face more beast than human. The way his amber eye seared through me when he sensed the powerlessness of my right hand still haunts me.

"Are you loyal to me?" he asks, his gaze piercing me as surely as he will drive a knife into my heart if I lie to him.

I relax a little as we settle into the routine that I'm accustomed to. "I am."

His eyes narrow, the amber in his wolf's eye brightening while the gray of his human eye is cold as stone. "Will you betray me?"

I'm emphatic. "Never."

Usually, he would let me go at this point and tell me to prepare myself for the fight ahead, but today, he continues with a dangerous growl on his lips. "Remember what you stand to lose."

My sister and brother.

I fight the sudden clench in my jaw.

It's been a while since he reminded me about the leverage

he has over me. It's been even longer since I saw my siblings at anything but a distance.

Kedric and Maybelle adopted them and within a year, they started dying their hair brown. It makes them much harder to pick out from a crowd—which is the point, since they're a much less visible target to other humans.

I've heard that they work with Kedric now, building and repairing homes. Apparently, Tamra designed a better roofing system to cope with the rain, and Gallium figured out how to improve sanitation.

Their minds were made for creating infrastructure and I'm grateful that the Vandawolf has chosen to give them that freedom.

But he has made it clear to me that he will cut them down in a heartbeat if I betray him.

He finally releases my arm and steps back, taking his body heat with him.

Above us, the clouds are beginning to churn, turning a dangerously crimson hue.

Another raindrop splashes to the stone between us, a bloody stain that divides us.

Him and me. Vandawolf and Blacksmith. A master and his captive weapon.

Across the city, the bells start to ring, a call to the soldiers to hurry to the wall, and a warning to civilians to get inside, take shelter, and pray.

Their fate is once again in my hands.

CHAPTER 7

As the bells continue to ring, a final gust of wind plucks my robe open, chilling me to the bone.

The Vandawolf is already prowling past me into the room beyond the balcony—my room—but his focus flickers briefly to the sash now whipping freely at my side.

He catches it before it can fly free, wrapping the strip of material around his fist as easily as he ties me to his will.

His gaze pierces mine, but in the next moment, his back is to me.

He steps into the shadow of my room, moving quickly now.

Every piece of furniture inside the room is made of wood, cleverly constructed without a single nail. Even the hinges on the door are made of a combination of wood and hardened resin, attached to the stone doorframe by boring holes, filling them with resin, and sinking wooden pegs into them.

The Vandawolf takes no risks with me. He restricts my access to metal to the fullest extent possible.

That's despite knowing full well that I can't forge anything without my hammer.

Ordinary metal does not obey my will. Not unless I

submerge it in forge-fire and shape it with my hammer to imbue it with my magic. Only then can I create weapons from it.

I remain on the balcony as the Vandawolf throws the far door open to the four human guards waiting outside my room—three men and a woman.

"Rachel, bring in Asha's armor," the Vandawolf orders the woman.

"Yes, lord," she says. The humans have come to address the Vandawolf as 'lord.' At one point, they wanted to crown him king, but he wouldn't have it. He rules over them with a council at his side.

"And hurry," the Vandawolf continues. "The magic beyond the wall is building faster than usual."

He turns to the tallest of the men, who towers in the doorway beside Rachel. "Braddock, guard Asha carefully."

"Always, lord," Braddock replies, his voice rough.

Oh, he will.

He doesn't dare look me up and down as often as he used to, but he won't let me out of his sight.

He takes up his usual position leaning against the back wall, scrutinizing me with faded-brown eyes, while Rachel hurries to follow him inside, her arms full of armor.

Braddock is aging now—probably approaching forty—but he's remained broad-shouldered and muscular. His complexion is ruddier these days, which I suspect is from drink, and his brown beard has hints of gray. He's just as quick to anger as he always was.

He doesn't trust me, and I don't trust him.

Rachel rushes to spread my armor across the bed. She has brown hair and brown eyes like the majority of the humans in the city, although her skin is paler than most. She was younger than me when the Vandawolf annihilated the Blacksmiths, and she wasn't in the crowd that night.

She's always polite—and also warier of me than Braddock

is. Possibly because it's her job to tie off all the belts and buckles on my armor that I can't reach, which means she has to come closer to me than the other guards do.

The power building in the sky warns me we don't have long.

I'm itching to step inside, conscious of the new drops of blood-rain splattering the balcony beside me.

But I make myself wait while Rachel loudly and deliberately counts the pieces of metal on my armor, pointing at each one for the Vandawolf to see.

It's so that I don't try to secretly add another buckle to my armor while I'm in the wasteland.

I'm not sure how I would do such a thing, but again, the Vandawolf takes no chances.

Not that he couldn't tell at a glance if I were hiding a Blacksmith's weapon on my body.

Just as he can sense the magic growing in the wasteland, he can identify Blacksmith magic immediately.

This whole charade is for the humans' benefit.

The Vandawolf waits near the door, his weight shifting from side to side, a sign of growing impatience as he also waits for Rachel to finish counting.

"Twelve steel buckles," she announces. "The same as always."

"Good," the Vandawolf says. "Bring Asha to the northern gate as soon as she's dressed."

His hair is covering his wolf's eye now and his shoulders hunch a little before he stalks from the room.

I won't see him again until I reach the city walls.

He alone will bring me my tools. He won't allow anyone else to touch them, and he's wise to be cautious—the transformation magic within the metal is dangerous to humans.

Another raindrop falls on my shoulder. A quick glance

upward tells me that the clouds are boiling, seething like a pot that's about to spill over.

Even the light around us is turning red.

My silver-blonde hair is reflecting it.

Across the distance, Braddock's eyes narrow at me. "Devil girl," he mutters beneath his breath.

No matter what he calls me, I let it wash over me.

Rachel steps back from the armor. "Lady Asha, we're ready for you."

She calls me 'lady' like I'm some sort of noble. Some of the humans who guard the wall do, too.

I don't know how to put a stop to it, since I'm prohibited from telling any human what to do.

I focus on my armor, hurrying toward the bed and the blood-red leather bodice, tunic, pants, and crimson cape spread across it. Colors that match the rain and won't show the blood so badly.

I carefully hold the diaphanous robe close to my body until I reach the bed. Snatching up the pants, I pull them on first before turning my back, removing the robe, pulling on the tunic, and then positioning the bodice over the top.

Rachel pulls the harnesses tightly across my back and around my arms and I test my movement before thanking her for her help. We may not be friends, but she has the power to leave my armor loose, which would make me vulnerable, yet she always tightens it perfectly.

I welcome the warmth and the strength in each piece of my armor. The bodice extends up to the base of my neck, protecting all of my vital organs while the plates across my shoulders mold to the curve of my biceps. The Vandawolf surprised me with this armor when I was eighteen. Before then, he sent me out wearing nothing more than a tunic and pants.

In hindsight, I'm lucky I survived those early battles.

But then, the monsters weren't as strong as they've become in recent years.

Once dressed, I take a moment to breathe deeply and quiet my pounding heart.

Then I turn back to Rachel and Braddock. "I'm ready."

Braddock inclines his head toward the door, and I know the drill.

Rachel goes first. I follow her. Braddock brings up the rear. The other two guards waiting outside the door flank me when I exit the room. All four of them will escort me to the wall.

The corridor outside is short but wide, leading to an equally wide set of stairs. Down we go. Flight after flight of stairs, five in total, before we reach the base of the tower, where we exit directly into the courtyard.

Malak's anvil is long gone. The courtyard now contains a few potted plants, although they struggle to grow.

Crops and trees only thrive on the southern side of the city, farthest from the damaged wasteland that lies to the north. The fields on the southern side have been individually walled off in case of attack, creating segments of land that stretch nearly to the mountains.

It's a straightforward walk from the castle to the northern gate along a wide, cobbled path. There are direct paths, like the spokes of a wheel, from the castle to each of the four gates, one in the north, the south, the east, and the west. The southern and western gates give access to the crop fields. The northern and eastern gates let out into the wasteland.

All gates are heavily guarded.

Rachel keeps a quick pace and I walk in time with her.

I'm conscious of the tense silence around me as we hurry along the deserted path.

When the bells ring out, the city becomes deathly quiet, its inhabitants hiding themselves away behind barricaded doors and windows. Tamra and Gallium will be among them, staying safe with Kedric and Maybelle in their home on the southern side of the city.

The humans are never so united as they are in fear.

Finally, we reach the wall.

All along the top of it, soldiers have gathered. Each of them is wearing armor and carrying long spears—weapons forged by human metalworkers.

A group of soldiers has also gathered in front of the gate. There are about twenty of them, standing three rows deep. They are the brave souls who will follow me out into the wasteland, forming a second line of defense should I fail to kill what needs to be killed. They will stay far behind me, and they won't come to my aid if I fall.

They are colloquially known as *the Wasteland Warriors* and they train as hard as I do, even though I've never let a monster get past me.

The Vandawolf waits in front of them, his presence dominating the space, his shoulders still slightly hunched and his hair falling firmly across his wolf's features.

He stands to the left of the table that holds my tools.

It's only ten paces away now, but even from this distance, the energy radiating from the metal pieces makes my skin tingle.

Somehow, this magic diminishes everything else around me —everything, that is, except the Vandawolf.

Now that the sky has turned to blood, and the air is filled with a crimson gleam, a shimmer of magic is visible to me above my tools.

It rises up and swathes the Vandawolf's broad chest in ribbons like heat waves.

Blacksmith's magic is drawn to itself.

The humans won't be able to see it and that is probably for the best.

Right now, he must look human to them.

Rachel steps out of my path and the soldiers on either side of me peel away. They take up position with Braddock at my back.

I'm now wedged between the guards at my back and the Vandawolf and a legion of soldiers in front of me.

I pause on the front foot, waiting for the Vandawolf to give me permission to approach the table.

He doesn't waste time. "Approach!"

Quickly stepping up to the table, I take stock of my tools.

I call them *mine*, even though they were Malak's.

Just like Malak's anvil, this waist-height table has grooves carved into its surface to securely house the hammer and three titanium medallions. The Vandawolf doesn't give me the tongs since I don't work with fire.

Hovering my hand over the medallions, I take a moment to close my eyes and sense the ebb and flow of the power rippling through them.

My stomach churns as the dark energy calls to me, a seductive pull that reeks of violence.

I tell myself it's a necessary evil.

I convince myself that this magic may bind me once I pick up my tools, but I am still *me*. My will is stronger than the destructive desire Malak left in this metal.

I tell myself this, repeating it like a mantra as I open my eyes and reach for the hammer with my left hand. I need only tap the medallions with the hammer to awaken the power within them, and then I can leave the hammer on the table. I will take only the medallions with me.

I'm an inch away from touching the hammer when the Vandawolf grabs my wrist.

I gasp with surprise, my fingers splaying.

"Kill the monster," he snarls, low and dangerous. "Anything less is betrayal."

I know this.

The fact that he feels the need to remind me, and in front of all of these humans, makes my forehead crease.

I study his visible eye—the human one—trying to discern his thoughts. There's a tightness around his lips and eyes that could indicate heightened anxiety, more than usual, but I can't be certain.

I want to ask him what's going on, but I'm conscious of the intensifying stares around us.

It's rare for the Vandawolf to lay a hand on me in public. That first night at Malak's anvil was the exception.

Still, he grips me, and I refuse to look away, even though my eyes are now watering.

I speak my promise through clenched teeth. "I'll tear the monster apart."

Finally, he releases my hand.

Free from his hold, my palm plummets to the hammer, faster than I intended.

Power strikes through me so quickly that it stops the breath in my chest.

Energy explodes through my arm, washing across my body like a wildfire burning through my muscles, filling my mind with unquenchable desire.

The desire to mold the world, the humans, and the very earth beneath my feet into whatever form I want them to take.

Malak's desire. Not mine.

The impulses within the hammer rage through my mind, commands that I fight with every beat of my heart.

Take control of the light and the dark.

Shape the living to match your needs.

Make them yours.

All of them...

I push back against the twisted power, focusing away from the things I could harm and to the top of the hammer's head and the medallions that will soon come alive at my touch.

I tell myself: The *medallions* are mine to mold.

Not the humans. Not the earth. Not... the Vandawolf.

Dear saints, I'm even more conscious of the heat in his body now. Through this lens of power, he's a burning presence at my side, more alive than any nearby human, his wolf's nature writhing within him. A fierce beast he barely controls.

It's in these moments, when I see into the heart of his inner turmoil, that I recognize the depth of the lie he lives.

He pretends to be civilized. Controlled by rules and decency.

It's a fucking façade.

He wants to give in to the wild as badly as I do.

CHAPTER 8

The fire within the Vandawolf is like molten metal waiting for me to shape every inch of muscle...

Fighting the groan rising to my lips, I grip the hammer more tightly, smothering the overwhelming impulse to reach out and close the gap between him and me.

Three droplets of rain fall to the table and it's the cold distraction I need.

I'm lucky the clouds haven't opened up already.

The threat is growing beyond the city, and I need to hurry, but I can't rush this part of the process or I'll risk losing control.

Lifting the hammer, I strike down. *Hard.* Connecting with each of the medallions, one after the other.

Each *clang* rings out, a sharp, echoing sound that makes the humans wince. I'm conscious of the way they edge away from me. If I were really aggressive about it, the clangs could make their ears bleed.

Along with the noise, I know how the power surging within my body will appear to them.

My pale skin takes on a metallic sheen, becoming silvery. My hair glistens, reflecting even more of the crimson light around us. My eyes will gleam a deceptively soft and gentle shade that's neither pure blue nor green nor gray, but moves between all three depending on the angle of the light.

With each strike, sparks of dark light shoot up from each medallion. They glow brightly as they respond to my magic, awakening from their sleep, and then they fade again, as if they're waiting expectantly.

Striking them brings some relief from the intensifying impulses within me. I won't be completely in control until I can craft each band into the weapon of my choosing, but I don't dare do that until I step through the wall. Any sooner would be interpreted as a threat to both the Vandawolf and the humans, but damn, it's taking all of my willpower to resist.

Moving quickly, I return the hammer to its place on the table, even though my instinct is to place it in the harness at my waist like Blacksmiths of old.

Continuing to use my left hand, I position each medallion against my right bicep, one beneath the other, using the power streaming through me to mold them into snug armbands.

Now that the medallions are awake, they will give me continuous access to my magic for as long as they're near my body.

Carrying them on my right arm means I can easily remove and transform them with my left hand when I need them.

My hands are shaking by the time I finish.

The surge of power within me is unbearable now.

I barely recognize my voice when I say to the Vandawolf, "Let me through the gate."

I expect the three rows of soldiers to part and let me through like they usually do at this point, but the Vandawolf says, "One more thing."

He turns to the soldiers and gestures toward the back row. "Gallium, step forward."

Gallium?

I stiffen, suddenly alarmed.

My brother can't be here. He isn't a Wasteland Warrior.

The front two rows part and Gallium steps through.

I barely recognize the grown man who stops several paces from me, but his green eyes are unmistakable. He stands as tall as the Vandawolf with shoulders just as broad. His biceps are visible beneath a short-sleeved tunic, and they're clearly defined, no doubt from years of construction work. In his face, I see the shape of our mother's eyes and the strong cut of our father's jaw.

Nobody would call him small for his age anymore.

He's dressed in the same armor as the warriors, and he carries a sword at his back and a dagger at his waist.

He looks completely comfortable with the weapons.

"Asha," he says, greeting me with a solemn nod, his voice a deep baritone. "I'm coming with you."

My rejection is sharp. "You will *not*."

Shaking my head, I take a quick step back, conscious of the way Braddock is suddenly breathing down my neck. The bastard must have edged forward to get a better view of my family reunion, and now he's in danger of stepping too close to me while I'm connected to my magic.

The darkness within this power would love to smash him into a pulp—a violence I must reserve for the monster in the wasteland.

So now I'm fighting both my impulses and my heart.

I can't allow Gallium to be endangered outside the wall, but I also never wanted him to see me this way.

I never wanted him to see my body light up with the magic that only brought him pain. I don't want him to watch me at my worst when the magic has full hold of me and I give in to the impulses raging through me.

If I'd known Gallium was here, I wouldn't have picked up the hammer in the first place.

My brother's jaw clenches at my response, but I'm already spinning away from him to the Vandawolf.

I keep my voice low, but I have no doubt everyone can hear me, especially now that the wind has died down. "I refuse to take my brother with me."

I meet the Vandawolf's hard eyes. "You promised to keep my siblings safe."

"Which is why your sister is sheltering on the southern side of the city."

"*Both* of them," I say.

His expression softens, but not by much. "Gallium isn't here at my command. He asked to go with you. In fact, he bargained for it. If you have an issue with it, you'll need to take it up with him. My mercy only stretches so far."

I whirl back to Gallium, incredulous, but he doesn't back down even when my left hand rises toward the medallions on my bicep.

"I'm coming with you, Asha," he repeats, his hand hovering over his dagger's hilt, as if he's willing to take me on should I disagree.

My thoughts are churning. I need to find a way to make him stay here in safety, but I also need to move. The longer it takes me to get out into the wasteland, the closer the monster will make it to the city before I can fight it.

The longer I wait, the stronger my power and impulses grow.

I squeeze my eyes shut, fighting the darkness that will soon cloud my thoughts and dominate my emotions completely.

Take control of the light and the dark.

Shape the living... Mold them... Mold them...

Power is building like a scream inside my mind.

I need to move.

My eyes snap open and I glower at Gallium. "Keep your distance, brother, if you don't want to get hurt."

Then I stride toward the soldiers blocking the gate. "Get the fuck out of my way."

Let me go kill a monster for you.

I step out onto the ashen field just as the wind picks up.

The air is cold and smells stale no matter how hard the breeze blows. This close to the wall, the layer of ash covering the ground is thinnest, making the ground solider beneath my feet, but by the time we make it a hundred paces out, our feet will sink into the drifting white-gray powder.

A splatter of rain in front of me indicates the downpour is only seconds away now. We need to make it much farther out before that happens because visibility will be impaired.

The sky is as dark as dusk now even though it's early afternoon.

Gallium steps up behind me, but I don't wait for him.

I need to keep moving and I need to maintain a safe distance between him and me so I don't hurt him.

He keeps pace with me but remains a step behind and to my right. He's wise to stay on that side of me since my left hand is curled into a fist and tingling with magic.

My heart may be filled with the hunger to transform all living things around me but that doesn't mean I'm not hurting right now.

"This isn't the reunion I wanted," I grind out as I glance back at him.

"It was the only way that worked," he replies.

I miss a step because his answer implies that he tried other ways and failed.

He confirms it when he says, "Tamra and I have been searching for a way back to you for years."

"This is not a good way," I snap. "It isn't a safe way."

Gallium is quiet and when I glance back at him, he wears a small smile. It surprises me. He's incredibly calm in the face of my anger.

"No way is a good way back to the Left-hand of Malak," he says.

I shudder as he uses the name some humans call me. "Are you trying to insult me?"

He shakes his head. "You use Malak's hammer and you're left-handed. You're *feared*, not despised."

Fear that the Vandawolf takes full advantage of. Killing monsters out in this wasteland isn't the only task he sets for me.

Gallium is still speaking. "The only safe way to associate with you is as one of your guards—and unfortunately, the Vandawolf won't trust me with that—or as a Warrior. At least this way, I learned a few new skills."

He taps the dagger at his waist.

My forehead creases as I resume plowing through the dust, kicking up ash. It floats around us like snow flurries as we reach the first line of skeletal trees.

I'll need to stop soon to determine where the creature will rise, but for now, I continue onward. Behind us, the Wasteland Warriors are spreading out. They will stop when they reach these trees and fan out to cover as much ground as they can.

"You've been training with the Vandawolf." It's a guess on my part, but Gallium confirms it with a nod.

"For the last four years," he says.

I pull to another stop. "Four *years!*"

Gallium shrugs. "I was playing the long game."

I stare at him, wishing that the magic coursing through my body wasn't veiling my vision in a lens of power.

He arches an eyebrow at me. "You realize Tamra chose to design rooftops because she thought it would bring her closer to you in your tower?"

I shake my head.

Gallium gives a rueful shake of his head. "Sadly, there are no roofs tall enough."

My heart pangs at the realization that she tried. That

they've both been trying to reach me all this time. "If you trained with the Vandawolf for four years for the chance to speak with me, then you must have something to say to me."

He's quiet for a moment. "We missed you."

I take a shaky breath, pushing hard at the darkness, needing to put voice to what I've felt ever since the night they were taken away from me. "I missed you, too. Both of you."

I take a step toward him, wishing I could hug him. At the very least grasp his shoulder in the way of one soldier to another. But it only triggers another surge of overwhelming power.

I try to shake it off. An impossible task. Especially when my emotions are clouding my judgement.

I pin him with my gaze as I say, "You can't have done all this just to tell me you miss me."

His expression hardens a little. "We wanted to see how you were being treated."

"By the Vandawolf?" My forehead creases. Then I shrug. "He keeps me where the humans can't kill me in my sleep. He gives me food and armor—"

"And sends you out to fight his battles for him," Gallium says, all gentleness gone from his expression.

Now there's only the look of a warrior on his face.

I glance back to the wall. Over the years, I've ascertained that the Vandawolf has much sharper hearing than any human. Chances are that he can hear us even now.

Regardless, my answer would be the same. The truth. "It isn't cowardice," I say. "If he died, the city would descend into chaos. I would be killed. You would be killed. So would Kedric and Maybelle for taking you in."

I sigh before I turn away and resume plowing through the field. "Our fates are tied to his."

"But will he free you?" Gallium asks.

"Not as long as there are monsters to be killed," I say.

Monsters in the wasteland. Others who live in the dark spaces of the city—humans who break the Vandawolf's laws.

But my thoughts are churning again because I don't believe Gallium has been upfront about his real purpose. He can't have trained for four years just to tell me he misses me and ask me how I am.

He asked me if the Vandawolf will ever free me, and now I wonder if his question was loaded.

I veer so sharply toward my brother that he has the good sense to backpedal away from me instead of standing his ground.

My voice carries all the danger of my power as I prowl after him.

I will be menacing if it means I get the truth.

"Do you mean to free me?" I demand to know. "Is that why you're here?"

Gallium tips his chin up and digs his heels in, forcing me to come to a standstill.

"We do," he says. "We *will*."

CHAPTER 9

S udden fear spikes my blood and it only makes me angry. "You will not speak of my freedom, brother. That is treason, and it will only get you killed."

Gallium stands his ground and doesn't look away. "I remember every detail of that night," he says. "I remember the look in your eyes, Asha. You did everything in your power to protect us." He thumps his chest, his voice rising. "We aren't children anymore. You don't need to give up the rest of your life for us. There has to be another way."

There isn't.

I've had years to think about it and I've come up with nothing. Even if we ran into the mountains—assuming we could survive the terrain—the Vandawolf would find us. We have no allies. Nobody to run *to*.

I squeeze my eyes closed, fighting back the burn of tears, the last of my human emotions welling hot inside my heart.

Above us, the clouds rumble with thunder, but I'm grateful there are no flickers of lightning behind my closed eyelids.

Lightning produces the most dangerous monsters.

But the thunder tells me I'm out of time. Gallium has

snatched this moment with me, paid for with four years of training, but now it must come to an end.

I speak softly. "Very soon, I won't be myself. I need you to steer clear of me and protect yourself at all times. Don't follow me into battle. Hang back." I raise my eyes to his. "When it's over, I'll find a way for us to speak again. I promise."

He nods, but his jaw clenches. "If you're in trouble, I won't sit by and watch you die."

My heart squeezes and the echo of his young voice returns to me: *I will fight with you, Asha.*

Still, I give a firm shake of my head, the magic within me giving me confidence. "I've fought countless beasts—"

"Not this one."

I peer at him. The edge of tension in his voice reminds me of the Vandawolf when he grabbed my hand and reminded me to kill the beast. If Gallium was training with the Vandawolf... in fact, if Gallium was with the Vandawolf right before the rain started... then maybe Gallium knows why the Vandawolf is so on edge. Maybe the Vandawolf said something to him.

"What do you know?" I try to keep the snarl out of my voice, but I'm losing myself.

Too quickly now.

Gallium hesitates. "I've never seen fear on the Vandawolf's face before today."

I narrow my eyes at him, needing more.

He shakes his head. "That's all I know."

I spin away from him. "Stay behind me."

We've reached the third line of skeletal trees now. Their trunks gleam with magic that has burned itself out, leaving them like fragile onyx statues.

On my far right, the Sunken Bog is a stagnant marsh. It's filled with soggy earth and misshapen trees. Those trees aren't burned out, but their trunks consist of perpetually rotting wood and have a strange, amber hue. Their leaves are dark brown and curl into shapes resembling insects.

I head in that direction, since the Vandawolf said the attack would happen near the edge of the bog.

Behind us, the Wasteland Warriors have now taken up position at the first line of trees. The outer gate in the wall finally closes with a *clang*, and I glance back once to make out the Vandawolf standing on the wall above the gate.

He'll watch from that vantage point until it's over.

The wall provides an illusion of safety for the humans in the city.

Every monster I've faced on this battlefield—even the weaker ones—could scale the wall within moments.

At least there's only ever one.

One beast to slay and then it's over until the magic in the ground delivers yet another storm and another monster to kill.

We're nearing the edge of the bog, more than five hundred paces out, when the storm clouds finally open up.

Blood-rain pours around me, even colder than the wind, and the sudden pounding weight of liquid drives me to the ground.

I'm prepared for the onslaught and briefly take a knee.

Behind me, five paces back, Gallium drops to the ground, and then I lose sight of him within the thick curtain of rain.

I push back to my feet, sensing every strike of magic in the raindrops.

It only makes me stronger.

My hair is plastered to my head, although my armor is designed so the liquid runs right off it. Visibility is terrible, and the ground beneath my feet is quickly turning to sludge.

But the rain is useful.

It always pours the thickest where the monster will appear.

I scan my surroundings, trying to breathe without inhaling blood, searching for the spot where the rain falls the heaviest.

My forehead quickly creases with confusion.

The Vandawolf said he sensed that the attack would come from the northeast at the edge of the Sunken Bog—in fact, he made a point of repeating it—but the rainfall closest to me is the lightest.

The strongest downpour is off to my left near the center of the field. *Away from* the bog.

Dropping back to a crouch, I press my left palm to the muddy earth at my feet, accessing my magic through the medallions and allowing it to flow into the ground and connect with the environment.

At my touch, a flash of energy streaks from a point in the center of the wasteland. It shoots across the earth so fast that I would have missed it without my heightened vision.

It leaps up from the sodden ash beneath my palm to bite my bare skin.

Quickly retracting my hand, I rub my palm against my thigh.

The energy definitely traveled from the wasteland, not from my right near the bog. What's more, the wind suddenly gusts from the same point in the wasteland, bringing an intense heat that sharply counters the otherwise freezing temperature.

My confusion increases.

I don't know why the Vandawolf would have lied to me.

If he didn't lie, then I'm not sure how he could have been so mistaken.

I take another glance at the edge of the bog. Then all the way back toward the wall.

The rain is easing up and my line of sight takes me past Gallium, where he has remained crouched and watching me.

The Vandawolf will be watching me, too.

My magic makes me a bright spark across the distance—he told me that once—and he will follow my every move, even within the barrage of rain.

He's capable of seeing nearly seven hundred paces out. Not every detail, but he'll know if I move off the course he set for me.

Fuck.

But I have to trust my instincts.

If the monster rises from the wasteland instead of the bog, and I don't intercept it, I'll be blamed.

Pushing through the mud and rain, I veer toward Gallium and shout, "Stay there! The monster is this way. I'm going to it."

He squints at me through the downpour and cups his hand behind his ear, an indication that he can't hear me.

"Stay there!" I shout again, pointing to the ground at his feet, nearly choking on the rain as I inhale it.

He finally gives me a nod and remains crouched where he is.

I plow through the mud back into the heart of the waste-land, pushing against the wind until it's beating at me in heat waves.

I'm forced to drop to the ground before it knocks me over.

My heart is pounding.

It's the final burst of fear before the calm sets in.

It won't be long now.

Each creature is unique. Some resemble the wild beasts that used to roam this land when the forest was alive—bears, wolves, and stags. Others resemble slugs and creatures that crawl through the mud. All on a much larger scale.

Some rise from the sodden ash beneath my feet. Some rise from the Toxic Thirst in the east. Some emerge from the onyx trees.

Rarely, they take shape from lightning strikes. Those monsters are the hardest to kill, but luckily, there's no lightning today.

Until I see the monster, I won't know what weapons will be

most effective against it. If it's covered in spikes, I'll need spears so I can fight it from a distance. If it has tough skin, I'll need short daggers. If it has claws, I'll need a shield, although I can only create a small one with the medallions that I have.

I won't know any of that until the rain stops.

That's when the creature will form.

The rain begins to ease around me but pours for a few seconds longer onto a spot only thirty paces away.

It's a brief, final intensification of energy that signals the exact spot where the creature will rise.

I focus on that location, my left hand hovering above the medallions, my muscles tense.

I wait for the rain to stop and the silence to fall.

The final raindrops splatter across the ground in front of me.

One droplet hits my cheek, but I don't wipe it away. I let it run like all the others. I'll only add more blood to it soon.

Now comes the calm.

I exhale the last of the fear that keeps me human, and I give in to the impulses within me.

Rise up and fight me, beast. I will make you mine.

The downpour stops, leaving the blood-rain to swirl through the white ash around me.

The silence is heavy, broken only by drips from nearby tree branches.

My fingers twitch above my medallions as the seconds extend into a long, silent minute.

Finally, ahead of me, the mud begins to stir.

A spiked object emerges from the ground, slowly at first and then faster, rising upward. It's craggy like the burned tree trunks around me but much thinner. Maybe only as thick as my arm.

Its silver color is disconcerting. It could mean this beast will have skin as hard as metal.

Another spike surfaces, poking up through the mud, but it's about four feet from the location of the first spike. Then a third and fourth barb appear, then a fifth and sixth, each one close to the one before.

My forehead creases in concentration until the emerging shapes become clearer.

Antlers!

Each point is deadly sharp and the distance between them tells me this beast will be larger than most.

Its head begins to appear, also a shimmering silver color, although it remains lowered and its eyes are closed.

The beast's formation is much faster now, but still, I force myself to wait.

Wait, I tell myself. *Wait...*

I need to see more of its body to understand the full threat it poses.

It means losing the advantage of killing it before it wakes, but I learned the hard way not to throw myself into an attack before knowing what I'm up against.

Impaling myself on a backbone of bony protrusions would be a bad way to die.

This creature's neck is as long as a stag's and when its back appears, it becomes apparent that its body is covered in interlocking silver plates.

I won't know what they're made of until I touch them. It could be organic material that only *appears* metallic, but I suspect it will be as hard as stone.

There's a pattern to the plates. Swirls across its back and down its legs.

I don't have the luxury of admiring its beauty.

It may have the head and antlers of a stag, but it has the body of a bear with sharp claws, and all of them are extending and retracting as the creature finishes forming and slowly opens its eyes.

I don't waste another moment.

Remaining low to the ground, I slap my left hand to the uppermost armband.

A surge of power and malice, a potent combination, bends the metal to my will. It's like pouring lava through my palm and fingertips, the heat making the band malleable. The force of my will is like a hammer that extends the band into any shape I want it to take.

I picture the spear I need. Long enough to use it to vault across the beast's back. Strong enough to impale the creature through the eye while avoiding its antlers.

The spear is strong. Perfectly formed. I deftly transfer it to my right hand, using my left on the second medallion. It quickly elongates into a dagger, long and curved, its blade gleaming red in the crimson light. I secure it in my belt and then I prowl forward, toward the threat.

The beast shakes his head. Shivers cascade across its body, sending mud sloughing off it onto the ground, revealing the full extent of the protective plating across every inch of its body.

It's as sleek as a blade itself. Larger than any bear. Its antlers are long enough to impale three men standing back to front.

It opens its eyes, a deep brown color, and then it focuses immediately on me. Its nostrils flare and its claws dig into the sodden earth, scraping so deep that little valleys form as it snorts at my approach.

There's always a moment... an impossibly quiet moment... when the last of my humanity surfaces and I hope that the beast will simply back away. Turn and flee into the distant mountains, never to return.

This creature is a product of the transformation magic that remains in this land.

It's a creature of the mud and ash.

It's not my enemy until it threatens to harm me.

I hold my breath and slow my pace as the stag waits a beat longer than the monsters usually do, watching me with eyes that spark with intelligence.

It's so impossibly *alive*.

The magic churning within its body is as alluring to me as the magic that writhes within the Vandawolf himself. It's both beautiful and horrifying at once.

Then it roars, spitting blood-rain across the ground, and the moment breaks.

Its teeth are sharp enough to rip off my limbs. Its mouth is large enough to chew through my chest, armor and all.

I can't help the smile spreading across my face as every-thing else disappears and all of the malice in the medallions surges through me.

It doesn't matter how much the beast roars.

It's mine now.

CHAPTER 10

The beast charges, its claws flashing.

The ground vibrates with every thudding step it takes and its roars are deafening.

Within my mind, all is quiet.

Every sensation rushes across me. The brush of air as I raise my right arm, spear in hand. The slosh of mud that gives way beneath my feet as I leap to the right, avoiding the dangerous swing of the stag's antlers.

The strength in my legs takes me high, the agility of my torso allowing me to twist midair.

My left arm snakes out and I catch hold of the beast's outer antler, letting its momentum throw me farther upward.

Magic floods through my left hand, spearing through the antler. I can't change the beast's emotions, but I can change the nature of its hide.

I have a single thought.

Soft.

I sense the instant change in the surface of the antler, its steely construction softening beneath my palm. If it were as easy as touching the beast and stopping its heart, I would, but I can only change what I can touch, sending my magic across the surface of its skin.

The moment my magic flows across its antler, the beast reacts, rearing up on its hind legs.

The tip of the spike tears off within my hand, but I was ready for it. I don't try to hold on, allowing its upward momentum to throw me into the air, where I fly high above the creature's head and spin to control my trajectory.

I grip the spear in both hands as gravity takes hold once again, and then I plummet toward its neck, the spear's tip pointed downward, the air rushing around me in hot gusts.

The ripple of my magic through the antler is visible to me, a dark light that I pray will reach the back of its neck by the time I make contact.

One heartbeat. Two.

The beast isn't waiting for me to strike. It leaps forward, forcing me to adjust the angle of the spear at the last moment.

A split second later, I crash onto its back, farther to the right than I wanted, but my magic has flowed to the hard plates at the back of the beast's neck and done its work.

The spear drives down through the plates as easily as if they were paper. My strength drives the weapon through the rest of its neck.

The creature rears up again, but I continue to move fast, bracing against its back and using every muscle in my body to rip the spear back out, screaming with effort, before I throw myself from its back.

Landing in the mud, I roll clear of its falling body.

The *thump* as it hits the ground vibrates through the earth, so heavy that it rattles me.

It has fallen onto its side with its back to me. Its antlers—the ones that remained untouched by my magic—have plowed into the ash and dug out little valleys.

I can't see its face to gauge its status from its eyes, so I watch its sides, the up and down movement of its breathing, as I remain crouched, spear in hand.

Its breathing is unexpectedly steady and my forehead creases.

The spear should have done mortal damage, the blood loss should have been catastrophic and death nearly instant, and yet...

As I watch, the metallic plate at the back of its neck seals up, the pierce point disappearing.

The beast takes a deep breath, shuddering as it pushes up to its feet again.

Oh... fuck.

No monster has ever healed itself before.

The first hints of fear return to me, a cold trickle down my spine.

If I can't kill it, then I can't stop it. If I can't stop it...

I slap my left hand against the medallion still resting against my bicep and the surge of power puts a stop to my threatening panic.

I chance a brief glance back at Gallium across the distance, reassuring myself that he has remained at a safe distance, even though his focus is firmly on me. He won't be able to see that the beast isn't dead until it gets back up. I'm sure he'll think that I've killed it.

But the Vandawolf...

I check the far ramparts of the city wall. He's a bright spot in the distance. For now, he, too, has remained where he is.

I banish the last of my fear, grit my teeth, and rise to my feet.

"Come on, you bastard." I growl at the stag. "It's time to come for me. Come wreak your violence."

The beast launches itself back to its feet, its antlers leaving a glittering arc in the air as it swings back to me.

I focus on the way its muscles ripple, seeming connected to

the metal plates encasing its body. All I need is to find its weak spot. A gap between plates where I can connect with sinew and bone beneath the outer layer.

My left hand twitches, my fingers curling toward my palm.

The beast roars at me, spitting blood. It may have healed, but I certainly hurt it.

It lowers its head as if it's going to charge me, its eyes gleaming. They're swirling red and black orbs as if they're filled with silver and reflecting the seething clouds above us.

"Come on!" I scream at it. "Come for me!"

The beast charges, its paws digging turrets in the mud, its claws gouging deep.

I make myself wait the awful heartbeats, judging the distance between the creature and me.

Closer... closer...

Just as the monster would reach me, I launch myself forward, using my spear as a vault, driving it into the ground and leaping upward.

I let go of the weapon, leaving it behind, before I sail directly up and over the stag's antlers. I twist in the air, snatching the dagger from my waist and gripping it in my left hand as I descend once more onto the creature's back.

This time, I don't try to use my magic.

I drive the blade down as hard as I can against the creature's right shoulder, seeking a gap—*any gap*—between the plates protecting its body.

The sharp blade grates down the animal's hide, screeching so loudly that a human's ears would bleed if they were standing nearby. Sparks of dark light fly off the blade as I allow myself to fall, dragging the weapon down the beast's hide as I drop.

It's a horrible risk.

But I need the beast to react. I need it to thrash. Only with movement might the plates on its back separate enough that I can drive my dagger between them and expose its body beneath.

The animal shudders at the sound of grating metal.

It bucks and rears up, roaring as it tries to bat at me with its left paw.

And then—

The blade catches.

The sharp metal slips between the edges of two plates on the beast's lower right shoulder that separated when the beast tried to dislodge me.

My fall stops abruptly and I need to act fast.

With a scream of effort, I drive the blade deep, thumping my right fist against its hilt, wedging it in the monster's flesh to keep the plates separated.

But to drive it deep enough, I'm forced to remain in the path of its claws for a heartbeat too long.

A heartbeat during which I register the danger but can't do anything about it.

My muscles are bunching, my instincts screaming at me to leap away, but there isn't time.

Silver claws drive deep into my armor. The leather rips and a chunk of armor tears free. Air rushes in, beating at my side.

I'm aware of the thick, crimson leather separating from my bodice, pulling away from me as the beast's claws tear deeper.

Deep into my torso.

Then it's all far away. A distant pain as the monster hurls me through the air.

Its claws recede from my body as I'm flung across the field. I'm aware of the hot wind rushing around me, and of the ground spinning beneath me, up and down, around and around, before I hit the ground.

I slide and come to a stop, lying on sodden ash. A river of blood spreads out around me. Some of it will be mine.

I find myself facing upward, staring past the skeletal tree

I've landed beside, and up at the flickering clouds. Little pulses of strangely-golden light dance through them. A ripple of energy high above me.

How can such a beautiful sky be so deadly?

At the back of my mind, my thoughts are cold and clinical. I wanted to wedge my weapon between the plates across the beast's back and expose its skin, and I succeeded.

But the cost was high. I'm wounded—how badly, I'll soon discover—and my blurred vision tells me I have a concussion. My spear lies in the mud too far away to reach, and my dagger remains in the beast's hide.

I have only one more medallion.

But I'm breathing. My lungs must not have been pierced. I guess that's something.

The same clinical reasoning within my mind registers the animal's pounding paws as it rages toward me. It will be upon me in seconds, and I need to get up.

Right now.

Even if it means I'll have to face the damage to my body and the pain that comes with it.

I've barely twitched when Gallium shouts, "Asha!"

I blink as he jumps over me, landing at a crouch between me and the oncoming beast, a dagger in his left hand, the spear in his right.

"Get back!" he roars at the beast.

No, Gallium.

The creature slows—but only a little—before it roars back at him, its mouth opening wide enough to bite off his head.

He launches himself forward, springing up, mud spraying around his feet as he leaves the ground.

My breath catches at the strength in his jump, the way his muscles bunch as he draws the spear back and throws it right into the animal's open mouth. He doesn't have the Vandawolf's speed or strength—that would be impossible—but he's far stronger than an ordinary human.

His spear flies into the beast's mouth and through its right cheek. On impact, the stag skids to a halt, its eyes wide as it thrashes its head.

For a moment, I think it's hurt.

Then it chomps down on the wood, splintering the spear's shaft as easily as it might snap a toothpick.

It spits out the pieces, spraying wood as it screams again with rage.

Gallium leaps back to me as debris spears the air, turning his back toward the spray.

Turning himself into a shield.

The way I once shielded him.

My eyes burn with gratitude despite the horror of the beast bearing down on us. It's a moment where I remember what it was like to have family.

Then I grit my teeth and tell myself to *get the fuck up.*

If I don't, I'll lose Gallium when we've only just been reunited.

My left hand flies to my remaining medallion, my palm closing over it and steadfastly holding on. I draw on the cold anger within the titanium to dull my pain as I roll onto my right side and push up with my right arm. This position has the advantage of hiding the damage to that side and I don't intend to look down.

I'm hurt, and I know it's bad, but taking the time to stop and check means death.

I make it to my knees and then up to my feet.

"Gallium!" I cry. "Get down. Now!"

My brother obeys my command just in time to evade the next swipe of the beast's paw.

I launch myself at its extended limb, pulling the medallion

into my left fist so I'm free to wrap my right hand around its swinging limb and use it to propel myself upward.

Back toward the dagger I left jammed in its side.

I reach out with all my might, my right hand closing around the dagger's hilt, before I pull myself up onto its back.

My left hand is shaking violently.

I've never held a medallion for this long without transforming it into a weapon. With every passing second of contact, the impulses within the metal are becoming an irrepressible command within my mind.

Mold the living to match your will.

Fight the old and find the new...

I don't fight back. Don't resist.

Leaning to the right—so far that I'm in danger of sliding off head-first—I slap my left palm onto the creature's exposed skin. The medallion rests squarely between my hand and the stag's skin, a powerful conduit between my will and its body.

The animal is plowing forward, charging at Gallium, but the medallion is already amplifying my power.

"*Ash!*" I scream. "*You will be ash!*"

CHAPTER 11

B urning malice flows through me, so hot, it feels like my
body is freezing.

Dark light ripples out from my hand, spreading
across the beast's back like a shiver.

Its legs buckle and it drops to its knees, sliding through the
mud and stopping only inches from Gallium, who launches
himself away from it.

My brother lands at a crouch, his head raised, the tension in
his body telling me he's ready to move again if he needs to.

Hairline cracks form in the metal plates across the
monster's hide, shooting out from my position, all the way up
across its head and through its antlers.

Then the plates beneath me give way, cracking and crum-
bling and turning gray.

I throw myself off it while it remains solid, snatching up the
medallion and my dagger, taking handfuls of ash with me.

A trail of dust follows me to the ground, where I land heavily, stumbling and barely getting my feet under me in time to
stay upright.

The creature's face is turned in my direction.

Its crimson and black eyes become glassy, then dull, then gray. A final breath sighs from its mouth before its chest becomes still.

It has become... *ash*.

Just as I willed it.

A gust of wind plucks at the dust across the fallen beast's back, picking up the powder and swirling it into the air.

I stand in the silence, gripping the medallion in my left hand, but even through the veil of malice and power, I feel regret.

Like me, this creature didn't choose the parameters of its existence. It was born from this earth, only to be driven back to the mud from which it rose.

Along with sadness, fear stabs at the edge of my mind.

I've never used my power like this before. It scares me how easy it was to kill a living thing.

I can barely breathe as I reach toward the ashy statue the beast has become, but the next burst of wind razes across the stag's form and it disintegrates in front of me, its body collapsing.

Within moments, it's nothing more than another pile of ash on this barren field.

"Asha?" Gallium's voice breaks through my dread as he steps carefully toward me. "You're hurt."

"Stay back!" I cry, attempting to twist toward him but barely able to move. "I'll hurt you."

I need to place the medallion back on my arm and I need to retrieve my spear—I can't let Gallium touch any of these weapons—but I can't seem to function.

I wobble backward, grateful when Gallium keeps his distance.

"I saw what you did," he says, his green eyes wide and his face pale in the growing dark. "Is that how you always end them?"

"No," I whisper, a strangled exhalation of sound. "I've never done that before."

I fumble with the medallion, trying to return it to my arm, but my fingers are stiff and the titanium sticks to my hand and I don't know why.

Is it sticky with blood?

Why won't it let go?

I turn my left palm over, only to find that the medallion doesn't slide off. Before my eyes and against my will, the ends of the band curl around the back of my hand, clinging to my bare skin as if it were a part of me now.

"No." *This malice can't be a part of me now.* No matter what happens, I can't lose myself to it.

With a cry of effort, I press my left palm to my right bicep and give a snarled command, a cold order. "*Armband.*"

The medallion stops curling around my hand, stills for a moment, and then it obeys me, curving in the opposite direction and around my arm.

But now I'm faced with the extent to which the power within the medallion was keeping the pain at bay.

My surroundings rush in and so does the agony. I force myself to consider the wound—a gut wound, the kind that will kill me. How fast depends on how much blood I lose.

My hands are suddenly shaking violently, and I know I'm about to go into shock. I have enough mental clarity to transfer the dagger into my left hand, transform it back into a medallion, and slap it to my bicep before it, too, can curl around my left palm.

As soon as the second band touches my arm, the full force of magic recedes, leaving me to deal with the consequences.

My scream breaks the heaviness in the air, the sound piercing as anguish burns through me. I drop to my knees, trying only to breathe through the moments, to get to the next moment without losing my mind.

"Asha!" Gallium is no longer keeping his distance. "You're bleeding out!"

He's right. Blood is flowing down my right side, not so fast that I'll be dead within minutes, but fast enough that I won't live beyond the next hour.

I'm faced with a choice. The magic in the medallions was keeping me in one piece, but to hold them in my palm again means losing myself.

My choice now is to die as myself or to live pain-free—but probably for not much longer—while this awful magic turns my thoughts against me.

My brother gives a roar of frustration, his fists clenched, as he paces away from me and back again. "You have to let me help you," he says. "Take off the bands. Let me bind your wounds."

"Bind them with what?" I moan, looking up at him through tears of pain, my mind foggy and my thoughts slow.

He's ripping off his armor, unbuckling the protective plates and tugging at the tunic beneath them. Of course. His tunic. And there's my tunic, too. What's left of it.

I reach for the medallions, ready to let them fall to the ground and be rid of them. That's when movement in the far distance catches my eye, and I freeze.

The Vandawolf is like a beacon, a spot of firelight that seems to burn brighter with every passing second. That burning spot of fire launches from the top of the wall, jumping a full hundred feet down and landing on the field below without stopping. It's a jump that would have killed a human.

Is he coming because he heard me scream? If only he were that merciful. There has to be another reason...

The line of Wasteland Warriors scatters before him, allowing the Vandawolf to sprint through. I imagine him shouting orders at them, but I'm not sure if he'll tell them to stay back or come with him.

My head has tipped to the right now, my torso sinking toward that same side, and once again, the golden light flickering above me registers in my senses. I try to ignore it, try to focus on getting the bands off my arm, and then—

My eyes shoot wide.

Wait... no.

Flickering light means lightning. Lightning means a monster.

The worst kind of monster. The hardest to kill. But there's never a second beast. Not right after the first.

Curse my foggy mind!

Dread burns through me as I stare upward at the glittering streaks of golden light that are growing stronger.

No... please...

But there's no denying it. The back of my neck is prickling and the increased magic in the air is humming through my body, taking away some of my pain all on its own.

Shouting harshly at myself within my mind, I take a good look at the mangled mess on my side. If I were human, I'd be dead already. But I'm not.

I'm a fucking Blacksmith.

It's time to die as what I am.

"Gallium, get back," I say. "Get to safety. Now."

His armor already lies on the ground and his shirt is halfway over his head. He lets the material fall back to his chest as he steps toward me, every tense muscle in his body telling me he's ready to argue, but then the golden electricity crackles sharply above us, and he, too, looks up.

I use the distraction to press my left palm to both medallions, pulling them from my arm and back into my fist, holding them there. Once again, the ends of the medallions curl around the back of my hand, fastening themselves to me.

Immediately, the pain eases and so does the blood loss.

Whatever power Malak infused into these metal bands, it's effective.

"You have to go!" I cry to Gallium. "I'll live long enough to kill the monster. Promise me you'll get to safety or all of this was for nothing."

My shout is drowned in a crack of thunder that booms across the sky. It's followed by another streak of lightning, which splits in the middle, each subsequent strand reaching down toward the ground like clawed fingers.

My brother meets my eyes across the distance, his face lit up golden and, in this bright light, the silver-blonde of his hair shines through.

My breath catches to see it.

There must be some small level of Blacksmith's magic left within him for his body to react like this when surrounded by such a strong tide of power.

I'm suddenly afraid for him, and not because of the monster. If the Vandawolf senses that my brother still carries some power, then Gallium is a dead man.

Another burst of lightning streaks and crackles overhead, this one much louder. It reaches toward the earth on my far left but doesn't hit the ground yet.

Gallium pulls out his dagger and gives me a nod, as if I asked him to stay instead of telling him to leave. "I'll fight with you, Asha."

The cold power in the medallions is once again taking over my mind, much faster than it did before. My humanity is nearly gone, but I manage to whisper, "So be it, brother."

Then I turn away from him and crouch low to the ground.

Pressing my left palm to the earth, the medallions sitting neatly between the earth and my skin, I wait for the energy within the ash to streak across the ground toward me. The point of origin will tell me where the lightning will strike and the creature will form.

It shoots from a point on my left. Right at the edge of the Sunken Bog. Right where the Vandawolf said the attack would happen.

Of course it fucking does.

Overhead, the storm clouds thicken, and within mere heartbeats, it's as if the darkest night has fallen across the field.

I'm grateful for the oppressive dark because it makes it easier to ignore the desperate state of my armor and the deadly wounds I've sustained. I can pretend that I'm fresh from the castle, not exhausted and barely alive.

In the far distance, I'm aware of the Warriors rushing in my direction, but now they halt and resume the formation they always take. The difference is that this time, they're much closer to the threat.

If even one of them dies, the humans will blame me. All of the soldiers heard the Vandawolf warn me of the threat. It will be my fault for misinterpreting what was coming.

I turn my back on all of them. Even on the Vandawolf, who is still two hundred paces away from me and closing in fast.

I break into my own run, hobbling and limping, forcing myself to keep going. Veering briefly to the right, I scoop up my dropped spear, which gleams in the unnatural light.

The medallions I'm already gripping stay put as I transform the spear back to a strip of metal and the final band settles around my fist.

The pain all but disappears.

So does my fear, my concern for Gallium, my awareness of anything but the power now surging through me.

A power I intend to use to its full effect. I will have no need of weapons if I can touch this beast, skin on skin.

The amber trees within the bog are black in the darkness, the marshy earth glistening. Above me, the sky is suddenly heavy with silence. It means that the final lightning strike is near.

Thunder rumbles through the air, a soft growl increasing to a roar.

Then comes the *crack*.

Golden light strikes vertically from the sky, a thick, jagged rope of power. It hits the earth only twenty paces ahead of me. The dazzling shot explodes with energy and takes on a life of its own, roaring outward like a spreading fire for five feet in every direction.

The dome it forms is so bright that I can't see a thing.

Flinging my left arm across my eyes, I drop to a crouch, making myself a smaller target.

The humans are shouting in the far background. The explosion must have impacted them all the way back near the wall. At the corner of my vision, on my right, I manage to make out Gallium through the crack between my arm and my face. He's also dropped to a crouch, shielding his face.

I cry to him, "Stay back, Gallium! Don't come closer!"

I'm aware of another energy source, this one raging toward me.

The rest of us may have dropped to the ground, but the Vandawolf hasn't. He'll reach me within a minute, maybe less.

Anger swirls inside me and my thoughts grow colder by the second. He must think that I'll fail. That I'm too feeble to kill a creature of lightning, even though I've ended these monsters before. He dares to shame me and make me look weak—

I shake myself, trying to dislodge the irrational anger. There's a part of me that recognizes my thoughts stem from the bands, but that part is disappearing fast.

I focus on the lightning's point of impact as best I can through the gaps in my fingertips. The gleam is beginning to fade, but the influx of energy was so great that the air continues to sparkle.

Tiny, gleaming spots float across my vision.

I make out ragged earth at the edge of a shallow crater

where the lightning struck, the uneven outline of a burned-out tree next to it, and the silhouette of something big curled over within the crater.

The creature unfurls, a rising outline in the fading light.

Gleaming sparks of light float inward toward its edges, seemingly drawn to its shape, lighting up its body once more.

My eyes widen.

No, this can't be right.

I lower my arm, needing to fully see what I can't believe.

The silhouette now backlit by sparkling light is human.

CHAPTER 12

The monster is human.

And with a clearly male profile.

He hunches close to the ground, side-on to me, the muscles across his naked back bunched and tense. His head is lowered, but his left hand quickly rises. It's a big hand, proportionate to the breadth of his left bicep and the expanse of his chest. He's wearing little more than torn pants that are ripped around the ankles.

He hasn't looked up yet.

Instead, he turns his hand back and forth, his fingers splayed as if he's studying them. Behind the strands of his bronzed hair, his forehead is creased, his wide eyes reflecting the light that continues to swirl around him.

"What the fuck?" he whispers, as if he doesn't recognize his own hand.

I'm frozen where I stand, trying to breathe despite the overwhelming strength of the power in the sparks of light that gather across his broad shoulders and bare chest. They settle against the shape of his muscles and gleam across his ragged, black pants like brilliant snowflakes.

The *pull* toward him is electric.

It's as strong as the magnetic pull I feel toward the Vandawolf.

It's Blacksmith's magic, drawn from the very earth I'm standing on. Luring me in, just as I was pulled toward the stag. Just as I'm drawn to the Vandawolf.

Power attracts power.

I recall the vehemence in the Vandawolf's voice when he took hold of my arm in front of the soldiers.

He told me: *"Kill the monster. Anything less is betrayal."*

But... is this man a monster?

Will I betray the Vandawolf by letting this man live... or by killing him?

The cold and destructive malice flowing from my left hand tells me it doesn't fucking matter. The dark impulses within the medallions strike at me like commands.

Mold him!

Do it while he's vulnerable!

"No!"

I only realize that I shouted when the man's head snaps up and his bronzed gaze crashes into me.

His eyes widen as his focus shoots across my face, my silvery hair, and my damaged armor. I'm covered in blood, but it won't mask the way my skin glistens or my hair catches the golden light.

"Fuck." He lurches to his feet and I'm not sure if he intended to step toward me or to move away, because he immediately sways on the spot.

His left hand flies to his head, fingers gripping his forehead, his eyes squeezing closed while his shoulders hunch. His legs buckle, but he manages to stay upright.

"Who are you?" He groans as he speaks. "And where the fuck am I?"

I slowly hold out my hands, lifting them from my sides, palms up, an attempt at a gesture of peace.

"Easy," I say, keeping my distance from him, fighting the *pull* toward him with all my might. "I'm not here to hurt you."

It tastes like a lie, even though I mentally scream at myself that it's true, because with every breath I take, I'm fighting the darkness that tells me to crash into him and use my power on him.

I wouldn't turn him to ash. No, I'd shape him into a form I want.

A weapon of bronze and scales...

A thing of beauty...

He lowers his hand, squinting at me, a pained crease in his forehead. "The blood you're wearing would say otherwise."

As he speaks, his gaze passes across my outstretched arms. Right then left. He must be checking for weapons, but the moment he reaches my left palm, he freezes, suddenly fixated on the medallions.

I regret holding my hands out where the bands are visible. More than that, I regret the dark light that's growing around my palm—a light I can't control that wants to be released.

I snap my fist closed, but I can't hide it. The dark light streams between my clenched fingers.

"You're a Blacksmith." The stranger's voice is like a rumble of thunder. His features fill with unmistakable fear and hatred and the deepest anger, and it's so much like the fear I've encountered my whole life that it's a whip cracking across my chest.

He's a stranger to me, but somehow, he knows what I am.

"You're a fucking Blacksmith!" Every muscle in his body appears to tense as he rapidly lifts himself back to his full height, not once taking his bronze eyes off me.

Eyes that remind me of burnished metal in a face that could belong to a vengeful god.

"I am," I whisper, exhaling slowly.

"Then you're here to take what's left of me and mold me to your will," he snarls.

I'm horrified that he knows my thoughts. That, somehow, he knows enough about Blacksmiths that he recognizes exactly the threat I pose to him.

The coiling of his muscles, the way he's preparing to fully turn toward me, the flex of his biceps, and the clench of his left fist all tell me...

He won't run.

Just like the stag, he's preparing to fight.

I don't know where this man came from, who he is, or how he got here. I can't possibly predict the extent of his knowledge about Blacksmiths.

But I know that there's nothing I can say to him now that will make him trust me.

Still, I try.

"I won't hurt you." My voice is quiet but strained as I force myself to keep my distance from him. "I only kill monsters."

Darkness suddenly plays across his face. "What if I am one?"

The light around us begins to change, the golden hues that are still clinging to his body darkening to crimson waves as bloody as the sky. I'm wary of the change in the light, uncertain if it's caused by the environment or by this stranger, since it grows darker in time with his rage.

He adjusts his balance, his left foot crunching in the ash at the edge of the crater, but still, he hasn't turned fully toward me and I sense that when he does, he will attack.

My response is delayed a beat too long and he roars at me. "What if I've become a monster? What will you do then, Blacksmith?"

My left arm is shaking violently, the influx of magic in the air shuddering through me. My mind is in turmoil, but a single, clear thought surfaces.

Not my thought or my wish.

It's cold and dark and I can't stop the words spilling from my lips. "I will make you mine."

The corners of his mouth turn down. His eyes narrow and the air charges between us.

For the briefest moment, his focus flickers to a point to my right, and that's when I'm horrified to realize that I lost awareness of my surroundings.

Somehow, everything else around me has simply faded away. I don't know where my brother is, nor the Wasteland Warriors, nor worse—the Vandawolf. I know he must be close, too close now, but I can't sense him within the intensity of the magic swilling in the air around me. Clouding my thoughts and senses.

My moment of distraction seems to be all the stranger needed.

I catch a flash of bright light, and a glint of gold, as he launches himself out of the shallow crater and across the gap toward me.

It's a short gap. Too short.

Every instinct in my body says to stay right where I am and let him crash into me, but there is still a very small part of me that remembers who I am.

A small spark of sanity screams through my mind, growing like wildfire, reminding me that I need to regain control or my family will pay the price.

I leap backward, a rushed, defensive move, trying to evade the stranger's tackle.

My backward jump takes me into a new storm.

To my horror, the Vandawolf's footfalls are right behind me, a sudden blast of heat through the thick torrent of power.

Just as the Vandawolf rages past me, the stranger's

outstretched left hand reaches me, his fingertips touching the ends of the flying strands of my hair.

At the same moment, the Vandawolf's palm plants on my lower back and the moment freezes.

Every sensation rushes through me. The burn of the Vandawolf's hand like a brand, heated by the magic that lives within his body. The release of the power through my left hand as the medallion floods with malice. The surge of energy across my chest from my left arm to my lower back because this impulse that I was already fighting breaks through the barriers I was trying to place around it.

The kick in my heart as power sizzles, not only toward the Vandawolf, but toward the stranger as well, shooting through my flying hair toward the tips of the stranger's fingers.

Most of all, I feel fear.

Overwhelming terror because I'm not in control of this anger, this hateful power, or this need to remake the world so that it's mine.

Mine.

At the last possible moment, the force of the Vandawolf's shove registers. A push so fast and hard that my bones shift as I'm propelled away from him and the stranger.

There's a stomach-churning *thud* as the two men collide in the space I left behind.

The Vandawolf's left shoulder was already lowered, allowing him to catch the stranger across his chest, a perfect tackle.

That's all I see before I gain air.

A heartbeat later, the ground flies toward me. My left arm hits first and my shoulder crunches. My scream of pain is strangled because I can't draw enough breath. The energy that would have surged into both men crackles against the ground.

The bright sparks sputter and die, but *oh!* The pain that suddenly thrums through me feels like revenge. As if the dark magic in the medallions is turning on me for failing to set it free.

The world spins, mud splatters around me, and I tumble across the ground before coming to a stop, nearly paralyzed by the agony shooting through my side.

I'm facing away from the fight, overshadowed by a warped tree whose branches seem to crane down toward me, the lowest of its sharp twigs hanging near my eyeline.

I can't move. All I can do is close my eyes and try to breathe.

Behind me, it sounds like thunder. Thudding. Fists or feet I'm not sure. Both, probably.

I make out shouted commands and recognize Gallium's voice.

"Shields and arrows!" he roars.

A chorus of voices roars back and there are the sounds of weapons being drawn.

I need to see what's going on. Need to know what fight is being fought. I tell myself to move, rise to my feet, but my insides are boiling. The medallions are seething and there's a dam of power building within me. It's filling up and can only spill over.

Maybe I should let it.

It might finally consume me, and this war within me can end.

Oh, not an option.

With a groan, I compel myself upward, managing to turn and struggle to my knees, but no further. The twisted tree branches prick my back, but I don't have the energy to move away from them.

I can finally see what's happening.

Across the way, the Vandawolf holds the stranger in a head lock. Both men are on their knees, a pair of near giants struggling for supremacy.

The Warriors have formed two rows in the shape of a half-circle. The front row of soldiers has taken a knee, shields to the front, while the back row stands with bows and arrows nocked and pointed at the stranger.

Gallium is positioned on the far side of them, his keen focus on the Vandawolf now, as if he's waiting for a command.

Above us, the gold and crimson lights continue to swirl, but not too intensely now, a fading power.

"Who are you?" the Vandawolf roars at the stranger.

The stranger's response is to ram his left elbow back into the Vandawolf's side, trying to free himself, but the Vandawolf is relentless, holding on.

"Why are you here?" the Vandawolf tries again, but again, the stranger is tight-lipped, responding only with attempts to free himself.

"You will yield!" the Vandawolf shouts, the muscles in his arms visibly straining. "Or I'll break your fucking neck."

The stranger continues to struggle, but this time, he responds, his voice strangled. "I will not yield to someone who protects a Blacksmith."

"'Protects'?" the Vandawolf snarls.

My forehead creases at the stranger's assumption that the Vandawolf pushed me out of the way to help me.

How little this newcomer knows.

The Vandawolf growls before he raises his voice again, and this time, I know he's speaking to me. "You betrayed me, Asha."

I freeze at the accusation made so openly in front of the Wasteland Warriors. A flood of fear overwhelms my physical pain. Not fear for myself, but for Gallium, who is suddenly like stone where he stands.

I fight to draw breath against the dread filling my body. "But this man is human," I whisper, knowing that the Vandawolf can hear me even if my voice is barely louder than a murmur. "He hates me. He's human." My voice slurs as I try to gather my thoughts. "He... hates me..."

Damn, why is it so hard to think right now?

A fog has fallen over my thoughts, but I have enough clarity to wonder if I failed to kill the stranger because of compassion, or because the power within me wanted to keep him alive.

"Your mercy is misplaced, Asha," the Vandawolf replies, quieter than before, but the softness of his response scares me more than if he'd shouted.

He wrenches the stranger farther to the left, fully exposing the newcomer's right side and that's when I finally comprehend...

The stranger's right arm is...

No. This can't be.

His right arm is covered in fine, bronze scales as burnished as his eyes.

CHAPTER 13

L ike a serpent's hide, bronze scales extend across the man's right shoulder and up the side of his neck. Also down his side under his arm, stopping only above his waist.

How did I not see them before?

But his right side was concealed from me because of the position of his body when he first appeared. The lightning left the air glowing and that further hampered my vision. Then he'd run at me and I'd finally caught the flash of gold, but the Vandawolf pushed me out of the way before I could process what I was seeing. Even now, my vision is blurring as the extent of my wound takes its toll.

Across the distance, the stranger's bronzed gaze catches mine, but this time, his feelings are hidden behind a wall, his expression unreadable, and once again, I ask myself: *Who is he? How is he here?*

The lens of power that continues to flow from the medallions is rapidly clouding my perception of both men. Every burst of energy through their muscles flares within my vision. While the Vandawolf's beastly nature churns within him, the stranger is like heated metal, a glow so bright that I can't see beneath the surface. I can't discern his true nature. He's like a sheet of bronze that is yet to be shaped...

The stranger's voice cuts the silence as he casts a rasped accusation at the Vandawolf. "You have aligned yourselves with Blacksmiths."

"We have not," the Vandawolf replies, pulling his arm more tightly around the man's neck.

"But you shield that one." The stranger gurgles. Even with crushed vocal cords, his voice is like slender wire coiling across the air toward me. Wire that I want to wrap around my hand as tightly as the medallions...

"Asha is mine to command," the Vandawolf says, speaking through gritted teeth. "And mine to kill when I choose."

Across the distance, his gaze blazes over me. Under his scrutiny, the crease in my forehead vanishes and my expression becomes like stone.

I am blank. I will show nothing of my feelings.

But inside, my heart pricks. A quiet stab. Powerful in its unexpectedness.

Even after all these years, I am still a thing to be killed.

I harden my heart. After all, this is not news to me. Every time the Vandawolf sends me out to fight monsters, he's sending me to my death. Hearing him affirm his intention to one day end me shouldn't bring me pain or surprise.

I become as emotionless as the mud beneath my knees—a filthy surface soaked with blood and unwanted power.

The stranger's quick gaze seems to miss nothing.

His lips part in apparent surprise, his eyes narrow, but he grinds out, "Then I will yield."

The Vandawolf doesn't let up on the man's neck. "Gallium!" he shouts. "Do what Asha could not and chain this monster."

The stranger's gaze hasn't let up on me. His narrowed eyes

raze across me, as if he's reassessing his first impressions. His focus lingers on my wounded side, and the crease in his forehead becomes puzzled. If only I could see what thoughts lurk behind those beastly bronze eyes. A monster's eyes that are clear to me now that the power in the air is fading, no longer impeding my vision.

The stranger's lips part. It must be very difficult for him to speak now, but he tries anyway. "Your Blacksmith is—"

The Vandawolf's arm is already tightening around the man's neck, his hold changing. I recognize the maneuver. It will make the stranger pass out. The Vandawolf could have used this tactic before now, but he must have wanted the man to speak.

The man's eyes roll back and he passes out a moment later.

Across the way, Gallium is already retrieving a set of iron shackles from one of the Warriors. If he thinks anything of what the Vandawolf said to me, he doesn't show it. A tiny spark of pride lifts the heaviness of my thoughts since Gallium has learned to control his emotions so well.

As Gallium approaches, the Vandawolf allows his captive to slide into the mud.

"He won't be out for long," the Vandawolf says. "Once he comes to, you will escort him to the prison beneath the castle. Make sure he's guarded at all times. Do not underestimate him. I will deal with him once I've dealt with your sister."

"Yes, lord," Gallium replies. He glances at me. "But with respect—"

The Vandawolf growls, the pure sound of a wolf, and whatever Gallium was going to say, he stops. I'm glad he does. Anything he tries to say right now will only make my situation worse.

My brother's jaw clenches as he bends to the prisoner, and the clanking of iron soon fills the tense silence.

The warriors keep their arrows aimed at the unconscious

stranger, and the Vandawolf takes a step back, allowing Gallium to work, but he doesn't appear to relax even when the shackles are secure around the man's wrists and ankles.

That's when the Vandawolf finally prowls toward me, the furrow in his brow deepening as he approaches.

I've remained on my knees, my shoulders hunched. I know I need to get up, but I... *can't.*

With the Vandawolf's back turned to him, Gallium's worry suddenly shows through. His lips press harder together the longer I stay kneeling in the mud.

Gallium knows how badly I'm hurt. The Vandawolf does not.

"*Get up,*" Gallium mouths at me. "*You must get up.*"

I can't respond and, despite my best efforts to stay upright, I lean farther to the left with every passing second.

It's dawning on me that I may not be able to stand, after all. Even the power from the medallions seems to be deserting me.

Despite that cold thought, I tell myself that I'm simply waiting for the Vandawolf to give me my next orders. Then I'll get back to my feet and do whatever he commands me to do.

He's still ten paces away when the tree beside me creaks loudly and snatches my attention. It's an ominous sound as the plant sinks another inch into the ground right before my eyes. I wonder, if I were to huddle close enough to it, if its branches would form a cage of sorts around me and take me down into the mud with it...

"You're hurt."

I'm startled to find the Vandawolf already crouched in front of me. Somehow, I missed his final approach.

In any other circumstance, the fact that I'm wounded would have been obvious from my ripped armor, but it was reasonable for him to assume that I'm covered in the stag's blood. Or simply soaked in blood-rain since the ash has turned red with it.

I don't lie. I give a single nod. "I'm hurt."

My eyelids feel so damn heavy and my thoughts are floating like feathers in a soft breeze. I squint at the Vandawolf as his silhouette blurs and then doubles. Triples.

The medallions don't seem to be protecting me from the pain anymore. In fact, at some point in the last minute, since the stranger was knocked out, they've become cold against my palm.

My thoughts, as fuzzy as they are, seem to be my own again.

I must be succumbing to delirium from blood-loss and shock, but the rational part of my brain that allows me to recognize that I'm in trouble is fading fast.

"Asha." The Vandawolf snaps my name, his wolf's tooth appearing and his lips drawing back into a snarl, as if the fact that I'm injured causes him fury. His voice is harsh, a barked command. "Asha, look at me."

I try to comply.

My brow furrows when his features bleed across my vision, his white tooth blending in with the contours of his strong chin, and his wolf's eye becoming a gleaming amber streak across his upper face.

"Please don't punish my family," I whisper, all of the fight leaving me. "I did what you asked. I killed the stag. Please don't..."

As I speak, I lean farther to the left, unable to keep myself upright.

His big hand snaps out toward my shoulder—the one that's descending toward the mud—but then his focus falls to my lap.

My left palm rests there, upturned.

The medallions curled around it are a clearly visible threat. They may not be thrumming with dark light anymore, but they are still a danger to everyone but me.

He can't touch me.

Without anything to halt my fall, I collapse onto my side, finally crumpling into the dirt. My left hand slips to the ground, my arm outstretched.

"Asha!"

There's a sharpness in the Vandawolf's voice that I've never heard before and I'm not sure what to make of it. I can't read his face. I can't focus on anything... except the medallions.

While everything else blurs, the bands of black metal are clear. Before my eyes, they peel up at the ends, as if they know I'm dying and they want to be rid of me now.

I suppose it's a good thing.

I would rather perish as myself than as a vessel to this magic.

The Vandawolf's shout turns into a roar of frustration. His anger beats across my still form in waves as hot as a summer wind, a strangely welcome heat that comes with his nearness.

He jumps to his feet, moving fast, his boots splashing through the mud as he races to my left.

The nearby tree rustles, its branches thrashing at the corner of my vision.

Then there's a *snap*, followed by several *cracks*.

The sounds make sense when he returns and bends to the medallions.

He's holding a short section of branch. One by one, he scoops the medallions up into the hollow wood without touching them. It's a tight fit and the last piece sticks, but he turns the section of branch upside down and rams it against the ground over and over until the medallion disappears inside it, along with a pile of muck.

His fist closes around the branch and then I don't know what happens to it because his shadow drops over me. His figure is hunched, but his purpose seems unyielding.

Without a word, he scoops me up out of the mud, drawing me close to his chest.

He doesn't command me to look at him.

For once, he seems to have no orders for me.

Instead, the fast, wild thud of his heartbeat fills my ears while he adjusts his hold so that he's supporting my head.

A moment later, he breaks into a run, gripping me tightly against him.

I try to stay awake, but all I catch are fading glimpses of my surroundings: my brother, the Warriors, the prisoner—who's stirring where he lies on the bloody ground.

Then I slip into a darkness that swallows me whole.

CHAPTER 14

I wake with a jolt, a rush of pain strangling the cry that rises to my lips.

My ears fill with the sound of boots crunching on pebbles, but the rapid *crunch-crunch* is drowned in the next moment by the Vandawolf's shout. "Petra! I need Petra! *Now!*"

He's still gripping me tightly in his arms, although my left arm now drops at an awkward angle, and his breathing is ragged. His heart is working fast, pounding against my right ear. Sweat drips down his face above me, droplets clinging to his shadowed jaw.

I'm surprised that I'm still alive but, *oh*, there's a frail part of me that never would have chosen to wake to this agony and disorientation. It takes everything I've got to make sense of where I am and what's happening around me.

Night must be falling because the light around us is dim but clear of any crimson glow. Far above us, thin, white clouds stretch across the sky. The threat of monsters is over for another day.

I recognize the courtyard within the castle, but the path the Vandawolf races along is one I'm forbidden to walk.

It leads to his personal quarters in the tower diagonally opposite mine.

There's a scurry of movement around us, followed by a jumble of voices and the sounds of more quickly-crunching boots.

I isolate the voice of my personal guard, Rachel, from the thumping heartbeats at my ear. "Petra isn't here, lord. We'll spread out and find her."

At Rachel's promise, multiple footfalls hurry away and I imagine the other personal guards are going with her.

The woman the Vandawolf called for—Petra—is a healer he favors to attend to him if he's injured.

Even though I've crossed paths with Petra a few times, she has chosen never to speak to me. If the Vandawolf is summoning her to help me, she won't be happy about it.

Braddock's voice sounds next, slightly puffed. "Lord, the prisoner is being escorted to the cages beneath the castle. Gallium has him under control."

"Good." The Vandawolf's reply is clipped. "I'll deal with the prisoner later."

The late afternoon sunlight vanishes as the Vandawolf hurries into a corridor beyond the courtyard, his footsteps never slowing, not even when he ascends the first flight of stairs.

I know the layout of this tower because of my explorations when I was a little girl—before the Vandawolf freed the humans. Like in my tower, there are five flights of steps and as many levels, although each level only contains one room. The library is in this tower, one of the few places I miss visiting.

I'm vaguely aware of a hard object pressing against my back where the Vandawolf holds me—maybe the branch that carries the medallions.

We reach the top of the second flight of stairs, turn right, and enter another corridor. This one has bare walls. The echo of multiple footfalls tells me there's still another person following us—a heavy tread I continue to recognize as Braddock's.

He finally darts ahead and opens the door the Vandawolf is headed toward.

Before the Vandawolf can proceed through the opening, Braddock snags his arm.

The Vandawolf grinds to a halt, a growl on his lips.

"Lord, I would never question you in front of the others." Braddock speaks in a hurried whisper, his mouth twisting in an expression of distaste when his gaze flashes to me. "But wouldn't it be better to let the Blacksmith die?"

The Vandawolf's lips draw back from his teeth. "Do you want to lose an arm, Braddock?"

The scarred man seems to realize the danger he's in. His cheeks pale and he takes a hurried step back, releasing the Vandawolf's arm and clearing the doorway. "No, lord."

Without a second glance at Braddock, the Vandawolf charges into the room, still holding me close. "Shut the fucking door," he snaps. "And make sure the corridor is guarded. Nobody enters but Petra."

Braddock acknowledges the command and quickly pulls the door closed.

The room the Vandawolf carries me into is far more cluttered than I was expecting, the shapes of its contents coming in and out of view within my hazy vision.

The far side has a window seat swathed in rugs, the weave of the material indicating that they're finely-spun wool. The window itself is wide and made of intricate stained glass—all pale colors that allow the first rays of moonlight to shine through.

A large, four-poster bed rests up against the right-hand wall, the bed's surface scattered with plump cushions that are probably filled with duck down. A desk sits on the right-hand side of the bed, resting between the bed and a wide, wooden closet. The closet's doors are slightly ajar and clothing spills through the opening.

It's a messy space, but even through the fog of pain, I identify patterns in the mess. Cushions, blankets, and clothing seem to be built up to form...

Burrows.

This room is like a den.

The Vandawolf continues to move fast. He kicks clothing out of the way as he carries me to the bed and lays me down on it, not seeming to care about the blood that I'll leave on the fine blanket.

An object drops to the bed beside me, released from his fist, and I recognize the stubby branch that holds the medallions.

He snatches it up and quickly deposits it onto the table before turning to the closet.

It seems uncharacteristically reckless of him to leave the tools within my reach, but the weak beat of my heart probably reassures him that he would have no trouble stopping me from taking them.

The dark energy in the tools would normally call to me, but now they seem dull and restrained. It's as if they're waiting, like I am, to see if I'll live longer than the next few hours.

The Vandawolf digs through his closet, grabbing multiple tunics, again seeming not to care when a pile of them fall to the floor behind him.

Returning to my side, he pulls off my boots before he reaches for a dagger from the belt at his waist.

I'm incapable of feeling alarm right now, but any need to fear his intentions fades when he begins cutting the belts on my armor. He rapidly peels the plates away, revealing the worst of the damage.

I can't lift my head to see the wounds—can't do much of anything except focus on continuing to breathe—but I know

I'm lucky the monster's claws drove in and out of me like a knife instead of tearing through.

The Vandawolf still hasn't said another word to me, although he must be aware that I'm awake. My eyes are half-open and my heartbeat would give me away.

Still, his focus seems to be consumed by my injured body as he rips my tunic all the way from the base up to my breasts. Next, he pushes my long pants down my hips, far enough that the material is barely concealing my pelvis.

I have no sense of indignity in these moments.

My body is mortally wounded.

I am his to heal or to throw away.

My wounds are finally exposed for him to see and for a second, he pauses, his breath stilling.

He expels his breath with a curse. "Fuck."

His jaw clenches and then he's moving again.

He still doesn't speak to me, barely glancing at my face as he proceeds to wrap the soft tunics around my stomach and ribs. Reaching around and beneath me, he lifts me easily, his touch firm but careful as he pulls the wounds closed with the bandages and finally stems the blood.

I want to ask him why he's helping me, since Braddock was right: It would be far easier to let me die.

I try to bring moisture to my lips so that I can speak. Even then, the best I can do is a slow, quiet whisper. "Why?"

His jaw clenches again. He continues tying off a knot at my side and I'm not sure if he'll answer me—assuming he can guess what I'm asking.

His hands finally still. He glares down at me. His hair is tucked behind his ear and his wolf's features are fully visible, his tooth sharp and his amber eye bright, his deeply furrowed brow making him appear angry as fuck.

"Do you want your family to die?" he asks.

My eyes widen. "No."

"Then you will continue breathing," he says, as if he's daring me to disobey his command.

Of course.

I bartered my life for theirs. If I die, they will no longer have the Vandawolf's protection. The humans will go after them. He may even kill them himself.

Even so, he has no reason to care about their welfare. My death would allow him to rid himself of us, once and for all.

But then... who would fight the monsters?

My thoughts go round and round, but before I can attempt to speak again, the door bursts open.

Petra rushes into the room, her long, mauve skirt hitched up in one hand. She's tall with an oval face, pointed chin, and large, brown eyes. Her light-brown hair is dyed purple in thick streaks down each side and then braided back in two braids. The healers all dye their hair in streaks. Purple marks her as a senior healer.

In the background, Braddock pulls the door closed behind her, but before he does, I catch sight of my other personal guards. Rachel is bent over, puffing and leaning on her thighs as if she'd run hard and fast to get here. The other two men are also trying to catch their breath.

Likewise, Petra's chest is rising and falling rapidly and a sheen of sweat glistens on her brow.

She hurries directly to the Vandawolf and plants her palms on his chest, her face upturned to his. "You called for me. Where are you hurt?"

I suppose she's choosing to ignore the obvious.

He scoops her hands firmly away from his chest and directs her to turn to me. "I need you to help Asha."

Her expression shifts the moment she's no longer facing him, but her tone conceals nothing of her distaste. "The Blacksmith."

"Yes."

She casts a sharp look across my bandaged torso, taking in the makeshift wraps and the blood that's seeping through them.

A very small smile touches her lips, but her voice is tightly controlled. "Gut wounds kill slowly. She'll be dead in a day, maybe two if she's unlucky enough to suffer that long."

She wipes her expression clean before she turns back to the Vandawolf and shakes her head. She speaks more softly. "I can't heal her. I swore I would never help one of her kind after what they did to my family."

Judging by her appearance, she would have been a year or two younger than I am when Malak was killed, but if she showed proficiency at healing from a young age, then she would have been forced to work for at least one of the Black-smith families.

The Vandawolf's voice also lowers. "I'm asking you to do this, Petra," he says. "Not for the Blacksmith, but for me."

I recognize the restraint in his tone. He must be trying to be patient. He may command me, and he may be the humans' ruler, but he can't force Petra to do anything. She's the daughter of the human metalworker who sits on the council. To force her hand would only pit the Vandawolf against her father and the other council members.

She stares up into his face, paling a little when she seems to register the sight of his fully visible tooth.

For some reason, he isn't choosing to hide his wolfish features right now.

"I can't." She squeezes her eyes closed and a tear escapes down her cheek, as if she's truly regretful. "Forgive me, lord, but I won't."

She steps back from him. "I'm sorry."

His jaw clenches. "Then you must leave."

She gives him a single nod before she turns to the door. Her movement slows as her gaze rakes up over my wound a second time and then stops on my face. She sounded sorry that she couldn't help me, but the twist of her lips, the gleam in her eyes, and the pure hatred in her expression tell me she isn't.

It's a hatred I'm accustomed to, and I don't have to suffer it for long, since she speeds up again.

Within moments, she opens the door and disappears into the dimly-lit corridor.

Braddock reaches in to pull the door shut behind her, a barely concealed smirk on his face.

Once the door closes, the Vandawolf is like stone. He remains standing at the side of the bed, as frozen as a mountain of rock as he stares at the back of the door.

Slowly, very slowly, his posture and expression change. Incremental shifts that make him appear wilder. The drawing back of his lips in an animal's snarl. The tightening around his eyes as if he's targeting prey. Growing tension in his shoulders and the flex of his biceps.

I'm not under any illusion that his anger is directed at the departing woman.

"I could have killed you a hundred different ways, a hundred different times," he says to me. "I've ordered you to fight monsters to the death on so many occasions that I've lost count. I've watched you succumb to Malak's power and I've witnessed you tear beasts apart with more savagery than any wolf or bear."

He stops speaking for a long minute.

Then he says, more softly, "But neither of us has any power to stop your death now."

CHAPTER 15

The Vandawolf snarls like the beast burning within him as he crosses the distance between us.

Within seconds, his hands drop to my shoulders, pressing me down onto the plush bedding. "Asha Silverspun—"

Shouts from the corridor interrupt him. A commotion that can't be ignored.

A clear, female voice sounds through the door. "Stand aside, Braddock. Let me pass!"

"I will not." Braddock's response is harsh. "Your sister's already dead, Tamra. Accept it and fuck off."

"Now, hold on a minute." That voice is Rachel. She sounds like she's still puffed, but her voice is raised loud enough to be heard through the door. "This decision is not ours to make, Braddock. We can't turn Asha's sister away without seeking the Vandawolf's orders first."

"Tamra." My whisper comes out as a groan as I struggle to get up, fighting the constant pain as I push against the Vandawolf's hold. "Don't hurt her."

He restrains me easily, but his eyes—both eyes—are

suddenly bright. The smile that crosses his lips is shocking in comparison to the fury he wore only seconds ago.

"Always, you will fight for your family when you won't fight for yourself." He lifts off me a moment later, strides to the door, and flings it open, revealing the corridor outside.

I manage to turn onto my side, trying to sit up, my protective instincts in full swing. I can't see clearly all the way through the doorway, but I make out Braddock's form. His big hand is wrapped around my sister's upper arm. Unlike Gallium, she has remained petite, and Braddock has lifted her so high that her left foot dangles above the ground.

She's wearing a black tunic and black pants. Her boots appear to have solid heels and my first thought is that she could break Braddock's bones with them if she wanted.

Tamra's face is pale—Braddock must be hurting her arm—but she focuses past him to the Vandawolf. "Lord, please let me see my sister. I can help her."

"Asha's dying," the Vandawolf replies, a cold declaration. "What makes you think you can save her?"

Tamra takes a deep breath and her voice is strained. "The same way Gallium and I survived all these years. A gut wound is the least we suffered."

I close my eyes, my heart hurting to hear of the harm they suffered.

"No healer would touch us, so we learned their ways and treated ourselves. I know how to deal with my sister's injuries." Tamra's lips press together for a moment. Her green eyes are wide, desperate, but there's a hint of accusation in her voice. "Unless you want her to die a long and painful death."

"I would not let that happen," the Vandawolf replies.

Tamra draws a quick breath at the implication that the Vandawolf would end me rather than let me suffer. I wonder if that's what he was going to tell me when he pressed me down onto the bed just now. Perhaps he was going to tell me to prepare myself for death.

But he still hasn't given Tamra permission to help.

She bites her lip as he remains silent for a long moment. Like my brother, she seems to know when to speak and when to remain quiet.

"I will let you try," the Vandawolf finally says before he inclines his head at Braddock. "Let her pass."

Braddock reluctantly unwraps his hand from my sister's arm.

Tamra drops to the ground, landing lightly. She immediately scoops up an object from the floor—what appears to be a basket. Then she darts past Braddock and into the room.

She's quick. As agile as Gallium as she steers clear of the Vandawolf and heads straight for me. She drops the basket at the side of the bed. "Asha."

Her voice is quiet, and her eyes brim with tears.

"Tamra." I can't stop the burn in my own eyes. To see her is a gift I wasn't expecting. "You've grown so much."

She takes my outstretched hand and presses it to her heart as she bends to me.

Her expression fills with rapidly changing emotions, worry and sadness first, her wide, green eyes glistening with the tears she doesn't try to hide.

Her hair is dyed brown like Gallium's and her skin is tanned, presumably from time in the sun. The hand she presses over mine is no longer small and fragile, but strong. I note the contour of the muscles on her arms. She has wielded a different kind of hammer for most of her life now, and I sense the strength in her hold.

There's a soft click as the Vandawolf closes the door and leans up against it, keeping his distance. I'm aware that he's watching us, but nothing is so important to me in this moment as my sister.

It's been ten long years.

"Oh, Asha." Her voice is barely above a whisper as she presses her forehead to mine. "You're too pale. Gallium warned me about your injuries, but I fear it's worse than he described."

I give her a smile. "Nothing... hurts... now that you're here..."

She drops a kiss to my forehead and I wish I were more alert in this moment, more capable of taking in the enormity of seeing her again.

I couldn't hug Gallium and now I'm too injured to hug Tamra. It's been a long time since I've felt the caring of family and a simple sisterly kiss is making my heart ache.

She's already setting to work, pulling the basket up from the floor and retrieving items out of it, including a contraption that looks like two blades placed tightly together with a hinge in the middle.

"Cutters," she explains, lifting them up for the Vandawolf to see from a distance. It's a smart move, given that anything sharp is a potential weapon against him. "I designed them. They have no sharp outer edges so they're safer to use than a knife."

When he relaxes against the door again, Tamra returns her attention to me. "I need to remove your clothing now, Asha. I don't want to risk not knowing about a hidden wound."

I lie back against the bed with a brief nod. Maintaining whatever small scrap of dignity that I've retained is not worth my death.

Tamra sets about snipping off the remains of my ripped tunic and then cutting down each outer side of my pants. Her cutters must have strong blades because they slice easily through the leather.

I'm a little surprised when the Vandawolf averts his gaze and turns his face toward the window as soon as Tamra starts pulling off my clothes.

Without even looking at him, she seems aware of his action and her expression immediately hardens. "Don't look away on my account, lord," she snaps. "I know my sister has no privacy in your presence."

He abandons the pretense, his eyes narrowing at Tamra's back.

Her tone was far sharper than it was before and I'm worried that I might have been wrong. She may not know when to remain silent, after all.

Her focus returns to me, although it's clear she's still speaking to the Vandawolf. "Braddock tells anyone who will listen about every indignity you put Asha through. We've all heard about those transparent fucking robes and your midnight visits to her room."

Tamra grits her teeth and throws the Vandawolf an angry glance. "If I were Asha, I would have crushed your skull with that black hammer years ago."

My hand snaps around her wrist, my eyes wide with warning. It is *not* smart to threaten the Vandawolf. No matter how outraged she is about the robes. And, as for the midnight visits, they aren't what they appear to be.

The Vandawolf's rage is sudden, but what he says surprises me.

"I do what's necessary to keep Asha alive," he snarls. "If I had a choice, I would never humiliate her in this way."

Tamra is stiff, her shoulders rigid. "Because Malak killed the human king with a medallion concealed in the lining of his cloak."

"I don't fear such a threat," the Vandawolf replies. "I would sense any Blacksmith weapon hidden on her body, but my people won't forget the past. I do it to appease them. As for Asha's feelings about it, she loves you too much to make an attempt on my life. Or protest about what it takes to ensure she protects you."

Tamra instantly deflates, her tone bitter now. "You recognized Asha's capacity for love from the moment you saw her. You latched on to it and never let go."

"Love is more powerful than hate and fear combined," the Vandawolf growls, softer now.

Tamra gives a quiet sigh before she pats my hand, as if to tell me not to worry about her, unfurling my fingers from her arm. "So it is."

She doesn't speak again for long moments as she finishes checking my arms, my legs, and my back. It's a hard task that requires me to move around and she was right—it *hurts*.

"There are no hidden wounds." She gives me a quick smile, but it looks like she's steeling herself as she pulls the blanket over my lower half to cover me again. "Now for your side."

Quickly, she sets about removing the makeshift bandages and assessing the damage. I wince with every move she makes, every tug of the bandages, but I'm relieved when her expression grows more confident.

"I can stitch this, starting from the inside and working outward." She casts her eye around the room. "But I need a surface for my implements."

She speaks far more politely than before. "Can you bring me that table, lord?"

The Vandawolf lifts himself from the door and does what she asks, clearing the table by pushing everything toward the back of it and onto the floor. He doesn't seem to care about the mess and nothing seems to break. Probably because there's a layer of clothing to cushion the fall.

The branch containing the medallions is the only item he keeps with him, carrying it back to the door with him and placing it on the floor where he takes up position once more.

Tamra begins pulling more contraptions from her basket, including a spool of thin thread.

The Vandawolf watches with sharp eyes, although he keeps his distance. "That isn't the usual thread healers use."

She stiffens a little. "It's from a vine that grows in the Sunken Bog. It dissolves over time without leaving any toxic residue so it can be used within the body."

There's a pause and I wait for the Vandawolf to express his wrath.

"It's forbidden to leave the city walls without permission," he says, a low growl.

Tamra barely glances at him. "Would you have given me permission if I'd asked?"

"No."

"Then that's why I didn't ask."

His eyes narrow. "You admitted to disobeying my laws. What do you expect me to do now?"

She gives him a brief, hard stare, and I'm starting to recognize that she has two gears. One is quiet and considered, the other is as hard as titanium.

"What you do is up to you, lord," she says. "But if you ask me questions, I will tell you the truth. I would suggest that you choose your questions more wisely. The truth is often unpleasant. I may give you *many* answers you don't like hearing."

Again, I worry for her safety, but if the Vandawolf wanted to lash out, he could have done it before now. I can only assume that he must be prepared to tolerate whatever she says as long as she's working on me.

Even so, his brow furrows to a dark glower.

When he doesn't immediately rebuke her, she continues, more softly. "The Sunken Bog may be dangerous now, but it also contains many wonders. Not everything the Blacksmiths created was with the intent to harm humans."

She pauses as if she's waiting for his response.

She's increasingly tense when his silence stretches.

He's clever. He may not like every answer she gives him,

but he could take any information she offers and use it against her or me, including her assertion that the Sunken Bog isn't entirely dangerous.

When he still doesn't speak, she focuses back on me. "I'm going to knock you out, Asha. You shouldn't be awake for what comes next."

She pours liquid from a small bottle onto a soft-looking cloth and holds it against my mouth and nose. "Inhale the fumes. Don't fight them."

It smells like roses. Rose water, maybe. But within seconds, my head is fuzzy.

In the background, the Vandawolf jolts away from the wall again, as if this new substance alarms him more than the thread did. "What are you doing?"

"It's water from the Toxic Thirst," she replies. "Lethal to drink. But the fumes are safe to inhale. It will make Asha sleep while I stitch her wounds. She will wake soon enough..."

My sister's voice rapidly fades.

So does the Vandawolf's tense form until he's a raging shadow within my mind.

CHAPTER 16

I wake to the soft tug of material being wrapped around me.

My eyelids part, but only barely, allowing me to recognize the hue of early morning sunlight.

The room is quiet.

Tamra's hands are gentle, but her movements are slow. Her basket sits on the side of the bed and all of her instruments appear to have been put away. There's a clean blanket beneath me and a sheet carefully draped across all my naked parts.

By some miracle, my pain is minimal.

If Tamra worked over me all night, she must be exhausted.

She's intent upon the bandaging and doesn't seem to notice that I'm awake. I would speak, but my throat is too dry and my lips are too cracked, although I'm grateful that my mind and vision are much clearer.

I'm not sure where the Vandawolf is until he moves in the background, and then I locate him sitting in a chair in the far corner behind Tamra.

He will know that I'm awake from the inevitable change in my heartbeat, but he doesn't draw attention to my wakefulness.

He remains where he is, leaning forward, his elbows on his knees, his hands clasped, and his shoulders hunched. He looks haggard and I can only imagine what sort of medical miracles Tamra performed on me during the night and how many times he demanded to know what she was doing.

Despite that, his next words indicate that she may have stopped lashing him with her truths some time ago.

"You've been quiet for too long, Tamra Silverspun," he says. "Say what you're thinking."

My sister places her hand on my heart, her gaze moving to my eyes. She gives me a soft smile. She must think the Vandawolf believes I'm still asleep because her response treads perilous ground.

"You didn't want Asha to die."

His back stiffens. "Of course I don't," he snaps. "She kills monsters for me."

Tamra leans back from me, resting slowly down on the edge of the bed with a tired sigh. "I'm not talking about the events of now. I'm talking about ten years ago."

The Vandawolf's expression is suddenly like stone.

A muscle ticks in his jaw, but that is all.

"She offered you her life in exchange for ours." Tamra side-eyes him and I wish, for her sake, that she didn't have nerves like titanium, because the storm building on the Vandawolf's face can only mean real danger. If she's finished helping me, then he won't have a reason not to lash out.

"You *chose* to keep Asha alive," Tamra says.

"That fact is self-evident."

Her eyes narrow slightly, but there's no hint of anger on her face. "Then last night, you let me help her when you could have had me forcibly removed."

His scowl deepens, but only briefly before a smile grows on his face. It isn't a kind smile. "To lay hands on you would risk breaking my promise to Asha that you will live a long life."

"Because you could hurt me?" Tamra asks.

"I could break your neck in seconds."

Truth.

"But you won't because of your promise," she says.

His lips part, twisting as if he would utter a harsh response, but he pauses. "What is your point?"

Her voice lowers even more. So quiet now. "You don't want Asha to die."

"We've established that."

Tamra leans back and folds her arms, pinning him with her sharp, green eyes.

A crease forms in the Vandawolf's forehead when she says nothing more.

"What do you want from me, woman?" he asks, suddenly seeming more perplexed than angry.

She doesn't answer. With another tired sigh, she unfolds her arms and reaches out to squeeze my hand before she rises from the bed.

The fight seems to drain from her. Her shoulders droop and the rings under her eyes appear darker.

"I've given Asha medicine for the pain. If you want her wounds to heal, she must not be moved for another three days at least. After that, she should keep physical activity to a minimum for at least three weeks to ensure the wounds do not re-open. She will need steady fluids. She lost a lot of blood."

Three weeks. *Impossible.* A monster will rise before then.

Tamra bends to me, pressing a kiss to my forehead. I close my eyes and drink in the rare, gentle contact.

"I love you, Asha," she whispers. "Stay alive."

She smooths down her shirt before she scoops up her basket and heads for the door.

The Vandawolf steps into her path. "You will not leave yet."

I can't see her expression since her back is to me, but she's suddenly stiff.

"I have a task for you," he continues.

She takes a moment. "What do you want of me?"

His wolf's eye gleams. "You will take your sharp tongue and pay our new prisoner a visit."

She remains stiff. "Lord?"

"You will extract any truths you can from him. I have no doubt he will have resisted all efforts made so far to ascertain his identity, and Asha isn't in any state to undertake his interrogation, so you must try instead."

"Interrogation?" Tamra's head tips a little to the side, as if she doesn't understand what he's talking about, and then I catch her sharply indrawn breath. "Asha undertakes interrogations...?"

"Killing monsters is not all she does for me," the Vandawolf replies, as if he's talking about nothing more heinous than a splinter in his finger. His smile is unsettling. "You offered me the truth. I will do the same."

Inside, my stomach is sinking and my heart is heavy. I never wanted my sister to know that I do these things. I didn't think that the Vandawolf would want anyone to know, either.

What Tamra described as the Vandawolf's 'midnight visits' to my room are the cover he uses to conceal the times when he asks me to use my power against humans.

For the most part, the humans appear to respect the Vandawolf, but there are those who would rise up against him. After ten years of his rule, there are growing rumblings about needing a 'fully human' leader, not a man changed by magic.

The vastness of the city means there are plenty of spaces for such uprisings to grow.

I'm the blade that keeps them from flourishing.

The interrogations I conduct are not intended to preserve life, so nobody has ever lived to tell of them. They are the

Vandawolf's ugly secret and one of the reasons he has maintained power for so long. I've nipped rebellions in the bud at least five times. As for the bodies, a death in this city can easily be made to look like a robbery or an act of violence between rival families.

The humans may have been united in their fight against the Blacksmiths all those years ago, but alliances soon became conflicts.

As for the impact the interrogations have on me, the darkness in my tools gives me the distance I need from my actions. It's the same barrier that preserves my heart and mind when I kill monsters in the wasteland.

It's Malak's evil, not mine.

The Vandawolf continues to Tamra. "You have no need to fear for your safety. Your brother will be there and, if Gallium has followed my orders, the prisoner will be fully chained."

Tamra seems to recover some of her nerve. "Why would I do this when you have soldiers to do your bidding for you?"

"Because," the Vandawolf says, taking a step toward her, towering over her petite form. "If you gain useful information from the prisoner, I will let you see Asha again."

Her voice becomes bitter. "You're good at making deals, aren't you, lord?"

His response is calm. "If I wasn't, I wouldn't be alive."

I sense the way she's torn, read it in her hesitant posture and the way she bounces a little on the balls of her feet.

I want her to say *no*.

Making deals with the Vandawolf never ends well. I'm already concerned about the price Gallium paid to see me yesterday.

Tamra twists to look back at me and her expression softens, her green eyes luminous in the early morning light. The glistening silver highlights in her hair shine through the dye she uses to cover her true coloring. Yesterday, I sensed that Gallium had retained some of his power and now, I wonder, if Tamra has too.

"I'll do it," she says quietly.

"Good. You have until this afternoon to extract any information you can."

When the Vandawolf opens the door, I spot Rachel standing guard outside. I'm relieved that Braddock isn't with her—or if he is, I can't see him—since he's far more likely to harass Tamra as she leaves.

Rachel simply gives my sister a firm nod.

Then Tamra disappears from my world again.

The Vandawolf pulls the door closed and his hand lingers on the knob.

It's a steel knob.

I've already identified that the closet handle is also metal and, no doubt, so is every nail that was used to construct each piece of furniture in this room. There are silver embellishments on the posts at every corner of his bed and several small tin cases are now scattered on the floor.

I may not be able to bend any of this metal to my will unless I can hammer it with my Blacksmith's hammer, but I'm aware of every piece of it.

Too many items in this room are forbidden to me.

My sister told the Vandawolf that I should not be moved, but he will never let me stay here. I imagine he only brought me here because he thought Petra would help me and this was the nearest room.

He has remained with his back to me. He's still wearing yesterday's armor and his hair is disheveled. But it's the increasing tension in his shoulders that worries me.

"I have no use for an injured Blacksmith," he says.

I'm already turning on to my left side—the uninjured one—so I can plant my hands on the edge of the bed and leverage myself up into a sitting position. It's too difficult to hold on to the sheet at the same time, so I abandon it until I'm sitting up, after which I pull it back to my chest.

The skin across my wound pulls in unpleasant ways, the room spins, and I take a moment to catch my breath.

Across the room, I sense the Vandawolf's deep inhale, followed by the slow release of tension from his shoulders as he exhales.

He begins to speak. "But I do want—"

At the same time, I rasp, "I need clothing."

My forehead creases as I register that I spoke over him, but he's already spinning to face me.

For the briefest moment, he looks surprised to see me sitting up.

Did he think I'd complain?

I meet his unflinching gaze and repeat in a hoarse whisper, "My armor is ruined. I need something to wear."

I'm walking a fine line with him now. He accused me of betraying him in front of his Warriors. Braddock isn't the only one who will whisper to anyone who will listen. News of the stranger and my part in his appearance, along with my near-death, will have spread like wildfire through the city. In fact, there may already be rumors that I'm dead. Gallium and Tamra will have no chance of keeping any of that talk at bay.

My family is only safe while I live.

I will only live as long as I can serve the Vandawolf.

To keep them alive, I must prove to him that I'm still useful to him, no matter how much pain it causes me.

CHAPTER 17

I'm defiant as I gesture to the blanket I'm clutching to my breasts. "Unless you want me to walk back to my tower wrapped in this sheet?"

The movement of my right hand was a bad idea. It pulls the stitches and I wince, my stomach churning at the sudden, sharp pain.

The groan in the back of my throat becomes a snarl as I force myself to my feet, dragging the sheet off the bed with me.

"*Our* deal still stands," I say with all the strength of the anger and pain growing within me. "My life is yours and my family is safe—"

"Stop," he says, but there is no mercy in his expression. Only a sharp tooth and angry eyes. "Stay where you are."

He saunters to the closet, rifling through clothing until he reaches the very bottom.

He pauses for a moment, and I catch only a glimpse of black material before he stands and turns back to me.

"This," he says, walking the garment over to me.

The soft material floats into my arms, light as air and smooth as silk, but it may as well be a dagger at my throat.

I recognize this dress.

It belonged to Malak's sister, Milena. She was killed in a failed uprising by the humans when I was five, soon after I first attempted to use a hammer. Malak's revenge on the humans was horrific and it continued for weeks afterward.

I'll never forget this dress. Milena was wearing it when she handed me the hammer that proved me defective. I remember thinking how she seemed to glide across the throne room's inky, marble floor, her long, black hair gleaming like a starry night.

The dress is designed to wrap around the body, kept in place with a sash. It has an opaque inner layer that covers the torso and thighs while the elbow-length sleeves and long skirt flow in gauzy layers.

I want to ask the Vandawolf why he has it. He might not even know it was hers. He would have been barely six years old when she was killed. It may very well have been bundled up with all the things that were left in the castle when my people were overthrown.

Despite the memories it brings back, it's a good choice for me right now. It can wrap as loosely around my torso as I need it to, while concealing my bandages.

If I hold myself upright, I may not even appear injured.

Turning my back on the Vandawolf, I take what little privacy I can get before I drop the sheet and attempt to find the edges of the dress. Finally locating the right arm hole, I manage to slide my arm through it, but the left is much harder. It requires me to reach with my right hand, which pulls again on the stitches, making the room swim.

I don't realize that I groaned until the sleeve of the dress lifts at my side and the Vandawolf's hand comes into view, holding the material ready for me to slip my arm through it.

"You think I'm cruel," he says, his presence at my back like a constant wall. A wall that both cages me and shields me from the humans who wish me dead.

There is no easy or right way to answer his question.

He told me never to forget that he's a monster.

"I think you're built for survival." My voice is flat. "Sometimes survival requires cruelty."

His fingertips brush my arm as I pull the dress carefully up my arm and manage to draw it closed at the front. The sash has also fallen to the sides, hanging down from the loops at the waist. He gathers up each side and slips his arms beneath mine to wrap the material around at the front.

He moves carefully, taking time to smooth out the sash without pressing on my wounds before he draws the straps to the back again. The soft tugging sensations tell me he's either tying them in a knot or a bow, but either way, the material is secure.

His touch feels different and I don't know what to make of it. It's gentler, less tumultuous, and yet somehow... resigned.

He asked me if I thought he was cruel, but what I really think is that I will never truly know, or understand, his mind.

The only times I have a sense of his impulses are when I hold my tools and can discern the wolf whose instincts drive his own.

One of his palms flattens against my back, positioned on the left of my spine right on the other side of my heart.

His voice is low and soft, but there's an edge of steel in it. "Are you loyal to me?"

My heart calms at the familiar question and my breathing evens out. "I am."

But it seems he's prepared to change the script today because he asks, "Did you intend to betray me?"

My response is immediate and truthful. "No."

His palm presses more tightly against my back. "Were you too injured to kill the prisoner?"

My eyes widen. My thoughts churn.

The truthful answer is no, and I'm sure he knows it.

I could have killed the stranger despite my wounds. The power in the medallions was surging through me and all I needed to do was connect with the stranger's body and command him to become ash.

But the Vandawolf has never asked me a question like this before. The way he speaks, the tone of his voice, it's as if he's telling me to rewrite my thoughts in the moments when the stranger first appeared to me.

I was already badly injured.

The stranger attacked me.

He was strong.

I was too hurt to fight back.

It's a plausible story that would be believable to the council and to his people. What's important is that betrayal and disloyalty have no part in it. But if this is the story he wants known and repeated, then it will have other consequences for me.

It says that if I'm hurt badly enough, even when I have my tools, I can't defend myself.

Of course, the humans already know that I'm mortal, so perhaps it's not so bad...

When I hesitate, the Vandawolf's other hand closes around my right shoulder and he repeats his question through gritted teeth. "You did not betray me as I first thought because you were too injured to kill the stranger. Is that correct?"

"Yes."

The lie is sour on my tongue.

"Good." The Vandawolf turns me carefully so that I'm facing him. His hands drop to his sides. "Will you ever betray me?"

Without reservation, I reply, "Never."

He takes a step back, his expression shuttered now. "You will walk across the courtyard, accompanied by your guards. Do not go quickly. You will ensure that as many people see you alive as possible. Tonight, at midnight, you will be ready to come with me to the prison to interrogate the prisoner. I will let you have your tools again then."

I'm surprised by his final command that I will go to the prison since he already told Tamra to question the stranger today.

Ah, but he's strategic.

If Tamra reveals that she's my sister, she will be the face of powerless Blacksmiths. She may even lull the newcomer into a false sense of security before I stand before him and extract whatever information the Vandawolf wants.

Assuming I *can* still stand by then.

I school my voice so I don't reveal my pain. "I'll be ready."

I draw a deep breath, preparing myself for what it will take to hold my head high and walk the distance to the tower without passing out.

"Boots," he says gruffly when I move straight past them.

"I can't put them on," I reply, already picturing myself trying to reach my feet and compressing the wound in my side.

He gives a huff that sounds more frustrated than angry, and the fine line I'm walking rears its ugly head again.

"I don't need them," I insist, but he stops me before I can take another step.

"Sit," he orders me, pointing to the chair by the door.

The branch containing my tools rests on the floor right beside that chair and I've deliberately avoided looking at it. My tools didn't exactly help me heal on the battlefield, but they kept me in one piece and they dulled my pain. I can't ignore the possibility that they could accelerate my healing, but I can't ask for access to them.

Asking for my tools will always be interpreted as a threat.

I crossed that line yesterday on the balcony and the Vandawolf responded by demonstrating very effectively how much stronger than me he is. I don't need an altercation with him in my current state of health.

"You want your tools," he says matter-of-factly. "Your heart-beat increases every time you look at them."

I try to moisten my lips as I lower myself onto the chair. "They kept me alive yesterday."

"Did they?" he asks softly as he picks up my boots and carries them to me. "Or did the power within them merely create that illusion?"

My forehead creases as he kneels in front of me and captures my right foot.

"Malak was convinced that the medallions made him invincible." The Vandawolf's palm rests beneath the arch of my foot and my limb seems so small against the size of his palm. "It was trickery. He died like all the others after him."

The Vandawolf slides his hand to my heel as he angles the first boot onto my foot and then the second.

His hands glide in a slow stroke up my calves between the top of my boot and my knee before he wraps his hand around my lower thigh. His touch is soothing to my frayed nerves but very much at odds with his next command.

"Walk as if you aren't injured," he says, his voice much harder than his hands.

I give a curt nod and rise to my feet when he releases me.

Outside, Rachel and two other guards stand in the middle of the walkway, facing the direction of the stairs as if they're guarding the corridor and not my room.

"Trouble in the night?" the Vandawolf asks.

Rachel spins at the sound of his voice. Her jaw drops when she sees me standing in the Vandawolf's shadow.

She recovers quickly. "A little, lord, but nothing I couldn't handle. However, I'm sure you were already aware of those commotions."

"The council members can fucking wait," he replies.

A disturbance outside this door means others might have

tried to gain entry and it sounds like it was either council members or emissaries they sent on their behalf.

The other two guards have immediately stood to attention, their surprised gazes passing from my head to my booted feet.

The Vandawolf addresses each of them in turn. "You will take a message to each council member. Tell them I will meet them tomorrow afternoon in the throne room. At that time, I will give them the answers they seek."

His voice lowers to a snarl. "You will also remind them that I won't tolerate impatience or division."

The two guards acknowledge the order and hurry away.

"Rachel, you will escort Asha to her tower."

"Alone, lord?"

He gives her a wolfish smile. "Are you concerned for your safety?"

"No, lord, only... Are you coming with us?"

"I am not."

She gives him a brief nod before she gestures me forward. "Lady Asha, this way please."

I step out from the Vandawolf's shadow to walk ahead of Rachel.

The black dress swishes around my legs as light as silk, while my boots thud a hard beat. Every step drives nails into my bones. Every breath brings tears of pain to my eyes.

Still, I remain dry-eyed and force myself to walk onward down the stairs, taking each agonizing step evenly, and into the outer corridor, where I enter the abnormally busy courtyard.

There are a far greater number of people milling about than usual, all of them appearing to have some purpose in being here.

So fucking contrived.

The castle grounds are usually restricted. I have no doubt that Braddock must have 'forgotten' to order the gates be closed.

I recognize humans who are part of each council member's staff, and I suspect they were waiting for news of my death.

I don't pause when the courtyard hushes, carving a steady but slow path from one corner of the yard to the other. The light breeze plucks at the black dress and I keep my head high, glaring at anyone who stands near to my path.

They hurry to get out of my way.

The whispers start and repeat in waves, loud enough for me to hear.

"She's alive."

"The Blacksmith still lives."

"How did she survive?"

"She doesn't even appear hurt..."

One by one, they peel off from their positions and head for the portcullis, casting glances back at me. It's obvious they're going to report to whomever sent them.

As cruel as the Vandawolf's orders may be, to appear weak will only invite a knife in my sleep.

I'm relieved to make it all the way across the courtyard and into my tower without stumbling.

After reaching the stairs at the base of my tower, I manage to ascend to the top of the first flight before I wobble, unable to stop myself from veering toward the side of the stairwell, seeking its support so I don't fall.

"Lady Asha. Let me help you."

"No," I snap at Rachel. "I don't need your help. I'm not hurt. Just tired."

I drag in a breath, slowly pushing myself upright again.

I find her standing with her hand outstretched, but her shoulders are hunched and her expression is defeated.

It's not the response I was expecting.

"I understand that cruelty can masquerade as kindness," she says. "But you have my word, I won't take your hand only to push you down these stairs. I also want you to know that I don't spread stories about you, Lady Asha. I don't try to weaken you in the eyes of my brethren. I saw your wounds. No human could have survived injuries like that. Let alone walked as far as you already have. You are strong enough in my eyes."

Through my pain, I take the chance to look at her—really look at her. I know nothing about her or why she's on my personal guard. I certainly can't fathom why she calls me 'lady.'

"Who are you, Rachel?"

The crease clears from her forehead. "I'm nobody. Truly."

I narrow my eyes at her as I suddenly realize... "You don't fear me."

"Why would I fear a woman who fights to protect her family?"

My eyes burn. My head lowers and I can't ignore the pain any longer. "Why do you call me 'lady'?"

She slips her arm around my back, a slow and tentative movement, as if she expects me to push her away.

When I don't, she says, "Many decades ago, my grandmother's life was saved by a Blacksmith. She remembers a time when they wielded their power with benevolence. They were lords and ladies then. Your people were not always as evil as they became."

Hot tears trickle down my cheeks. "I would give anything to have been born in that time."

Rachel takes my other arm, supporting me. "As would I, Lady Asha."

Exhaling slowly, I say, "I won't make it up these stairs without you."

"Then I'll help you to the top," she says. "After that, I'll bring you food and water, although you'll need to eat and drink slowly until your wounds heal."

It's a painful ascent up each flight of stairs and by the time I reach my room, I'm passing out.

Rachel manages to get the door open and help me to my bed.

After that, the moments blur.

As she promised, she brings me food and water—and helps me to eat and drink. She brushes the knots out of my hair as well as she can while I'm lying on my side. Then she gives me more water, lifting the cup to my lips once more.

Finally, she sits in the wooden chair in the corner of my room, watching over me while I fall asleep.

In all my life, I've never given even a moment of trust to a human.

As I fall asleep, I can only pray she doesn't betray me.

CHAPTER 18

S hadows grow long behind my eyelids, but none are so dark as the Vandawolf's.

His big body blocks the moonlight, his appearance at the side of my bed drawing me upright with a groan. "I'm awake."

I force my stiff body up from the bed, noting the empty chair on the other side of the room. I'm not sure when Rachel left. It could have been hours ago, or only minutes.

"I dismissed her," the Vandawolf says, apparently noticing the way I peered at the empty chair.

Normally, when the Vandawolf comes to my room at night, he would hand me my armor, but tonight, I'm surprised when he passes me the wooden box that houses my tools.

I can only assume that he's transferred the titanium bands from the branch back into this box where they will now sit alongside my hammer.

He usually waits until I'm standing in front of the target to give me my tools. It's all part of a dark game that aims to elicit responses from them. The fear that grows when I tap the bands and bring them to life can make even the most tight-lipped human speak.

I don't immediately take the box.

Slipping my legs over the edge of the bed, I give myself a moment to adjust to being upright. My hair hangs loosely down my back. The black dress is tangled around my torso and thighs, but I don't bother adjusting it. After all, he's seen my legs before.

"Why have you brought my tools so soon?" I ask before I can stop myself from questioning him.

"This prisoner will not be easily intimidated," the Vanda-wolf replies. "You will strike hard and fast."

I try to see his expression within the gloom. His silhouette is backlit with moonlight, which is making it difficult. "What did my sister find out?"

"Only that he wants to speak to you."

But he hates Blacksmiths.

I set aside my uncertainty.

The stranger's origins and identity are a mystery. Too much is unknown and unexplained. The sooner I'm prepared to face him, the sooner I'll have answers.

I move quickly.

Taking the wooden box, I open the lid and scoop up the medallions along with the hammer. Quickly closing the lid and resting the box on my lap, I lay the medallions in a row on top of it and place the hammer to their left. All of this, I do with my right hand.

I take a moment to breathe and prepare myself.

My senses are going haywire with the need to claim the power within these tools and use the strength they give me.

But always, this final moment before I awaken the medallions is the last moment that I am truly myself. As weak and injured as I am right now, my mind is still my own.

I won't remain that way once I pick up the hammer with my left hand.

I don't delay any longer. Without the grooves beneath the bands, they could slip when I strike them, so I place my right palm over the top ends of all three.

Exhaling slowly, I count through the breath and prepare myself.

Power strikes through me the moment my left hand closes around the hammer. The pain in my side reduces significantly and I can't stop the moan of relief that leaves my lips.

The tension in my shoulders releases—so much tension that I only now realize how stiff I was. Even my facial features feel as if they're smoothing out, the strain of physical pain leaving my body and mind.

Carefully controlling my strength, I strike lightly on each medallion.

One, two, three.

The soft clangs ring out and dark light shoots from each band as it awakens. Without a second's hesitation, I place the hammer onto the wooden surface and plant my left palm over all three medallions at once. They curl around my palm, sitting neatly side by side.

Every last shred of pain within my body vanishes as intense energy flows through me.

A silvery, metallic sheen dusts my arms and legs, glistening beneath the flowing dress. My hair shines where it rests across my shoulder, gleaming all the way to my waist. I'm aware of the changes that are flowing across my face, the color that will make my cheeks radiant and the shifting hues of my irises from green to blue to gray to green.

As I slip off the bed, fully mobile now, the light radiating from my body invades the shadows that were concealing the Vandawolf's face, exposing his features.

He's standing closer to me than he normally does when I trigger my tools. Dangerously close. His head is tilted, the wolfish side of his face turned toward me. His left hand is raised at his side, high enough that he could touch me if he took a single step forward. His lips are slightly parted and a gleam brightens his eyes.

I've never seen such a look on his face before.

I'm not sure how to interpret it.

It pulls me toward him, but not because my power tells me to mold him. No, this pull is something else.

So strange.

Opposite me, the Vandawolf's fingers slowly close into a fist and the gleam in his eyes vanishes. Gone so suddenly that I fear I imagined it. Whatever *it* was.

I gather my thoughts, refocus, and let the power surge through me once more.

Carefully pressing my left hand to my right bicep, I command the medallions to transform into armbands that sit neatly around my arm.

My expression is blank when I turn back to the Vandawolf.

I have a task to do.

The dark energy in the bands will let me do it.

Tipping my head back to see his eyes, I say, "As you asked, I will strike hard and fast."

With that, I round the bed, scooping up my boots on the way to the door. I can function much more easily now that the medallions are masking my pain. Still, I don't put the boots on right away since I can walk more quietly in bare feet.

The Vandawolf quickly snaps the toolbox closed and stashes it in the base of my closet. The closet has a false bottom, beneath which the toolbox will remain hidden until I return with the medallions.

He shadows me as I slip along the empty corridor and down the stairs, gliding down each step until I reach the base of the tower.

There, I pause.

The glow from my power would be a problem if I had to access the cages by walking around or across the courtyard, but there's a second entry—a hidden one—at the far end of the corridor at the base of my tower.

There was a time when I thought the Vandawolf chose this particular tower for me because of the proximity to the cages, since he could throw me into one faster from here. Too soon, I discovered it was because it gave me easy and secretive access to any prisoner he was holding there.

I dart along the corridor—in the direction away from the courtyard—and reach the heavy door at the end. It opens into a small and dingy storage room filled with wooden buckets and broken tables and chairs.

I navigate through the narrow space between damaged objects to reach the concealed trapdoor in the floor on the far side. Its handle masquerades as the broken leg of a chair and its edges are irregular, mimicking the uneven planks that make up the rest of the floor.

By turning the handle—the broken chair leg—clockwise, the trapdoor clicks open.

Within moments, I've stepped down into the darkness of the stairwell beneath the floor, leaving the door open for the Vandawolf to follow me in.

I'm already halfway down the stairs when he closes the door above me, dropping us into darkness again—a darkness broken by the power streaming through my body.

Three paces from the bottom of the stairs, there's another door. This one is wooden on this side but wears a layer of stone on its other side that makes it invisible from within the prison's rock walls.

It would seem impossible to fuse rock to wood like this, but Malak accomplished it.

He created this dungeon and each of its unbreakable metal cages.

The Vandawolf was the only one who ever escaped them.

I push the door open but pause to pull on my boots, slipping them easily onto my feet without any of the difficulty I experienced before I put on my medallions.

Hurrying along the hallway toward the cages, I quickly scan the cells on both sides of the walkway. They're constructed of steel bars, each an inch apart, that have been driven up into the rock ceiling and down into the floor, making them immovable.

I locate the prisoner chained within the farthest cell on the left, his arms and legs spread, his wrists and ankles shackled to taut chains. The ones attached to his wrists extend from the ceiling while the chains around his legs are bolted to the floor.

My lips press together when I see that there are bloody lash marks across his bare chest. When the Vandawolf said that the prisoner would resist other attempts to elicit information from him, I should have guessed those attempts would have involved a lash.

As I approach, I make out the way the cuts glisten a little, and I detect the scent of salve—the same scent that lingers on my own skin. My sister's medicine.

My footsteps slow as I draw closer.

Every muscle in the stranger's body tenses as he watches me approach. His bronzed eyes graze me from my head to my toes, following the silvery strands of my hair to the folds of my dress where they float around my legs as I walk. Then back up to the black bands resting around my right bicep.

There is no longer lightning swirling around his form, no glittering sparks of energy clinging to the shape of his muscles, but the pull toward him is unrelenting. I have no doubt that if I crouched and pressed my hand to the floor right now, the energy that tells me the location of a monster would shoot from the rock where he stands.

His body is *flooded* with Blacksmith's magic.

While the Vandawolf stays in the shadows of the corridor, I step inside the cage.

I promised the Vandawolf that I would strike fast, but I also need to control my own reactions, the irresistible pull, and the hitch in my breathing.

The position of the stranger's body fully exposes the scales that shine down his right side—scales that gleam in the dim light—and they're fucking beautiful. Like plates of bronze begging to be shaped.

His right fist clenches the closer I get to him and for a moment, I consider if his scaled arm could be strong enough to break the chains that keep that arm shackled.

I suppose I'll find out if he thrashes.

Strike fast, the Vandawolf said.

I don't hesitate a moment longer, striding right for the prisoner, my left hand outstretched.

He must have expected me to approach him slowly, to let his fear build, because his eyes briefly widen.

He appears about to speak, his breath catching, but my palm slaps against his chest, silencing him.

"Who are you?" I demand to know.

I speak before I register the power beneath my hand.

Too much power.

My heart stops. And then beats harder. I sense his sweat and blood and the thump of his heart as clearly as the warning bells that ring out when a monster is about to rise. Burning heat scorches my palm where my skin presses to his chest while the medallions on my arm are suddenly searing.

It isn't like touching the monsters that appear in the wasteland.

It feels exactly like those long-ago moments when I picked

up Malak's hammer for the first time and my legs were wrapped around the Vandawolf's waist.

In those moments, I connected with more than the malice in the metal. I connected with the wild power in the Vandawolf's body, just as I'm now connecting with the ferocity of the power that rages within this stranger.

I expect him to try to wrench away from my touch, but he presses into it instead, his muscles tensing, as if he's daring me to use my power on him.

"Do it," he says. "Use your magic and show your master what you really are."

My eyes widen a little at the way he's trying to goad me into using my power, but to what end?

Maybe to demonstrate that *I* am the monster here.

Regardless of his reason, I recognize that his speech is calculated to elicit a response from me. If I had any doubt about how dangerous this man is, it disappears in an instant.

"I act only at the will of the Vandawolf," I say, restraining my magic and lowering my voice. "Tell me who you are."

"What do you want from me, Blacksmith?" he asks, a soft rumble, much like the sound of growing thunder. "My name? Or more than that?"

"Everything," I say before I catch myself and clarify my meaning. "I want to *know* everything." I claw my fingers against his chest to emphasize my next words. "You will answer every question I ask. You will only tell me the truth."

"And if I don't?" he asks.

"If you refuse to answer or you lie to me, I will create instruments with my medallions that will cause you pain beyond any you've ever experienced."

"Like a true fucking Blacksmith," he replies, any softness in his expression disappearing.

For the first time since I stepped into the cage, he wrenches on the shackles that bind his arms, pulling downward so hard that I'm sure he's in danger of breaking his wrists. I press my palm firmly against his chest, never allowing him to avoid contact.

"Those shackles are unbreakable," I say, quietly ignoring his rage. "They were forged by Malak himself." I go on in the next breath. "Now, tell me your name."

"I'm called Thaden Kane."

Despite my threats, I wasn't expecting him to answer, but I'm not about to show my surprise. "Why are you here, Thaden Kane?"

His expression hardens. "Why are *you* here, Asha Silverspun?"

I'm a little surprised he knows my full name, but I assume one of the prison guards, or even my sister, must have mentioned it. His response sounds like he's throwing my question back at me, but there's a glint in his eyes, an intensity that indicates his question is more than insolence.

I hesitate for the moment that gives him the chance to lean in a little. "Why are you here doing the bidding of a wolf?" His focus flickers to the Vandawolf, who hasn't moved from his chosen position in the shadows. "When you could raze this city to the ground."

Again, it feels like he's goading me. Or is there a hint of confusion in his eyes? Because to an outsider, it must seem strange that someone with my power has submitted to being ruled.

"Enough!" I whip my left hand away from his chest, slap it against the topmost band on my right arm—which immediately curls around my left palm—and back against his heart.

He draws a quick breath and freezes, the muscles across his shoulders and sides bunching.

The band sits neatly against his chest, and I will it to soften a little to conform with the contours of his chest while I take a few moments to let his fear build.

The influx of power hums through my body and I take deep breaths, controlling my impulses.

For now.

"Answer me," I whisper.

His gaze falls to mine, but he doesn't otherwise move a muscle. "I was sent here."

My eyes narrow and my brow furrows at his unexpected response. "Sent? By whom?"

He exhales slowly and some of the fight goes out of his body. "I was sent by the Blacksmith who created me."

CHAPTER 19

There can't be another Blacksmith. The Vandawolf killed them all. He brought their empire to its knees and left me and my siblings the last of our kind.

I meet Thaden's eyes, the bronzed color of them so unnatural in the dim light.

A Blacksmith created him?

Not possible. Only Malak succeeded in creating a living, breathing beast. No other Blacksmith even came close.

He's telling me lies.

Rage floods my body. An irrational and uncontrollable rage. I can't fight it and it's the opening of the flood gates that allows the malice in the bands to take over.

Pure cruelty shoots from the armbands to my heart and all the way up into my mind, consuming every shred of compassion and empathy within me.

Smothering every shred of *me*.

I feel only hatred and anger now and the overwhelming desire to hurt this fucking liar for trying to play on my emotions. For suggesting that I'm not completely alone. Even if the Blacksmith he speaks of may be an enemy.

EVERLY FROST

He begins to speak again. "The Blacksmith sent me with a message—"

I'm already pushing forward, rising up on tiptoes, my head tipped back, my chest nearly pressing to his. In this position, the fingertips of my left hand brush the edges of the other two medallions that sit across my right arm while the one in my left hand softens like putty between us.

It's ready to transform into any weapon I wish. Or turn him to ash at a single command.

"You're lying!" I snap, pushing the metal band against his heart so hard that I force him back against his chains, making his muscles strain. "Every other Blacksmith is dead."

Instead of attempting to retreat, he leans forward into me, squishing my palm between us, his muscled chest suddenly hard up against mine.

"They are not," he snaps. "*She* is not."

"Oh, a *female* Blacksmith?" I ask, goading him now. "Just like me?"

"Nothing like you," he snaps. "She does what she pleases. She answers to nobody. She hurts whomever she wants to hurt. And she's coming for—"

With a furious scream, I step back from him and close my fist around the putty within my hand. "Do you think I won't hurt you for your lies?"

Blade! I shout within my mind. *Sharpest blade!*

The medallion transforms, elongating into a needle-sharp spindle, a thin spoke with a solid handle. It's long enough to impale him by inches and it will extend all the way through his chest at a mere command from me.

There's no surprise on his face, only a quick flash of resignation, as if he knew I'd attack him eventually.

I stab the weapon at his right shoulder, aiming for the fleshy part at the edge of his bronze scales, intending to inflict pain without any real damage.

Just as the tip reaches his chest, the air moves at my back and the heat of a wolf's body fills my senses.

"Stop," the Vandawolf growls at my ear.

For ten years, I've obeyed him to the point where my body's response is instant, and I fucking hate it.

The sharp tip of the black dagger halts, piercing Thaden's skin right at the edge of his scales.

A single drop of blood drips down his chest.

I stare at it, following its path, knowing all it would take is the lightest touch and I'm sure I could transform his blood into boiling lava. As hot as the power I sense within him.

"Step back, Asha," the Vandawolf says, his voice and his presence allowing no disobedience.

For so long, I've complied with every command the Vandawolf has given me. I've feared reprisal and the repercussions for my family. But I've also never imagined there could be another Blacksmith out there.

That possibility has filled me with turmoil. And right now, with Malak's dark power surging freely through me—the kind of surge I usually only experience out in the wasteland—the storm of emotions within me has no outlet except violence.

It's a violence that suddenly surpasses the control the Vandawolf has over me. Despite obeying him before, I can't stop my refusal now, even if there's a very small spark of myself screaming at me to obey him.

"No," I say, a harsh whisper, my voice sounding nothing like my own.

"No?" His rebuke is stern, but it contains a hint of disbelief.

I spin to the Vandawolf, the dagger in my hand.

"No." I'm aware of my glistening hair swaying at my back, the black dress that belonged to Malak's sister swishing around my legs, and the darkening glow from the remaining medallions casting shadows across my right arm.

At my declaration, the Vandawolf's expression becomes

like stone. If he's surprised, he doesn't show it and he certainly doesn't back off. He towers over me, a beast's growl on his lips, his amber eye and sharp wolf's tooth fully visible. "Asha, you will do as I say—"

"Which command?" I ask, stepping into his space. My hand is so tight around the dagger that I'm cutting off my own circulation, but I don't care. "Kill the monster? Interrogate the monster? *Don't* hurt the monster?" My voice rises. "Which command do you want me to follow?"

He gave me the bands and told me to put them on. He ordered me to strike hard and fast. Every time I wear this metal, I've been told to carry through with the violence that follows.

This time, he's changed his mind.

Except that it's too late.

The malice has me.

His left hand rises, palm up, but it's a warning, not an appeasement.

"Asha." His tone is harsh. "Remember the consequences."

I narrow my eyes at him, my voice cold. "I don't care about consequences."

In this moment, I only care about the power streaming through me. A power that tells me to subdue the Vandawolf.

Drive him to the ground.

Finish what Malak started...

A new command comes easily to my mind as I draw my left hand back.

Chains.

Power rushes through the dagger I was holding, transforming it quickly as my hand darts forward.

A fine, black chain streams from my palm, flying straight at the Vandawolf's throat. I keep hold of the end of it and spin at the same time, ensuring the chain arcs.

The Vandawolf is fast, but at this proximity, he can't avoid the wire altogether.

It wraps around his neck, the metal hissing through the air like a snake.

The Vandawolf's hand snaps up between the chain and his throat so that it doesn't immediately cut through his skin, but he can't stop it from tightening.

Within heartbeats, it wraps neatly around his neck, its shape thinning as power continues to stream through it from my hand where I hold the other end of it. Faster than I can follow, the metal becomes longer and thinner so that it wraps around and around... Snapping and winding like a tornado...

The Vandawolf is immediately on his back foot, but it's not a defensive move. I recognize the way he's preparing to lunge at me.

It would be the first physical contact between us for ten years while I'm wielding my tools.

"Asha!" he rasps. "Don't make me fight you. It won't end well for you."

"Will you cut off my hand?" I ask as the chain tightens across the back of his hand and blood trickles down his arm. "Or tear out my heart?"

Shadows descend over his face and for the first time in ten years, I witness the wild I saw all those years ago.

The killer who reaped justice on my people.

I'm sure he will finally retaliate.

I'm sure that, finally, he will let loose the wolf and allow it to dominate his thoughts.

My forehead creases when he stays right where he is, pulling at the wire wrapped around his throat, and doesn't lunge at me after all.

"Asha..." He drops to a knee, blood dripping from his fingers and down the sides of his neck. "This... isn't... you..."

My eyes widen as a spark of myself cuts through the thick mire of cruelty and anger within my mind.

My left hand starts to shake, my hold on the chain loosening.

"How would you know?" I ask, pain bleeding into my speech. "How could you possibly know who I am? I'm nothing but a soldier to you. A thing to die at your whim."

A growl leaves his lips, but nothing more. The band must be too tight around his throat for him to speak now and the threat of his death is very real.

I glimpse the wolf rising within him as he snarls up at me.

It has vicious teeth and mindless anger and it won't let him die. I know this with every fiber of my being.

In another few seconds, it will take over and then we'll discover which of us is stronger—

Sudden movement at the corner of my vision startles me.

I spin back toward Thaden, but it's too late.

There's a flash of bronze, the sound of grinding metal, multiple ear-piercing shrieks, and then his furious body collides with mine.

My left hand opens, releasing the chain around the Vanda-wolf's neck a split second before I gain air. I hit the ground and tumble, my consciousness consumed by Thaden's large body as he rolls with me along the prison floor. I register smooth scales, broken skin, the weight of muscles, and a sudden influx of power.

I don't have time to breathe, let alone process the danger I'm now facing.

All I have is a single, startling thought:

Thaden broke his shackles.

Shackles forged by Malak himself.

In the next moment, I hit the side of the cage, a crunching impact that reduces my thoughts to instincts.

Thaden has landed half over me, one knee between my legs, both arms free, putting him at the advantage. I already let go of my first medallion, but the other two bands remain against my skin, feeding strength and speed into my muscles.

Using that strength without hesitation, I punch upward, my left fist colliding with Thaden's chest—right where my dagger pierced his shoulder. He gives a grunt of pain as my punch pushes him backward. The new gap between us allows me to use my own momentum to twist to the right, making it up onto my knees with my back against the cage bars before he reaches for me.

He doesn't take a swing at me, one hand closing around my shoulder.

I knock it away, attempting to get to my feet.

His other hand lands on my other shoulder, forcing me back to my knees.

I punch that hand away, but he's already reaching for my other side, seeming infuriatingly intent on keeping me on my knees.

It's only been seconds since he launched himself at me, but behind him, I'm aware of the Vandawolf hurrying to unwind the black chain from around his neck. He's still kneeling, but I'm acutely conscious of his deeply indrawn breath as the chain falls from his neck.

He's seconds away from joining the fight.

The perilousness of my current situation is not lost on me.

The consequences are suddenly sickening.

What have I done?

I have few choices now. None are good.

I don't fight back when Thaden abandons my shoulders and his hands shoot toward my sides instead, aiming for my ribs beneath my breasts. I allow his palms to close around me. He pushes me back against the bars, lifting me upward at the same time, but not so far that my feet leave the ground. His bronze hair falls across his face and conceals all but the determined set of his lips. "Be still, Blacksmith."

No.

His hold around my ribs has freed up both of my arms and there's enough space between our chests for my left hand to snake toward my right bicep.

I snatch at the two bands.

To my dismay, Thaden is faster. As fast as the Vandawolf.

His right hand—the one covered in bronze scales—angles across my body. His fingers close over the medallions before I can reach them.

In that instant, I realize he grabbed me around my ribs for the same reason I let him hold me in that position. We were both going for my medallions.

My palm hits the back of his hand, and even though I try to pull his fingers away from me, I can't stop him from plucking the bands right off my arm.

For a moment, my palm rests over the back of his scaled hand as he closes his fist around the medallions, but his scales are an effective barrier between me and the bands.

The power drains from me.

My eyes widen. Fear floods my body and mind.

I catch the flash of energy in Thaden's eyes, the sudden glow around his form as the magic in his body reacts to the power in my tools.

He shouldn't be able to touch the medallions without harm and yet...

Dark light explodes down our arms, a final burst of energy.

Then, with a savage roar, Thaden twists and throws the bands across the cage. They hit the back wall and clatter to the stone floor.

His chest is heaving, his focus remaining on the medallions for another moment while his left hand presses hard against my right side—my wounded side—keeping me pinned against the bars at my back. And causing me excruciating pain.

Now that my tools are gone, so is the overwhelming malice

that was dictating my actions. So is my strength and my ability to protect myself.

I have no power to fight back.

His hand is like a vise and the pain in my side is unbearable. I sense the blood drain from my face and I can't stop my scream.

Thaden swings back to me, his bronze eyes filled with wrath, his lips pressed hard together, but his face falls when his focus drops to my side.

He quickly pulls his hand away, revealing his palm smeared with blood.

It must be seeping through my bandages, although not easily visible because of the black dress.

I'm shaking too hard to remain upright and without Thaden holding me against the bars, I crumple to the ground, tremors racking my body.

I am nothing more than a wretched heap swathed in black silk and all I have now is fear.

I'm vaguely aware of the Vandawolf's roar as he plows toward Thaden, a roar so ferocious that it drowns out my own cry—a cry of pain and rage and complete powerlessness.

What have I done?

CHAPTER 20

T he Vandawolf's fist cracks against Thaden's jaw, a hit so hard that if Thaden were completely human, his bones would have shattered.

Instead, he seems to absorb the blow, lurching backward with a grunt, but he doesn't try to fight back.

Thaden drops to his knees, his hands upraised.

"I have no war with you, Vandawolf!" he shouts as the Vandawolf draws his arm back to strike again. "My war is with Blacksmiths!"

The Vandawolf pauses. His neck is smeared with blood. So is the fist that hovers over Thaden's head. Wounds that I'm responsible for.

Through the sweaty, bloody strands of the Vandawolf's unruly hair, I glimpse the wolf.

"Hurt Asha again and I will tear out your fucking throat," the Vandawolf says.

Thaden's gaze flashes upward, his eyes narrowed. He seems to swallow his first response before he snaps. "You're welcome."

Technically, Thaden helped the Vandawolf by attacking

me. He pushed me away when I was threatening the Vanda-wolf's life.

The Vandawolf's lips draw back in a snarl that makes his sharp tooth appear even sharper. His amber eye gleams while his human eye is as cold as titanium. "If you want to stay alive, Thaden Kane, cuff your left hand to the floor."

Thaden's left hand is the one that isn't strengthened or protected by scales.

Across the way, the shackles that secured his ankles lie mangled on the ground, although one of them appears to be in better shape than the other. Both of the shackles that were attached to the ceiling are damaged beyond repair. One hangs from the ceiling by a mere strip of metal. The chain-links of the other are twisted out of shape and swing gently back and forth, making a soft clanking sound.

Thaden shuffles toward the chains on the floor, reaching the first one and discarding it. Picking up the second, he studies the wide band that remains of the shackle before he presses it around his left wrist, using his scaled hand to force the edges closed.

The tortured metal groans in the silence.

Once finished, Thaden settles onto the floor. "Done."

The fact that he has the strength to bend the metal manu-ally around his wrist means he can also open it, but I suppose the Vandawolf is counting on the shackle slowing Thaden down for a second or two if he tries to escape.

Even through the fear clouding my mind, I'm cataloguing every seemingly impossible thing Thaden has done. He broke the shackles, touched me while my power was in full force, and seized my medallions, all without apparent harm to himself.

I look up when the Vandawolf's shadow drops over me.

He lowers himself into a crouch in front of me, far more slowly and calmly than I was expecting.

He's quiet, but I detect pain in the tightness around his eyes and lips.

I hurt him. My chains broke the skin around his neck.

He could have retaliated and killed me, but... he didn't.

My chest suddenly squeezes because in a perfect world, I wouldn't hurt this beast, who, like me, didn't ask to be what he is.

I'm not sure what will happen now, but I won't look away from what I did.

I meet his eyes as I promised myself I always would.

"I don't expect you to let me live," I say quietly. "All I ask is that you allow my family to leave the city. The wasteland and the mountains are dangerous enough that there's only a slim chance they'll survive. Please don't hunt them down."

He gives a slow nod, as if he agrees, then a quiet exhale before he reaches for me. His hands are far gentler than I anticipated, especially since, even without Malak's power rushing through me, I can sense his wolf's nature driving him right now.

I expected the creature to be volatile and vengeful, so its restraint is baffling.

"I'll check your wound now." The Vandawolf slips his arms around me, drawing me away from the cage bars to loosen the bow at the back of my dress and unwrap the sash. He carefully separates the dress at the front, but only a few inches to the right to expose the bandages on that side.

He's leaning close to me while his palms skim my body, avoiding pressing my wound while he checks the bandages.

His unruly hair brushes my cheek, a faint tickle while he works to pull one of the bandages back into place before he straightens the dress and reties the sash.

With every passing second, I expect to be rebuked, anticipating the harsh words and the accusations that are coming my way.

He finishes tying the sash but doesn't move away.

"This was my fault," he says.

His gaze rises to mine while his hands drop from the back of my dress to rest lightly on my hips.

My lips part in surprise, but my forehead quickly creases.

I can't have heard correctly—

"You were already in pain," he continues quietly. The wolf's growl in his voice is like a soft hum, strangely calming to my nerves. "Malak's cruelty was strongest when he was hurt. Strongest before his final breaths." The Vandawolf's lips press together briefly, his eyes suddenly haunted. "I always wondered if his final pain tainted his tools with even greater malice. I shouldn't have asked you to use the medallions tonight. Not until you were healed."

I'm frozen where I sit. "But..."

His voice instantly hardens. "Do you wish to argue with me, Asha?"

"No," I whisper, desperately trying to understand his feelings. "But... will you punish my family?"

He shakes his head. "They will not be banished or harmed."

I don't understand.

I remember the way he seemed to pull my thoughts from my mind on the night we first met. I wish I had that power now because I need to comprehend his motivations.

I need to understand his mind, now more than ever.

He tilts his head to the side, a very human gesture, as the wolf seems to fade from his face. "I'm not incapable of taking responsibility for my mistakes. Even if I rarely choose to do so."

Before I can say anything, he continues. "Your tolerance for pain is much greater than that of a human. Soon, I will order you to rest and heal. But first, I need you to remain here with me for a while longer. Can you do that?"

He's... asking me...?

My focus drops briefly to his injured neck, then rises back

to his eyes. He hasn't made any move to wipe away the blood or tend to his wounds. I'm lucky that the injury appears superficial, given that his speech hasn't been affected and he's fully functional.

"Yes," I say.

"Good. Stay where you are." He gives me a firm nod before he stands and turns to Thaden.

Thaden's bronze eyes are sharp. I haven't missed the fact that he's been watching us and listening intently.

The Vandawolf rises up to stand at my side before he folds his arms across his chest.

"What creature?" he asks, inclining his head at Thaden's scales.

Thaden's expression is inscrutable for a long moment while the Vandawolf waits for a response.

When Thaden finally speaks, it isn't with an answer. "In the north there are stories," he says, still watching us carefully. "Fables of an immense, walled city in the south that is ruled by a wolf. It is said that the wolf is served by a female Blacksmith." Thaden's gaze passes over us. "I never believed those stories."

His jaw clenches as he continues. "Then I was captured and taken from my village by a Blacksmith, and I thought *she* must be the one in the stories, because she hates this city. She calls this place *Svikari Traidor*: Home of Traitors."

The Vandawolf unfolds his arms, his stance becoming threatening. "What creature?" he repeats, his tone far from calm. "Do not evade again."

Thaden grits his teeth. "I also grew up hearing stories of dragons that live in the mountains that divide the north from the south," he says. "I had even less faith in the truth of those stories than the fable of a wolf living in harmony with a fucking Blacksmith."

The Vandawolf's expression is suddenly unreadable. His voice is quiet. "Dragons."

Thaden closes his right fist, clenching and unclenching it. He tugs on the shackle around his left hand and, with a deep exhale and barely any visible effort, he pulls his hand free.

If that is the strength in his left hand, then I can only imagine the power in his scaled arm—power enough to hold my medallions without harm.

The twice-broken metal chain clanks to the prison floor.

"A dragon," he says.

CHAPTER 21

My eyes are wide with disbelief and I'm certain my heart missed a beat.

Aside from requiring us to believe that dragons exist... which is a challenge in and of itself... *What Blacksmith could possibly achieve the combination of a human and a dragon?*

Tension radiates from the Vandawolf's body as he prowls to the left while Thaden remains sitting on the prison floor.

I didn't believe Thaden when he said that a Blacksmith created him. It doesn't fit with my understanding of how the power that pollutes the wasteland works. It certainly doesn't match with how monsters have appeared there before. All of them rose from the mud and ash—even the lightning monsters, although they appeared at the instant of the lightning strike.

But the way the Vandawolf asked Thaden what kind of creature he is indicates that the Vandawolf believes Thaden's story.

The Vandawolf proved to me many years ago that he can sense Blacksmith magic in another being. He sensed it in me— along with the absence of it in my brother and sister.

I wonder how soon he, or his wolf, recognized the presence of the beast whose soul Thaden claims was combined with his own. It might have been out in the wasteland, which would explain why he gave Thaden the chance to speak and didn't kill him on the spot. Maybe he was hoping my sister would glean more from Thaden.

But if Thaden is telling the truth, then he really was somehow *sent* to the wasteland. All the way from the north.

Now, the Vandawolf considers Thaden with hooded eyes, his wolfish features half-hidden by his hair. He stops pacing and tips his chin in an acknowledgement of sorts. "Dragon."

Thaden's expression is like stone, but he inclines his head, as if returning a greeting. "Wolf."

Very slowly, Thaden rises to his feet, standing as tall as the Vandawolf and just as broad in the chest. "I was human and made into a monster," he says to the Vandawolf. "Just like you were. We have no reason to be enemies."

The Vandawolf's expression barely changes, but there's a tightening around his eyes. "I believe your claim about your origins, but as for being enemies, that will be determined by your willingness to answer our questions."

"Ask," Thaden says, his hands rising as if he has nothing to hide. "You already know the worst."

I'm not so certain that he'll be forthcoming. All of his answers so far have been evasive.

I'm surprised when the Vandawolf defers to me. "Asha?"

I take a beat but recover quickly. Now that the malice in the medallions isn't dictating my actions, I have a greater capacity to approach Thaden as a human would. And perhaps, that is the better way.

Quietly, I ask, "Do you have a family, Thaden Kane?"

His brow furrows at my question.

The Vandawolf also casts me a curious glance, but he doesn't interject.

I'm sure they both expected me to ask Thaden something about his power or about the Blacksmith who sent him. I need those answers, but I need to test Thaden's ability to tell the truth first. Lies are often exposed in the details—in the things that don't seem as important.

Thaden takes a moment to answer, as if he's expecting me to abandon the question. When I don't, he says, "My father was a farmer."

"*Was?*"

"He was killed. My mother died many years before."

"Any brothers or sisters?" I ask.

"None," he replies. "And if you were about to ask: No, I don't have a wife or children."

"So you're alone in the world," I say.

He folds his arms across his chest. "It would seem so."

I let that sit for a moment. "How old are you, Thaden Kane?"

"I was born twenty-one winters ago."

That makes him five years younger than I am. Six years younger than the Vandawolf.

But it's the fact that he measured his years by winters, not summers like the humans in this city do, that matches with his claim of living in the north. The winters in the south are relatively mild compared with the cold and bitter months that prevail beyond the northern mountains. Only in the north do they refer to their years as 'winters.' At least, according to the texts in the library that I read when I was younger.

"The village where you grew up—is it far north of the mountains?" I ask.

Thaden shakes his head. "It's called Myrkur Fjall. It means *in the mountain's shadow.* It's a harsh place with some forest but mostly barren ground. Bad for growing crops, so farming is hard. Farther north, there's more fertile land, but those lands are riddled with war between feuding queens. Myrkur Fjall was the only place we could find peace." His expression darkens. "Until men from our village started disappearing."

Men. More than only him.

"When were you captured?" I ask.

His brow furrows and he takes longer to answer. "The passage of time is murky. I spent a long time in darkness. It could have been a month or possibly more."

I expected the Vandawolf to interject before now, but he hasn't, so I continue. "The Blacksmith who sent you. What can you tell us about her?"

Thaden grimaces and, for the first time since he snatched the medallions from me, his focus moves to the bands. They're dull now, appearing like ordinary metal where they lie scattered on the prison floor.

"What do you want to know?" he asks.

I shrug, as if it doesn't matter too much. "What does she look like? Does she have a name?"

"She has dark hair," he says, still staring at the medallions. "As black as your tools. Eyes just as inky. In terms of her stature, she's small." His lips twist. "Fragile." His focus returns to me. "Her name is Milena."

I stiffen. So does the Vandawolf.

Milena was the name of Malak's sister, but Thaden can't be talking about the same person.

Thaden turns to the Vandawolf. "She told me that the wolf who rules this city killed her brother." His lips thin. "And that the Blacksmith who serves that wolf is a traitor to her people."

I let the accusation wash. Of course any Blacksmith would think of me as a traitor. Only a betrayer could survive the annihilation of her people.

"Milena died years ago," I say, shaking my head. "I was only five, but I remember it distinctly. Malak went on a rampage because of it."

Thaden shrugs. "I don't know anything about that. This

woman is very much alive. She told me her name. She told me she was called a Blacksmith. She used black metal bands like yours. She also had a hammer, tongs, and an anvil that felt like ice at my back." He winces as if with remembered pain before he stares at his scaled hand. "If I'd known these dragon scales would allow me to handle the bands safely, I would have fought back sooner."

I struggle to my feet, the dress I'm wearing suddenly feeling like it's lined with lead and dragging me back down.

Milena's dress.

My heart is thumping and my voice is strained. "*How* did she send you?"

He shakes his head. "I'm not sure. She gave me the message she wanted me to relay and then stepped away from the anvil. I was trying to free myself from the chains that bound me, and I'd nearly succeeded when I heard a clang against a surface behind me. It sounded like her hammer hitting the stone wall. Then there was a flash of energy."

His forehead creases as if in concentration. "A glowing line appeared in the cave ceiling like a thread of fire suddenly streaming across it. The line of energy raced down the wall, connected with the side of the anvil, and then—"

He gives a sigh. "Then I found myself in a field of ash, facing another Blacksmith: you."

The Vandawolf finally steps forward, his voice not so calm now. "You said Milena sent you with a message."

"A message for you and your Blacksmith." Thaden takes a deep breath and rolls his shoulders as if he's shaking off bad memories. "She said to tell you: She wants her city back."

170

CHAPTER 22

The Vandawolf's expression is once again like stone.

"What is Milena planning?" he asks Thaden.

The other man shrugs. "She didn't say. But if she supposedly died years ago, then she's had a long time to prepare."

"Some kind of attack," I whisper. "If Milena has attained the same power as her brother—transforming humans—then she could have amassed an army of her own making by now."

"Assuming they will willingly follow her," the Vandawolf says.

The Vandawolf had no reason not to kill Malak. Malak had already destroyed the Vandawolf's family, killed his brother, so he had no leverage to wield over him. I wonder if Milena has had more foresight than that.

I ask Thaden, "You said that other men were taken. Did you see other prisoners while you were there?"

He nods. "When she took me from my dark cage, I passed many prisoners. Some I recognized from my village. Others I'd never seen before."

I'm more hesitant as I ask my next question, since it reflects my own situation. "Would these men have families they want to protect by doing Milena's bidding? Assuming she were to threaten them?"

Thaden is quiet for a moment. "I don't have any family left, which could be why she chose to send me here, but many of the men I recognized have loved ones they would want to protect."

"Then that's how she'll gain their cooperation," I say, my voice flat, emotionless, despite the burn of the Vandawolf's eyes on me.

"We need to prepare for war," the Vandawolf says, turning his attention back to Thaden. His forehead creases, his expression becoming perplexed. "In the meantime, you've created a dilemma for me, Thaden Kane."

Thaden lifts himself to his full height, nodding his head. "You need to decide what to do with me."

The Vandawolf rubs his forehead, appearing deep in thought. "I do."

When the Vandawolf remains silent for a moment longer, Thaden gestures at the cell we're standing in. "I understand that my presence is a problem for you. After all, I can break out of this prison, so there's no point trying to keep me in here. What's more, I can overpower any human guard."

The Vandawolf grunts.

"But you can't let me walk around freely, even if you trust me, since that would cause unrest within your city," Thaden continues. "Of course, you could try to kill me, but I've seen Milena's home. I've experienced her magic. I have knowledge that you might need."

"Indeed," the Vandawolf says, as if he's testing Thaden. "So what options does that leave me?"

Thaden's focus flashes to me. "Only one. The Blacksmith should guard me."

I'm instantly wary of his suggestion. In my current state, I'm no stronger than a human. The only way I can successfully guard Thaden is if I'm given my tools and I... *can't...* touch them again. Not yet. Not until I'm healed. I've already proven that I can't control the anger in the metal while I'm injured.

Maybe that's what Thaden wants. He made it clear that his war is with Blacksmiths. I'm sure he will have guessed that the humans tolerate my existence as long as I obey the Vandawolf. But if Thaden could make me lose control like I did in this cell, especially in a public way, then the humans will turn on me.

"Agreed," the Vandawolf says. "The Blacksmith will guard you."

No.

I'm shocked that the Vandawolf acquiesced so easily. I'm preparing to protest when he stares me down, his wolf's eye bright. When I swallow my objection, his lips soften to the smallest smile, confusing in its unexpectedness.

He continues, "But not tonight."

Thaden was on the front foot, as if he was preparing to leave the cell, but now he halts, a glower growing on his face.

"Tonight, you will stay here," the Vandawolf says to him.

"But—"

"It's true that you can break the shackles—I did it myself—but you won't bend the bars. Believe me, many years ago, I tried to get past this metal." The Vandawolf reaches out to close his fist around one of the solid poles that extends up into the ceiling. "These cages don't break."

Thaden's lips part as if he's going to argue the point—maybe he believes his scaled arm is strong enough—but the Vandawolf stops him. "I have good reasons for asking you to stay here, Thaden Kane. Tomorrow afternoon, I'm meeting with the council. I need time to convince them that you can be let out of this prison. Once I have their agreement, I will release you into the Blacksmith's care. In the meantime, as proof of your willingness to cooperate, I'm asking you to remain here without a fight."

Thaden's scowl indicates he isn't happy about it, but, with a heavy exhale, he finally gives a nod. "I will comply."

"Good," the Vandawolf says before he steps across to the nearest abandoned medallion.

The metal appears cold and should be safe to handle—at least for him. Never for a human. Still, I'm prepared for him to ask me to retrieve the bands, readying myself for the effort required to bend and pick them up.

Instead, he slips off his tunic, wraps the material around his hand, and scoops up the medallions one by one. Once he has all three of them, he quickly pulls the material off his hand, forming a pouch and tying a knot in the top of it before he approaches me.

He holds his free hand out to me as if to help me. "Asha."

I was stealing myself for the difficult walk back to my tower and I'm thrown by his gesture. More so because he's standing on my left and it's my left hand he seems to want to take. My *powered* hand.

I hesitate, but he doesn't back down.

The wolfish smile he gives me throws me completely.

What is he doing?

Watching him carefully, I slide my hand into his. Even without access to my power, energy tingles across my palm. A quiet warmth. Instinctively, I lean into him, accepting the way he takes my weight.

Within moments, we're stepping out of the cell. The Vandawolf keeps hold of my hand, continuing to support me while he pulls the door closed and locks it.

"The guards will return in a few moments," the Vandawolf says to Thaden. "They will keep their distance this time."

Thaden prowls back and forth inside the cage as he watches us go, his stare scalding across my back.

Then we're moving beyond the cells into the corridor and out of his sight.

I expect the Vandawolf to let me go now, assuming his show of support was somehow for Thaden's benefit, but he doesn't.

By the time we reach the hidden door and enter the dark stairwell, I'm leaning on him far more than I want to admit. I resolve to push ahead of him when we reach the base of the stairs so I can reassert the barriers between us.

"I can do this on my own," I say.

"You don't have to," he replies gruffly.

Despite my claim, I'm leaning too heavily against his side to pull myself upright with any kind of speed. My shoulder and arm are pressed against his bare chest, his big arm cradling me.

I tip my head back to see his face, all shadowed in the dark, especially now that I'm not glowing with power. I can't read his expression, can't find the answers I seek about his motivations.

He speaks, and the snarl returns to his voice, a snarl I'm used to. "I have no use for an injured Blacksmith," he says. "With every step you take, you're hurting yourself. Therefore, I will carry you back to your tower."

"Carry—?"

He scoops me up before I can blink, hoisting me off my feet and into his arms.

Damn, that feels better.

I tell myself that I'll accept his help, even though, in reality, I couldn't make it on my own right now. With every step he takes, I feel heavier in his arms, all of the tension leaving my body, my head sinking against his chest and my eyes slowly closing.

I try to remain aware of our progress up the hidden stairwell, through the small storeroom, and then back up the stairs within my tower.

I expect to find the corridor outside my room empty. At night, there are two guards and they rotate shifts, but on the nights when the Vandawolf dismisses my guards for his 'midnight visits,' they're ordered not to return until dawn's first rays.

It's still dark out there. Dawn is at least an hour away.

Yet Rachel waits at the door. And she's not alone.

"I returned as directed, lord," Rachel says, stepping aside to reveal my bleary-eyed sister.

Neither of them comments on the state of the Vandawolf's neck, although Rachel's focus narrows on it for a moment.

Tamra's eyes are only for me. She takes one look at me in the Vandawolf's arms and her forehead creases fiercely. "What have you done?" she snaps at the Vandawolf. "I told you not to move my sister and now her wound has clearly opened up again."

"You also told me Thaden gave you nothing," the Vandawolf replies, at which my sister stops in her tracks.

"Should I believe one claim as truth when the other was a lie?" the Vandawolf asks.

My sister's cheeks are suddenly pale, and her reaction concerns me. Indignation on her part would indicate that she didn't lie, but the way she worries at her lip tells me there's something she didn't tell the Vandawolf.

Keeping secrets from him can never end well.

She doesn't address his accusation, quickly deflecting by gesturing to the basket at her feet. "Rachel told me to bring my medicines." She tips her chin up, seeming to rally. "Did you summon me here to help Asha or not?"

The Vandawolf gives a grunt that seems to mean *yes*.

Rachel quickly opens the door for him, and he proceeds into the room with me.

Tamra hurries in after him while Rachel remains outside. Before Rachel pulls the door closed, the Vandawolf throws her a brief order. "You know what to do."

Rachel gives a nod.

He adds, "You must not be seen."

"I won't be." A moment later, Rachel closes the door and I catch her quiet footfalls disappearing down the corridor.

I'm too exhausted to wonder what they were talking about.

The Vandawolf places me carefully onto the bed. It's suddenly cold away from his chest, but he doesn't linger, prowling across the room toward the bathroom.

Tamra seems to take quick stock of the room, pulling the lone chair over to the side of the bed to arrange her tools on its seat. She casts dissatisfied glances around at the sparse furniture, the threadbare blanket I'm lying on, and the opening on the far side that leads to the balcony.

"It's freezing in here," she says, scowling at the Vandawolf when he reappears from the bathroom. "Can't you close off the balcony?"

He's retrieved a small cloth and is wiping his neck with it. His skin is remarkably smooth and unmarked where he wipes away the blood.

Without comment, he saunters past the bed, drops the towel onto the floor, and takes hold of the creaky partition that slides across the opening to the balcony. It doesn't close all the way and the wooden surround cracks when he tries to force it. Several shards of wood fall to the floor before the partition sticks completely.

He scowls back at me. "How long has this been broken?"

"A long time," I say on a sigh.

I guess he never had to pay attention to that door before. After all, it doesn't matter if it's open or closed. I can't fly, so it doesn't affect the security of my cage.

"I'll have it repaired," he says, his voice disgruntled.

Tamra responds before I can, her tongue sharply sweet. "Only if it's not too much trouble, lord. While you're at it, you might consider giving my sister some warm blankets. I know you don't care if she dies from the winter sickness, but I do."

"Asha never asked for blankets," he snaps.

Tamra widens her eyes at him. "Oh, so she has to ask for the basic necessities? I suppose she has to beg for her food too?"

"Of course not."

"Only blankets, then." Tamra turns back to me with a disgusted huff. "I'm glad we sorted that out."

Behind her, the Vandawolf shakes his head, grumbling, "I should have prepared myself for your sharp tongue, Tamra Silverspun."

"Yes, lord. You should have."

While she was snapping at him, Tamra retrieved her cutters from her basket and now she angles them toward the sash around my waist.

I stop her. "Don't cut this dress."

I groan with effort as I roll myself onto my left side. It's the position I'll need to be in anyway, but it means I'm now facing the Vandawolf and taking the brunt of his scowl.

Tamra quickly unties the sash, managing to slip it out from under me.

The folds of the dress fall to either side of me, although I catch the top of it before it exposes my breasts, pinning it in place by holding my upper arm across my chest.

Tamra quickly wraps the blanket around my legs and sets to work cutting off my bandages and reassessing my wounds. She's quiet as she works, finally reaching for her needle and thread again, along with the bottle of liquid that put me to sleep.

She freezes when the Vandawolf speaks.

"That thread doesn't grow in the Sunken Bog," he says. "There is no such plant."

Tamra has stiffened so suddenly that her hand clamps around my arm. When the Vandawolf first observed this thread, he said he'd seen nothing like it before. Tamra told him she found it in the Sunken Bog and that not everything out there was harmful.

But now, he seems to be challenging the truth of her claim, and I'm not sure why. I peer at him as he prowls forward, heading around the bed.

"As for the liquid you supposedly skimmed off the Toxic Thirst to help your sister sleep, if the fumes from that lake had that effect on people, we would find sleeping bodies at the lake's edge, not dead ones."

Tamra is as frozen as a rabbit that has just become aware of a predator.

"Damn," she whispers. "I was worried the story about the Toxic Thirst had flaws, but it was the best I could come up with."

"You were clever, I'll give you that," the Vandawolf replies, nodding his head as he finishes rounding the end of the bed. "You knew your heartbeat would betray you, so you told a story about going into the Sunken Bog. I'm sure you hoped I would attribute your guilty heart to your supposed admission about breaking my laws."

He stops mere paces from Tamra. Certainly close enough to strike if he chooses. "You hide behind that sharp tongue of yours, Tamra Silverspun."

My hand closes over my sister's arm while she remains frozen and suddenly very small beside me. "Tamra, what's going on?"

Her tanned cheeks are pale as she stares down at me with wide, green eyes, full of fear. "I... can't..."

"Your sister's power has returned," the Vandawolf says, a low growl. "And she's been using it."

CHAPTER 23

I can't breathe.

The Vandawolf only spared Tamra's life because she was powerless. If what he says is true, then she's in danger.

Real danger.

I struggle to rise upward, fighting the pain, especially now that my wounds are exposed. My arm shoots out like a shield in front of her, releasing my dress, but I can't care about that right now. "I won't let you harm her."

Tamra's cheeks are ashen, but she pushes me back to the bed, adjusting my dress to cover me. "No, Asha. You can't save me from this. I won't allow it."

She pulls away from me before I can grab her, whirling to the Vandawolf and stepping forward so she stands between him and me. A shield like I once was.

"What did you expect me to do?" she asks him. "The humans hate us. They came at us whenever they could. Unlike Asha, we didn't live in a tower where their blades couldn't reach us."

Her hands are visibly shaking and her voice is quavering,

fear rising off her body in palpable waves while the Vandawolf towers over her, silent and dark.

"Kedric and Maybelle were targeted too," she continues without taking a breath. "They were the only ones who treated us with kindness and, for their compassion, they were punished. One night, when I was thirteen, a group of thugs led by that bastard Braddock broke into our home. They stabbed Maybelle and she was..."

Tamra finally gasps a breath, words tumbling from her. "Maybelle was dying. I didn't know until that moment that my power was coming back, but that's when I felt it." She holds up her hands, curling her fingers into fists. "It was pushing at me, screaming to be released, and I couldn't ignore it. I wouldn't let Maybelle die. Not when I could save her."

She takes another breath and I hear how she's gritting her teeth now, her voice seething with anger. "I had no idea I could use my power to heal people, but I'd do it again in a heartbeat. Fuck your rules. Fuck the consequences."

I hover at the edge of the bed, blood slowly trickling down my stomach, preparing to fight for my sister if I need to—despite her wishes.

I quickly assess the location of my tools. The Vandawolf is holding my medallions in the makeshift pouch at his waist and my hammer is within the toolbox in my closet. I tell myself I'll be fast enough to get to them in time, even though I know he could break Tamra's neck before I've even taken a step.

He stares down at her, the hair falling across his human side for once, only his wolf's features visible and oh-so-completely savage.

He raises his voice, his focus shifting to the door behind Tamra. "Rachel?"

Her voice sounds from the other side of the door. "We're here, lord."

"Bring Kedric in," he says.

Tamra takes a step back, swinging to the door and then back to the Vandawolf, her eyes wide. "No, he isn't responsible—"

The door opens and Rachel steps in from the shadowy corridor with Kedric close behind her.

It's been a long time since I saw the older man up close. He's aged, and there are silver highlights in his brown hair and short beard, but he appears healthy and fit.

He's holding two wooden boxes, and I'm astonished to recognize them.

They each contain my parents' tools.

"Lord," Kedric says, bowing his head to the Vandawolf.

Rachel steps back as if she'll go back to guarding the room, but the Vandawolf halts her. "You can return home now, Rachel. Say nothing of what you've seen here tonight."

"I won't betray your trust," she says before she pulls the door closed.

The Vandawolf takes a deep breath, his features calming a little. "Explain to me what's in those boxes," he orders Kedric.

Tamra flies toward the Vandawolf. "No, it's not Kedric's fault—"

She meets the Vandawolf's hand, his arm slipping easily around her, deflecting her without any effort before he places her two steps away from himself. He gives her a firm order. "Stay there, Tamra Silverspun, and hold your tongue. Anything you say will only make things worse for Kedric."

He turns back to the older man, who holds up the wooden boxes on his upturned palms, one box on top of the other, like an offering.

"Lord Vandawolf," Kedric says quietly. "These boxes contain the Blacksmith tools of the late Ayla and Kalith Silverspun, Tamra and Gallium's parents."

"Tools that I ordered be destroyed," the Vandawolf says.

"Yes, lord."

"Yet you kept them."

"Yes, lord," Kedric replies.

The Vandawolf pauses, as if he's waiting for more. "Do you have any excuse?"

"Only that I thought my children would need them one day, lord."

"*Your* children, Kedric?" The Vandawolf's eyes narrow and his next words carry a sharp barb. "You have none."

A muscle in Kedric's jaw clenches and now his voice is harder. "Tamra and Gallium, lord, who became my children when you asked me to raise them." Kedric's gaze finally rises to the Vandawolf's. A look of steel.

"They are *my* children, lord, as surely as if Maybelle had given birth to them. And I will never abandon them. They deserve the chance to determine who they are. To understand their power and decide for themselves how they'll use it."

The steely look on Kedric's face softens when he looks at Tamra, who has tears in her eyes. "I will take whatever punishment you deem necessary lord, but I have no regrets about my choices."

My heart is heavy. Despite everything my brother and sister have faced, they have love in their lives. True loyalty and kinship.

The Vandawolf's expression is inscrutable as he folds his arms across his chest, his lips drawing back from his teeth. I brace for his wrath, preparing to throw myself between him and Kedric.

"That's why I chose you, Kedric." He inclines his head at Tamra. "Give Tamra her tools."

Kedric blinks at the Vandawolf, clearly as thrown as I am by the Vandawolf's response.

Opposite me, Tamra is also a picture of shock and confusion, her brow creasing as she stares at the Vandawolf.

"Lord?" Kedric asks, peering at the beast.

"Tamra needs her tools if she's going to heal Asha," the Vandawolf replies.

"Y-Yes, lord." Kedric passes one of the wooden boxes to Tamra—the one I recognize as containing my mother's tools. Each of their boxes was specially designed, not makeshift like the one that the Vandawolf uses to house Malak's tools. My parents' boxes have grooves carved into the top to hold the medallions steady while they're awakened. Inside, they're lined with velvet that cushions the medallions and the hammer.

Tamra takes the box, her lips still parted in surprise as she stares from Kedric to the Vandawolf.

The Vandawolf's expression hardens again, any softness fleeting. "I will make myself clear and you will both obey me: Once Asha is healed, both sets of tools will remain with me. Tamra will have access to them when I see fit, just as Asha does."

"Thank you, lord," Kedric says, handing the Vandawolf the second box.

Neither Kedric nor the Vandawolf has spoken of Gallium and I don't dare ask if my brother's powers have also returned. Out in the wasteland, Gallium fought with strength beyond a human's capability and I was fearful that remnants of his power remained, but that doesn't mean his power has returned in full force like Tamra's apparently has.

I vow to ask her if the chance presents itself.

"You may leave now, Kedric," the Vandawolf says, "but if you love your children as much as you claim, then you were never here." The Vandawolf taps the box. "And these tools don't exist."

"I know nothing of any tools," Kedric says, his expression carefully blank. He doesn't look at the boxes again, and it's as if they no longer exist in his eyes. "I slept soundly this night and never woke."

He pauses another beat and I assume he's waiting in case the Vandawolf has more to say.

When the beast remains silent, Kedric heads to the door and disappears through it into the corridor's gloom.

Tamra doesn't seem to want to take any risk that the Vanda-wolf will change his mind. She hurries to my side, sweeping her medical supplies off the chair and into her basket, which she places on the floor. Then she props herself on the edge of the bed beside me with her toolbox.

When she lifts the lid, I catch a glimpse of the purple velvet inside it and a flash of silver as she sweeps the hammer and medallions into her hand.

Our mother's tools are made from a silver alloy and they shine even when they're sleeping.

Tamra appears to have no reservations about holding our mother's hammer—unlike me when I'm required to pick up Malak's tools.

Closing the box with a snap, she positions each of the three bands in the grooves and strikes each one lightly.

They make melodic clangs, ringing out like pretty chiming bells. Light radiates from them, a sharp contrast with the gloom around us.

Tamra lifts each one and places them on her left bicep but keeps the final band in her right hand, pressing gently so that the ends curl around her palm and stay put.

The silver strands of her hair gleam brightly, shining right through the dye she uses to mask her true coloring. Her green eyes glow like emeralds and her skin becomes luminescent as she gives me a small smile.

She appears completely calm and at peace, none of the malice in her eyes that I'm sure dominates my expression when I awaken Malak's tools.

I wonder if there's any remnant hatred in my mother's medallions, but if there is, it doesn't show.

"I'll heal you now, Asha," she says. "Please relax and trust me."

CHAPTER 24

Tamra lowers her palm to my side and I'm not prepared for how calming her power is.

It flows through me like sunlight, warming me from the outside in, easing the tension in my mind and my heart.

I close my eyes and accept it.

I don't fight the tears that burn behind my eyes and I don't try to wipe them away when they fall.

"I would have healed you before now," Tamra murmurs, "if I thought I could do it without endangering us all."

I open my eyes as she continues to press her hand to my side, the concentration on her face intense.

"You did the right thing," I say.

She gives me a nod and after that, we're both quiet.

So is the Vandawolf. At some point, he retrieves the empty chair from near Tamra and carries it silently to the far side of the room near the drafty door.

I'm not sure why he would subject himself to the cold side of the room, although it does give him a full view of Tamra and me.

Tamra's healing power doesn't work instantly. She swaps the medallion she's using three times during the process and she doesn't lower her hands for half an hour. I'm not sure if it's because of the complexity of my wounds or because this is simply how her power works.

When she finally finishes, she slowly pries the third silver medallion from her palm and returns it to the box next to the hammer, where it becomes dull again.

Her shoulders hunch and she exhales slowly, rubbing her eyes for a moment before she sinks back to the bed. I'm still lying on my left side so she sits close to my back. Her hand closes around my shoulder in a gentle gesture. "You're healed now, Asha."

My pain is gone and my skin is smooth. I brush across the healed skin. I can't quite believe it, even though I'm seeing it. "Not even a scar."

She gives me an apologetic smile, some of her previous spark returning. "Sorry."

I catch her hand, conscious of the Vandawolf's presence but uncertain when I'll next have the chance to speak with her.

"How can your Blacksmith power do this?" I ask her. "I never heard of any Blacksmith healing others."

She grimaces. "Actually, I was hoping you might have answers for me."

I shake my head, but then my mother's long-ago scream returns to me in a flash. On the night our parents died, they tried to grab Tamra and Gallium and use them as living shields. At least, that was my assumption. But maybe they knew Tamra's power was unique. They must have known she could heal them if they were mortally wounded.

And maybe... Malak drained her power, not to make himself generally more powerful, but in a bid to make himself invincible.

I'll never know for sure, but I can tell my sister what I *do* know.

"Part of Malak's mission was to change the nature of life itself." I speak carefully, aware of the Vandawolf listening to everything I say. "He wanted to control more than metal. At its heart, I suppose that's what you're doing. You're transforming broken flesh into whole flesh."

She sighs. "Organic material is actually all I can transform," she says. "Plants, people's wounds. I suspect I could transform animals, but I would never try." Her focus flashes to the Vandawolf. "I'm not saying that because of present company. I don't use my power for the sake of it. I've only ever helped my family. And worked on plants so that I can treat my family using the usual healing techniques of stitching and medicine if I'm unable to access my tools."

I'm surprised, not by her determination to help her family, but by her statement that she can only use her power on organic, living things. "Are you saying you can't transform metal?"

She nods. "I've tried and failed. I can't create weapons like you can. I can't change a medallion's shape. I only use the medallions as a conduit between my power and the person I need to heal. Or the plant I want to change."

I'm dying to ask about Gallium, but Tamra has fallen silent, and I decide it's an unwise topic despite my intense curiosity.

"I wish I could transform broken minds and hearts as easily," Tamra says.

She leans over me, pulling the blanket over my chest. "You're healed, but I've used some of the energy within your cells to make that happen. You need to rest."

She lifts her gaze to glare at the Vandawolf. "I mean it, lord. Let Asha rest for at least three hours or she'll collapse."

He gives my sister a firm nod. "Understood."

With a soft exhale, Tamra drops a kiss to my forehead. "I'm

glad I could see you again. I'll let Gallium know that you're okay now."

She closes her toolbox and carries it to the Vandawolf. "As instructed."

He takes the box without fuss, resting it on his lap. "I've acted in good faith, Tamra Silverspun. I've allowed you to see your sister. Will you now be honest about what Thaden Kane said to you?"

She steps to the side, glancing back at me before she gives a resigned sigh. "He said he knows how to navigate the northern mountains, since he grew up in their shadow."

The Vandawolf's forehead creases. "Why would he think that was relevant to you?"

She's tense again, but she looks the Vandawolf in the eye. "Because he wants to get the hell out of here, and so do I."

If the Vandawolf is angry, he doesn't show it. "You dream of escape, Tamra Silverspun."

"Every damn day, lord."

The Vandawolf's lips press in a wry line. "Did Thaden also speak of his hate for your sister?"

Tamra's eyebrows rise. "N-No..." She falters. "But I didn't tell him that..."

"You didn't tell him that Asha is related to you," the Vandawolf finishes for her.

Slowly, he rises to his feet, gripping the toolbox in his left hand. "Our prisoner is dangerous, and he's hiding more than he's sharing. Your honesty is appreciated, Tamra, so I will repay it with a warning: Be wary of Thaden Kane."

Her surprise fades, a stubborn scowl marring her forehead. "Spoken by a ruler whose control could be threatened by a newcomer with strength that rivals his own."

The Vandawolf acknowledges her allegation with a nod but says, "Your time with your sister is at an end."

Tamra gives a visible shiver. She rubs her arms as she

crosses the room back to me. Then she hugs me one last time. I close my eyes and soak it up.

She scoops up her basket and within moments, she's gone again.

I tug the blanket up to my chin, needing to close my eyes. I tell myself that if the Vandawolf has a new order for me, I'll stay alert to it, but as long as he remains quiet, I'll rest.

"It's fucking freezing over here."

He sounds disgruntled.

I crack one eye open. He's remained where the drafty door won't close and I can feel the crisp, early-morning air wafting from that direction. What's more, he's shirtless. Having stood over there myself from time to time, I know that the breeze can feel like it's passing through my very bones.

His shoulders are hunched and the corners of his mouth are turned down. "Why didn't you ask for more blankets?"

I allow my eyes to drift closed again. "Was I allowed to?"

"Of course."

"Hmm." My disbelief must be evident because I'm aware of him approaching the bed now, probably to order me out of it for some reason. Maybe he'll tell me to get the blankets myself.

The bed dips, causing me to tip forward.

My eyes fly open to see the Vandawolf perched on the edge on the other side. There are twin thuds as he drops his boots to the floor before he settles onto that side of the bed, facing upward. The bed is wide enough that there's a foot of empty space between us. He folds his hands over his chest, closes his eyes, and becomes perfectly still.

"What are you doing?" I whisper.

He grumbles, "I'm resting my eyes."

My forehead creases. "Do you intend to sleep here?"

I'm not sure when he would have last slept and, if I look closely, I'm sure I can detect darkening circles under his eyes.

191

"Fuck, no," he says without opening his eyes. "This bed is too soft."

My eyebrows rise. "It's as hard as stone."

"If you say so."

I settle back onto the bed, but I don't take my eyes off him, even when he remains exactly where he is, his chest rising and falling evenly.

I'm starting to relax again, my own eyes drifting closed, when he takes a deep breath and speaks quietly. "I thought I could control Braddock by keeping him where I could see him."

Is he trying to apologize?

My sister said that a group of thugs led by Braddock had broken into their home and stabbed Maybelle. I can only imagine how hard Gallium, Tamra, and Kedric fought to make sure nobody else was hurt. Or maybe they were and Tamra didn't want to say so.

My own concerns right now are more about the present than the past. I need answers and since the Vandawolf seems open to conversation, I'm not going to let the opportunity pass. "When did you know my sister's power had returned?"

"For certain? Only today." He sighs. "But I suspected that your siblings' power would return as they grew older. Like a tree stump will sprout new leaves. You have to cut it out of the ground to end it." His forehead creases as he seems to rethink. "Even then, other creatures will use a hollow tree as a home to foster new life."

"Burrows," I whisper, suddenly thinking of his room. "If you knew their power would one day rejuvenate, why did you let my brother and sister live?"

He opens his eyes and turns to arrest my gaze. "I told you: Love is more powerful than fear and hate combined."

"What has that got to do with it...?"

"They love you as much as you love them," he replies, his tone full of steel.

Oh.

All these years, my brother and sister were the leverage the Vandawolf needed to keep me under control. But it only now occurs to me that *I* was the leverage keeping my brother and sister under control, too.

"I kept you in balance by keeping you apart," the Vandawolf says. "But I knew this day would come."

"When you have to end us," I say, a deep sense of dread filling me.

"No," he says. "The day you're stronger together."

CHAPTER 25

T he Vandawolf's response throws me like a whirlwind spinning inside my mind.

If my family is reunited, then we'll become a threat, and that can't be a welcome possibility to the Vandawolf.

Certainly not to the humans.

I prop myself up on my elbow, peering at him across the distance, desperately needing to know his thoughts. So desperate, I feel like I'm going to burst out of my own skin.

"What are you saying?" I ask, praying for clarity.

"I'm saying that it's time for you to work together."

My lips part in surprise. "Us? Gallium, Tamra, and me?"

He appears fully awake now, his eyes brighter, as if the two-second nap he took has replenished his energy. Maybe it has. For all I know, he doesn't need anywhere near as much sleep as I do.

"I've been training Gallium for the last four years," he says. "As soon as he came to me, trying to bargain for the chance to speak with you, I saw my chance. His power gives him strength that equals mine—although to his credit, he's hiding it. Obviously for fear of discovery and the repercussions that would follow. I wasn't aware of the details of your sister's power before today, but I already chose to turn a blind eye to the fact that Kedric kept your parents' tools."

"Wait... You knew about that before today?"

He arches his eyebrows as if he's surprised I'd doubt it, but there's a darkness in his expression when he says, "I killed every Blacksmith but you and your siblings. I counted every death, and I also counted every set of tools that was melted down. Even the spare sets."

"But what could you possibly gain from allowing us to combine forces?"

Now his expression shifts to the countenance I'm accustomed to. The angry wolf.

"There isn't a single human in this city strong enough to fight Milena or her army," he says.

My eyes widen. "You want us to fight her together." I'm already shaking my head. "Okay, I can see how that makes sense. We're disposable. It doesn't matter if we die in the fight, as long as we kill her too. But you only found out about Milena today. You couldn't have anticipated any of this four years ago—"

I gasp as he launches himself across the bed, his hands landing on my shoulders as he hovers over me.

"No more." He growls down at me. "No more!"

No more... *what?* My eyes are wide as I stare up at him, my lips pursed in shock.

"You will not speak of your death as if I don't care," he snarls, his tooth fully bared and his amber eye as fierce as a wild wolf's. "You're more to me than just a soldier, Asha."

My heart suddenly hurts and I don't know what to do with this feeling that threatens to burn through my chest. How can I believe him when everything he does dictates my very existence? When he sends me out to die over and over again?

I speak quietly as I quote him. "'Asha Silverspun is mine to kill when I choose.'" I don't release him from my gaze. "That's what you said."

"Yes," he snaps. "Because if I claim that right, then nobody else can. *That* is how I can protect you."

"But I believed you," I whisper, years of pain rising into my voice. "All this time, I've never doubted that you would one day end me. Either by your own hand or by sending me out to fight a monster."

His eyes become dull. "You are the obedient Blacksmith who lives at my whim. I am the ruthless wolf who would kill you without warning. Our survival depends on these lies. Lies that have become so ingrained, they may as well be truth."

He lets me go, returning to the other side of the bed, where he stares up at the ceiling once more.

My eyes are suddenly brimming with tears—hot, unbearable tears—and I find myself struggling to process the shift in my perception of him. Once again, I need to understand his mind, but maybe... the path to comprehending his thoughts needs to start small. And maybe... it starts with action instead of speech.

Very slowly and very hesitantly, I untangle myself from the blanket. I pull the threadbare material with me as I slide across the bed toward the Vandawolf. He eyes me warily and I watch him just as carefully, alert to any indication that he's going to react badly to my approach.

He lets me come.

Once at his side, I angle myself over him and cautiously lay myself down on his bare chest, my ear pressed to his thumping heart.

His arms remain at his sides, his body tense beneath mine. His voice is rough as he asks me the same slightly alarmed question that I asked him earlier. "What are you doing?"

"I'm listening to your heartbeat."

He relaxes a little and stays quiet for a long moment. "Are you surprised I have a heart?"

I give a small shake of my head, aware of my hair dragging across his chest with the movement. Even more aware of the goosebumps rising up across his skin. Without lifting my head, I tug the blanket over him so that it partially covers us both.

"I'm trying to determine if your heart belongs to you or to the wolf," I say.

A low rumble thrums through his chest, vibrating at my ear. "I *am* the wolf."

There's a truth in that simple statement that says so much.

He's a wolf with a wolf's instincts, nature, and needs.

There used to be many wolves in the forest that grew where the Sunken Bog now lies. Those wolves ran in packs. They exhibited loyalty and caring for each other while also reacting with ferocity and violence toward humans and Blacksmiths. They weren't built to be alone. And it was certainly not in their nature to live peacefully among humans.

I've witnessed the war inside of the Vandawolf when I put on my medallions. My power allows me to see the energy of the beast that he keeps constrained, but I've often viewed it as a separate part of him. Something that was imposed on his human self.

I realize now that I shouldn't have thought of it that way because the wolf *is* him.

Its needs are his needs.

His family is gone, but he chose all those years ago not to destroy mine. He kept Tamra and Gallium alive and now he's giving us the excuse to work together, and I wonder if there's a part of him that needs the same. To become *pack.*

I speak quietly and just as hesitantly as I approached him across the bed. "In the past ten years, I've never disobeyed you. Not even once. But yesterday, I allowed Thaden to live against your command. Then I tried to kill you—an even more grievous betrayal. Despite all that, you're offering to reunite me with my family. And I understand that the threat of another Blacksmith must be met with as much force as possible, but you could have resolved to keep us apart regardless."

"You would not have killed me," he says.

I don't dare lift my head to see his expression. "How can you be so certain?"

"For the same reason you didn't kill Thaden," he says.

My forehead creases. "But that was a betrayal on my part."

He makes a low humming sound that vibrates through his chest. "I thought so at first. I was certain that a monster was going to rise from that spot in the wasteland. When the lightning struck and you held back, I believed you'd disobeyed me. But you couldn't kill Thaden any more than you could kill me."

Now, I lift myself up, catching a glimpse of how peaceful he looks, only to watch a scowl swiftly descend over his features when I separate from him.

Again, I ask, "What makes you so sure?"

He speaks quietly but with a conviction I wasn't expecting. "Because when you look at me, you see a person, not a monster."

My eyes widen and my lips part softly. In my eyes, the Vandawolf has always been a beast, ferocious and unrelenting, but from the moment I saw him I never doubted that he had a heart and a soul.

I draw a ragged breath, trying to find my voice.

"You've offered to reunite me with my family and I'm grateful," I say, hoping he will hear my sincerity. "No matter what happens, I will value every moment I spend with them. I want you to know that I wish your family were still here, too. I'm sorry they were taken from you. You didn't deserve to be alone."

His scowl fades, his features smoothing out again.

He gives me a small, slow nod.

I draw back, wary that I've invaded his space enough for now and intending to move away, but his right arm slips around me. Not tightly. The lightest pressure.

"Stay." His lips part as he inhales a deep breath. "Please."

I don't push back. He and I have had enough conflict between us for the past ten years that I don't want any more. Not right in this moment. Not when he's started speaking openly to me for the first time.

Even if I were willing to bring about conflict, my heart won't let me. We were made into enemies. We didn't choose this.

It feels dangerous to wonder who we would be if we'd been born in a different time—a time of peace—but I allow the question to linger in my mind.

In another era, would I have allowed myself to believe that it feels right to fall asleep listening to his heartbeat? That there's a sense of belonging here?

Settling back down onto his chest, I shuffle myself into position so that I can comfortably curl across him with my head on his heart again. The blanket comes away in the process and the edges of the wrap dress pull apart a few inches, but there's enough material between us that we aren't skin on skin.

Well, not to any significant extent.

His heartbeat is lulling and I listen to it for long moments as my breathing deepens and so does his.

I'm sure he thinks I'm asleep when he speaks so quietly, it's barely louder than an exhale. "I'd give anything to have my family back. At least I can finally give you yours."

I don't reply. If he wanted my acknowledgement, I'm sure he wouldn't have waited until now to speak, but my heart feels lighter as sleep finally claims me.

CHAPTER 26

I'm not surprised to wake up alone.

I *am* surprised to find myself wrapped in a warm blanket. It's pulled all the way to my chin and tucked in on both sides of me.

The brightness of the sunlight streaming through the gap provided by the broken door tells me it's past midday. Somehow, I slept more soundly than ever before. Possibly because of the blanket.

By habit, I immediately check the color of the sky beyond my room, looking for telltale crimson hues. The sky is visible through the crack where the far door doesn't close properly and it's a calming blue with a few wisps of cloud.

A perfect winter's day.

The Vandawolf may already be in his meeting with the council, but I won't know the outcome unless he chooses to tell me about it. I've never attended the meetings with him since the council would view my presence as a threat.

Sliding to the edge of the bed, I pull the blanket with me because—*damn*—this material is too soft to let go of it just yet. I pause to assess my wounds, which is an easy task because the dress falls open beneath the blanket as soon as I stand up.

I take a moment to feel gratitude for Tamra's healing power.

My mind is clear and my body feels strong again.

Even so, my sense of peace doesn't last long.

I've barely emerged from the bathroom before a loud knock sounds at my door.

Without waiting for an answer, Braddock bursts into my room with a barked order. "Strip."

He stops and shoves a gauzy, white robe at me.

I consider the garment with surprise. I'm only required to wear these robes when the Vandawolf visits, but he should be meeting with the council now, not on his way here.

I hesitate a moment too long and Braddock steps into my personal space. His cheeks are flushed and his breath reeks of alcohol. "Fucking strip or I'll do it for you."

I will never allow this man's hands to touch my body. In all of the past ten years, I've avoided his every maneuver and I'm not about to fail now.

Snatching the garment from his hand, I veer toward the balcony, only for him to close his fist around the edge of the material so that I'm forced to halt, the robe stretched between us.

He gives me a vicious grin. "Somebody snitched," he says beneath his breath. "The Vandawolf's taking me off your personal guard and putting me on the wall instead. I've been fucking demoted."

"Snitched about what, Braddock? How much ale you drank last night?" I ask, remaining calm, although my thoughts fly to the story Tamra told about Braddock attacking her home.

He takes a step toward me, yanking on the dress—probably intending to upset my balance so I'll stumble toward him.

I simply let go of the material and his own momentum takes him backward.

He barely maintains his footing, bumping into the chair beside the bed as he spews hatred at me. "You and your fucking family will burn—"

Brisk footfalls sound in the corridor and Rachel appears in the open doorway. She narrows her eyes at Braddock but doesn't make any comment about his flustered appearance.

He promptly falls silent, still clutching the gown.

"Lady Asha," Rachel says, staring pointedly at the robe. "You must prepare for the Vandawolf."

I hold out my hand for the robe now dangling from Braddock's thick fingers.

He pushes it at me once again and this time, he lets me take it. He begins his usual check of my room—searching for anything metallic that I might have stashed here—although he's much rougher about it today. Biting my tongue and turning away from the mess he's creating, I head for the partition between my room and the balcony.

On the way, I slip off the black dress, allowing it to fall to the floor before I quickly pull on the robe.

Then I grab the edge of the partition, attempting to pull it open. Thanks to the Vandawolf's efforts to close it last night, the damn thing is well and truly stuck.

He normally only comes to me when there's a monster and I'm supposed to be standing on the balcony when he arrives—away from any possible weapon within the room—but I don't have a hope of opening this door.

After the events of the last two days, these extreme precautions—the transparent robe, upturning my room, and waiting on the balcony—seem completely irrelevant. But Braddock and Rachel don't know that. I have to be seen to comply with the usual requirements or questions will be asked.

As I grip the broken edge, desperately ignoring the splinters from the timber pricking my palms, I'm aware of Braddock's growing smirk behind me.

I'm also conscious that his focus has shifted to my waist, where my wounds have healed. I've never been badly injured, so for all he knows, I have accelerated healing—or the wound wasn't as bad as it first appeared. Even so, it would be dangerous for him to start asking questions.

Now that he's present and watching, Rachel is unlikely to help me. What's more, the heavy footfalls of my other two guards are rapidly approaching.

No, make that *three* sets of footfalls.

The heady presence of the wolf gives my heart an unexpected jolt and then my breathing calms.

I step aside as the Vandawolf looms behind me, reaching past me to take hold of the door. He's dressed in black pants and a dark, short-sleeved tunic. It looks like formal attire. Far more formal than his regular training clothes.

Without speaking to me, he gives the door a shove. "Rachel," he says, his muscles bunching as he speaks a command back into the room. "I want the carpenters to fix this as soon as possible."

"Yes, lord," she replies. And then, "Will I bring in Lady Asha's new armor now?"

"Yes. And count the buckles while you're at it. I don't have time to waste."

The door finally gives way with a tortured groan, nearly bumping off its tracks with the force of his push.

The moment the space opens up in front of me, I dart onto the balcony, taking up my usual position to the left of its center. Not too close to the railing. Not too close to my room.

The sun is warm and the breeze is light. Nothing like the chill that falls over this tower at night—which is probably why the Vandawolf never realized how cold it gets.

He steps up beside me, standing closer than normal. His

expression is inscrutable, but the tension rising off him is palpable.

Last night's events may as well have not happened.

We survive by these lies.

"You will come with me to the council meeting today," he says, a terse order. "You will not react to anything I say." He finally pins me with his wolf's gaze. "No matter how you feel about it."

I'm concerned that he's warning me not to react, since it indicates he's going to do or say something that could upset or inflame me.

Still, I give him a single nod. *I am the obedient Blacksmith.* "I will do as you say."

"Good." He turns away from me to ask Rachel, "Is the armor ready?"

"Yes, lord."

She's spread my new armor out across the bed and I take a swift look at it before the Vandawolf indicates I should put it on.

Braddock sidles up to him. "The room is clear, lord."

The Vandawolf inclines his head sharply at the door. "Join the others outside."

Braddock's smirk hasn't disappeared. He waits a moment too long, casting his eye over me. One last insulting look.

The Vandawolf steps between him and me, blocking Braddock from view.

"*Get the fuck out!*" the Vandawolf roars, making Braddock jump.

Sweat breaks out across the older man's now-pale brow as he hurries to obey.

"Be grateful you're still breathing," the Vandawolf throws after him before he turns to Rachel. He asks her, far more calmly, "Is the armor ready?"

She lifts the armored pieces with a nod.

It's rare for the Vandawolf to stay while I dress and, despite the fact that I'm already wearing next to nothing, I feel oddly self-conscious.

I relax a little when he leans up against the far wall and averts his gaze. He stares at the other wall on his right while he taps his fingers impatiently.

I don't delay. Within minutes, Rachel ties off the last buckle and I test out the movement of my new armor, finding it a little lighter than my old suit. A little easier to move in, too.

The Vandawolf must have been watching more than he let on, because the moment I allow a smile to cross my features, he says, "Let's go."

CHAPTER 27

I t's a short walk to the throne room, but it isn't a path I've taken for ten years. I haven't set foot in that room since the night my world changed.

As if timed to perfection, Gallium approaches us at the same moment that we cross the courtyard.

He's leading a group of Wasteland Warriors who are flanking Thaden Kane on all sides.

I catch the clanking of chains, although it appears that Thaden's wearing only shackles around his wrists and nothing around his ankles. It's a token restraint. He could break the shackles in seconds, but it seems he's continuing to comply with the Vandawolf's wishes.

The Vandawolf instructs Gallium to follow us, and I catch my brother's eye before I turn to walk ahead of him.

The worried crease in Gallium's brow eases after he takes stock of me. Tamra will have told him I was healed, but I guess he needed to see it for himself.

I hate that I can't speak with him. Can't even give him a smile before my back is turned and we approach the wide throne room doors.

A hum of sound indicates that the place is already full.

The council is made up of the heads of the various guilds: farmers, metalworkers, healers, weavers, carpenters, and merchants. The Vandawolf himself controls the military.

The doors are wide open and the black marble floor extends ahead of us. A large, rectangular table has been positioned in the center of the room, but the space is so large that the table looks small.

Every chair at the table is occupied, but there's space at the far end where I presume the Vandawolf will stand.

The Silver Throne has remained in the room, although it's covered in a black cloth that looks a little dusty. The throne clearly hasn't been sat in for a while. Maybe not since Malak last used it. Even this far away from it, I have to suppress the shudder that runs through me—not from the memory of hiding in its shadow, but from the cold malice I remember feeling within its metal.

It's a malice I embrace every time I pick up my tools.

The congregation hushes as soon as the Vandawolf appears, although my appearance a step behind him quickly causes a ripple of whispers among them.

Rachel and my other two personal guards peel off from beside me as we enter the room. They head to the left of the room, all three lining up along the wall.

Behind me, the Wasteland Warriors also separate, although half of them head to the left and the other half to the right. The last two Warriors pull the doors closed behind them and, within seconds, there is a firm military presence around all edges of the room.

Casting my gaze casually to the side while I continue to follow the Vandawolf to the head of the table, I ascertain that Gallium has remained with Thaden and they're proceeding with me.

Once we reach the table, I watch for the Vandawolf's silent

commands. When he inclines his head to his left, I head in that direction.

Gallium and Thaden stop on his right—also obeying a mere nod of his head.

I quickly assess the council members.

Petra's father, Nero, who is the leader of the metalworkers, sits to the Vandawolf's right. He's a heavily-built man with a shaved head. To the Vandawolf's left is the head of the healers' guild, a woman named Sybil who has a wide streak of bleached, white hair framing the right side of her face.

Farther back, I recognize the leader of the farmers. While the other trades seem to follow the humans' traditional expectations of the roles of women and men, the head of the farmers' guild is a woman.

Her name is Genova. Her light brown skin is weather-beaten, her frame is lean and muscular, and her eyes are bright with intelligence. She's known to be protective of her guild—and fiercely at odds with the metalworkers.

It's a rivalry that's been burning for the past ten years as both guilds have vied for greater power. Without the farmers and the farming land that takes up the vast south of the city, there would be no food. Without the metalworkers, there would be no weapons or tools. Somehow, the Vandawolf has managed to keep both guilds on his side.

Now, most of the council members can't seem to decide where to look: at me, at my brother, or at Thaden and his scaled arm.

Genova is the only one whose focus is firmly fixed on me.

The Vandawolf breaks the silence, addressing the council without ceremony. "You have questions. Ask them."

Nero immediately launches in. "Well, to begin with, you can explain why you've brought our enemies into this room."

"What enemies?" the Vandawolf asks, his expression completely deadpan.

Nero blusters. "The Blacksmith, her brother, and the..." He waves at Thaden but doesn't seem to know what to call him. "*Creature.*"

The Vandawolf appears to chew on his thoughts, a dark cloud descending over his features.

Thaden himself twitches, his brows drawing down. His treatment in the prison should have prepared him for the humans' animosity but I wonder if he thought their leaders would treat him differently.

"This *man's* name is Thaden Kane," the Vandawolf says, placing emphasis on the word 'man.' Turning briefly from the councilors, he gives Thaden a nod. "You can free yourself if you wish."

Thaden pulls his hands apart, snapping the metal shackles at their hinges.

There are gasps around the council table at the ease with which Thaden breaks the metal.

He catches the broken chains before they can fall to the floor. Approaching the table carefully, he places the shackles and chains on the surface in front of the Vandawolf before stepping back into position.

The Vandawolf gestures at Thaden's compliant stance. "As you can see, if Thaden were here to attack us, he would have done so already."

"Then what purpose does this man have here?" Genova asks, her voice far quieter, but just as commanding, as the other councilors'.

"Thaden brings a message." The Vandawolf plants his hands on the table beside the broken shackles, his wolf's features concealed. I can't see his right side from my vantage point, but I imagine his human countenance is as unyielding as stone.

"He's here to warn us," the Vandawolf says. "Death is coming."

209

The council is suddenly in an uproar and their questions come so thick and fast that the Vandawolf doesn't have the chance to answer.

"Death? In what form?" Sybil demands to know.

"Is it the monsters?" another councilor asks.

"What the fuck are you playing at?"

The last question is shouted by Nero. It's a far more aggressive response than is wise in the Vandawolf's presence, but before the Vandawolf can react, Genova speaks up again.

"It was already clear to me that we face a new threat!" she cries, loudly and clearly, causing the other councilors to turn to her in surprise. "All of the signs point to it."

"Signs? What signs?" Sybil splutters, the thick, white streak in her hair falling forward as if to mirror her indignation.

Genova is unflinching. "Few of you connect with the land like the farmers do," she replies. "In the last week, the animals have been unsettled to the point where we've nearly had stampedes. The edges of the crop fields are suddenly decaying, covered in slime. We've kept the Sunken Bog at bay for a decade, but our defenses won't last forever. The magic in the wasteland is growing stronger." She eyes me with sharp intelligence. "So, I would wager, is the strength of the monsters that rise within it."

I'm not sure if I'm allowed to speak, but the Vandawolf gives me a nod, his expression concealed from me beneath the strands of his hair.

"The monsters are stronger than they've ever been," I say.

The leader of the carpenters' guild—an older man named Vincent, who is known to have retained his position through guile, rather than through physical strength or skill—practically spits at me. "Your people continue to attack us from the grave."

I don't react. My own parents became afraid of the wasteland because of the built-up magic out there. Even now, their whispered conversations echo back at me about the danger in the north.

"What of *him*?" Nero asks, pointing a finger at Thaden. "What is he, if not one of those monsters?"

"I'm human," Thaden snaps without waiting for permission from the Vandawolf to speak. "Changed by a Blacksmith. I have even greater reason to hate them than you do."

Nero turns his glare on me, as if he thinks *I* was the Blacksmith responsible for Thaden's situation.

Not so for Genova, who wears a resigned expression, as if her worst fears have been confirmed. "Now we come to the heart of it," she says. "Another Blacksmith lives."

Her declaration is met with both shocked gasps and stares of disbelief.

"Impossible," Nero snaps.

The Vandawolf doesn't hold back, injecting himself into the conversation. "Malak's sister, Milena Ironmeld, is alive."

Nero jumps up so quickly that he sends his chair spinning. "Like hell she is. I watched that bitch die."

The other councilors are nodding.

"Nero witnessed her death," Sybil says. "Poison, wasn't it?"

"The only time we got close enough to kill one of them," Nero replies before he throws an acknowledging glance at the Vandawolf. "Before you, that is, lord."

The Vandawolf is calm in the face of the councilors' disbelief, but Thaden has stiffened, a dark glower descending over his features.

I suppose he's insulted that Nero thinks it's a lie.

"Milena is alive," Thaden says. "And she's more powerful than you can imagine."

Nero scoffs, but Thaden doesn't let up.

"This Blacksmith you think is dead," he says, "she made me into the beast I am now. She did it by capturing a dragon—a fucking *dragon*—and combining its soul with mine. A Blacksmith with that much power could burn this city to the ground on a mere whim. I don't know what you saw in the past, but clinging to the belief that Milena Ironmeld is dead will only get you and your loved ones killed."

Nero plants his hands on the table, but the glare he casts at Thaden isn't as dark as before. "Maybe the Blacksmith you met lied about her name," he suggests, and there's a hint of desperation in his voice now.

I recognize that his bluster and his anger is founded in fear. The Ironmeld family were the most powerful. The prospect that one of them survived must be chilling the humans to the bone.

Thaden gives a heavy exhale. "It's possible she lied for the purpose of creating fear, but answer me this: The black medallions that Asha Silverspun now wears belonged to Milena's brother, correct?"

Nero nods.

"I'm still learning about Blacksmiths," Thaden continues, "but I believe that the color of their medallions was often unique to their family. Is that also correct?"

Again, Nero nods.

"Well, the Blacksmith I encountered wore bands just like them," Thaden says. "Three of them on her right arm."

The blood drains from Nero's face. "Only the Ironmeld family carried black medallions."

"Then she wasn't lying about her identity," Thaden says.

The fight appears to be knocked out of Nero's body. He takes a deep breath before he retrieves his chair and sits down once more at the table. "We're doomed," he whispers into the silence.

Thaden turns to the Vandawolf, who remains unusually quiet.

A reluctant smile tugs at Thaden's lips and he shakes his head as he returns his attention to the councilors. "You aren't doomed, and I'll tell you why. Because in the short time that I've been here, I've witnessed the extent to which the Lord Vandawolf protects you. As much as I disliked my stay in his prison, he was right to put me in there until he could determine if I was a threat to you. Even on my walk to this room, I witnessed all the ways in which he protects this city—the guards, the wall..." Thaden's gaze flashes to me. "And the Blacksmith whose power he bends to his will."

"But what of you, Thaden Kane?" Genova asks. "Where do *you* stand in all this? It's clear you could have attacked us if you wished, but the fact that you haven't doesn't mean you're an ally, only that you've refrained from violence thus far."

"As I said, I'm human," Thaden replies. "I will fight to protect humanity against all Blacksmiths. I will stand beside the Vandawolf in this fight, and I believe you should, too. You should trust in whatever plan he has to fight Milena."

Thaden steps back and all eyes are now on the Vandawolf.

Despite the lingering fear on their faces, each of the councilors nods until the room is humming with quiet agreement.

"Well, then, lord," Nero says, his former bluster gone as he addresses the Vandawolf. "How do we repel this threat?"

"We don't," the Vandawolf announces, and even Thaden looks surprised.

The Vandawolf turns to consider me with a glint in his eyes as he continues, "Asha will."

Genova is the first to find her voice. "How?"

"I'm sending Asha north," the Vandawolf says. "To find Milena and kill her."

CHAPTER 28

I'm frozen beneath the Vandawolf's burning gaze, mentally screaming at myself not to react.

Be still.

Don't move.

He warned me that I might not like what I hear and he told me to remain calm, but he was right to be concerned about my reactions.

I'm not an assassin, and now he's sending me out as one. Sure, I've ended monsters, and even human lives, when the Vandawolf ordered me to, but I've never hunted another creature for the purpose of killing it. And I never killed one of my own people.

What's more, my absence from this city can only leave my family vulnerable. My presence may not have completely deterred human attackers in the past, but if I'm gone, the animosity my family faces can only get worse.

Around the table, the council is once again hurling questions at the Vandawolf thick and fast.

"Surely, you don't intend to set Asha free?" Sybil asks, sweeping her white hair back.

"No, Asha must return to the city once her task is complete," the Vandawolf replies.

Nero huffs. "Why would she do that when she could simply walk away?"

"Because her sister will remain here," the Vandawolf says. "If Asha wants to see her family again, then she will return to us."

"What if she joins forces with Milena against us? What then?" Vincent demands to know, his wrinkled brow fiercely furrowed.

The Vandawolf's response is cold. "Her sister will pay the price." His wolf's eye gleams at me through the strands of his hair. "To ensure the consequences of betrayal are clear, Tamra Silverspun will be relocated from the safer southern side of the city to the northernmost home. She will be guarded day and night until Asha returns."

I try not to flinch, keeping my expression blank. On the other side of the Vandawolf, my brother is also like stone.

Unfeeling.

It's as if we don't care.

Even if, every time the Vandawolf mentions my sister's life, my stomach turns.

I tell myself to hold on to the scream that's building within my throat. Hold on until I reach my tower and I can muffle it with my new blankets.

Around the table, the barrage of questions continues.

"What of Asha's brother?" Vincent asks, his faded eyes considering Gallium with a look of suspicion. "You speak of Asha's sister, but not of her brother."

"Gallium will go with Asha," the Vandawolf says.

I'm acutely aware that Gallium has remained impassive, although I catch the twitch of his fingers at his side. He asked to be sent out with me into the wasteland, but I'm sure this isn't what he had in mind.

The Vandawolf continues. "Having one of her powerless siblings at her side will motivate Asha to fight Milena with all her strength."

"And Thaden Kane?" Sybil asks.

"He will be their guide," the Vandawolf replies. "He alone can find Milena's stronghold. He has every reason to want her dead, so I don't doubt he will assist with this. However, he is free to make his own choices. He isn't our prisoner."

On the other side of the Vandawolf, Thaden appears surprised. "I'm free? But I thought—"

He thought I was going to guard him.

I also believed that was the Vandawolf's plan.

The Vandawolf answers Thaden without missing a beat. "You're free to move about the city, but for tonight, I ask that you bring yourself to the western tower. Many of my people will see you as a threat and I would warn you to conduct yourself carefully." The Vandawolf turns back to the councilors. "I'm counting on each of you, as leaders of your guilds, to spread the message that Thaden is our ally."

They murmur their agreement.

Thaden's surprise hasn't faded, but he responds to the Vandawolf's words with a nod. "Then you have my strength on your side, Lord Vandawolf. But once Milena is defeated, I will return to my home in the north."

"As you wish," the Vandawolf says.

The councilors continue to nod with what seems to be general agreement to the Vandawolf's plan.

Only Genova remains stiff in her seat, a deep furrow growing in her brow.

"Lord Vandawolf," she says. "This plan seems sound, but it ignores the more immediate threat. While Asha's gone, how can we keep the city safe?"

The Vandawolf doesn't appear perturbed by her question. "I've already ordered an increase in the number of guards along the wall. To do that, I've relocated some of our best warriors to new positions there. This includes each of Asha's personal guards except for Rachel, who will continue to guard Asha tonight."

"Huh." Nero arches his eyebrows. "So that's why you moved Braddock to the wall."

"It is." The Vandawolf's reply is firm, as if there couldn't be any other reason. "I also need volunteers from each of the guilds to boost numbers. The guard must be doubled around the clock."

"We will ask for volunteers," Sybil replies, and the others murmur their agreement.

They may wish for increased power, but they don't take the threat of the wasteland monsters lightly.

Genova, though, has remained stiff.

"I agree that the wall should be fortified," she says. "That is a good plan. But with respect, Lord Vandawolf, that wasn't my greatest concern. Who will fight the monsters in the wasteland while Asha's gone?"

"An excellent question," Sybil chimes in, leaning forward as if she were thinking the same thing. "It's not as if the monsters will stop rising from the cursed ground while she's gone."

The Vandawolf squares his shoulders as he considers each of the councilors in turn.

He responds with a determined growl. "I will fight them."

My heart plummets.

While the councilors respond with hushed whispers and furrowed brows, my anxiety triples.

Out in the wasteland, Gallium asked me why the Vanda-wolf doesn't fight the monsters himself and the reason for that hasn't changed. If the Vandawolf dies, the city will descend into chaos. Members of the rival guilds will fight for supremacy and innocent people will lose their lives.

My sister and her adoptive family will be the first to burn.

Even with Tamra's healing power, she can't save what's already dead. And with Gallium gone, she'll be more vulnerable than ever.

What's worse is if the Vandawolf dies without killing the monster, the monster will scale the wall and Tamra will be one of the first to perish. Even if she survives the first attack, there will be other monsters.

They won't stop rising.

Despite the fear building within me, I nearly stay silent.

I tell myself I'll find a way to protect my family.

But just as I resolve to obey the Vandawolf, to suppress my reaction, he leans a little toward me. I catch the flash of his amber eye, relive the scent of sweat and blood that coated him when we first met, feel again his hand around mine when he could have ended me but chose not to.

Suddenly, all I hear is his heartbeat. The heart of a man who became a wolf against his will.

Through the mire of shock about his plans for me, one thing is clear: The monsters will tear him apart. If I don't do something, he'll be killed.

I raise my voice. "No."

The Vandawolf stiffens before he turns to me.

His eyes are cold and his lips are pressed into an unyielding line. "No?"

I stand firm in the face of his anger, but my voice lowers. "You won't survive."

There's a flicker of surprise behind his eyes, quickly gone as he draws the hair back from his wolf's features, baring his sharp tooth and towering over me.

He speaks in a threatening growl. "You stay silent while I speak of sending you out to fight, yet you object to me protecting my people."

I refuse to back down. "If your plan means walking to your

death—*yes*, I object. What use will you be to your people if you become yet another corpse in the wasteland?"

He's a tower of quiet fury, his teeth gritted and his jaw tightening, but again, there's a flicker of uncertainty behind his eyes. The fact that he hasn't immediately retaliated—verbally or physically—tells me I have a chance to make him listen.

Probably a small chance, and it most likely won't end well for me, but I only have heartbeats to make myself heard.

I step into his space, my head tipped back to maintain eye contact. I'm aware of the shocked silence around me, the gaping mouths, even my brother's wide eyes and the way he's shaking his head as if he's warning me to stop.

But the moment I move into the Vandawolf's shadow, a calm descends over me. A strange sort of bubble forms around us, as if everyone else disappears and it's just him and me.

"The last monster I fought had the ability to heal itself," I say, speaking only to the Vandawolf. "I drove a spear through its brain and it revived within seconds. To kill it, I had to use my power in a way I'd never used it before, and even then, I was injured. If you doubt the truth of my words, ask my brother. He saw the monster regenerate. He saw what it was capable of."

The Vandawolf doesn't turn away from me. "I don't doubt the truth of what you're saying about the monster's strength," he says softly. "But I'm hearing a problem, not a solution."

He's right to be frustrated. While I'm gone, there's nobody stronger to fight the monsters than the Vandawolf himself. He's the only one with any chance of survival.

But even with all his strength and speed, he doesn't have the ability to turn a beast to ash. He wouldn't defeat another monster like the stag.

I resist the urge to reach for him and close the distance between us, keeping my arms firmly at my sides. Despite the whirlwind within my mind, the tangle of my thoughts is straightening and a path is becoming clear.

A dangerous path. For me.

"Let me be the solution," I say, holding my breath for a moment. "The reason you're sending me to kill Milena is the same reason you should let me help you protect the city."

His brow furrows. "You can't be in two places at once."

"No, but I can give you the weapons you need."

He tips his head. "I'm listening."

"Let me use my power like my ancestors did." I speak carefully, my tension increasing since my suggestion is unlikely to be welcomed. "Give me three days with my tools. Let me be what I was born to be. I will create weapons for you to take down any monster that might rise against you. Weapons that will give you a chance of survival."

I sense him withdrawing from me, his expression becoming closed, even though he asks, "What weapons?"

I force myself to breathe through my anxiety, allowing my deeper instincts to rise in a way that I usually only permit when I'm out in the wasteland. They're the same instincts that tell me what kind of weapon I need to fight a particular monster. The same instincts that whisper to me to mold other beings into the shape I want them to be.

"A harpoon," I say. "One that can anchor a monster to the spot so it can't get close to the city. And a crossbow—a large one that can be fired from the wall, without anyone needing to get close to the danger." I rush on as images of weaponry flood my mind. "A net with which to tie the creature down once it's trapped. Chains with weights on each end to hobble its legs or arms or whatever limbs it has—"

"All in three days?" he asks, interrupting me.

I clench my jaw with determination. "As many as I can make. I'll work hard—"

I want to say more, but he steps back abruptly and that's

when I'm aware again of the people around us and the sheer uproar that I've triggered.

It billows around me, an unpleasant storm of sound.

"You can't allow her to use her power within the city," Nero shouts.

"It's too dangerous," Sybil cries.

Vincent is nodding furiously, and so are the other councilors.

Once again, Genova is the odd one out, sitting quietly in the back, although she's peering closely at the Vandawolf and me.

The Vandawolf turns to face the councilors and I anticipate the way he'll silence them, remembering the force with which he once bellowed at his people.

His chest fills with air, but before he can let loose his roar, Genova lifts her voice.

"We should consider it," she says.

The other councilors spin in their chairs, their disbelief evident in their raised eyebrows and wide eyes.

"No, we should not," Nero snaps, rubbing his brow with fingers smudged with coal dust.

Genova pins him with a sudden glare. "Why not, Nero? Is it because you're worried about what this might mean for your guild? Heaven forbid, Asha creates weapons in three days that your people have been struggling to forge for a decade."

Nero blusters. "Well, I..."

Genova gives a heavy sigh. "It's reasonable that we're struggling to support the use of Blacksmith power within our city. The darkness of that power led to atrocities and trauma that we will never forget. I feel this in my very bones."

At her words, every councilor becomes quiet, the shadows of the past seeming to descend on the room.

"But we face a new threat," she continues. "One which must be fought with every means at our disposal." Exhaling deeply, she returns her attention to the Vandawolf. "Lord, I trust you to make the right decision. What is your judgment in this matter?"

The Vandawolf considers the council for a moment before he speaks, far more quietly than I imagine he would have if Genova hadn't calmed the mob for him.

"Ten years ago, I fought to free each and every one of you," he says. "Since then, there have been times when I've made decisions you haven't agreed with. I understand there are competing needs and priorities within this city. But I have never once endangered you."

Sybil slips her white hair behind her ear as she leans back in her chair. "This is true," she says, and several of the other councilors nod.

The Vandawolf raises himself up to his full height. "What I'm about to say is also truth, although you may be reluctant to hear it."

He studies each of them before he continues. "Over the last ten years, Asha Silverspun has left the city walls time and time again to fight monsters for us. Yes, they are her peoples' legacy, but she was not the one responsible for creating them. For ten years, she has obeyed my laws and followed my every command. She has never harmed a single one of you. Not before her people perished. Not after. She has never retaliated or sought revenge. Even when given her tools before she leaves the city walls, she has never used them against us."

My heart is hurting at the way the Vandawolf is speaking about me. I feel my brother's eyes on me, and Thaden's. In addition, the burn of the councilors' scrutiny is a weight that pushes down on me.

"There are still some among us who remember when Blacksmiths were our allies," the Vandawolf says.

"A golden era that no longer exists," Vincent grumbles, but the force of his anger has faded.

"Nevertheless, Asha is not our enemy," the Vandawolf declares. "It is my judgment that she will be allowed to use her tools, but only under my strict supervision."

His lips pull back from his sharp tooth as he speaks to me. "You have three days."

Without waiting for me to reply, he turns back to Nero. "You will ready a forge closest to the northern gate for Asha to use."

Nero's lips immediately pinch. "If you wish, lord, but I believe there's a problem you're not considering. Our human forges are useless to Asha Silverspun without crimson coal, and we all know it's gone."

The Vandawolf's eyes suddenly gleam. "Is it?"

"Of course it is." Nero fidgets a little. "You decreed that it should all be destroyed."

The Vandawolf continues to stare at him. "I did."

Nero begins to squirm. "Lord?"

The Vandawolf plants his hands on the table and leans toward the older man. He speaks low and soft, but the threat in his tone makes me shiver. "You will bring every lump of crimson coal that you hoarded in contravention of my laws to the forge for Asha to use. If you 'misplace' even a single piece, I will deal out the punishment you have avoided all these years."

The blood drains from Nero's face. "I... You... How did you...?"

The Vandawolf raises his hand. "Make sure the forge is ready by first light."

Nero remains tense. "Yes, lord."

The Vandawolf steps back from the table, as if he considers the conversation to be over, but Genova raises her hand. "Lord, if I may ask one last question?"

The Vandawolf pauses before giving her a curt nod. "Yes, Genova?"

She speaks carefully, her bright eyes on me. "If Milena is so powerful, how can Asha beat her?"

A smile grows around the Vandawolf's mouth, but it makes me shiver with dread. "Asha's own people underestimated her. Milena Ironmeld will underestimate her. But I never will."

At that, he gives the councilors a final nod. "We're done here."

They all stand, but he doesn't wait for their salutations before he turns to Gallium. "Show Thaden where to find his rooms in the western tower." Then to me: "Asha, you will come with me."

On the other side of the Vandawolf, my brother is already stepping away from the table. I try to catch his eye—and I sense him hesitating a moment as if he's also trying to make eye contact—but the Vandawolf steps between us.

The force of the Vandawolf's glare pins me to the spot.

Enough rules have been broken. I can't be seen to be colluding with my brother.

As I turn in the direction the Vandawolf is directing me— around the side of the table opposite to the one my brother is walking—my mind is spinning with everything I now face.

Three days of working with my tools in the hope of creating weapons that could save the Vandawolf's life, and by extension, my sister's life. Then a journey north into the wilderness with Gallium and Thaden to find a Blacksmith I believed had died years ago.

I can only hope that the Vandawolf will give Gallium access to his tools on our journey so that he can fight at my side, despite the statement the Vandawolf presented to the councilors about my brother being powerless.

I'm aware of Thaden proceeding toward the door on the other side of the table and I feel the weight of Thaden's stare until Rachel hurries forward and takes up position once again at my back.

I can only guess what Thaden's thinking. How he feels about accompanying Gallium and me into the wilderness.

I have no doubt he wants Milena dead. He's made no secret of his hate for all Blacksmiths.

But that includes me and my brother.

If we survive the fight with Milena, we'll have to watch our backs.

CHAPTER 29

I t's darker outside the throne room than I was expecting, the sun already descending toward the horizon. My stomach growls with hunger since it's been a long time since I've eaten. I try to ignore it as I quicken my pace and hurry to keep up with the Vandawolf.

He's making a straight line for my tower.

Rachel stays close behind me, but it's not her footsteps that suddenly crunch on the courtyard pebbles.

I'm unsettled when Thaden appears beside me, hurrying to overtake me and reach the Vandawolf.

"Lord Vandawolf, I can help Asha."

The Vandawolf doesn't slow down. "I know you can. You can lead her through the mountains. That's why I've asked you to go with her."

"No, I mean with the weapons."

The Vandawolf stops so suddenly that Thaden nearly overshoots.

"Speak quickly," the Vandawolf orders him. "As much as I respect your freedom, I'm out of patience right now."

Thaden seems to take the Vandawolf's warning seriously.

"My father was a farmer, but we didn't have access to a metal-worker, so by necessity, we had to work iron ourselves to make farming tools. I have some basic skills. I can work the forge with Asha."

The Vandawolf's scowl darkens. It's a look that would make most humans scurry away, but Thaden doesn't back down.

"You've given Asha three days, but even a delay that short could backfire if Milena makes a move sooner," Thaden says. "With my help, Asha can work faster."

The Vandawolf's jaw tightens, but again, Thaden persists.

"I'm the only one who can help." He raises his right hand as if to emphasize his point. His scales gleam in the early evening starlight. "I can handle a Blacksmith's tools safely."

"Fine," the Vandawolf snarls. "Be at the forge at first light. Gallium will give you directions."

Thaden smiles, his bronze eyes clashing with mine as he steps back. "Asha." He gives me a polite nod and I'm unsettled by how pleased he looks.

I don't have time to wonder why.

The Vandawolf is already plowing forward, and I hurry to follow.

When we reach the stairs at the bottom of my tower, the Vandawolf barks an order at Rachel. "Fetch Asha a meal. Her growling stomach is blaring in my ears. Leave it at her door and then guard these stairs from here. Nobody but me is to come up these stairs tonight."

"Understood." She's wide-eyed as she watches us go.

I turn the corner at the first landing and then she's out of sight.

The Vandawolf's speed only increases until we reach my room and he shuts the door behind me.

I'm suddenly confronted with the full force of his feelings.

"Defying me in front of the council was reckless!" he snaps at me, his fury beating at me like a furnace.

It's true. What I did was dangerous. Speaking up was a risky move, let alone asking for access to my tools.

Even so, the chains that bound me in the past are breaking. The rules that kept me silent are disintegrating.

I'm not sure exactly when it started. Maybe it was seeing my siblings again, knowing how strong they've grown and hearing about their determination to escape this life. Maybe it was my near death.

Or maybe it was lying on the Vandawolf's chest and listening to his heartbeat thump calmly at my ear. And recognizing that he's as alone as I am.

"I'm not the one who's being reckless." My chest hurts as I speak, an inexplicable feeling. "I understand the need to send me out before Milena arrives at the city walls. It's a tactical choice and a sound one, but if you balance the risks, is it really better than keeping me here where I can protect you?"

He abruptly stops pacing. "Protect me?"

"Yes. You." My response is certain. I feel it in my heart, but suddenly, I falter. "I mean, my family. And Kedric and Maybelle. And Rachel..."

The Vandawolf's lips rise into a smile that sends a shiver down my spine. He advances on me, step by predatory step. "No, you were talking about me."

I stop myself before I retreat. I don't have anywhere to go anyway. The door is at my back, but it's not as though the stairs will give me freedom.

I have to face this beast in all his complexity.

I speak quietly. "You send me out to atone for my peoples' crimes, and I go willingly. But not because of shame or regret. I go because it's how I can protect the people I care about, and whether you like it or not, that includes—"

His growl is short and sharp. "Stop speaking."

Only days ago, I would have obeyed.

"No," I whisper, even though my throat is dry. "I won't stop." I swallow hard and hurry on even as the storm grows darker on his face. "I go out there to protect you, too."

"Why?" he asks, his voice harsh and raw.

"Because we're more alike than I thought possible."

The furrow in his brow only deepens, but a small spark of curiosity flares behind his eyes despite his denial. "We are not alike."

I arch my eyebrows at him. "You rule this city for your people. To do that, you balance their needs against your own. You wield me as a weapon when you need to. I also act for my people—my family. I consider their survival with every choice I make. I obey any rules and fight any fight to protect them. You and I are the same because we're both surviving within the boundaries of the hand we were dealt."

As I speak, and he listens, the hardness in his expression fades. The crease in his forehead eases out. The tension around his lips disappears.

He's quiet. Remarkably so.

I swallow again and continue, even though I'm stepping onto even thornier ground. "That's why, even though we were born into a time when we were destined to be enemies, I don't want you to die a senseless death. I don't want you to lose your life to a monster in a field of bloodied ash. Not when I can do something to prevent it."

His chest rises and falls deeply before he takes a step toward me.

He lifts his right hand toward my shoulder, and asks, "May I?"

I'm not exactly sure what he's asking permission for, but I take a chance and nod.

Carefully and slowly, he presses his palm to my chest above

my heart. His head tilts, his gaze becoming far away, as if he's listening to something I can't hear.

"Your heart is pounding in my hearing," he says. "Yet it feels steady beneath my palm." He pauses. "I don't know how both can be true at once, but they are."

His gaze lifts to mine. "This is the way I see you. As two opposing natures constantly in conflict with each other. Fragile but strong. Fearful yet unafraid. Compliant but deeply defiant. There is only one respect in which you are constant."

I wait for him to tell me what it is and when it seems he might not, my lips part to ask.

He smiles, a brief flicker of rare appreciation, as if he'd been waiting for me to give in to my curiosity. "You're limitless."

My forehead creases as I wonder at this assessment of me.

I'm not sure what aspect of me could possibly defy limitation, not when so much of my life is confined to these walls.

"When I first came upon you in that throne room, I sensed fear but not hatred," he says, seeming a little less confident now. "Why have you never hated me?"

I give it thought. "You had every reason to want justice, but you didn't hurt me."

"But I could have," he says with conviction. "And then I did." He gestures with his free hand at the room around me. "I took you from your family and put you in a cage in the sky."

I remember the bargain I tried to make with him. I'd asked for death and he refused. "You kept me alive when I thought my only option was death."

He scoffs. "I put you in a drafty tower to freeze at night. I ordered you to slay monsters at the risk of your own life. I made you wear clothing that left you effectively naked and demeaned you in front of my people. I took away your power and then forced you to use it at times that suited me, despite the malice that lives within your tools and the effect it has on you. And even after all that..."

He shakes his head as his palm presses gently against my heart. "There *must* be hatred in you. How do you hide it from me?

"I can't hide what I don't feel." I dare to place my smaller hand over his.

He immediately turns his hand, lifting it off my chest and lacing his fingers with mine. His touch is warm, comforting, but the brush of his thumb across my wrist is tantalizing in a way I don't have a name for.

I catch my breath. "Tomorrow, I'll create weapons that you can choose to use. Or not. It's up to you." I meet his eyes, my voice husky as he continues to stroke my wrist. "What's important to me is that I've given you the choice."

"Then I accept," he says.

He steps back from me, lowering our joined hands and slipping away from me.

I want to ask him to stay, but I'm not sure how to voice the request.

How can I tell him that I crave the warmth of his body? That I slept better last night than I ever have before?

"Wait," I say.

He pauses at the door, half-turned, a hulking figure.

I start to speak, but suddenly, deep within me, a spark of fear bursts into life. I've convinced him to let me use my tools to create weapons, something he never would have agreed to before, and a sliver of doubt has unfurled within me.

Are my intentions as pure as I believe them to be?

What if the Vandawolf was wrong, and my violence toward him when we were in the prison with Thaden wasn't because of my injury?

I have to consider the awful possibility that when I used the medallion out in the wasteland to turn the stag to ash—an act of transformation that Malak would have smiled upon—a touch of his darkness may have taken root within me.

231

That darkness could be quietly manipulating my thoughts and behaviors now, and leading me into using his hammer. I've never had extended contact with it. Never had to defy its malice for more than a few moments.

What if I'm not strong enough to resist it?

As the Vandawolf waits for me to speak, I trip over my speech. "I... uh..."

I squeeze my eyes shut for a moment and, rather than asking him to stay, I stumble onto another question instead. "Why are you allowing Thaden to walk free?"

The Vandawolf smiles. Not a happy smile. But a quietly pleased one. "I'm not."

"But I'm not guarding him."

The Vandawolf nods. "As I promised Thaden, a Blacksmith will guard him. That Blacksmith is not you."

My lips part with surprise. He can only be referring to my siblings. "Tamra or Gallium? Or both?"

His smile broadens. "Your sister seemed the best choice. That's why I sent her to the prison to tend to his wounds. She'll watch him without appearing to watch him."

I blink at the Vandawolf, a little in awe of the way he maneuvered the pieces into place. Sending Tamra to the prison where she would befriend Thaden. Publicly putting Gallium in charge of showing Thaden around. By doing so, he nudged them into each other's lives before announcing that Thaden would lead us through the wilderness.

But by doing so, he's put my family in a dangerous position, given Thaden's feelings about Blacksmiths.

I narrow my eyes at the Vandawolf. "Does she *know* she's watching him? Or will you spring questions on her at a time of your choosing?"

He shrugs, a non-committal response, and I suspect it's the latter.

Despite his apparent nonchalance, worries continue to

flood me. "What if he senses her power?" My voice rises, my fear in full swing. "What if he hurts her?"

"I recognize your concern," the Vandawolf replies, his smile vanishing and his hand lifting in a reassuring gesture. He crosses the distance between us, quickly returning to me. "You don't need to be worried. Thaden is already aware that Tamra and Gallium are your siblings. I told him before the meeting today. As it turned out, that information wasn't new to him. Gallium had already said something. I'm not sure how that conversation transpired, but there's no enmity between them. In fact, I believe Tamra is the reason Thaden offered to help build the weapons."

I'm even more alarmed. "How so?"

"He wants to keep her alive as much as you do."

I'm stunned by the Vandawolf's assertion, my lips pursed in a questioning "*Why?*"

The Vandawolf's lips set into a wry line. "Your sister has a way of opening eyes and changing minds," he says. Then adds, "When she wants to."

My concerns are not completely dispelled, but they aren't rampaging wildly around my mind anymore.

He seems to sense it and turns back to the door, blithely throwing back, "Thaden's having a meal with your family tonight."

My eyes widen again, but the Vandawolf continues.

"You have no reason to be alarmed. I'll be watching from a distance. That's where I'm going now. If there's trouble, I'll step in. Not that your brother should need any help."

With that, the Vandawolf closes the door behind him.

I'm left staring at the wooden surface.

My protective instincts remain in full swing. I should be with my family. I don't want this danger for them, not in addition to the threats they already face on a daily basis.

Unless the Vandawolf's right.

233

If Thaden will listen to my sister, if he could possibly be open to believing that not all Blacksmiths crave blood and power, then he could become an ally and not an enemy.

It's a horrible risk.

But it comes with a huge benefit if it means we can trust Thaden to take us safely through the mountains.

I try to breathe through my tension and my sense of powerlessness.

Anything that happens tonight is completely out of my hands. I can't influence any of it.

I remind myself that, even though Thaden is strong and fast, so is the Vandawolf. So is my brother. Tamra may not have their physical strength, but she's smart and perceptive.

I tell myself they'll be okay. I have to believe it or I'll lose my mind to fear.

Fear for my family, but also fear of what I'm about to do.

When I pick up Malak's hammer tomorrow, I vow that his darkness will not take hold of me.

I will not succumb to his cruelty.

CHAPTER 30

Dawn breaks across the horizon as I follow Rachel down to the courtyard, where the Vandawolf waits. He stands in the shadow at the side of the portcullis. His dark-gray hair is messy, the wolfishly textured strands falling across his features. The visible parts of his jaw are shadowed with growth, making him appear even wilder.

He's holding my toolbox, clasped tightly in one big hand.

With the lid closed, the energy radiating from the tools isn't as strong. Even so, my body tingles as the magic, amplified by the Vandawolf's nearness, seeps out through the joins in the toolbox and reaches across the distance to curl around my chest.

It pulls me forward, but I force myself to move slowly, steeling myself for the enormity of the task ahead of me.

It would help if I were better rested. I tossed and turned all night, and I struggled to eat the breakfast Rachel brought me this morning.

She draws me forward now, as bleary-eyed as I am since she was required to guard me all night after being awake all day yesterday.

As soon as we reach the Vandawolf, I ask, "My family?"

A little of the sternness in his expression fades. "They're fine. No troubles there."

I'm relieved about my family, but the way he speaks, it sounds like there may have been trouble elsewhere. The dark rings under his eyes certainly indicate that, like Rachel and me, he didn't sleep much.

The softening of his features doesn't last long and I remind myself that our interactions aren't private. We're visible to everyone around us. The chains that once bound me may have broken, but I have to proceed carefully.

To Rachel, the Vandawolf says, "Go home. Get some sleep. I'll summon you if you're needed."

Rachel rubs her eyes and barely stifles her yawn. "Thank you, lord, but if it pleases you, my grandmother's home is along the northern walkway. I'd like to walk with you as far as that."

"If you wish," the Vandawolf says before he sharply inclines his head in that direction. "This way."

I inhale the crisp, morning air, attempting to clear my head. At the same time, by habit, I check the sky for discoloration and rain clouds.

It's another perfect day, but that doesn't mean it will stay that way.

I'm not prepared for the hustle and bustle of the city, which hits me as soon as I step through the portcullis. Even at this early time of morning, the walkway is busy with humans already going about their day. Chattering voices float from open windows in nearby buildings and the scent of freshly baked bread fills the air, along with the soft clank of coins.

Whenever I've left the castle over the last ten years, the city has been deathly quiet.

Hushed beneath the threat of a crimson sky.

Now, it's filled with life and for the first time, I have the chance to appreciate this metropolis as the peaceful and prosperous place that the Vandawolf has enabled it to be.

As we proceed along the street, the humans greet him with solemn reverence, each one murmuring, "Good morning, Lord Vandawolf."

Their expressions quickly harden when they see me. Some take glances at me before they hurry away. Others usher their children indoors. Still more stare coldly at me, their hatred evident in the twists of their lips and the narrowing of their eyes.

I'll take their glares over stones thrown at me like that first night when the Vandawolf had brought me out of the throne room into the crowded courtyard.

Despite the passage of time, I understand the extent of the pain that lies at the foundation of their feelings. They still wear the physical scars my people inflicted. I'm sure they'll never forget what was done to them or the fact that I'm capable of hurting them just as badly as my predecessors did.

I keep my focus firmly fixed on the Vandawolf's back, forcing myself to ignore the toolbox he grips so tightly and ensuring I don't make any sudden moves or gestures that might cause a riot. It helps that Rachel stays close behind me.

Halfway along the main northern walkway, we approach a portion of the city that contains a larger number of homes. An elderly woman waits in front of a thatched cottage with patches of herbs growing beneath the front windows—thyme and rosemary, judging by the scents that waft toward me.

Rachel leaves her position at my back and surges up to my side, a soft smile growing on her face, which is answered by the older woman ahead of us.

The woman's hair is silvery gray and her eyes are faded brown, but her cheeks are rosy and there are smile lines around her mouth and eyes. Her face wears the marks of happiness as well as hardship.

The Vandawolf slows his pace and greets her with nearly as much reverence as the townspeople greeted him.

"Mother Solas."

My forehead creases because I recognize her surname, but I'm not sure where I've heard it.

"Nanna," Rachel says, embracing the older woman. "May I introduce Asha Silverspun?"

Rachel's grandmother gives me a gentle nod. "Well met, Lady Asha."

I'm worried that she has greeted me too politely when there are passersby within earshot and other humans clearly watching us from partially shuttered windows.

Mother Solas immediately leans in. "Don't mind them. It's fear that drives them, not hatred."

"I understand, but my worry is for you, not me," I say.

She gives a little shake of her head and her lips form a mysterious smile. "Oh, they won't bother me, don't worry about that." She quickly changes the subject. "I'm told you intend to forge weapons today. I want to give you something for the task."

She reaches for my hand and presses a small, metal object into it.

I gasp when it touches my palm, an instantly warm feeling racing through my arm and into my chest.

Mother Solas's hand is wrapped around mine and I can't yet see what she's given me, but I know, in my heart, that whatever it is, it carries peace and hope with as much strength as Malak's hammer carries cruelty.

"Your grandmother gave this to me for safekeeping," Mother Solas says. "It was the last object she forged and I watched her pour all of her goodness and heart into it. She prayed that the next generation of Blacksmiths might rise up against Malak and that *this* would help them." Mother Solas's voice becomes grave. "But Malak was shrewd. He killed every Blacksmith who opposed him, including her."

I'm saddened by this news, but not entirely surprised since my parents refused to speak of their own parents, so I assumed there'd been some kind of rift between them.

Mother Solas slips her hand away from mine and I can finally see what she's given me. It's a pin the size of my thumb that appears to be made from silver and forms the shape of a crescent moon. It's the emblem that was once associated with my family. The Silverspun crest.

Mother Solas's faded, brown eyes become shadowed, as if remembered horrors are rising within her mind. "It was a terrible day. A light went out of this world when your grandmother died. Made worse when your mother stepped over her body and pledged allegiance to Malak."

Mother Solas squeezes her eyes shut for a moment. She exhales, as if expelling the bad memories, and when she opens her eyes, her smile has returned. "I see your grandmother in you, Lady Asha, so I know there's hope for you."

Hope.

It's as dangerous as love.

CHAPTER 31

I close my hand around the pin, looking to the Vandawolf for permission to keep it.

Only to gasp at the sudden brightness around his form. It catches the silver highlights in his hair and lifts the darkness from his eyes. For a second—a heartbreaking second—I'm able to picture him in his purely human form. The man he was. Simply fighting to protect his family.

It takes me longer than it should to realize that the brightness around us is caused by the magic within the pin. I'm reminded again that Blacksmith's magic is drawn to itself and now the light in the pin is radiating around us both.

Just as Malak's darkness rises to curl around the Vandawolf's chest when he stands near my tools, so too does the peaceful light of my grandmother's pin.

I don't think the humans can see it.

Even the Vandawolf tilts his head to the side, a curious crease appearing in his forehead. "Asha?"

I bite my lip, unable to explain the peaceful light to him in this moment. Instead, I say, "I don't know my grandmother's name."

"Her name was Accalia," Mother Solas says.

The Vandawolf still wears a puzzled expression, but he inclines his head onward. "We need to go."

I quickly attach the pin to my tunic, right above my heart, taking comfort from the peace that lives within the metal, hopeful that it will shield me against the cold malice in my tools.

Then I bow my head to Mother Solas. "Thank you, Mother Solas. Your gift means so much to me."

I want to stay longer, but the Vandawolf is already stepping away, so, with reluctance, I walk on, leaving Rachel and Mother Solas behind.

It takes us another ten minutes to reach the vicinity of the forge, which is located at the edge of the buildings in the north. I want to ask the Vandawolf for more information about Mother Solas, but there are still too many people around.

Soon, we approach the forge, which is located so close to the gate that the wall looms in the distance. It would be worrisome to the humans to live this close to the wasteland, so most of the buildings now surrounding us are industrial. It makes sense that the forge, where the guards can replenish their weapon supply, would be near the gate.

Here, the street is deserted and the windows of the surrounding buildings are closed and barred.

"This part of the city has been vacated on my order," the Vandawolf explains. "I spent much of the night dealing with belligerent workers."

That would explain why he has such dark rings under his eyes.

"The metalworkers can't be happy," I say.

"Neither were the carpenters," the Vandawolf says, pointing to a closed-up building I identify as a carpentry workshop and then to the warehouse beside it. "Or the weavers."

Now that there are no longer any passersby around us, I

dare to admit, "Mother Solas's name is familiar to me, but I'm not sure why."

The Vandawolf casts me a sharp glance. "She was the cousin of the last human king."

My eyes widen. "She was human royalty?"

The Vandawolf nods. "Left alive as a reminder of the royal family's death. Her son was later killed, but Rachel survived. Neither Mother Solas, nor Rachel, has a strong claim to the throne, since they aren't direct descendants of the old king, and the guild leaders won't support a new monarchy."

I remember Rachel asserting to me that she is nobody—an important claim given that some humans might feel threatened by her existence.

"The guild leaders must dislike the possibility," I say, thinking it through. "By placing Rachel on my personal guard, it keeps her close to you, where it's safe. You're protecting her, aren't you?"

The Vandawolf's sharp tooth appears. "In the only way I can."

I exhale quietly. It's taken me far too long to realize that nothing the Vandawolf does is without purpose and reason. Even when I can't anticipate his intentions or don't yet understand his motivations, he follows a carefully considered path. Even if it winds and twists in a way that makes his purposes a mystery to me.

In light of that, it stuns me even more that he's letting me forge weapons today, since I sprung the idea on him.

Now, the forge is only fifty paces away. It's a large, stone building with a wide window at the front. The only open window in the vicinity.

I'm surprised to see crimson smoke already wafting from the chimney on the roof, but not surprised that Thaden Kane waits out front.

He appears far more relaxed than he did yesterday. His

bronzed hair is slicked back and his broad shoulders carry none of the tension of our previous encounters. His sleeves are already rolled up and his forearms are dusted in soot that sparkles across the scales on his right arm. It's crimson soot.

"Lord Vandawolf. Asha." Thaden greets us as he closes the distance between us. "I've taken the liberty of lighting the coal."

I narrow my eyes at him. It's not a simple task to light crimson coal. Once lit, the coal will continue to burn for days, since fire already lives inside each piece and it needs only to be brought to life. Which also makes it incredibly hot and dangerous in unskilled hands.

I give him a quick visual check, particularly his hands and arms, looking for burn marks.

The corners of his mouth twitch upward. "If you're worried, don't be. Gallium and Tamra warned me about the coal and told me how to light it safely." He lifts up his arms. "See? No burns."

"Good." My response is clipped since I'm still wary of him. Now that I'm standing closer to him, the magic in the pin radiates outward, drawing out the copper in his hair and eyes, but, oddly, not as brightly as the Vandawolf.

His focus drops to the pin for a moment, a crease appearing in his forehead, but I'm already moving past him.

The color of the smoke draws me toward the forge door, the warm scent of the coal filling my mind with echoes of my past.

The moment I step through the door, everything else disappears around me. Even Thaden and the Vandawolf.

Oh, that scent.

I inhale deeply and close my eyes, my thoughts consumed by the sweet honey of the crimson smoke and the metallic tang in the air.

It calms me like the pin did. Calms my heart until I'm floating in memories of my parents lighting their coal, of watching the blood-red sparks fly across the air like little stars, hearing the sharp clang of hammers on metal. A pounding sound that mimics a heartbeat, a rhythm I could get lost in.

They're selective memories.

They don't have any hint of the bloodshed that was happening around my parents.

The happiness within the memories is an illusion, and my recognition of that fact brings me abruptly back to myself.

At that same moment, the Vandawolf steps up behind me, and his strong presence dispels the past. Especially because the toolbox he's carrying now radiates with power, as if it's reacting to our environment, the energy within it tingling sharply across my back.

The darkness contained within the toolbox clashes with the peace in the pin I'm wearing.

The dark and the light are colliding within me.

I take a deep breath to center myself before I quickly consider the forge's interior. On the far side is a waist-height fireplace that has bellows at the side to feed air across the coals. An open hessian bag brimming with crimson coal—so much of it, I'm not sure how Nero ever thought he could get away with hoarding it—rests beside the furnace. A large anvil is positioned toward the center of the room but near to the furnace. Large tongs sit on top of the anvil.

The wall behind the anvil is filled with other tools that hang on nails in the wall, including multiple tool belts. Lastly, there's a bench sporting a large pot of water that the metalworkers must use to cool whatever implement they've created.

I won't need the water. I only need the fire, the anvil, and my tools. And, of course, chunks of metal to mold.

Stepping up to the anvil, I run my hand over its smooth surface, which reflects the glow from the crimson coal.

A basket of random-shaped metal chunks sits beside it. They appear to be a motley mix of offcuts and discarded pieces, no doubt the metalworker's most unwanted and unworkable metal.

They would never leave me their finest iron.

It doesn't bother me. My parents could turn the ugliest, most impure metal deposits into beautiful implements. What's more, they could make a small amount of metal go a very long way. I once watched them fashion five swords from a lump of steel no bigger than my father's hand.

I tell myself I can do the same with these discarded pieces.

Acting quickly, I choose a tool belt from the wall and tie it around my waist, preparing for when I need to holster my hammer while working with both hands.

By the time I return to the anvil, Thaden has slipped into the forge behind me, heading to my left and keeping to the space near the window.

The Vandawolf prowls toward me, his silhouette backlit in the red glow from the fire. He sets my toolbox onto the iron surface without taking his eyes off me.

I brace myself, my left hand pressing to the pin.

When the Vandawolf opens the box, the hammer and medallions gleam as if they're alive, and the magic within them reaches out toward me, plucking at my soul.

The pull is terrifyingly strong, amplified by the scent of the burning coal, the warmth of the room, and the magic that lives within both the Vandawolf and Thaden.

My mind spins with the heady rush of it.

Already, I'm overwhelmed by Malak's impulses, which stab across my thoughts in sharp bursts.

Take control.

Shape the living.

Fight the old.

Find the new—

The Vandawolf's voice cuts through the storm. "No matter

how afraid you are, you have the strength to fight the cruelty in this hammer."

I open my eyes, unsure of when I closed them, only certain that they're watering with pain.

His voice is filled with conviction. "You *can* fight Malak's anger and find your peace."

I focus on the Vandawolf, and only him. The way the glow from the fire plays across his face and chest, seeming to dance across his broad shoulders and messy hair. The shadows in his eyes, but at the same time, the way the light from the pin eases his sternness, revealing the little lines around his mouth and eyes where he might once have smiled or laughed. Or loved.

My fear fades and Malak's cruel impulses are pushed to the side like shadows disappearing in sunlight. They will return, of that I have no doubt, but for now, they've lost their strength.

I'm calm again.

The Vandawolf seems to sense it.

With a brief nod, he takes a step back. "Now, claim your tools, Asha Silverspun."

CHAPTER 32

I don't hesitate.

My left hand closes around the hammer, and the instrument's icy power flows through me in a rush that defies the warmth in the room.

I inhale a deep breath, controlling the power that fills my body and mind, balancing the dark with the light.

I'm even more acutely aware of the two men whose bodies thrum with the same energy I now control, the strength that flows through them, and the animals they both constrain.

A wolf and a dragon. The way their energy sparks tells me that neither one was ever tame. Both were wild and free and now they're somehow so *present* that they amplify the power surging through me.

It doesn't scare me. Every ounce of energy that surrounds me can only help me finish this task.

I turn to the basket of discarded metal pieces, intending to choose my first piece, only to find Thaden already whisking the tongs up off the anvil.

He quickly chooses a chunk of iron. Not a bad chunk—in

fact, it's the one I would have picked. Thrusting the iron into the fire, he submerges it beneath the burning coals.

"How long?" he asks me, his face alight in the wash of brightness from the fire, his bronze eyes gleaming.

Now that the hammer is in my hand, I can sense every piece of metal in this room.

The softening iron he's holding beneath the coals calls to me the loudest.

"Count the heartbeats," I say. "One... Two... Three..." And *there*. I sense the metal's readiness as the energy within the crimson coals prepares it for the hammer. "Bring it to me."

He quickly withdraws the tongs from the fire and places the chunk of iron in front of me. It glows a perfect amber color.

A moment of uncertainty passes through me.

I've never done this before. Never imbued metal with enough magic that I can mold it to my will, but not so much magic that it takes on the life of a medallion and will be dangerous for humans to touch.

I was never given the chance to practice my skills, only to watch my parents, and even then, they didn't greatly care if the metal they forged was harmful to humans.

I can only hope that my instincts will prevail, the same way I taught myself to transform medallions out in the wasteland.

Allowing myself to move without doubt, I tap the softened iron with the hammer, a light touch to begin with.

It's a greeting of sorts. And a request. I'm asking the iron to come on this journey with me. To accept my will because I won't betray its natural form. I will only ask it to be what it's capable of being.

At the hammer's strike, a perfect *clang* rings out through the forge.

The sound is as pure as a chime, rising up within the building and floating beyond it.

Oh, how I missed the melody within that sound.

The sense of release within me is immense. It's like letting go of all past pain and embracing what could be.

Any remaining uncertainty melts away and a soft sigh leaves my lips.

Finally. The cage within which I've kept my magic is open.

The cold malice within the hammer is subdued, the strength of hope in the pin prevails, and my own magic, my power governs them both.

The lump of iron has no motivations, no greed, no anger, nothing to taint its form. My power can flow in its natural rhythm, not for the purpose of harm, but in the quest for creation.

My next hit is harder, light sparking between the two colliding surfaces.

I sense the iron responding with willingness to accept my magic, and then the rhythm takes over. My muscles flex as I continue to beat it, gently but firmly, flattening it down into a near-perfect circle.

When it's smooth, I use the tongs to fold the metal in half. Beat it again. Fold it again. Over and over until it's growing cold.

Without me asking, Thaden whisks the metal disc back into the fire, and I watch him whisper through the heartbeats, counting to three before he passes the disc back to me again.

I beat and fold, beat and fold, until sweat drips down my forehead. Even as my muscles work mercilessly and my palms start to bleed, my mind is crystal clear.

There is no right or wrong here. No fear or hatred. Only me and the metal and the impulses in the hammer.

Take control of the light and the dark.

The impulse within my mind doesn't carry the cruelty it once did. Everything has light and dark and both must be in balance.

With every beat of the hammer, the iron becomes darker,

slowly but surely taking on the properties of the hammer until the iron is as black as a raven's wing.

That's when I know it's done.

To beat it any longer would create a medallion, and I don't want that.

Slipping my hammer into the belt at my waist, I place my left hand over the disc I've created.

It's silken against my skin.

Closing my eyes, I sense the extent to which I can stretch this single small chunk to create multiple pieces.

The harpoon must come first. I'll need to fashion the spear part of it, as well as the mechanism to release the spear, and a stand that can be anchored to the wall to hold the weight of the large weapon while also being capable of swiveling to follow the movements of a creature. The purpose is not so much to kill the monster—although that would be welcome—but to tether it so it can't get close to the city.

The crossbow will need to be similarly designed with multiple bolts and another stand, also capable of taking the weight of the weapon while swiveling from side to side, up and down.

The energy within the metal tells me I will only be able to fashion the harpoon's spear and parts of the swiveling mechanism from this single piece. If it could be a smaller spear, I could make more of the mechanism, but I need this weapon to be large enough to take down a creature the size of the stag or even bigger.

The metal won't stretch as far as I hoped, but I resolve to get on with it.

"Stand back," I say to Thaden, who has remained close by.

He doesn't immediately obey me. "I can do more."

My eyebrows rise. "You can't use my hammer."

"No, but I can use a human one," he replies, looking to the

Vandawolf, who has remained on the other side of the forge. "With a hammer, I could—"

"You can't use my magic," I say firmly to Thaden. "You can't help with this."

"Are you sure?" he asks, taking a step closer to me, lifting his right hand. "I know you felt it when I took the medallions from your arm."

His gaze burns into me, and I'm not sure what he wants me to say. Yes, I sensed the sharp energy that stung the air between us, but I'm not sure what that has to do with him helping me now.

"There was a spark," he continues. "A *transference*. If I can wrap a medallion around my right hand and use a human hammer, maybe I can transfer some of the magic from the medallion into the metal. I could beat it like you do. At least to get it started. You can then finish the piece and ensure it works the way you need it to."

My eyes have widened at his suggestions. "What you're proposing is incredibly dangerous. To you, to the Vandawolf, and even to me."

His jaw clenches. "I know you don't trust me."

"Because you want me dead."

"Is that what you think?" he counters.

"Of course that's what I think. You declared it."

He gives a heavy exhale as he rubs his forehead. "I *did* want you dead. I wanted all Blacksmiths dead because of what was done to me." He grimaces. "But you could have killed me and you didn't. First out in the wasteland. Then in the prison. And now, for the last three hours, you've had countless chances to simply turn around and end me. But you haven't."

It isn't the conviction in his voice that shakes me so much as his mention of the time.

"Three hours?" I cast around, seeking the light shining at the window, praying he isn't correct.

The intensity of the sunlight tells me it's at least mid-morning, which means it really has taken me three hours of hammering to imbue my magic into a single piece of metal.

Three hours and I haven't even fashioned the spear yet.

"Damn." My lips press together before I turn to the Vandawolf. He hasn't interjected like I thought he might. "It's not my decision to make."

The Vandawolf surprises me when he replies without hesitation. "If Thaden accepts the risks, then you should try it."

"I accept the risks," Thaden says.

I'm incredibly unsettled by how quickly they reached agreement.

"No." I nearly grab Thaden's arm before I stop myself, recognizing the danger of accidentally transferring the energy of the hammer into him. "Why?"

"Why what?" he asks.

"Why do you want to help?" I search his eyes. "You're offering to risk your life, which is foolhardy if you're supposed to lead us to Milena. Maybe you want to protect the humans in this city, but this risk is far too great."

His jaw clenches and his expression hardens. "You won't like my reason."

"I'd rather be told a truth I don't like than be fed a lie."

He nods. "Okay, then. It's a risk I'm willing to take because when we reach Milena, I'm not going to wait around to be killed. If she overpowers you, I want to know that I can take your medallions and use them in your stead."

"You don't believe I'll end her," I whisper.

Thaden glances at the Vandawolf. "The Vandawolf believes you will, but I've seen Milena in action."

I take a shaky breath, my hand instinctively slipping from the iron disc on the anvil to my hammer. I tell myself to shake off the doubt and the fear. I force myself to focus on the more immediate danger.

"If you prove to yourself that you can safely handle a medallion and, what's more, transfer its magic into a piece of metal, then how can I trust you won't use my medallions against *me*?"

"You can't," Thaden replies. "But I think that's a risk your leader is willing to live with."

I'm surprised by the Vandawolf's continued silence, and even more disconcerted by his increasingly relaxed demeanor as he watches my exchange with Thaden.

I remind myself that how he presents in public has a purpose and isn't necessarily indicative of his true thoughts or feelings. Right now, I imagine it's more important for the Vandawolf to keep Thaden on his side.

"I don't have to *live with it* because it isn't a risk," the Vandawolf says. "Thaden won't kill you, Asha."

A curious expression descends over Thaden's face, as if he's intrigued by the Vandawolf's certainty. "I won't?"

The Vandawolf shrugs, but his voice is a low growl. "A shrewd warrior would never melt down the perfect sword. You would pick it up and wield it. Asha is one such powerful weapon. To destroy her would be a foolish thing to do. I don't take you for a fool, Thaden Kane."

A smile flickers around the corners of Thaden's mouth. "I would certainly like to believe I'm not." He considers me from the corner of his eye before he turns to face me fully. He rubs his forehead again, then he gives a heavy exhale. "Your sister's voice is inside my head."

My eyebrows rise. "What did she say to you?"

"That her hope lies with you."

My chest hurts. My lips part, but I'm not sure what to say. My siblings want our freedom and for a short time, Gallium and I will be able to leave this place. This journey will, at the very least, show us a safe way through the mountains, a path that Tamra may now see as our only hope for escape in the

---

future.

Thaden adds, with a shrug of his shoulders, "And that I'd better not betray you."

I smother my smile since that certainly sounds like something Tamra would say. In the last few days, she's demonstrated that she has no hesitation speaking her mind.

Thaden shakes his head. "I can't place the crimes of another Blacksmith on your shoulders, Asha Silverspun. I'm prepared to trust you. In return, I ask that you give me a little of *your* trust."

I slowly exhale. It's true that I'm more of an immediate threat to him than he is to me. Here I stand with my hammer, and the medallions within my reach, and not once have I thought to use them against him.

It also now occurs to me that Thaden won't be able to wake up the medallions on his own. They require the hammer, and it can only be wielded by a Blacksmith. So the danger to me only arises if Thaden takes the medallions after they're already awake.

At least it will stop him from using them to kill me in my sleep.

"I'm willing to try," I say.

His eyes crinkle with humor. "Willing to try *trusting* me or willing to let me try using a medallion?"

I clear my throat. "Both."

Turning to the wall of tools, I choose a sturdy-looking hammer that's made entirely of steel so it will have a good chance of conducting magic. Then, using my right hand to minimize the impact of the magic on me, I take a single medallion from within the toolbox.

Placing the medallion onto the anvil, I tap it lightly to wake it. It feels natural now that I've spent the last three hours using the hammer, and the sound it makes is like a softer echo of the beating of the hammer against iron.

254

I step back from the anvil, making room for Thaden before I gesture to the medallion. "The risk is yours."

CHAPTER 33

Thaden's right hand hovers over the medallion and the increasing tension around his eyes tells me he's not so indifferent to the risk as he made out.

His broad chest rises and falls with a deeply indrawn breath before he lowers his bronze hand to the medallion.

The moment he makes contact, light bursts around his palm.

His jaw clenches and his nostrils flare with a sudden, sharp breath. "Fuck."

He recoils, immediately lifting his palm.

His face is pale and the corners of his mouth turn down as he glares at the metal band. "I felt its anger in the prison, but I thought it was *your* feelings flowing through the metal."

I give him a small smile. "Cold, isn't it?"

"Fucking cold," he whispers, sucking in air as if he's still trying to catch his breath. "It wants death and dominion."

I speak quietly. "Malak poured all of his cruelty into these medallions. I have to resist their nature every time I put them on. There's no shame in giving up."

"No," Thaden says, a dark cloud descending over his features. "I need to do this."

He nods with determination, as if he's trying to bolster his resolve. "Like I told you, Milena has bands like these. You have to fight like with like. Cruelty with cruelty. I need to know that I can pick these up and use them if needed."

This time, he plants his hand firmly on the medallion, his eyes squeezing shut. A pained groan leaves his lips and his human fist thumps the top of the anvil. Sweat breaks out across his forehead and a visible shudder runs through him.

Across the way, the Vandawolf has risen from his lean against the wall, a suddenly sharp expression on his face. He throws a warning glance at me.

We need Thaden alive.

"It's fighting you," I say, reaching for Thaden's hand, preparing to wrench the medallion away from him if I need to. "You should stop—"

A second later, the ends of the band curl up on either side of Thaden's palm.

The moment the metal accepts him, his shoulders relax.

The fist he thumped against the anvil uncurls and he releases a soft breath.

Then he opens his eyes. Bright bronze like they're made of metal. "I'm fine."

He considers me calmly, no hint of the pain he was experiencing only moments ago, before he reaches for the human hammer. He tests its weight in his hand, turning it over a few times before he says, "I think this will work."

I watch carefully, prepared for the situation to change, as he takes the tongs and chooses a new piece of metal from the basket. It's a particularly twisted chunk that appears to be made up of both iron and copper.

He pushes it into the fire and counts softly before he pulls out the glowing piece and positions it on the other end of the anvil.

There's enough space for both of us to work.

"The moment of truth," Thaden says as he lifts the hammer.

The black band in his palm glistens, throwing light across his hand and accentuating each perfect dragon scale.

The metal clangs and the hum it leaves in the air is pure and clear.

I sense the flow of magic down his arm and through his scales—the magic that was imbued into him to make him into the dragon. It intensifies at the point of his palm and then flows onward throughout the hammer and into the metal.

"Don't force it," I warn as he strikes the twisted chunk harder than I would have.

He gives me a grin. "I won't."

I watch him for another moment, processing the fact that it's working. He can actually help me.

Finally, I relax, exhaling my tension.

Across the way, the Vandawolf resumes his lean against the wall.

Then I turn my attention back to the silken, black disc and the weapon I want to create.

By the end of the day, the pieces of both the harpoon and the crossbow are ready to be assembled, right down to the last hinge and bolt. The space inside the forge isn't large enough for us to carry out the assembly, but there's a back room where I can store the weapons' components, ready for tomorrow.

We work without stopping, taking sips of water every now and then until moonlight streams through the forge window.

It's only when I place the hammer back into the toolbox, forcing myself to let go of the power it gives me, that I become fully aware of the burning ache in every muscle in my body.

My back thrums with pain, the muscles in my arms are seizing up, and my legs are unsteady when I try to take a step.

With a groan, I lean forward, gripping the edge of the anvil with both hands, arching my back in an attempt to stretch it out.

Beside me, Thaden is rubbing his neck, wincing as he stretches it from side to side. His back audibly cracks when he twists.

"You both need food and rest," the Vandawolf says.

My attempt at agreement comes out as a vague hum.

Thaden gives a grunt, then another groan as he rolls his shoulders.

The Vandawolf continues. "Thaden, you're free to go. Be back here at first light if you still want to help."

A hard edge appears on Thaden's face, as if he's insulted the Vandawolf thinks he might give up. "I'll be here. Don't doubt it."

He steps up to me and I startle when he scoops up my hand. He clasps it only for a short moment, and I'm ready to pull back, but his touch is light and the way he positions my hand, on top of his scaled palm, gives me enough freedom that I don't feel trapped.

"Thank you for trusting me today," he says, his bronze eyes dull with fatigue but his voice strong.

He lets go of me, and my palm is left tingling with the remnant energy that must have stayed in his scales even after he put down the medallion.

Moments later, he's gone, and the Vandawolf closes the toolbox and tucks it under his arm.

The calming power of my grandmother's pin is enough to

give me strength to walk, but speech defies me as we make our way out into the cold night.

Silently, I follow the Vandawolf back through the city streets toward the castle that looms at its center.

Rachel waits at the base of my tower and once again, the Vandawolf asks her to bring food.

She pauses only to ask, "Will I guard Asha tonight, lord?"

He shakes his head. "I will stay with her."

I'm too exhausted to wonder at his motivations or reasons, other than to rationalize that he wants Rachel to be well-rested for some other task tomorrow. Though I'm not sure when he himself intends to sleep.

A moment later, I register Rachel's retreating footfalls and then my own heavy tread fills my ears, every step feeling like I'm climbing a mountain.

When I turn the corner at the second landing, I find the Vandawolf waiting for me.

"Will you be insulted if I carry you the rest of the way?" he asks.

He's helped me up stairs before, but that was when I was deathly injured.

"I'm insulted that you offered." I tip my head to the side and follow with a bold smile. "Of course, you could give me my hammer and then I'm sure I'd skip the rest of the way like a sprightly deer."

"Wolves hunt deer," he replies, his lips pulling back to expose his sharp wolf's tooth.

He scoops me up and, even though the toolbox presses into my back, I can't help my sigh of relief.

It isn't only the weight that lifts off my legs but the nearness of his body to mine. The magic within him glows softly and up close, I not only sense the human he used to be, but the wolf he has become. A creature capable of caring for a pack.

His people are his pack.

I stifle my yawn and mumble against his chest. "If you plan to guard me all night, when do you intend to sleep?"

"It's my intention to sleep all night," he rumbles.

My forehead creases. "How will that work?"

"Well, first I'll close my eyes and then I'll sleep."

I try to see his face, but mostly, I get a view of his shadowed jaw. "Are you making fun of me?"

"Making fun, yes," he says. "But not of you."

I'm quiet for a moment. "I didn't expect you to have a sense of humor."

"My family often found comfort in laughter," he says. "It defies the darkness."

I wonder at that. "I can't remember the last time I laughed."

Not even before my people fell.

He pauses at the base of the last flight of stairs, finally looking down and meeting my eyes. "I didn't leave any space in your life for laughter, Asha. For that, I'm sorry."

The darkness of the rings under his eyes is acute. He may not have worked all day like I did, but now that I think back on it, during those small snatches when I was aware of what he was doing in the forge, I remember his constant tension. The unfailing tilt of his head as if he'd been listening to every sound within our surroundings.

The constant hammering must have been intense in his sensitive hearing, and it would have made it harder for him to hear what was going on outside.

Even his posture... It wasn't so much like he was watching me, but rather, watching *over* me.

"Maybe one day, when we're old, we'll find the space to laugh together," I say, my eyes drifting closed.

He exhales a heavy sigh. "Creatures like you and me rarely have the chance to grow old."

His words strike me hard.

It's been ten years since my people fell and in that time, I've obeyed the rules, followed every command. It's only in the last few days that I feel like I've started living, and now, my remaining time could be short.

As I allow myself to close my eyes, I vow to fight for every moment I have left.

CHAPTER 34

oments later, we reach the corridor to my room, where the Vandawolf slides me back to my feet.

I shiver from cold now that I'm separated from the warmth of his body and stumble into my room, looking for a thick blanket. It's only when I reach the bed where the blankets are folded that I realize how filthy I am.

My clothing is black, so it hides most of the crimson soot, but when I check my hair, I find it tinted auburn and covered in a fine dust.

So are my arms and hands.

So is the Vandawolf.

"Oh, damn," I whisper. "All I want is to crawl into this bed, but I can't.

"Wash up," the Vandawolf says. "The bed will wait for you. In the meantime, I'll check the repairs on the door. It should have been fixed today."

I'm surprised to realize that it's not so cold in here as it was out in the corridor, and it appears I owe that to the fully closed partition on the other side of the room.

The Vandawolf heads straight for it and I hobble toward

the little bathroom. I'm reluctant to remove the crescent pin, but I can't keep it on forever. Unclasping it from my tunic, I place it on the little table in the corner of my room. When I place the pin away from me, the world around me looks and feels less bright, but it's a reality I can't avoid.

I continue to the bathroom and close the door behind me. The water only runs cold, so I usually reserve any sort of bathing for the middle of the day when the room is warmer.

Tonight, I'm so filthy that I have to brave it, pumping water into the small bath and bucketing the freezing liquid over myself until I'm shivering violently but as clean as I can be. I avoid washing my hair because it won't dry for hours, and sleeping on cold hair is worse than getting dust on my sheets, but I brush it out as best as I can.

Trembling and wrapped only in a towel, I hurry from the bathroom, seeking the quickest path to the nearest blanket.

"Here." The Vandawolf steps in from the side, a blanket already held in his hands.

Within seconds, he wraps me up in it and pulls me up against his chest, his body heat somehow making it all the way through the layers.

I'm astonished at the way he anticipated my need for warmth. "How did you...?"

"I could hear your teeth chattering the whole time you were in there," he says, one hand beginning a slow rub across my back.

His body is so warm, and his touch so soothing on my sore muscles, that I can't stop myself from sinking against him. It's impossible to keep my distance when he hugs me close, standing quietly with me for a long moment.

I'm vaguely aware of the delicious aroma of fresh bread and stew—probably vegetable stew—coming from two bowls steaming on the little table. Rachel must have brought them while I was bathing.

My stomach growls, but I have no wish to move from this spot.

Not yet.

Maybe not ever.

Every time the Vandawolf kneads my shoulders, I fight against uttering moans of relief as my pain eases. But I don't stifle my sigh when his fingers feather my neck. I fit my head to the curve of his shoulder, my ear pressed to his chest.

Little grains of crimson dust brush my cheeks.

"You're going to make me dirty again," I murmur, although I don't really care.

He doesn't seem in any hurry to move away. "I'll wash up once you're warm."

For another long moment, we stay right there.

When he stops stroking my back, a protest rises to my lips, but he picks me up, wrapped in the cocoon of the blanket, and sets me down in the lone chair next to the table.

"Eat," he orders me and, without another word, he prowls into the bathroom.

I'm startled to see that the toolbox now rests on the far left of the table next to my grandmother's silver pin.

I turn to call after the Vandawolf, but he has already closed the bathroom door.

Is he testing me? Tempting me to betray him?

Could he be trying to tell me he trusts me?

Or... could he simply be so tired—as I am—that he didn't really think about it?

I've never willingly picked up Malak's hammer. Even the first time was at the Vandawolf's command.

I don't intend to start now.

I reach for the pin instead, pulling it closer to me before I focus on the bowl of stew. Moaning with happiness, I spoon the tasty meal into my mouth.

While I eat, I'm aware of the sound of running water and splashing from within the bathroom.

Then a startling stream of expletives.

I fight my grin.

Yes, the water is fucking cold.

After using my bread to mop up the rich liquid that remains in the bottom of my bowl, I shuffle across to the closet in search of night clothes.

I keep the blanket wrapped as firmly around myself as I can manage, but I'm disgruntled by the fact that I'll have to drop it to get dressed.

Just as I slip it off my shoulders and to the floor, reaching for my night clothes, the bathroom door opens and the Vanda-wolf emerges.

"I didn't think about clean clothes," he grumbles as he attempts to wrap an insufficiently-sized washcloth around his hips.

The material barely stretches far enough to cover his pelvis, let alone his upper thighs. I've never seen so much of him, all the perfectly sculpted muscles, but I've also never seen the worst of his scars. A large, ropey one stretches across the front of his right thigh, cutting across the thick muscle. Another rests low on his stomach on the left side. Both appear to be knife wounds.

His focus rises to me where I stand naked in front of my closet.

I'm about to step toward him, to ask him about his scars—or maybe not because I don't know if he'll want to talk about them —but his eyebrows draw down into a deep scowl that halts me.

His gaze remains firmly on my face before he casts his focus sideways.

Folding his arms across his muscled chest, he glares stead-fastly at the wall. "I don't want you to have to stand naked in front of me. Ever again."

His reaction is so sudden and fierce that I'm frozen with one foot forward.

Well, oops.

I step back, grab the nearest tunic, and slowly pull it over my head, followed by long pants. All the while, I try to process this change of rules. "I don't understand."

Now that I'm dressed, he turns back to me. "You deserve more."

I'm stunned by his declaration.

In the past, I've done whatever was asked of me so I could keep my family safe. I never objected to the gauzy robes or stripping naked when ordered to do so. I *expected* to be treated as a deadly threat. The fact is, if I really wanted to, I could smuggle a medallion in my clothing and use it to kill him and any number of humans.

After all, that's how Malak killed the human king. In an underhanded act of treachery.

But now, I allow myself to accept the truth in his words, and I reply with a firm nod of agreement. "I do deserve better."

My response brings a calmness to the Vandawolf's face. The tension around his mouth disappears, his shoulders relax and so do his stomach muscles. It causes the cloth around his hips to slip dangerously, but I don't draw attention to it.

"Did you expect me to disagree?" I ask, keeping my own focus on his face.

One corner of his mouth rises in a half-smile. "I'm glad you didn't."

At that, the cloth slips, but he catches it before it would fall. Even so, it only covers the front of him.

Within seconds, he's scooped up a spare blanket and tucked it around himself, and then he meanders over to me. "Let me warm your feet. They must be freezing."

They are.

But my stomach is full and the rest of my body is warm.

Warmer when he picks up the blanket I dropped and wraps me up in his arms as if it's the most natural thing to do.

Carrying me to the bed, he lays me down and reaches for my feet under the blanket, all while managing to stay swathed in his own blanket. Well, at least to conceal his lower half. He doesn't seem to care when his blanket slips off his shoulders, leaving his chest bare.

"Icy cold," he murmurs as he kneels on the bed beside me, his warm hands closing around my feet.

He blows gently on my toes as he rubs the warmth back into them, his breath deliciously warm. And also tickly.

I bite my lip against my smile, my toes curling as the ice leaves them.

"Better," he says.

Seeming satisfied that I won't freeze, he reaches for another blanket—the third and remaining one. He wraps part of it around my feet, pulls the loose half of it up around my torso, and tucks it tightly around my sides. "Get some sleep."

It's an easy command to obey.

I'm warm. My heart is peaceful. The future and all it holds seems far away. The dangers ahead of me can't encroach on this space right now.

I struggle to keep my eyes open as the Vandawolf quietly eats his meal and then lies down on the other side of the bed.

When I turn over to see him, I find him staring up at the ceiling where the moonlight plays. There isn't so much light as there was when the partition was broken, but random beams steal through the cracks at the top and the bottom of the door.

The distance between us feels empty and unwelcome.

"Have you ever seen one?" he asks softly.

I'm puzzled at his question. "Seen what?"

"A deer."

Oh. I challenged him earlier to give me my tools so I could skip up the stairs like a forest creature.

I shake my head. "Unless I count the monsters, I've only seen them in illustrations."

"You might see one in the mountains," he says.

On my journey.

I want to believe that somewhere out there, the creatures of the forest survived Malak's assault on the environment and maybe even thrive. From deer and wolves to tiny field mice. They must still exist in the north—or creatures like them.

"If I see a deer, I'll tell you all about it," I promise.

He finally turns to me, and I'm floored by the intensity in his voice when he says, "Live every minute of it, Asha. Don't waste a second of your freedom."

My *temporary* freedom. But freedom just the same.

My heart is suddenly in my mouth. I struggle to suppress, or even to catalog, the wave of emotions I'm feeling. A sliver of anticipation. A wash of fear. But also, unexpectedly, sadness.

I'm leaving. I'm going in search of another Blacksmith, and I don't know what will happen when I find her.

Maybe I'll walk away alive. Maybe I won't.

Maybe there are things I need to say to the Vandawolf before I leave that I won't have another chance to say.

But I have two more nights to say them and for now, my exhaustion defies my will.

"I don't like this space between us," I murmur, fighting to keep my eyes open. "Will you come over to me?"

The bed dips as he shifts himself in my direction, dragging the blanket and a pillow with him until he's right beside me. He tugs at the edge of my upper blanket, pulling it over himself, too.

I shuffle forward a little, closing the gap and bringing my head to his shoulder. His upper arm curls around me, his fingers trailing through my hair before coming to rest on my upper back.

"Better," I say, closing my eyes.

The Vandawolf's breathing deepens and so does mine.

~

By the end of the second day, Thaden and I have created weighted chains to hobble a monster, and a net to capture it, along with the mechanisms to deploy both weapons from the top of the wall.

We work efficiently, and I'm surprised by how much progress we make.

What I thought would take three days only took two, and it leaves me with some uncertainty. I asked for three days. The Vandawolf granted them. Now that I've finished the weapons early, he's likely to send me on my journey sooner.

I tell myself that's for the best.

Milena could attack at any time and the sooner we leave, the better.

Stepping back from the anvil, my hammer still in hand, I speak to the Vandawolf, who leans against the opposite wall. "The weapons will need to be taken up to the wall tomorrow morning, but as for forging them, we're done."

I deliberately designed the harpoon, crossbow, net, and chains so that my tools aren't required to secure them to the city wall. In fact, the human metalworkers can do it. It was a deliberate decision on my part so that the humans can move the weapons and anchor them elsewhere if needed. I told the Vandawolf as much while I was working today.

He acknowledges my declaration with a nod, rising from his lean against the wall. He watched over us all day, a silent guard, but now he steps forward, opening the toolbox for me to return the hammer and medallion into it.

"My time forging weapons for the humans is at an end," I say, my heart strangely heavy.

Standing beside me, Thaden rests his scaled hand on the

anvil, the medallion wrapped around his upturned palm. "We worked well together," he says. "It's strange how comfortable I've become using this medallion. This power. Now that I'm done with it, I don't want to be without it."

The back of my neck prickles and some of my wariness returns. Malak's power is seductive. Its cold nature hurt Thaden to begin with, then it accepted him. But now, it seems, *he's* accepted *it*.

I begin to speak, a warning on my lips, but Thaden continues in the next breath.

"But I won't be sorry to put it away. Its heart is twisted." He looks to me, his eyes bright with the power still flowing through him. "I understand now the battle you fight to resist its pull."

My exhalation is shaky and I seek the comfort of my grand-mother's pin. It shielded me from the worst impulses in Malak's hammer, but Thaden didn't have any such defense.

"If I could have chosen my own hammer and forged my own medallions, they would be nothing like these," I say, firmly placing the black hammer into the toolbox.

The moment I release it, exhaustion hits me in a debili-tating wave. I wasn't expecting it, and I cry out in surprise as my legs give way. I knock into the anvil, banging my hip on its metal edge with a painful *thump*.

The Vandawolf jolts into action, spearing around the anvil toward me, but Thaden reaches me first.

Catching me before I hit the ground, his left arm wraps around my back and his scaled hand closes over my shoulder. His knees are bent and my lower half is pressed between his thighs.

But it's not his nearness that brings a scream to my lips.

The medallion is wrapped around his right hand, which is in turn closed around my left shoulder right above my heart.

The instant the metal band connects with my body, dark light bursts between us.

Malak's cruel power stabs through my chest. It's combined with an unfamiliar blast of heat, as hot as the lava of a dragon's fire. Ice and heat rage through me simultaneously in an agonizing rush.

I sense pain and anger, a beast's rage in its final moments, but within that moment of pain, there's also clarity.

When I've worn the medallions in the past, they've allowed me to discern the Vandawolf's wildest instincts, the wolf's nature that burns within him.

Now, the dragon whose soul was fused with Thaden is suddenly clear to me.

A young soul, not an old one. A vibrant creature with the power of light that has now turned inky dark.

When Thaden first appeared in the lightning strike, I sensed this beast within every tensed muscle in his body. The lightning had shattered around him, clinging to his form like firelit ash floating through the air.

Stone burned by a dying dragon.

A death that should never have been.

A majestic creature that should never have been destroyed.

I'm screaming. I know I'm screaming, but not only with pain.

A terrible, horrible grief claws at my heart and threatens to tear me apart.

CHAPTER 35

Thaden roars my name.

He reacts with near panic, his focus flying to the medallion. His eyes widen in a moment of apparent realization and his face fills with horror, but I'm already shoving at his chest. Needing to escape.

His arms fly wide and he jolts backward, pulling his hand from my shoulder even though the medallion clings between us, defying the separation, one side of it stuck to my shoulder, the other side wrapped around his thumb, forcing a connection.

But then...

A wolf's growl sounds at my back and the Vandawolf's arm slips around my waist from behind.

I'm filled with terror that the power in the medallion will surge through me to him. But the moment he touches me, the pin resting over my heart glows, its light bathing my chest and his arms.

The medallion stretches between me and Thaden, but it doesn't have the hold on my shoulder that it has on Thaden's hand. The metal shrieks as it releases me and snaps back to Thaden's palm.

Then suddenly, blissfully, the Vandawolf is pulling me to safety.

Tears stream down my cheeks as I land against his body and we hit the floor.

His thighs cushion my fall, but his soft grunt at my ear tells me he didn't fare so well against the stone surface.

My heart is pounding and I drag air in and out of my chest as the Vandawolf pulls me close, one arm wrapped across my shoulders, the other around my waist, allowing me to breathe but steadying me.

"You're okay," he rumbles at my ear. "Asha, you're okay."

But Thaden clearly isn't.

Opposite us, he has stumbled against the anvil and now he thumps his fist down on its surface, trying to dislodge the medallion.

Thump! He bashes his hand against the metal structure so hard, over and over, that the anvil's surface cracks down the middle.

"*Off!*" he roars, his eyes ablaze and light rippling down his scales.

Sparks burst around his palm and the medallion finally releases him, dropping to the anvil's broken surface.

The metal band glows for another second before it fades and finally loses its sheen. No longer awake.

Thaden staggers backward, his eyes dull and his face pale, until he hits the side of the fireplace and then veers toward the wall. He slides down it to the floor, landing with a soft *thud*.

His head drops into his hands.

"Fuck," he whispers into the silence.

My breathing has remained rapid and I struggle to get it under control. Even my grandmother's pin is no shield against the remembered pain echoing back at me.

"What happened?" the Vandawolf asks, a growl at my ear as I continue to rest in his arms.

"I saw the dragon." I gasp. "A fire dragon. I felt its anger as its soul was stolen. *Terrifying* anger."

Across the way, Thaden lowers his arms, his focus on me now intense.

"Did you see Milena?" he asks.

"No," I say, shaking my head. "It's not like that. I didn't see the past. Only the nature of the creature that lives within you. I saw its power and its rage."

I want to ask him how he controls it, but I'm worried that he's doing it unconsciously. I don't want him to question himself and by doing so, create cracks in his control.

"I felt its sadness." I close my eyes, tears dripping to my chin. To wipe them away, I would have to dislodge the Vanda-wolf's arms, and I'm not ready for him to let go of me yet.

When I open my eyes, Thaden is staring at the broken anvil.

On its surface, the medallion rests.

My jaw clenches. "It needs to be destroyed."

"Asha?" the Vandawolf's question meets my ears as I clasp his arms and force myself to push away from him and struggle to my feet.

I make my way to the anvil and glare down at the medallion.

Its surface is no longer smooth, but decorated with the pattern of scales, as if they'd been imprinted onto it by Thaden's palm.

"This medallion carries the power of dragon's fire now," I say. "I don't know for certain how it happened. But my guess is that by using it, Thaden has inadvertently imbued it with the beast's strength. I never anticipated this."

I draw a deep breath. "This imprinted medallion is far too dangerous to be used again."

The Vandawolf rises to his feet. So does Thaden. Both of them are shaking their heads with apparent disagreement.

"Are you sure?" the Vandawolf asks, reaching my side first. "You'll be left with only two medallions."

"Two is enough," I say, holding up my hands. "I can only carry two weapons at a time. The third was always a backup."

The Vandawolf studies me for another moment, as if he believes I'll rethink my decision, but I remain firm.

"We need to destroy it," I say.

"Very well," he replies.

Reaching for the tongs, he uses them to pick up the imprinted medallion and walks carefully around me, carrying the band toward the fire.

To destroy a medallion, it has to be held within the flames of crimson coal until the moment when it's about to melt. Then it must be plunged into water so that it becomes brittle. Icy water is best, but we'll have to make do with the stagnant bucket that has remained at the side of the forge.

Finally, the medallion must be lifted from the water and immediately smashed with a hard object, preferably an iron hammer or a gavel.

Before the Vandawolf can reach the furnace, Thaden steps in front of him, blocking the way.

"Stop." His protest is quiet but firm as he addresses me. "Asha, you can't do this. You're heading into a fight with a Blacksmith who is strong enough to kill the dragon whose rage you felt. You'll need that medallion if you want to survive."

"I can't use it," I say, a simple admission. "It nearly tore me apart."

"But I can," he replies earnestly. "I *am* that dragon. Its rage and pain are part of me. I can use the medallion if you need me to. If you ask me to, I will defend you with it."

I'm stricken by his declaration. The medallion initially caused him pain, but that seemed to ease—at least, it appeared to. But once the medallion formed a connection between us, its nature was changed. The way he fought to dislodge it indicated that it horrified him as much as it hurt me.

Still, he's offering to use it in my defense.

My decision is now driven by two opposing fears. One, the fear that this medallion is too powerful and needs to be destroyed. The other, the fear that I'll need its power if it means the difference between life or death.

I turn to the Vandawolf. "This is as much your decision to make as mine."

He shakes his head. "These are the only medallions you have. If I thought I could convince the council to let you make more, I would. But rightly, they will never allow it. And I swore I would never ask."

Once more, I stare down at the medallion, watching the light flicker across its new surface, as if it's coated in black dragon scales. I know, in my heart, that this medallion can only be used in exceptional circumstances. But I also tell myself that if I make it back from the mountains alive, I can always destroy it then.

The toolbox is perched precariously on the opposite edge of the anvil. It snapped shut when Thaden thumped his fist onto the surface and then it rattled its way to its present position.

Now, I retrieve it, open it, and use the tongs to place the imprinted medallion inside it.

The Vandawolf acknowledges my decision and beside him, Thaden exhales with a heavy sigh.

"You made the right decision," Thaden says, although the Vandawolf is quieter.

He takes the box from me once more before he addresses us both. "Your task is finished," he says. "I'll have the metal-workers complete the assembly of the weapons on the wall tomorrow morning."

To Thaden, he says, "Be ready to leave an hour after dawn.

You'll need to make it across the northern wasteland before night falls."

"Why not leave at first light?" Thaden asks, which is a fair question, given that we've started our day at dawn for the last two days.

"Because Asha needs to do something first," the Vandawolf replies.

I'm curious about what the Vandawolf intends for me to do, but I don't question him. If he wanted Thaden to know, he would have spoken more openly.

Before the Vandawolf can turn away, Thaden says, "We won't travel across the wasteland. We need to go through the Sunken Bog."

The Vandawolf's forehead creases. "That's far more dangerous."

"Only in the short term," Thaden replies. "The mountains directly north are impassable. If we travel east, we'll reach the safest pass through the mountain range. Once we've entered the pass, there are other, safer passages back toward the north."

"How do you know that?" the Vandawolf asks, a fierce crease in his forehead. "If you lived to the north of the mountains and not in the east?"

Thaden doesn't appear daunted by the Vandawolf's question. "I didn't always live in the north. My father spent years searching for a place to make our home. Even after we settled there, I hiked through the mountains whenever I could."

The Vandawolf seems satisfied with that answer. "Very well. Asha will meet you at the eastern gate. Gallium will bring supplies."

As I follow the Vandawolf from the forge, I glance back to Thaden where he has remained next to the furnace. His expression is worn, his focus on the broken anvil, but at the last moment before I turn the corner, he looks up.

That's when I see the sheer determination in his eyes. The hard resolve.

The fiery need for revenge.

If the dragon's pain I felt is what he has to bear in every waking moment, then I truly understand his need to end Milena.

It's a need that could surpass his declared intention to only use the imprinted medallion to help me. If it comes to it, the dragon's rage could overcome Thaden's reason.

I won't be collateral damage. And, I swear, neither will my brother.

When we reach the base of the tower steps, I hobble up them on my own, determined to walk by myself. With every step we take, I watch the Vandawolf's mask disappear. It's the face he wears for his people, the unfeeling leader, and slowly, it drops away.

That's when I ask him, "What is it that I'm supposed to be doing in the morning?"

"Genova asked to see you and I've granted her request," he says.

I'm surprised. "What does the leader of the farmers' guild want with me?"

He shakes his head. "I don't know."

I narrow my eyes at him. "But you granted her request."

"Because she's proven to me in the past that she never asks for anything unless it's important," he says.

I don't have the chance to say more because at that moment, Rachel appears coming down the stairs.

She's holding a large, wooden bucket and wears a warm smile on her face that dispels my dark thoughts.

"All done, lord," she says to the Vandawolf. And then, she adds, "Good night, Lady Asha."

She throws a mysterious smile my way before she continues on her way.

"What's 'all done'?" I ask the Vandawolf.

He grins at me—a rare trace of humor—but doesn't give me an answer.

Another mystery, then.

A few steps later, my muscles are screaming at me, and all it takes is a groan for the Vandawolf to scoop me up again.

I sigh against his chest. Tonight, he's carrying the toolbox in a satchel so it doesn't dig into my back. For a second, I wonder if he anticipated needing to help me up these five flights of stairs.

My pride stings, but I remind myself it's only because I worked the forge all day and that isn't going to happen again.

Still, I grumble, "This is becoming a habit."

He shrugs, and the movement presses me closer. "There are worse habits."

As soon as we enter my room, he sets me back on my feet. Ahead of us on the table are steaming bowls of stew, but that's not what immediately draws my attention.

"Bathroom," the Vandawolf says with a smile as he points to the open door on the other side of the room.

Even from this distance, I can see little wisps of white rising from the top of the bath. "Steam?"

I make a straight line for it, amazed to find the bathtub already full. When I kneel beside it and hover my hand above the surface, the warmth rising off the water pools against my palm.

I peer beneath the surface, puzzled by what looks like rocks in the bottom of the tub.

The Vandawolf steps into the space of the open doorway. He's no longer holding the toolbox, but he's brought clothing—

what looks like a tunic and pants—as well as a blanket. He places both on the little chair inside the door.

I point at the bottom of the bath. "What are those?"

"They're heating stones," he says. "Make sure you take them out before you get in. Trust me, you don't want to sit on one." He grimaces. "Jagged edges."

I allow the threads of steam to filter through my fingers, my forehead creased with curiosity. "Why are you doing this?"

"Because the water's cold."

I look up, seeking answers. "But why now?"

His smile fades. "There's hot water in the lower rooms of every tower. I assumed you had hot water up here, too. I should have realized years ago that you didn't." His jaw tightens. "There are a lot of things I should have given you right from the start." His speech slows and regret enters in his voice. "There are a lot of things I should have said and done."

I study his features, the wolf's face that he doesn't hide from me. When I look at him now, there's an emptiness behind his expression that I haven't seen since that very first night when he spoke about his brother's death.

It's *loss*.

It clouds his eyes when he looks at me.

He pulled me away from the imprinted medallion tonight. He saw what it did to me. My scream would have pierced his hearing. The same way he heard my scream all the way across the wasteland when the stag wounded me.

Loss. Sadness. I haven't seen them in his eyes since that first night in the throne room, but now they're bared for me to see.

It confirms to me what I've refused to acknowledge—what I've spent the last two days working hard to forget. But what Thaden has been trying to warn me about ever since he arrived.

I'm no match for a Blacksmith who can hunt and trap a dragon and cage its soul.

My only hope is to injure her enough so that Thaden and Gallium can finish the fight.

Quietly, I say to the Vandawolf, "I'm not coming back from this, am I?"

CHAPTER 36

The Vandawolf's jaw tightens again. A storm grows on his face as he crosses the distance between us and drops into a kneeling position beside me.

He reaches up to cup my chin, his fingers splayed across my neck and cheek. It's a soft touch that sends tingles to my toes, but his voice is far from gentle.

With a fierce snarl, he says, "Fear doesn't suit you, Asha."

I catch my breath.

When there were walls between us, I played my part and I played it well. I kept my thoughts and feelings to myself.

I had shields. Impenetrable ones.

My greatest defense was that I never gave the Vandawolf any ground.

And he never treated me with care.

Neither of those is true anymore.

I have no shields in this moment.

I lean forward and dare to press my cheek to his human cheek, the corner of my lips brushing his. His stubble scratches my chin and the wolfish texture of his hair tickles my forehead, but they're welcome sensations.

I sense the way he's holding his breath in the sudden stillness of his body. His hand lifted from my face when I moved and now it hovers beside my head, the lightest touch on my hair.

When he doesn't pull away, I turn my head, pulling back just the slightest so I can veer to the other side of his face. To the wolf.

He is frozen. Like stone as I carefully press my lips to the other corner of his mouth right beside his sharp tooth. "I was afraid," I say. "For a moment there. But I'm not anymore."

I pull back a little, reading a heat in his eyes that I've seen many times before, but the walls between us stopped me from recognizing it.

Need. Desire.

It couldn't exist in our relationship before, so I discarded what I sensed in him. And he certainly never acted on it.

His voice is a husky rumble. "Ask for anything you want between now and sunrise and I will give it to you," he says, making my eyes widen with surprise.

"You can have a late supper with your family," he offers. "Sleep at their home, if you wish. I'll take you there. You can read books about forest animals. I'll bring them to you. If you don't want to sleep, you can walk through the apple orchard. It's magical at night when the leaves sparkle—"

"Because of Malak's first discovery," I finish quietly. "The one innocent thing Malak ever did."

I sigh, a soft breath that whispers between us while our faces are so close. "My parents told me the story. An apple tree grew outside Malak's window when he was a boy and its branches creaked and groaned at night. It terrified him. One day, he decided to turn that beastly tree into something pretty. He took the terror away."

"Beauty instead of fear," the Vandawolf says, his fingers

connecting with my jaw again, softly tracing the contours of my chin and down my neck to rest on my collarbone.

He leans closer to me, his lips a hair's breadth from mine, and I want him to close the gap, but I made the first move and now I need him to choose his response.

"You can ask for anything you want," he says, drawing back even further while his fingers follow a path up to my lips. His thumb brushes across my upper lip in a meaningful sweep. "But you can't ask for this."

He slowly withdraws, his hand dropping away from my skin, breaking the contact.

I want to ask him why. I need to understand, but then I'm hit with a very real possibility.

My cheeks flush with unwelcome embarrassment. "There's someone else in your life."

I assumed he didn't have someone. The way he let me get close to him implied it. But now I think about it, I don't know that for certain. I remember the way Petra rushed to his side when she thought he was injured... "Petra?"

His eyebrows rise. "There isn't someone else. I can't get involved with anyone who could leverage my position for their own purposes. Especially Petra."

"Then... why?"

He doesn't look away. A rueful smile rests on his lips, but there isn't any bitterness in his speech. "Because I have too much power over your life, Asha. I can never be sure that your consent is given freely. I don't want this with you unless you're free to choose."

My heart hurts as he rises to his feet and steps away from me, heading to the door. "Think about how you want to spend this night, Asha. I'll make it happen."

I find my feet and brush moisture from my cheeks, trying to convince myself it's the humidity, not sadness.

He offered me time with my family, but if I do that, word

will spread. His people won't like it. My sister is remaining behind and it will only leave her more vulnerable to the humans' anger.

Before he can leave the bathroom, I say, "You never looked."

He pauses at the door and half-turns back to me, his forehead creased. "What are you talking about?"

I refuse to release him from my gaze as I say, "I stood in transparent clothing in front of you for years, and you saw me, but you never looked."

He never made me feel vulnerable that way. He only ever treated me like a warrior.

The crease in his forehead eases. He gives me a silent nod before he closes the door.

I'm left staring at the bath, trying to catch my breath.

I've taught myself to clamp down on what my body feels. To switch off all kinds of pain from lesser wounds to the freezing cold of this tower in winter. But that also meant switching off other sensations.

The only happiness I've experienced has been in the form of my family's love for me. A hug from my sister that brought warmth to my heart. The solidarity of a smile from my brother and knowing I wasn't alone in this fight. Then came warm blankets, and the Vandawolf himself eased my knotted muscles and brought my first experience of physical bliss into my life.

But there are facets of my body and my personality that I've never explored.

I *had* to shut them down, couldn't welcome them in, because when I picked up Malak's medallions, I needed to be able to fight my impulses.

I needed to know that I could remain in control. Always.

So I practiced control.

I would shout only when told to shout. Strike when told to strike. Resist my power. Resist. *Resist.*

I close my eyes as bitter tears burn them.

I've resisted the bad. But that has also meant never seeking the good.

With a quiet groan, I pull off my sooty clothing, pausing only to unclasp my grandmother's pin.

Reaching into the bath, I pull out each stone, and then I finally slip into the water.

I submerge myself completely, risking the inevitable cold of wet hair, hoping only that the water will dull my thoughts and stop this...

I don't even have a word for it...

This *heat* between my legs that I can't ignore any more.

My hands splay across my stomach, swilling the water, which is quickly darkening with crimson soot and tendrils of blood from the many cuts on my hands. The cuts smart in the water, but it's yet more pain that I've taught myself to ignore.

I'm suddenly, infuriatingly frustrated that the mechanics of sex were never explained to me. It's not like my mother ever sat me down to talk about it. Books only went so far: anatomy, yes, actual mechanics, no.

I can only remain submerged for another few moments, but I take a chance, giving in to my impulses. My fingers stroke down my stomach and slip between my legs, seeking the source of the heat.

It's not difficult with my knees bent practically to my chest in the little bath.

I find it, press lightly, and that single stroke shoots pleasure through my stomach and thighs.

It's so intense that I rush upward in surprise, breaking the surface and gasping for air.

My toes are still curling against the bottom of the bath as I process the sensation and its aftereffects.

I want more.

I grip the sides of the bath, trying to catch my breath, trying to steady my thoughts, but when I close my eyes, I feel again the tingle of the Vandawolf's shadowed jaw against mine. The shivery sensation of his fingertips brushing my neck and my lips.

He told me that I deserve more.

I wholeheartedly agree.

Pulling myself from the bath, I splash water across the floor before I quickly dry myself and attempt to dry my wet hair.

I'm warm from the water, but it won't last long.

I shun the clothing the Vandawolf brought me but take the blanket, holding it at my side as I open the door.

He's sitting in the chair at the side of the room, his shoulders hunched over, every bit the beast I first encountered.

He looks up and then straightens immediately when his gaze flickers across my nakedness. "Asha?"

"I want you to look," I say.

He's already shaking his head. "Asha, you—"

"I need you to hear me." I move toward him as I speak, grateful when he pauses, but now... *Now* I recognize the desire flaring in his eyes as I approach. The way his jaw clenches as if he's clamping down hard on his own impulses.

I stop in front of him, my hair dripping down my back despite my efforts, and goosebumps beginning to rise across my skin. Still, I refuse to pull on the blanket. "I want you to give me what I've never been given."

Heat flares in his eyes, but still, he doesn't respond. "What is that?"

"Pleasure," I say.

For a second, his muscles flex, as if he's about to rise from the chair, but again, his jaw tightens. Fiercely. "My reasons still stand."

"I understand," I say. "And I will honor your reasons if that's your wish. But I also have to face my reality: I will never be free. So to wait for my freedom is to create another cage around me."

He rises to his feet. Slowly. Towering over me. Regret is smothering his heat now as he seems to process what I said. "I hear you, Asha. I don't want that for you. But you can't have this with me. Not with the power I hold over you."

"Who, then?" I ask quietly, refusing to look away, trying to make him see that *he* is the one I want this with. *Him.*

"Am I to find some random man somewhere in the mountains who's willing to fuck me—" My forehead creases briefly. "That's what it's called, isn't it? Fucking?" I continue in the next breath even as his lips are drawing back and his wolf's growl fills my ears. "Some stranger who will fuck me in a dirty cave somewhere between here and my death—"

He moves fast, his arms rising around me, lifting me off my feet and pulling me to his chest.

My core presses against his hard body and my thighs clench against his hips.

"No," he snarls down at me, pure beast, pure guttural need. "*Mine.*"

"Then let me be yours," I whisper. "Accept my consent, because I'm giving it."

CHAPTER 37

The Vandawolf's palms sear my naked thighs as he pulls my legs around his hips where he stands. It isn't a gentle movement, but I didn't expect it to be.

My breasts are crushed against his chest and my core presses against his hard body, the pressure sending waves of heat to my toes. While his hands wrap around the back of my thighs, his thumbs stroke my naked skin. Pulses of pleasure ripple through me, intensifying when he swings us toward the bed, the movement grinding my center against him.

In the three steps he takes to reach the bed, my focus shifts to his lips. I need to explore the shape of his mouth on his human side, but more than that, I want to risk the danger of his wolfish side.

Before I can leverage myself upward to press my mouth to his, he lifts me higher, but not to kiss me.

His warm mouth closes over my nipple and a shock of pleasure beats through me all the way into my core. My thighs clench hard around his waist and a moan leaves my lips.

One of his big hands rests beneath my backside, the other

supporting me across my back as he lowers me onto the bed without breaking the connection. His wolf's tooth softly scrapes my skin, a mere tickle as he flicks his tongue over my breast, balancing himself over me with his other hand.

I'm aware that I'm lying diagonally across the bed now and he's kneeling between my legs with full access to my body. He's still wearing his tunic and pants. He's covered in coal dust, but it doesn't matter to me.

With every kiss he plants on my body, he smears me with crimson coal dust, leaving me painted amber and wanting more.

Finally breaking the connection, he rears upward to pull off his shirt. I reach for his naked chest as he lowers himself back to me. I'm determined to explore the shape of his muscles and trace the smattering of hair down his stomach to his pelvis, but he firmly pushes my arms back to my sides, his hands pressing first on my shoulders and stroking quickly down to my wrists. He presses them lightly against the bed as if to make a point.

"Your pleasure, not mine," he says in a husky growl while his gaze runs from my face all the way to my pelvis.

I'm incredibly exposed in this position, but I don't feel it.

He gives me a smile as his hands lift off my arms to glide up my inner thighs from my knees to my center on each side, burning a path and making my toes curl and my thigh muscles clench.

His left hand rests close to the center of my need, his thumb stroking softly back and forth while he runs his tongue across his other forefinger.

Again with a lazy smile as he explains, "If I could use my mouth, I would, but I won't risk hurting you."

The brief pull of his lips reveals the tip of his wolfish tooth —the same tooth that scraped deliciously across the side of my breasts but didn't cut me.

"Use your mouth for—?"

He answers me with a stroke of his wet finger against the sensitive nub at my core.

Oh dear... fuck.

I gasp. My breathing stops and then starts again as he strokes back and forth. Pure pleasure rides me, only intensifying when he leans down, plants his free hand against the bed, and lowers his mouth to my breast again.

A near sob tears out of me as I give in to my instincts and allow my body to rock against his hand.

The ache within me only increases. The burn only grows.

My center feels both heavy and light, and with every stroke of his hands and every soft, rumbling growl he makes against my chest, I become increasingly aware that there's a second source of my ache. It's deeper and he hasn't come close to touching it.

It doesn't seem to matter. My body is responding to his touch in ways I never dreamed possible, waves of heat and cold that build to a point where I feel like I'm breaking.

Tearing apart, coming together, lifting up, crashing down, a mindless release that leaves me gasping and trembling and yet so calm.

He lifts his head and his hand stills on my now overly-sensitive core.

Slowly, he slides forward and presses a kiss to my parted lips, only his human side touching mine. His chest presses down lightly on my torso, covering me while keeping himself balanced with the hands he's now planted on either side of me. His eyes close and so do mine. He stays right there for a few long seconds as my breathing evens out.

Then his arms slide beneath me and he rumbles something about the bath as he picks me up again. I curl my legs around his waist seconds before his hands glide across the backs of my thighs, settling me into position there.

My wet hair tumbles across his shoulder, turning the coal dust across one side of his chest and upper back into a thin layer of near-mud. His hands knead my lower back, and one palm slips up to the back of my neck as he carries me into the bathroom.

"The water will be getting cold," he says, his lips brushing my neck. "We need to make this quick."

I murmur my agreement a moment before he sets me back on my feet. Now that I'm separated from his body, the cold rushes in. I shiver but step into the bath, lift my hair up, and dunk myself up to my neck.

I emerge to the sight of a towel, which he wraps around me when I step out. It stops me shivering and I settle onto the little chair in the corner of the bathroom as he turns his back on me, drops another towel at the side of the bath, and steps in. There's a bucket at the side, which he uses to douse himself, all the while remaining facing away from me.

If I thought I had his permission to cross the distance and step into the bath with him, I would, but he made it clear that there are boundaries around his body.

Still, he didn't ask me to leave, so I take the chance to study the flex of his muscles across his broad back, his backside, and thighs. And the way the water runs off him, turning into a crimson pool around his knees.

To my surprise, heat pools between my legs and by the time he crouches to scoop up the towel, rubbing it across his messy hair, my body is prickling with renewed need.

I slip off the chair, my feet quietly slapping the floor.

The movement draws his attention and he glances back across his shoulder as I allow the towel to fall to the floor.

"Again," I say, my chest rising and falling more rapidly. "This time with your mouth."

I half-expect him to deny my wish, but his lips curl upward. Slinging the towel around his hips, he prowls toward me, whisks me off my feet, and within seconds, he's pressing me down onto the bed.

His hands clamp around my hips as he hovers above my pelvis, his focus intense. "Stay very still."

His head lowers and his tongue glides over me, slow and careful. I gasp at the warmth against my center, fighting the instinct to rock against him. Wrapping my fists with the blanket, I make myself lie still, beyond caring about the remnant dust clinging to my back and arms.

Let it smear my body.

All I care about is the gleam in his eyes and the curve of his lips when he glances up at me. He's careful, but the danger remains.

His mouth closes over me and then I'm lost to the sensations riding my body, the slow build and the rapid crash that takes me over a treacherous precipice. Into an abyss I never knew existed. A place of darkness and light.

I want more of it. As many times as he's willing.

Two hours later, I curl up against him, swathed in a blanket he firmly wrapped around me. My body feels light, but my eyelids are heavy. A tiredness that I can't fight much longer.

He hooks his arm around me and, even though he maintained a barrier between his body and mine while we were naked, now that he's dressed and lies beneath his own blanket, he pulls me close.

My eyes slowly close even as I fight sleep. "Have you ever imagined a world where we're allies?"

His fingers feather the side of my neck, trailing through my hair. "Right now, this cage in the sky is our world. We aren't enemies here."

I smile. "This room is ours. It can be the world we want it to be. Just here. From this bed all the way to the edge of the balcony."

"If I could have that world with you—" He exhales a shaky

breath. "A world where we can be completely honest with each other. Where there are no moves and countermoves, no commands, no subterfuge. No treachery."

He drops a kiss to my lips, the lightest touch, but his smile has faded when he draws back. "That world will never be ours, Asha."

I wish he wasn't right.

~

Hours later, when I wake before dawn, I find the Vandawolf already dressed. His big hand rests on my shoulder, a soft nudge bringing me back to complete wakefulness.

I can't read his expression as he speaks.

"It's nearly time. Genova will be waiting."

I'd forgotten about the meeting that the Vandawolf promised her.

He gestures to the bowl of porridge resting on the table and then to the armor he's laid out on the chair. I immediately notice the addition of a belt on the armor. Presumably to hold my hammer.

The hard reality of this day returns to me.

Rising and taking the blanket with me, I head to the bathroom, trying to shake off the memory of his hands and mouth. A little difficult when my body reminds me by heating at the mere thought.

I make myself dress and eat quickly. My final act is to attach my grandmother's crescent-shaped pin to my armor. And then I take a deep breath and prepare to leave.

He heads for the door, but his hand rests on the handle for a moment, and in those seconds, his features set once again into the fierce countenance with which I'm most familiar.

It's the face his people expect to see.

He is no longer the man who warmed my feet, tucked blankets around my body, and walked a dangerous line between pleasure and pain with me.

He is, once again, the Vandawolf who commands me.

I am, once again, the obedient Blacksmith who fights to the death for his cause.

He opens the door and growls, "The day begins."

CHAPTER 38

The apple orchard sparkles in the final darkness of night before the sun will rise.

Genova waits in front of the largest tree, which sits beside a small, well-kept cottage. She's wearing a dress of ochre-colored linen that falls flatteringly on her lean frame and accentuates her light-brown skin.

"You have until dawn," the Vandawolf says before he drops back, allowing me to continue on. Whatever Genova tells me, he will be able to hear it, but I suppose he's giving us the illusion of privacy.

"Genova." I greet her formally as I stop a non-threatening distance of five paces away from her.

"Asha Silverspun." Her eyes are bright as she gestures to the tree behind her. "Legend has it, this was the tree that started it all. Malak's fear of the dark drove him to do what was previously thought impossible: altering the nature of life itself."

Her focus shifts to the cottage. "There are many who think we should have burned down his childhood home. But I never want to forget that the seeds of our downfall were planted because a little boy was forced to deal with his fears on his own."

She peers at the cottage with eyes that are now dull. "What might have happened in that house that made him so afraid of the dark, I wonder?"

With a quick breath, she turns from the cottage. "Walk with me, Asha Silverspun. There's a small clearing ahead where we might speak more privately."

She waits for me to step to her side and then leads me along the rows of glowing trees to a clearing that has the appearance of a very small circular stadium. Three rows of stone steps are positioned around it, large enough to form seating.

Genova lowers herself onto the middle seat and gestures for me to join her. "Sit."

Again, I keep my distance.

She smiles at my effort. "You can sit closer if you wish." When I don't move, she continues. "I'm not afraid of you, Asha. I understand how your power works and right now, you're no stronger than I am."

I give her a nod but still don't budge.

She gives a little sigh before she moves closer to me, then gestures to the clearing. "The placement of these trees means the acoustics are jumbled for anyone standing nearby."

I consider our surroundings carefully. If this is a place where the Vandawolf can't hear, then, while it might afford us some privacy now, it could also be used for any number of clandestine meetings.

"Don't worry," she says quickly. "The Vandawolf knows. He and I have come to an understanding. He won't cut down these trees and in return I will tell him everything that happens here. I think you know better than most how good he is at making deals."

"I do," I reply stiffly. "But why am I here?"

Her eyes narrow, sharply perceptive. "You're here because

I want to tell you a story. But first, I need to give you something."

She reaches into the folds of her dress and produces a silver object, which she holds out to me. "Take it."

It's a spoon and, the moment I touch it, I ascertain that it's as ordinary as any other kitchen utensil.

It's also so sharply bent in the middle that the two ends nearly touch.

"Why have you given me this?"

She smiles, but it doesn't reach her eyes. "Did you know I used to be a midwife?"

I shake my head.

"The Blacksmiths often called upon me to deliver their babies. Of course, they stood over me with daggers in case I did anything underhanded, but I had a reputation for saving mothers and babies from difficult births. Sometimes, I would care for babies so their mothers might rest. It was important, in the time of Malak, to make yourself as useful as possible if you wanted to stay alive."

She folds her hands in her lap. "So, you see, I didn't ask questions when Malak's sister came to me one night with a baby in her arms and asked me to look after it for a night."

At the mention of Milena, my ears prick up, but I don't interrupt.

"She told me she would come back for the baby in the morning, which wasn't unusual," Genova says. "But then she said something very unexpected."

I wait for Genova to continue, even though curiosity is now burning within me.

"She looked me in the eye and told me *emphatically* that it was a human baby. I was not to tell anyone she'd brought it to me, and if anyone was to ask, I was to tell them that it was a human child."

"A human child?" I ask. "Why would she bring you a human child?"

"To this day, I don't know why she made that claim. It certainly wasn't her child. But you must understand, it was never wise to question a Blacksmith and certainly not Malak's sister." Genova points to the spoon in my hand. "But I knew she was lying when this supposedly human baby, which was obviously no older than a day, closed its fist around that spoon and bent it in half."

"Then... it must have been a Blacksmith child," I say, although that doesn't make complete sense because bending metal isn't something a Blacksmith baby can simply do. Sure, once I had strong enough hands, I could have bent this spoon without any power at all, and so could a human.

No newborn has that strength. Not without magic. "Why would she lie?"

Genova shakes her head.

"Was it a boy or a girl?" I ask.

Again, she shakes her head. "She didn't say and I didn't see. It didn't need its cloths changed before she came back for it not even an hour later."

Now, Genova's lips press together and tension appears around her eyes. "She was panicked and afraid. I had never seen fear on any Blacksmith's face before that moment. She told me her brother was coming for her. An hour after that, she was dead."

"It was that same night?"

Genova corrects herself. "I should say, it was the night we *thought* she died."

I'm puzzled by all of this. "There was never any mention of a baby in the stories I was told about her death." Not that there were really many details given at all.

"I kept my silence and never spoke a word of it," Genova

says. "Until many years later, only days after the Vandawolf slaughtered your people."

I wince since it's the first time anyone has referred to my peoples' downfall as a *slaughter*.

Genova's already continuing. "The Vandawolf came to me with some very curious questions about Milena and a baby."

I peer at Genova. "If you never told anyone, how did the Vandawolf even know about the child?"

"It seems Malak told him many things before he died."

The Vandawolf's younger voice echoes back at me: *"Before I killed Malak, he gave up all of his secrets to me. Even the secrets he kept from his own people."*

"Malak's secrets," I whisper, rubbing my forehead. "Why are you telling me this now?"

"Because apparently, Milena's alive." Genova is suddenly agitated. "If that's true, then nothing about that night is what it appeared." She reaches for my hand and her gaze is intense. "Who was that child? Were they important or nobody of consequence? Why did Milena have possession of them? And why would Malak falsify his sister's death?"

Genova's looking to me as if I might have answers, but I only have more questions.

"Falsify her death?" I stare at Genova. "No. Malak went on a rampage when his sister was killed. I was only five years old, but I remember his rage and grief."

"Rage that she was dead? Or rage that she fled from him?" Genova asks pointedly. "She was terrified that night and she told me her brother was coming for her. Now that there's evidence she's alive, I think it means she was either sent away against her will, or she ran to escape him. Either way, he must have known about it."

"But if Malak knew, then..."

Genova's gaze is piercing.

I start again. "If Malak knew his sister was alive, and the Vandawolf knows Malak's secrets..."

Genova finishes what I can't say. "The Vandawolf already knew she was alive."

CHAPTER 39

Too many questions rush through my mind, but one is the loudest. "If he knew about the threat, why keep it a secret?"

Genova peers at me. "Would you have stayed so willingly if you thought Milena was alive?"

"I..."

Would I have?

"You thought you had no allies," Genova persists. "You made the best deal you could to keep your family alive. Would your decision have been different if you knew she was alive?"

It's a question my younger self didn't have the chance to consider.

I don't know for sure what I would have decided, but if I'd known then that Milena had somehow made it safely across the wasteland and through the mountains, I certainly would have contemplated snatching my siblings and escaping with them.

I'm suddenly whisked back to the moment when I stood in the corridor outside the throne room and the Vandawolf had cleverly taken Gallium ahead with him. He halted my thoughts of escape in that moment.

"Yes," I whisper vehemently, allowing my anger to rise. "I would have made different choices. But what is this to you?"

She said she wasn't afraid of me, but her cheeks pale a little in the sparkling light, and I sense that my anger has made her nervous.

Dawn is only moments away now and soon the sun's rays will hide the beauty in these trees once more.

She swallows. "Milena was a powerful woman."

I'm not sure what she intends to convey with that statement, but I go with it. "Very," I say. "She made the hammers."

Including the one she handed me on the night I became an outcast.

"What does a powerful man do to a woman strong enough to challenge him?" Genova asks. "And before you answer, consider that I am a woman in a position typically held by men. I know what it's like to have to fight harder and never show weakness."

I already know the answer to her question.

"He destroys her," I whisper.

"By any means at his disposal," Genova says. "You might consider for a moment that you are a powerful woman, Asha Silverspun. And the Vandawolf is a powerful man."

My internal denial is instant.

He won't destroy me.

"I have never hated you, Asha Silverspun," Genova continues. "I never attributed your parents' crimes to you. Now, as another woman surviving in this world, I only want to arm you with information that I believe has been withheld from you. I don't mean to sway you in any direction. It's up to you what you do with this information."

At that moment, dawn breaks over the horizon.

Genova rises to her feet, smoothing down her dress.

I follow her up, my voice stiff. "If you made a deal with the

Vandawolf to always tell him what's said in this clearing, will you inform him about this conversation too?"

"He will guess what I've told you," she says. "He's far too clever not to figure it out."

She takes the first step up out of the clearing. "But if you think he will be concerned about your response, know this: In the night, Wasteland Warriors invaded your sister's home and took her away."

I freeze on the step, shock running through me. "What? No..."

The Vandawolf offered me the chance to see her. I don't understand why he would do that, only to have her apprehended.

My features set in hard lines, because, *no*, he knew I wouldn't take up that offer. He knew I would choose not to enrage his people and endanger my sister.

Bitterness fills my chest at the realization that it was an empty proposal. "They dragged her out in the night?"

"I've been trying to find out where she's imprisoned, but to no avail," Genova says. "The Vandawolf has hidden her well. He now holds your sister's life in his hands. He knows you won't risk disobeying him."

Because love is powerful.

And it drives every decision I make.

When I asked the Vandawolf why he was allowing me to reunite with my siblings, he told me that there isn't a single human in this city strong enough to fight Milena or her army.

When I asked him why he started training Gallium four years ago, at a time when he couldn't have known Milena was alive, he evaded the question.

But he *did* know.

As long as Milena held off attacking this city, he had time to wait for my siblings to come into their power so we would be strong enough to fight her together.

Of course, he would always keep one of us behind to ensure the other two did what he wanted.

And if Milena did attack sooner, well, I would do whatever he wanted me to do. I would give my life fighting her to save my family.

He must have had every possibility planned out.

He told me himself that he wished we lived in a world where there were no moves and countermoves. No subterfuge. No betrayal.

He warned me that a world like that could never be ours.

I chose to believe that he cared for me, not just as a warrior, but as a person. I held on to that hope because it meant there was a thread connecting us. We were both living at the hand of fate and we weren't truly enemies.

It was a fucking naïve belief.

I should have known that the Vandawolf plans ten moves ahead of everyone else. He maneuvers and makes deals. It's how he's held on to his control of this city.

He kept me completely focused on him all night.

Genova is speaking over the horrible buzz within my mind. "If I thought you'd listen to me, I'd tell you to never come back, Asha Silverspun. Never return to this kingdom of betrayal."

Her stern expression softens as she dares to reach for me, stopping me at the top of the clearing. "But you exposed your heart that night standing in front of Malak's anvil in the square. The way you held those children made it clear you would die for them."

With a rueful smile, Genova steps between the columns of apple trees until the Vandawolf is visible again in the distance.

"Our time is done." She gives me a nod. "Asha Silverspun."

Then she turns and hurries away, leaving me standing on a path where I can walk in only one direction: back to the Vandawolf.

He watches me approach with eyes that are like stone. His dark-gray hair is pulled back, his beastly countenance plain to see.

I stop in front of him, my heart cold. Iced over as if a chill breeze blows through this invisible cage I stand within.

"You knew what Genova was going to tell me," I say to him. "Why allow me to see her?"

Slowly, the Vandawolf breaches the distance between us, reaching up to brush his thumb across my cheek.

"It's a terrible instinct to tear down such fierce beauty," he says, his fingers coming to rest beneath my jaw.

What does a powerful man do to a powerful woman?

He fucking destroys her.

I fight the pain in my chest where my heart is cracking more painfully than I thought possible. "You betrayed my trust."

His hold hardens and his features darken. His wolf's eye is predatory and a growl vibrates through his chest. "Yes."

My eyes widen at his admission. "Why?"

His hand drops to my shoulder. His other hand rises to grip my arm. "I needed to destroy the spark of compassion in your eyes when you look at me. A spark dangerously close to love."

He asked me why I didn't hate him. He told me he thought I was hiding my hatred from him. And now I see that he was afraid I wasn't.

I rasp. "You *want* me to hate you."

His grip is painful, so much harder than the touch that made me moan with pleasure. I want to strike his hand away from me and give in to the anger rising within me.

It seems he desires the same thing.

"I want to see again the spark of cruelty in your eyes when you wrapped a chain around my neck and drove me to my knees," he says.

"I don't believe you." I try to see behind the menace in his expression to the man—the *wolf*—he is beneath it. I cling to a last hope that his actions now are yet another subterfuge designed to elicit a response from me and push me in a particular direction. "You don't want that. You don't—"

He pulls me close, so close that my chest is crushed to his and his lips are inches away from mine. His nearness triggers the heat within my core, the ache between my legs. It's a heat I don't try to fight or deny because it's part of me now, and I will never regret feeling it or experiencing it. Even if it was with him.

"I'm not lying to you, Blacksmith," he snarls. "This is me at my most truthful. There are no moves here. No countermoves. Either you embrace the gift of cruelty your tools give you and use it to fight for your life, or your family suffers. Only when you truly hate me will you fight for your freedom."

He presses his lips to mine, a sudden, hard contact.

His wolf's tooth is sharp against my upper lip, but a second before it would cut me, he releases me.

I wrench away from him, finally needing to acknowledge that there *is* a spark of cruelty within me.

Despite the protection of my grandmother's pin, all those hours of using Malak's hammer, along with the intense influx of power that rushed through me when the medallion wrapped around my hand the first time, have left a little of Malak's cold hatred within me.

A little of his mind and a little of his power.

Smoothly, I bow to the Vandawolf like a faithful subject, but I address him with the name my people gave him. "Beast."

When I look up, his expression is unchanged.

I search for even a spark of humanity in him, any remnant of the threads that connected us.

My soul quietly plummets when I find none.

He is unmoved.

I channel every spark of malice that the black hammer seems to have left in me as I say, "Take me to the gate. Give me my tools. Then get the fuck out of my way."

CHAPTER 40

Gallium and Thaden wait at the eastern gate. They're both dressed in sturdy-looking pants and shirts with coats rolled up and attached to the top of large satchels. A third satchel, which I assume is for me, rests on the cobbled path beside Gallium.

A row of guards looks down at us from the top of the wall and I'm aware of all the eyes on us.

I stop a few paces from the two men.

Gallium looks drawn and angry. His glare is furious enough to peel strips off the Vandawolf.

Thaden, too, appears disheveled as though he didn't sleep well, and I'm surprised when it's he and not my brother who greets the Vandawolf with a fierce accusation.

"Tamra Silverspun was prepared to go willingly," Thaden says. "There was no need to burst into her home and wrench her from her family in the middle of the night."

The Vandawolf responds with a soft growl. "There was every need," he says. "Asha's request to use her tools came with consequences. The metalworkers were preparing to take their frustrations out on her family. By making a show of force, I've appeased them. And now Tamra's safe where they can't get to her."

Thaden shakes his head, the corners of his mouth drawn down. He starts to speak again, but the Vandawolf cuts him off. "Did they hurt her?"

Reluctantly, Thaden shakes his head. "She was terrified, but she wasn't hurt."

My brother has remained a step behind Thaden. None of the anger has faded from his green eyes. "What of my parents? Will they be left to face the metalworkers' wrath?"

"They're being relocated to live with Mother Solas," the Vandawolf replies. "Rachel has been assigned to guard them there. They won't be harmed."

"Won't they?" Gallium's green eyes are bright with power as he glares at the Vandawolf. "You always have a smooth explanation. A seemingly flawless plan. But it's impossible to pick apart the truth from your lies."

The Vandawolf's expression was already like stone, but now it hardens even further.

Gallium takes a step forward with a vehement promise. "One day, Lord Vandawolf, my family will be free of you."

The Vandawolf inclines his head in a nod. "That may be so, but until then, you'll fucking obey me if you want Tamra to live."

In the far distance, the clanging of metal suddenly rings out through the morning air. I stiffen until I realize that it's not the warning bells that alert the city to a monster.

The metalworkers must have started assembling the weapons on the northern side of the wall. If they work quickly, they should be able to set up all four weapons within hours.

I turn to the Vandawolf. There's no use engaging him on the subject of my sister, so instead, I say, "My brother needs his tools."

"No."

I stiffen at the Vandawolf's response.

He hands me my toolbox and his hard eyes clash with mine. "The more vulnerable your brother is, the harder you'll fight."

I struggle to contain my own rising anger. I'm grateful now that Thaden stopped me from destroying the imprinted medallion, because it means there are still three medallions in my toolbox. One for each of us.

That is, assuming I'm willing to expose my brother to the malice that he once shrank from. I block out the memory of Gallium's cry from when the Vandawolf carried him toward Malak's anvil.

I remind myself that my brother isn't a child anymore. He's strong and he will fight at my side. If he needs to use Malak's medallions, then I know he won't hesitate.

I take my toolbox, crouch to the ground, and immediately pull out the hammer. I'm prepared for the influx of energy, welcoming the shield it provides against my feelings of vulnerability and helpless anger.

Quickly activating the other two medallions with light taps of the hammer, I place them on my right arm. I pick them up with my fingers, careful to avoid placing them anywhere near my left palm, where I sense they want to go.

As soon as I position them on my body, the pin begins to glow. White light and dark light alternate around me and I'm aware of the soft glow of my exposed skin, eyes, and hair.

I slip the hammer into the belt at my waist and the toolbox into my satchel.

I turn back to the Vandawolf. "There's nothing more to say."

His gaze rakes over me before he shouts to the guards. "Open the gate!"

The portcullis slowly rises, exposing the environment beyond it. The Sunken Bog looms, a vast, muddy expanse filled with rotting trees that are thin in some patches but also gath-ered so thickly in other places, we'll have trouble getting through them. We'll also have to be careful to avoid the Toxic Thirst, which lies dead ahead to the east.

Thaden and Gallium both bow stiffly to the Vandawolf before they hoist their satchels and stride through the opening, stopping on the other side to wait for me.

I reach the gate and there I pause, turning back to the Vandawolf one last time.

He stands alone on the path, his features set and coldly unfeeling. His thoughts are impenetrable.

But with my power, I can see his wolf.

What I see freezes me to the spot.

The burning flame of its soul is in terrible pain.

The wolf has always writhed within him, like a beast desperate to escape the boundaries of his body. A wildness that I glimpsed in the night.

But the agony I'm witnessing now is unbearable.

My breath catches and even my cold tools can't stop the responding ache in my chest.

Whatever plans the Vandawolf made in the past, it can't all have been a lie. Some of what he said to me, some of what he did, had to have been truthful.

What breaks my heart is that, like my brother said, I don't know truth from falsehood.

Now, all I want is to reach him in that cage in the sky. Go back a few hours and demand honesty. Pick apart the manipu-lations from the truth. Make him open his heart to me, even if I discover it's rotting on the inside. At least I would know what was real and what wasn't.

I step toward him, but he gives me a sharp shake of his head and turns away from me, a hulking form quickly disappearing back into the city.

The portcullis groans and I'm forced to step hastily through the gate.

It clangs shut, locking me out.

Damn.

I stare at the gate for a moment—just one moment of vulnerability to close off my heart—before I swing to Thaden and Gallium.

They're waiting for me beside the nearest rotting tree. Even this close to the wall, their boots are already sinking into the mud.

The tree trunks clustered within the bog have an unearthly amber glow while their dark brown leaves curl in ways that look like insects are resting on them.

"Asha." My brother steps forward and immediately wraps me up in a hug that knocks some of the sadness out of me.

For the first time since I started putting on the medallions, it's safe to hug my Blacksmith brother, whose power has returned, although he takes care not to brush up against the bands.

"I should have protected Tamra," he says, releasing me.

"You did the right thing," I reply. "It's difficult to trust the Vandawolf, but Tamra is his leverage. He can't afford to hurt her."

Gallium's lips thin. "A cold truth."

With a deep breath, I say, "We have to put it behind us and focus on our next steps. Surviving this journey is what matters now."

I turn to Thaden. "You said there was a pass through the mountains."

He nods and points, although I can't see past the patches of rotting forest. "Directly east, where the sun rises, there's a path where we can safely travel through the mountain range. But first, can you lead us through this bog?" He grimaces. "Now that I see it up close, I understand why you didn't want to go through it."

"We need to be careful and stay alert," I say. "But I can navigate us through. It's the mountains that worry me more and that's where we need you."

"Lead the way," he says, stepping aside.

Together, we step carefully into the dank forest of rotting trees, our footsteps slurping in the mud.

Within minutes, we enter a dense patch where the canopy is thicker above us and swarms of insects rise around us. They're strange critters, no bigger than my little finger with finely feathered wings and bodies like bees. They're harmless, but their buzzing is loud and sharp and *sounds* dangerous.

I gesture for Gallium and Thaden to crouch low each time we upset a new swarm so that the creatures can fly over us and away into another patch of decaying foliage.

Even with those interruptions, we make good progress so we're already half a mile away from the city wall when a droplet of liquid splashes onto my face.

I brush it off as humidity. I'm sweating horribly in my armor and regretting wearing it.

Then I glance down.

The smear of red on my fingertips makes me freeze.

Blood-rain.

CHAPTER 41

I stop so suddenly that Gallium bumps my arm.

"Asha?"

I tilt my head back and he follows my line of sight to the sky.

"Fuck," he whispers.

Above us, the clouds are tinted red, a subtle but undeniable change, and they're rapidly gathering to obscure the morning sun. The breeze picks up, fanning my sweaty skin, a brief relief from the humidity, but it brings the unwelcome and overwhelming scent of rain.

Behind us, Thaden swipes a drop of blood from his cheek. "What is this?"

"The only warning we get," I say.

I've never been outside the city walls this early in an attack before, so I'm not sure if it's too soon for the energy within the ground to tell me where the monster will rise.

Even so, I drop to the mud and plant my left hand in the muck.

I pray the creature will form far away within the ashen field to the north. Not here in the bog. And not close to the city.

Even now, the faint sounds of clanging tools tell me the metal-workers haven't finished assembling the weapons.

Allowing my energy to flow through my hand, I seek the location where the monster will rise.

Energy streaks from the north, biting my palm.

I draw a sharp breath when it originates from a spot much too close to the city.

Damn.

Just as I lift my hand from the mud, a second streak of energy, more intense than the first, bursts from a spot directly ahead of us. Maybe only a hundred feet away.

Damn, damn, damn!

I leap backward, catching my brother's arm. "There are two of them. One in the north and one right ahead."

"Which one is closer?" he asks.

"To us? The one ahead. But the monster to the north will rise near the city wall. I don't know if the metalworkers will finish in time."

Gallium's expression sets with determination. "We need to protect our family. Not only Tamra, but Kedric and Maybelle, too. We'll fight the monsters before we leave. Together."

His hand rises to my arm where the medallions rest, but I catch his wrist. "Not unless I need you to. These medallions are not like the ones you're used to."

"Asha isn't exaggerating." Thaden steps up behind Gallium with a shake of his head. "You only want to take one of those as a last resort."

To me, Thaden says, "I take it you've fought a lot of these monsters."

"I have."

"Then we should let you do what you do best."

He looks to Gallium, who finally gives me a nod. "We'll back you up."

"Thank you," I say, my nerves prickling.

The Vandawolf will sense the locations of both monsters and I hope he'll focus on the creature to the north and delay it from reaching the city. My focus has to be on the monster ahead of us, since the power I sensed from that spot is already stronger than the rising power in the north.

"We'll go this way first," I say, wincing as the energy in my medallions reacts to the increasing force in our environment. "But both of you, please keep your distance from me. When the sky turns to blood, these medallions..." I struggle to speak aloud what I've experienced for years. "I lose myself to this power. I don't want either of you to get hurt."

Thaden gives me a solemn nod. "I've seen you succumb to the cruelty in those bands. I'm here if you need help finding your way back to yourself."

When Thaden was in the prison, and I attacked the Vandawolf, it was Thaden who disarmed me.

Now, my gratitude feels small. "Thank you."

Up on the distant wall, the warning bells start to ring. The clanging sounds echo out across the bog, muted somewhat by the trees and mud. Soon, the city will be deathly silent, but in the minutes after the alert first sounds, there's an increase in noise as people shout to each other and hurry to seek shelter.

I pass my satchel to my brother, and then I move stealthily forward, aware of Gallium and Thaden keeping a safe distance behind me. The path ahead curves to the left, and they'll lose sight of me for a moment, but I trust they'll follow carefully.

I tread lightly, my left hand hovering over the two bands on my right arm, preparing to transform them into any weapons I need.

Halting at the bend in the path, I study the thatch of trees ahead. They form a screen that completely shields anything that might be hiding behind them.

Any kind of monster could rise from this muck. A stag-like creature or something akin to a giant bug.

I focus on moving silently as I take another few steps and then crouch again, pressing my left palm lightly to the mud.

The influx of power is intense. Blacksmith's magic, drawn to itself, shoots from a spot behind the curtain of trees and back to my position.

My forehead creases as I rub my smarting palm against my thigh. It's highly unusual for a monster to appear before the sky is boiling with clouds and right now, the air is merely hazy. The downpour hasn't even started.

Still, I prepare to open my mind to the malice in the medallions and use the power within them to defend myself, my brother, and Thaden at all costs.

A shadow moves up ahead, extending beyond the edge of the trees onto the path.

I'm startled that it's a person-shaped shadow. A small figure, too.

I straighten as a female face peeks around the edge of the trees and a whisper sounds. "Asha? Is that you?"

I gasp, clamping down on the power I was allowing to rise. "Tamra?"

My sister steps into view and hurries toward me.

I immediately let go of my medallions and rush forward. "Tamra!"

In the second before I reach her, I register her green eyes, her silver hair shining brightly through her hair dye, and that her left sleeve is rolled up to reveal three silver medallions sitting neatly around her forearm.

I never imagined that the power I sensed could be from another Blacksmith who was wearing their tools.

I can barely find my voice as I draw her into a hug. "Tamra! How did you escape?"

She pulls back, her eyes wide. "I didn't. He sent me."

My lips purse in surprise. "Who sent you?"

"The Vandawolf."

I stare at her in confusion because I don't understand what she means.

My sister's eyes remain wide. Her skin is pale. She's shaking as speech rushes from her. "This bog is fucking terrifying and it's worse in the dark, but he sent me out here, and I was sure he was trying to get me killed, but he gave me a message for you—"

"Tamra, slow down." My mind is buzzing, my thoughts crowding too fast for me to make sense of the fact that my sister is here and not trapped in a cage in the city. "The Vandawolf can't have brought you here. He was with me all night—"

I stop because that might not have been true. When I woke up this morning, it was clear he'd been awake for a while. He could have left and come back while I was sleeping.

"Tell me what happened," I say.

Tamra takes a deep breath. "He came for me very early this morning while it was still dark. He brought me out here while the guards were switching shifts so nobody saw us. I thought he was leading me to my death. But then he told me to find a place to hide and to put on my medallions. He promised that you would find me."

She reaches into her pocket and produces a small piece of parchment, which she hands to me. "He asked me to give you this."

My hands are cold as I take the paper.

I've never seen the Vandawolf's writing.

It's a rough scrawl, but it shatters my heart.

Take your freedom.

CHAPTER 42

My freedom.

I can't breathe. Can barely process.

He sent my sister out here after ensuring that his people would be certain she was locked away somewhere. He managed to get Gallium out here with me. And Thaden to take us safely through the mountains. All with his peoples' blessing. And none of them will expect us to return anytime soon.

He's giving us our freedom.

My hand flies to my mouth just as Gallium and Thaden hurry around the corner behind us, presumably because they heard our voices and knew it was safe.

I'm vaguely aware of them hurrying forward, of Gallium hugging Tamra and bombarding her with questions, but Tamra simply reaches into her satchel, draws out the second toolbox, and hands it to Gallium.

"The Vandawolf set us free," she says.

In the background, Thaden has drawn to a halt, his eyes widening at Tamra's statement.

Gallium stares at the toolbox for a long moment. "The Vandawolf did this?"

Tamra nods.

My legs wobble and I veer back against the nearest tree. Too bad it's rotting, so I nearly end up on my backside in the muck, except that Thaden's hand shoots out and he catches me.

His scaled palm wraps around my left arm. He doesn't make contact with my medallions, but before he rights me, energy travels between us, and I sense once again the ferocious dragon he keeps caged. "Asha? Are you okay?"

I take a shaky breath as my siblings and Thaden wait for my response. "Moves and countermoves," I whisper. "Every damn move he made in the last few days has led to—"

My voice chokes.

All of the moves. Right down to refusing to give Gallium his tools before we left. The Vandawolf *couldn't* give Gallium his tools because Tamra already had them.

Of all the cruel things the Vandawolf said to me in the last hour, one message echoes back to me with new clarity: *"I needed to destroy the spark of compassion in your eyes when you look at me. A spark dangerously close to love. Only when you truly hate me will you fight for your freedom."*

I sink to the ground, trying not to sit in the muck, ending up crouching instead. "I need a moment."

My brother crouches close to me. He rests his hand lightly on my shoulder. "We might not have a moment."

The air around us is quickly darkening. Overhead, a flicker of lightning makes me shudder. Bright spots remain in my eyes as the electrical pulses fade.

"Damn," I whisper. "Lightning is a bad sign."

"Asha?" Gallium looks to me, his voice heavy and quiet. "We have a decision to make."

I nod. "I know."

"Tamra isn't trapped inside the city anymore," he says. "If

the Vandawolf is giving us our freedom, then we should take it and run. We should get away from here as fast as we can and never look back."

Tamra isn't the only person I was worried about. "What about your parents?"

He runs his hand through his hair before twisting toward Tamra. "I can't make that call on my own."

Tamra was leaning close and now she crouches, too.

Her cheeks have remained pale, but she says, "Kedric and Maybelle would want us to go. They would want what's best for us. And... if we're gone... maybe they'll be left in peace."

I'm not so sure. The humans have proven to me that they can hold grudges for a long time, but I don't want to break my sister's hope.

"And Milena?" I ask, knowing I can't ignore the threat she poses to the city. In fact, there are no guarantees that the storm that's about to rage isn't heralding the arrival of an army. "Do we go after her?"

"Fuck Milena," Tamra says, color finally rising to her cheeks. "The Vandawolf can fight that battle on his own. *He* can go after her. He's proven he will always put his people first, so he'll protect them." Her voice grows quiets. "He'll protect our parents too."

Thaden has stepped back from my siblings, a new tension in his shoulders. He looks like he wants to interject, but I guess he's restraining himself.

"Thaden?"

He shakes his head before he gives a frustrated groan and speaks quietly. "I want Milena dead."

My sister twists at the waist to look up at him. "Vengeance means nothing if it kills you," she says. "Isn't your life worth more than that?"

He pauses before he scowls down at her. "Right to the point," he mutters.

"Always," she replies, arching her eyebrows at him with a small smile.

"We can decide about Milena later," I say, gathering my thoughts. "Whether or not we go after her, we have to travel the same way to the mountains."

A sharp crackle of lightning drowns my speech. Darkness drops over us so suddenly that I flinch. The scent of blood floods the air and I taste copper with every breath I take.

The influx of scent and sound is oppressive.

In the distance, I make out the frantic clangs of metal, ringing out between the chiming bells.

But with the increase of power in the air around me, so too comes the overwhelming cold of the medallions I'm wearing. I give my head a shake as the impulses within them strike through me, sharply and suddenly.

"Asha?" Gallium asks me, his focus on me intense. "Are we going or staying?"

Tamra speaks before I can. "We're going. We can't lose this chance."

I rise to my feet, tipping my head back to study the sky once more. The crimson hue reflects off my hair and body, radiating brightly between all four of us. A power none of us asked for but is part of us whether or not we want it.

I can't deny these impulses any more than I can ignore my feelings.

"The Vandawolf can fight this monster." Tamra's firm voice breaks through my thoughts. She gives me a hard look. "And the next monster. Just as he should have fought them from the beginning."

Despite the cold flooding my body—or maybe because of it—my chest hurts, and I press my palm to my heart, my fingertips brushing my grandmother's pin.

A spark of Malak's cruelty may now reside within me, but it can never destroy all of me.

I can't leave the Vandawolf to die.

No matter how much it hurt when I thought he betrayed me. No matter how uncertain I am about his true motivations and feelings. The weapons aren't ready. The storm is building too fast. And the scenario that I was afraid of is coming to pass. The Vandawolf won't survive this fight until the weapons are finished.

Making a decision, I bend once more, but this time to my satchel. This is the first chance I've had to take my hammer into a fight, so that's what I'm going to do.

Slipping the hammer onto my belt, I rise and turn to Gallium first, handing him my satchel as he also draws to his feet.

"I've left a medallion in my toolbox," I say. "Thaden can explain, but you shouldn't need to use it now that you have your own tools."

To Thaden, I say, "I'm trusting you to take Gallium and Tamra to the mountains. Tell me where to meet you, and I'll be there. I won't be far behind you. An hour at most."

Thaden gives me a solemn nod. "I appreciate your trust, Asha. Meet us at the pass I described earlier. There are caverns on the right-hand side. We'll shelter at the entrance to one of them so you can find us."

"Thank you."

Tamra is shaking her head as she jumps to her feet. When I move to hug her, she steps back from me, bumping into the amber foliage behind her.

"No," she snaps, her green eyes flashing at me.

"Tamra?"

Power flickers around her right arm. Her fingertips brush the leaves behind her and they brighten at her touch. She's spilling her healing magic everywhere, but it doesn't seem to assuage her own fears.

"I won't support this," she says. "You've given him enough."

I nod. "You're right. I have."

And now I'll give a little more because every instinct in my body is telling me not to leave. Not yet. Not when I need answers.

I need to know what was the truth and what was a lie.

"This time, I'm fighting for me," I say.

Tamra's forehead creases at my cryptic comment. She doesn't capitulate, but her expression softens slightly. "Then for fuck's sake, don't get yourself killed."

She turns away from me hurriedly, her eyes filling with tears.

I know she's angry because she's scared of losing what we've just been given.

I am, too.

Turning back to Gallium, I gesture to his toolbox. "Use your medallions and your strength. Go carefully through the bog. Avoid the Toxic Thirst. It's only two hundred paces that way. Ignore the insects; they won't hurt you. But watch for any creature that slithers in the mud—*those* can kill you. Please, brother, protect yourself and Tamra."

He places the toolbox and satchel on the ground to hug me. It's a strong hug. A determined hug. "Every instinct within me is telling me to come with you and fight beside you," he says. "But I fear this is something you have to do alone. Stay alive, Asha. We'll be waiting for you."

All I can do is nod. My heart is in my throat as I step back from him, turning quickly before I can question my own instincts.

All it takes is another glance at the sky for the energy around me to tingle across my body and banish any remaining uncertainty about what I need to do.

I don't have much time now. Above us, the crimson clouds are churning and a sudden downpour of rain sounds like drums on the canopy, splattering the ground around me before it ceases again.

Soon, the heavens will open fully and the heaviest rainfall will lead me to the place where the monster will rise.

Scanning my surroundings, I plot a path that will cut diagonally through the trees back to the wasteland and bring me close to the city wall.

It's not a good path. The mud is thickest that way and the chances of sinking are high.

Quickly visualizing the debris and fallen logs I can step on to avoid the worst of the muck, I convince myself that I can be as light as air.

I empty my mind of all doubt, and then I run.

My feet fly across the filthy ground as I leap from one motley surface to another—a stone, a branch, a patch of thick moss—darting around trees and even launching myself up at the dangling branches. They're brittle and they break easily, but they lift my weight off the ground at points where I would otherwise sink inches deep.

The farther I travel from my family, the colder the medallions grow.

The greater the power in the air, the less of myself I can feel.

The hammer bumps against my right thigh and I'm acutely aware that I'll have a nasty bruise tomorrow, but I no longer care.

Finally, I burst from the edge of the Sunken Bog onto the wasteland, a landscape dotted with dry, skeletal trees and swirling with snow-like ash, a sharp contrast to the dark environment I left behind.

But as I spin to the left, facing the direction of the city, I realize that despite my efforts, I've exited the bog farther north than I should have. I'm still eight hundred paces away.

In the distance, I make out the small shapes of guards standing on top of the wall. I don't see anyone outside the wall, so the Wasteland Warriors must not have been sent out yet. If the Vandawolf has sensed how close the monster will rise to the city, then he may have ordered the Warriors to join the wall guards, or even told them to form a line of defense inside the city.

The only figure outside the city is a single bright form in my vision, standing close to the northern gate.

The Vandawolf.

The magic within him is like a beacon to me.

As the cold wind blows around me and the ash rises in swirls that dust my armor, I crouch one last time to press my left hand to the ground and check the location where the monster will rise.

Dark light streaks from a spot six hundred paces in front of me—only two hundred paces out from the northern wall.

At the same moment, thunder beats across the sky and the clouds open up as if triggered by the influx of energy within the ground.

Blood-rain pours around me, flattening my silver hair and thumping onto my shoulders. It forces me to hold my breath and bend my knees to take its sudden weight, but I rise back up within it, narrowing my eyes as I seek confirmation of the spot where the monster will appear.

In the distance, the rain falls most heavily on the same location where the energy originated.

I don't waste another moment.

Leaping forward, I break into a run, knowing that I have too much ground to cover and not enough time. I've trained myself to sprint in this sodden ash. The rain tries to drive me to the ground, but my footing is sure and my speed grows as the energy around me feeds the medallions.

Feeds my focus on the Vandawolf.

With every pounding step I take, the dark impulses in the

hammer and the medallions grow. They're so much stronger now that both are in contact with my body at the same time. Too strong within this environment, which hums with transformation power.

He can be yours to mold.

The thought strikes through my mind and even as I try to shake it off, it increases in strength.

Make him yours and he will never lie to you again.

My arms pump and my hair flies behind me as I continue to race along the bloodied ground, pushing myself through the downpour, closer and closer to the Vandawolf.

I'm only two hundred paces away from him when a sharp crack of lightning bursts and sizzles across the air, forming bright-blue forks and tendrils in the sky.

All of the tendrils are short except for one, which streaks toward the city.

My breath halts as it strikes the ground exactly where I anticipated.

Light explodes across the distance, a crash so loud that it obliterates my hearing, and so bright that I can't make out the Vandawolf any longer.

The explosion spreads in every direction, all the way up the city wall where it casts the faces of the guards into sharp relief a moment before the force throws them back against the ramparts.

At the same time, the light also rushes toward me.

My ears are ringing and I experience a strange calm as the energy engulfs me like an avalanche.

Instinctively, I drop to the ground, my arm flung across my eyes until I realize that, although my hearing is impaired, my eyesight is clear.

Up ahead, a creature has appeared within the light, its body lying in a curled-up position that reminds me of a giant, sleeping cat. Its head and legs are facing me while its spine—

assuming it has one—is toward the city. Its face is tucked inward, its forepaws concealing its features, while its tail circles across the front.

Its fur gleams, each strand thick and appearing to have a sharp point. I have no doubt that its hair is metallic. By lying flat against its body, the fur will give it armor just like the stag—armor I'll need to get past.

In the background, many of the wall guards are struggling to rise. I have no doubt that many more are still crouched behind the safety of the battlements. What I can now also see is that only the crossbow has been fully assembled, positioned at a central point on top of the wall. The launching mechanisms for the harpoon, net, and weighted chains are partially constructed, but not complete.

The Vandawolf must be standing at the monster's back because I can't locate him right now.

I'm not about to wait for the monster to awaken.

I launch myself once again into a run, making it another hundred paces before the monster begins to unfurl in the fading light.

The color of its metallic fur becomes clearer. A dark gray. The outline of its ears appears and then its nose. It opens its eyes to reveal piercing and incredibly intelligent amber irises.

My heart skips a beat.

Of all the creatures that could rise from this cursed ground, I didn't expect a beast like the one that had been killed to create the Vandawolf.

CHAPTER 43

The giant, gray wolf rises up and swings toward me. It ignores the humans on the wall as its lips draw back from its sharp teeth.

It focuses on me and, as my hearing returns, its growl sends a chill to my bones.

I pull to a stop only forty paces from it now, my left hand hovering over my medallions while the monster towers over me, its eyes gleaming.

All is quiet now that the rain has stopped.

There's a hush at the top of the wall, the bells have ceased ringing, and the city is silent.

A final splatter of blood-rain falls from dead branches.

If the monster could speak, I have no doubt it would promise my death.

I don't feel dread. This giant wolf is beautifully fierce and the chill invading my body is thrilling.

We will see who dies today.

Its head lowers to the ground, indicating that its attack is only seconds away.

That's when I reach for my uppermost medallion and remove it with a silent command: *Axe.*

As soon as the weapon forms in my left hand, I pass it to my right. Then I press my left hand over the remaining band.

Power be mine, I whisper in my mind.

The medallion responds by curling around my left palm, forming a secure band across it. The rush of energy is heady and overwhelming, but it also clears my thoughts of everything except my need to defeat this creature.

With the medallion wrapped around my left palm, I have a direct conduit to my power. Provided I can make contact with the wolf's skin, I can turn it to ash, just as I defeated the stag.

The giant wolf gnashes its teeth and I don't wait another second.

Without any fear in my mind, I run toward it, my axe in my right hand and my medallion in my left.

I leap upward, an immense jump, aiming my blade for the creature's left eye. Once I connect, I'll be able to push my left hand against the bridge of its nose and turn this mighty monster to dust.

Just as my feet leave the ground, there's a blur of movement from my right.

A *gleaming* blur, followed by a violent *thud,* both of which happen so fast that my breath is snatched from my chest.

I register the Vandawolf throwing himself against the side of the wolf's jaw, his shoulder crunching into it.

The monster lurches to the side, the impact so sudden that it loses its footing and stumbles to the ground.

My target gone, I'm left to sail harmlessly through the air and land, stunned, in the open space nearby.

Across the way, the Vandawolf lands in the ash and rolls to his feet, his expression dark, the corners of his mouth turned down, and his eyes hard as stones. He's wearing black, supple-looking armor made of interlocked plates.

His glare is for me. "You shouldn't be here."

His voice carries to me, even though he doesn't shout.

He may not want me here, but he can't seem to hide the reaction of the wolf writhing with him. The agony in its energy eases, the sharp heat calming to a warm glow.

It was hurting, and now it's not.

I ignore his human voice, refuse to become angry about his rebuke, and respond to the beast within him. "I'm here for you."

As I speak, the giant wolf regains its balance and that's when I see what I missed before. Two tusks have formed on either side of its nose. They're shiny and smooth and look as if they're made from black onyx. Their wickedly sharp points gleam as brightly as the Vandawolf's body within my vision.

Oh, damn.

I only now comprehend that if I'd continued on my intended trajectory toward the monster's eye, I would have impaled myself on its rapidly forming tusks. I broke my own rule: Don't attack until the monster has finished forming.

My shock must show because the Vandawolf gives me a snarl. "This fight is mine."

I take a quick breath and shake my head, glancing up at the wall, where the humans are once again hurrying to complete the weapons, the clanging sounds resuming.

The monster's roar reverberates across the wasteland, its attention drawn to the wall, no doubt by the sudden flurry of activity.

As it moves, there are multiple clicking sounds. Black claws, as sharp as its tusks, appear on all four of its paws, clacking into place.

Nearby, the Vandawolf draws two daggers from a belt at his waist.

I ready my axe and clench my left hand around my medallion.

The monster twists, preparing to leap at the wall and take

me out along the way, its front claws swiping through the air toward me.

I'm already running. I leap in time to avoid the cut of its claws and launch myself at its nearest tusk.

At the same moment, the Vandawolf leaps for its back.

We make contact at the same time.

The Vandawolf's daggers drive down against the creature's spine, but its fur flattens, the strands fitting neatly together to create a smooth surface that causes the daggers to scrape across its hide without making a dint.

I don't fare much better, the monster wrenching its head to the side the second my left hand closes around its tusk. I'm jolted to the side and nearly lose my hold. Already, I can sense that trying to use my power on its tusk won't work. Its horns and fur are like armor that must be immune to my magic.

Just like with the stag, I need to make contact with this monster's skin before I can turn it to ash.

To do so will require provoking the sharpness of its fur to expose the body beneath.

I grit my teeth as I allow the monster to swing me sharply as it tries to dislodge me, using its momentum against it. On the next swing, I let go.

Somersaulting in the air, I adjust my trajectory and land at the base of the monster's neck, now straddling it.

We're closer to the wall now and I'm aware of the continuing commotion at its top. Out of the corner of my eye, I can see Braddock, my former personal guard, running along the rampart, but I can't make out what he's shouting.

I don't have time to worry about him.

Down on the ground, the Vandawolf launches himself forward again, his daggers slashing at the monster. As he flies through the air, his fierce eyes meet mine.

I read his anger in his raised arm, the sharp determination on his face, the tension around his mouth and in that moment, I know he's prepared to do whatever it takes to bring this monster to its end.

He will be the distraction.

The monster swipes at him with its claws and tries to gore him with its tusks as he lands blow after blow on its impenetrable hide.

I fight to stay on its neck as it thrashes, knowing I won't be able to hold on for much longer.

With both hands, I drive the edge of my axe down toward the gap between the monster's vertebrae, aiming precisely for the fine slit between the thick strands of its fur right at that spot.

Within my mind, I command my weapon to transform.

The edge of the blade becomes molten, liquid metal filling the fine gap and quickly hardening. I command it to split into two neat sides, forming a crowbar with enough power to force the strands of the monster's pelt to separate.

Of course, the monster isn't about to make things easy for me.

At the pressure of the crowbar, its fur shoots up.

Hundreds of sharp daggers rise beneath me, capable of shredding my legs and lower body.

I was prepared for that response. My weight is already on the crowbar, both hands gripping it, the muscles of my thighs and stomach tensed.

As soon as the creature's fur rises, I propel myself into a handstand, my body flying into a vertical position in the air. Every muscle screams with effort. I can't stay in this position for longer than a few seconds.

The crowbar has forced the sharp strands apart below me, exposing a small patch of the monster's body.

I focus on that patch, ignoring the fact that if I descend too far, sharp daggers will impale me.

I grit my teeth. Force myself to balance only on my right

hand so I can snatch up the hammer that's dangling from my waist.

As soon as my left hand wraps around its handle, with the medallion sitting neatly between my palm and the hammer's handle, a rush of power floods through me.

Too much power.

With a scream of pain, and remaining upside-down, I drop my left hand to the monster's body, planting the hammer's head neatly against its skin. Even with the extra reach that the hammer gives me, daggers slice across my armor, one tip impaling the top of my left shoulder.

But my power has met its target.

I sense the monster's nature through the hammer. I sense its rage, but also, its confusion. Moments ago, it came into being with no knowledge of this world, no motives except to survive.

Now I will end it.

Even as pain burns my shoulder, and my own death could be heartbeats away, I resolve that this monster will not be turned to dust.

As cold power flows through my arm, intensifying within my palm, and shooting through the hammer, I scream, "*Stone! You will be stone!*"

Dark light spears from my hammer, washing across the monster's back, rippling through its sharp fur and across its head. Crackling all the way to its tail.

Its movements become stilted, its body lowering toward the ground before it stops moving altogether, one paw frozen in the air, its tail pausing mid-swing.

I'm aware of the silence all around us now, especially the heavy pall that hangs over the ramparts. The humans have seen my power up close for the first time, but I can't worry about their reactions. The daggers across the monster's back are no less dangerous to me now than they were moments ago.

Even so, I have no regrets about my choice to turn it to stone.

I will leave this monolith of a wolf here outside the city wall, where it will greet the next monster that rises within this wasteland. Or, for that matter, anyone who dares attack this city.

My arms shake with the effort to keep myself vertical, but I prepare for one last leap.

Clamping my right hand around the crowbar while my left continues to grip my hammer, I propel myself back and to the right, managing to clear the monster's head and sail through the gap beside its stony neck.

I land hard, stumbling and dropping to the ground. The crowbar tumbles from my hand and into the sodden ash, forming the shape of a medallion again now that it has lost contact with my body. My hammer remains in my hand next to the medallion curled around my palm and the power flooding me is intense.

Unsustainable without losing every shred of myself.

With a cry, I open my hand and let the hammer fall to the ground. Then I pry the final medallion from my left palm, gasping with relief when it releases me.

I am myself again.

And now my focus is on the Vandawolf.

Five paces away, he drops to the ground, kneeling in the shadow beneath the monster's stone head. He's breathing hard and his hair falls across his face as his shoulders slump.

His chest is covered in blood. I could convince myself it was from the blood-rain except for the damage to his armor.

My own pain is forgotten. The fact that I can function without the medallions tells me I've only suffered flesh wounds.

Hurrying toward the Vandawolf, I scoop up the hammer and the dropped medallions with my right hand.

Within seconds, I reach the Vandawolf's side and allow all

of my tools to clatter to the ashen ground in a pile where they can't hurt him.

I reach out to him, fearful of the way his head is down and he doesn't acknowledge my presence. "Vandawolf?"

He slumps forward, but I catch him, taking his weight with an *oomph*. "Vandawolf!"

Panicked, I pull him toward the stone wolf's chest where it presses to the ground, using the surface to prop him up in a sitting position.

The giant wolf is facing away from the city and that means I can't see the humans any longer. Sounds are starting up again. Shouts. I'm sure the humans will spill through the gate at any moment, but my concern is for the Vandawolf's injuries. He's bleeding and I need to make it stop.

"Asha." He groans, one hand rising and brushing my arm.

I'm too busy peeling back the torn plates of his armor to answer. The largest chest-plate comes away, revealing deep gashes across his chest. One is bone-deep.

No.

My breathing is rapid, a fear growing within me that I haven't felt since my siblings' lives were threatened. A cold panic that becomes determination. I'm prepared to do whatever it takes to keep him alive. I'll rip off my clothing if I need to plug these wounds. I'll carry him across the wasteland to my sister if that's what it takes.

"You're not dying," I command him, reaching for the next plate of armor, needing to free him from it.

His voice is agitated. "Asha, look at me."

I can't ignore the distress in his voice. An uncharacteristic emotion that shocks me.

My eyes flash to his and I wince at the pain in his face. Sweat bathes his brow and his skin is pale.

"Stop," he rasps. "You have to go."

"You need Tamra's help," I say. "I'm getting this armor off you so I can wrap your wounds and then I'm taking you to her."

He shakes his head. His speech is slow and labored. "The Warriors will be here soon. They'll take me to the healers... Petra will help me. You can't be here."

"I'm not afraid of the Warriors," I snap. "They can't hurt me. But you—" My voice chokes. "*You* can hurt me."

I swipe at my cheeks, at the sweat that I suddenly realize is hot tears.

"Asha." He whispers my name, his hand rising to my cheek. His fingers tremble against my skin, a very bad sign. "I want you to have your freedom."

I try to see his eyes to know his thoughts. "Why?"

His palm rests against my cheek, dragging through my tears. A flicker of a smile cuts through the agony in his face. "Love is more powerful than hate and fear."

My heart cracks.

I force myself to speak. "We were enemies—"

His palm presses to my jaw. "You never looked away," he says, his voice raw. "Unlike everyone else, you look me in the eye. *Both* eyes. Wolf and man."

I recall the way his people bow to him, a gesture that hides the way they avert their eyes. The way he uses his hair to cover his wolfish features. But never when he's alone with me.

I made a vow that I would always face him. It was a promise I made to myself. I never imagined it would mean even more to him.

I reach up now, carefully tucking the strands of his hair behind his ear, starting with his wolfish side. His amber eye and sharp tooth. It's hard to face the pain he doesn't hide from me now, but I won't look away.

"You see me," he says. "You saw me from that first moment, and I couldn't tell you... All these years, I couldn't tell you what was in my heart."

I trace his features, the first time I've dared, before I lean forward and press a careful kiss to his lips. His sharp tooth nudges the edge of my mouth but it doesn't cut me.

Gently, I ask, "Why did you try to make me hate you?"

"I needed your anger so I could let you go."

His hand slides down my back and I can't stop my sob, choking on the quiet sound.

"I was never going to send you after Milena." His speech slows even more. "I finally had the chance to give you your freedom, and I took it. Find her or don't find her... Join her or don't join her... It's your choice now. Your family is with you. Your life is yours."

With a groan, he drops his hands to the ground and starts pushing himself upright, struggling to get back to his feet.

"No, don't try to get up—"

He snarls at me, forcing himself up on his own, even though I continue to kneel on the ground.

"Go, Asha." He growls down at me, ferocious, but one corner of his lips suddenly hitches into a smile. "Before I give in to my impulses and make you stay."

He turns away from me, leaning against the statue and using it to support himself as he takes a step away from me.

"Come with me," I whisper. I'm holding my breath, but I force myself to exhale. "We can have more than a cage in the sky."

He pauses, his back to me, and more than anything, I wish I were still holding my medallions so I could see his wolf and know his true feelings.

"Go," he says, a final command. "Don't look back."

I rise to my feet, conscious of the wound in my shoulder, the increasing pain. I focus on it because it's easier than confronting the tumult within my heart.

It's impossible to understand this incomprehensible, unpredictable, fierce, complicated man who kept me alive and now defies his people to set me free.

He steps out from behind the statue and into the ashen field, his shoulders held back, his head high, as if his armor wasn't torn apart and he isn't wounded at all.

Squeezing my eyes closed and gritting my teeth against the pain in my heart, I obey him one last time.

I turn away from him, and that's when I hear the *thump*.

I spin back.

A scream forms in my throat.

The Vandawolf lies on the ground, his legs folded beneath him, his left hand planted in the ash, his torso tipped toward me. Blood bubbles up between his lips and he gasps for breath.

The end of a crossbow bolt protrudes from his chest, its entry point in his right shoulder, its tip angled back toward the earth behind him.

It's one of the crossbows I made.

It can only have been fired from the wall.

Someone fired it from the wall!

"No!"

Rage, pure and cold, floods me. My feet are moving, my hand reaching for my tools before I even register what I'm doing. I ram the hammer against the medallions I'm holding, risking breaking my fingers as I run to the Vandawolf.

The *clang* my tools make is a melody I welcome.

The dark light bursting from them is mine to use.

The time for caution is over.

I throw myself in front of the Vandawolf, my feet digging into the ash as I turn myself into a shield and seek the traitor on the wall.

I stare up at ramparts filled with men I recognize as metalworkers and carpenters. There isn't a single wall guard or Wasteland Warrior among them. Nobody loyal to the Vandawolf.

Braddock stands behind the crossbow, his scars clearly visible in the emerging sunlight.

On either side of him are Nero, the leader of the metal-workers' guild, and Vincent, from the carpenters' guild.

All three men wear gleaming, gloating smiles.

A quick scan of the wall tells me that suddenly, like some sort of miracle, the other three weapons I created have been fully assembled, and, with sickening clarity, I realize that the workers' delay in assembling the weapons must have been deliberate.

"Thank you for the weapons, Asha," Braddock shouts down to me. "You gave us everything we needed."

My heart is racing, my breaths seething through my teeth, as I wrap one medallion around my bicep and allow the other to adhere to my left hand.

I expected the humans to come after *me*, not the Vanda-wolf, who fought for them and slaughtered an entire race to protect them.

"Betrayal," I snarl, but my accusation appears to have no impact on them.

Nero lifts his hands, his shaved head tipped back as he raises his triumphant voice to his people. "The Vandawolf's reign is over!"

A cheer goes up from the men on the wall. It's echoed from within the city, hundreds of voices rising up in celebration. Their jubilation washes over me in a wave, but I no longer hear them.

All I hear is the Vandawolf's breathing.

Soft, shallow breaths that won't continue for much longer.

"Go... Asha..." he rasps. "Be free..."

I turn and look him in the eye as I always will. "I'm no longer yours to command."

His stern features soften, the briefest acknowledgment,

before his eyes close and his body slumps to the bloodied ground.

I raise myself up to face the walled city because now I have a choice, and my choices whisper in my mind.

Save him.

Destroy them.

I inhale the tainted air and fill my heart with cold rage as I make a vow:

I will do both.

~

Continue Asha and the Vandawolf's story in
A Sin Like Fire.

A SIN LIKE FIRE
(KINGDOM OF BETRAYAL #2)

Betrayal is only a heartbeat away...

Content information: A Sin Like Fire is fantasy romance, enemies to lovers, the second in the Kingdom of Betrayal series. Recommended reading age is 17+ for sex scenes, mature themes, violence, and language. Ends on a cliffhanger.

BRIGHT WICKED

One forbidden touch.

I am the Bright Queen's Champion. The only fae to control the power of starlight, I am sworn to protect my people from the dark Fell who live in the wilderness beyond our border.

But when a Fell more powerful than any other challenges me, I'm not prepared for his fierce strength and skill.

Or the dangerous desire in his eyes when he looks at me.

Two champions bound to destroy each other.

One misstep is all it takes for me to invoke an ancient law that binds my fate to his. Suddenly, my life is no longer my own.

I am tied to him in a promise of pain and destruction.

Three days to live.

Now, I have only three days before I must fight him in a battle to the death that will determine the future of our two lands.

Every heartbeat counts.

But how can I kill the only man who sees me for who I truly am?

Content information: Bright Wicked is a fantasy romance, the first in the Bright Wicked series, a trilogy told over three consecutive days. Recommended reading age is 16+ for heat level.

ALSO BY EVERLY FROST

5. Rebels

6. Revenge

7. Rogue

8. Assassin's Match

SOUL BITTEN SHIFTER - COMPLETE
(Dark Urban Fantasy Romance)

1. This Dark Wolf

2. This Broken Wolf

3. This Caged Wolf

4. This Cruel Blood

DEMON PACK - COMPLETE
(Dark Paranormal Romance)

1. Demon Pack

2. Demon Pack: Elimination

3. Demon Pack: Eternal

SUPERNATURAL LEGACY - COMPLETE
(Angels and Dragon Shifters)

1. Hunt the Night

2. Chase the Shadows

3. Slay the Dawn

4. Claim the Light

DARK MAGIC SHIFTERS
(Dark Urban Fantasy Romance)

1. Wolf of Ashes

2. Bond of Flames

3. Crown of Fate

MORTALITY - COMPLETE
(Science-Fantasy Romance)

Mortality Complete Set: Books 1 to 4

1. Beyond the Ever Reach
2. Beneath the Guarding Stars
3. By the Icy Wild
4. Before the Raging Lion

Stand-alone fiction - dark romance

Corrupt Me: Immortal Vices and Virtues

ABOUT THE AUTHOR

Everly Frost is the USA Today Bestselling author of fantasy romance, urban fantasy and paranormal romance novels. She spent her childhood dreaming of other worlds and scribbling stories on the leftover blank pages at the back of school notebooks. She lives in Brisbane, Australia with her husband and two children.

- amazon.com/author/everlyfrost
- facebook.com/everlyfrost
- instagram.com/everlyfrost
- bookbub.com/authors/everly-frost
- goodreads.com/everlyfrost